The Puppy Papers

puppy sharon

and

Steven Toushin

Published by
Wells Street Publishing
1363 North Wells Street
Chicago, Illinois 60610
Printed in the United States

Copyright © 2004
ISBN 1-884760-03-1
First Printing 2004

Dedication

This book is for you submissive women and men who have acknowledged, understood, and accepted who you are and the submissive nature of your being. You have that precious inner strength that brings the peace and freedom to be who you are, without question. That inner strength brings the loyalty and devotion to service that we Dominants require, almost more than we require food and water. I thank you.

May there be a spark in puppy's journey to help and guide you in your own life.

—Steven Toushin

Table of Contents

Part I

Introduction

How did this book get started? I am a heterosexual Dom, and I began seeing puppy, a heterosexual female submissive.

There is a subtle game I play that tells me more about the person. This game also creates a connection and exercises control over them when I'm not with them. It is a homework assignment I frequently assign to some of women I play with. They have to write me 5 different scenarios on the same fantasy, which we will eventually play out. I also have options in discipline when the writings are poorly conceived, needing spelling correction, or don't provide enough description, besides rewriting and corrective homework. Each scenario has to be written in three or more paragraphs. The themes can be sexual, bondage, discipline, pick-up, chance meeting, abduction: anything, any time day or night. It has to include where this is to take place (the setting), like some area in the house, a park, beach, restaurant, car, movie theater, bar, a party, public rest-room, etc. I want them to establish a different mood and tell what dialogue goes to each scenario. I need to know how we should be dressed. I want her to dig into herself, her fantasies, and think about me, us, as 24/7 for a week.

With puppy, I changed the game a bit. I wanted her to write about a few of her sexual experiences and fantasies when she was younger and why they excited her. Well, she didn't know exactly what to write. So she started writing in descriptive detail the events that she experienced as a young teenager. As I read them, I realized how well she communicated in her writings and how involved I got in her stories. She made references to people, events, and organizations; I found myself asking her to elaborate in detail so I could learn more and have a better understanding of her life. When she sent me the e-mail about being forced by Blake and tied to a tree with vines, I was fascinated. I wanted to know what feelings that evoked in her. I was interested, and I had questions that I needed answered. When she wrote about young girls experimenting, I was hooked. It wasn't just about her thoughts and what she did alone in discovering her body and sexual self. It was about little girls together, and what they did to each other, their own collective sexual curiosity.

One thing that is never written about is young girls learning about their bodies and talking about those funny feelings. In our society, little girls do not do that; they are cute, adorable, innocent, untarnished. They do not have such thoughts and feelings, and we certainly do not talk about it. Where do we think little girls learn about their sexual and physical selves? Is it in church, or around the dinner table? For some reason, it is OK with boys; they're "different." We make movies of a young boy's first experiences. They have dicks that visibly get aroused, stiff when they get those thoughts, feelings. It is acceptable, somehow; they're boys; they learn how to touch themselves. Little girls can't see their sex, can't see their arousal; they can only feel it. Good little girls are not supposed to touch themselves, let alone get aroused.

Amazingly, puppy brings all this to light and will make you think about those years.

After 3-4 e-mails she wasn't just giving me what I wanted, she was giving me a lot more. So I decided to try something different, and my direction shifted to seeing where her words would take us in a more structured story. I loved the idea that her story takes its form in e-mail questions and responses. Each e-mail she wrote would bring up more questions about the events, which I then asked her. She would answer my questions 2-3 e-mails later, always keeping me intrigued.

As puppy's story unfolds, there comes a point that she lies dormant, only to awaken in the present by realizing her sub-missive needs, wants, desires and cravings. She discovers and jumps headfirst into the free-for-all, "Wild West" of the Internet, in search of what is missing in her life. Encountering her first

Master, her first taste of BDSM, and her experiences in interviewing and playing in the adult Internet world are all intertwined with the present. What is interesting is when puppy and I get together and talk, I would ask her questions she would verbally give me short, simple answers, but later on when she was home, she would answer my questions again in beautiful, humorous, eloquent, well-written detail.

As she wrote, I started visualizing in my mind's eye the structure: how we met, our daily communications, then her story from childhood interwoven with the present, interwoven with the recent past. It includes family, job, BDSM desires, play, connecting, respect, loving, becoming what she desired. No conflict, no regrets, no despair, no second-guessing. This is an onward, upward, positive journey, filled with humor and self-discovery.

This is puppy's story.

Steven Toushin

I would like to thank: Kym Olson for her many suggestions; slave patrick and Jack Rinella for directing me to Joanne; Joanne C. Gaddy for her wonderful editing; and, of course, puppy.

Ed. Note: All the names used in this book have been changed, with the exception of:

> - Monica, Chicago businesswoman and party hostess;
> - Jack Rinella, author of "Leather Views" in *Gay Chicago Magazine*, author of several BDSM books, and speaker at BDSM events;
> - patrick, Jack Rinella's slave; co-owner of *kinkybooks*
> - Karen (a.k.a., Femcar), Chicago submissive/slave; speaker at BDSM events;

➢ Guy Baldwin, Los Angeles psychotherapist, author of many BDSM columns and books;
➢ Steven Toushin, owner of The Bijou Theater and other adult-entertainment businesses.

Part II

How We Met

November 3, 2003

Steven Toushin wrote:

I'm working late tonight, went to *alt.com* for some relief, saw your wink, and read your profile. Slender, attractive, intelligent and kinky: fabulous attributes. You profile is short. You mention humiliation play: how have you played? You have read my profile; you know some things about me. I live and have my office and business on Wells Street in Old Town.

You use the word slave: is it just a fantasy? Have you ever entered into a slave contract, or are you a submissive who has served?

Please understand I enjoy and take my life, lifestyle and play seriously and with humor.

Please tell me some things about yourself: are you married, do you smoke, how long have you been playing? Please ask me anything you want. Here is my e-mail address: xxx@xxx.xxx. If you do e-mail me, please include a picture.

Thank you again for your wink.

Steven

November 4, 2003

Steven Toushin wrote:

When I got your e-mail, I was finishing up work last night. I was tired. I get e-mail from women who pretend, and I e-mail women who do not understand what a submissive or slave really is (their profiles read as if they have been doing this forever with the GODS). They think a little kink is what's it's all about. They are also not tolerant or understanding of other people's kinks or fetishes.

I do not know you, so I will take you at your short written profile word. I am very passionate about BDSM. Sex and BDSM have been my work for 37 years. I play and Top/Dom/ Master to my partners' capabilities. I have compassion and am compassionate in my play, all encompassing in my control and power over you. That power is given to me by you through respect, honesty, and chemistry. I do very much love the dance.

If we meet and agree to play, and if after that we decide that we should continue with each other, please address me as Steven (I do not go by any name other than my given name) until I have earned your respect to be called Sir/Master, if we should get that far.

Also I live by this rule: the world is not perfect and neither am I; I live with a margin of error.

Please tell me who you have served, what you expect of a Dom/Master, and what brought you to me. If I do not hear back from you, I will not bother you or e-mail you again.

Thank you again for your wink.

Steven

November 6, 2003

sharon smith wrote:

Steven,

i wrote two letters to you via alt.com & neither went through, so i will try this. i sent you a wink because i am a standard member & could not view your profile or initiate correspondence. Your profile was a pleasant surprise! i am intrigued.

i discovered BDSM about three years ago and have served one Master for most of that time. i'm sure you don't know him, as he is extremely discreet. i have also played with a number of others, both male & female, Dom & sub. i have never entered into a slave contract, so i guess you could say that i am "a sub who has served." i am married and so am not looking for a 24/7 relationship. i am, however, looking for an ongoing relationship. The thing that interests me is not so much the particular fetishes or kinks of BDSM (although i enjoy most all of them), but rather it is the control aspect that turns me on ... and, for some reason, the humiliation. It's not just the scening, but the ongoing power & control over me that i'm looking for. i choose to be submissive because it fills a need like nothing else has ever done. In my professional (health care administration) & everyday life, i have by necessity a strong personality ... in one way or another, i always get what i want.

However, D/s has changed my outlook & approach to things, for the better. i suppose i could psychoanalyze the whole thing, but i assume you've heard it all before. In the beginning of this submissive journey, i very much wanted to go to a club, but that has never happened. i did attend a "women's retreat" at Shadowfind in Niles, Michigan one time & chatted extensively with a number of women who were involved in a BDSM lifestyle 24/7 and who regularly visited the clubs. i was not impressed.

Most of them seemed desperate, cynical, bored, and bitter ... not to mention obese & downright ugly. i got the impression they became involved in BDSM only because they had nothing and no one else. That was a big disappointment for me because i had romanticized the 24/7 lifestyle & thought it was something i wanted to do. Since then, i think i have developed a more realistic concept of what i'm looking for. This is getting kind of long, so i'll quit for now. i'm very interested in hearing your thoughts on all this.

One more thing: i am a smoker, but i don't smoke around people who don't like it.

Sharon

[Ed. Note: Shadowfind is a lifestyle bed and breakfast in Niles, Michigan (www.shadowfind.com).]

November 6, 2003

Steven Toushin wrote:

Hello Sharon,

Thank you for the reply and for being open with me. *Alt.com* is kind of screwy at times if you are a standard member.

My life and businesses have revolved around sexuality and rough sex (BDSM). I have to start by letting you know a little about how I feel about BDSM so you can make a sound decision if you want to continue to talk with me. BDSM is romantic, consuming, and loaded with the ability to gain inner self-knowledge. That may not be the intended purpose, but it's there, improving your life as you learn about your inner core. If I sound like I'm preaching the Gospel of BDSM, then you're right; I am passionate about it. I feel that to be good at it, you need a partner with whom you can connect. It is a dance that transforms into a ballet; I am the leader and director, and you are the Prima Ballerina.

I believe in these four basic things:

1. Play with passion
2. Have compassion
3. Be compassionate
4. Have respect for each other

If that sounds diametrically the opposite of bondage, humiliation, flogging, role-playing, pain, serving, etc., it is not. Both sub/slave and Dominant/Master need to feed and fulfill each other's needs, wants and desires. Both must want to give each other what the other needs, no strings attached, to fulfill their dark forbidden fantasies.

So, communication is the key. The only control I have is the control you give me, which you can take away at any time. But in play I will be in control at all times; I will know where you're at. No matter how sadistic or punishing I may get, I have to always be aware of your headspace and safety.

Now, there are things that I have to learn from you. I need to know how you have played, where you go, and how your other partners took you there. I have questions on humiliation play: at what level of humiliation play have you played; give me an example; at the end of play, do you want to be left alone for a while to put yourself back together, or do you want to be comforted?

I laugh a lot and find humor in life and in my play.

You are very right; 95% of the men and women into rough sex are not very attractive.

I live and have my office and business on Wells Street in Old Town. If you want to talk, block your phone number, and call me at home or at my office.

Yours,
Steven

November 6, 2003

Steven Toushin wrote:

Sharon,

I hope I did not bore you or scare you away with my stream of thought on BDSM.

I did not tell you my full name or my address: Steven Toushin, I live at xxxx North Wells Street.

If we do continue to talk, I would like to see a photo and to learn more about your relationship with your husband, BDSM with a Dominant/Master, your marriage, and your relationship with your past Master, including why it ended.

I will also answer any and all questions you ask of me.

Steven

November 7, 2003

sharon smith wrote:

Steven,

i am sorry about not responding sooner. i have been dealing with a huge tragedy this week. A close friend of my son committed suicide at the age of 21. He was a brilliant, creative, fun-loving person who loved life & loved people ... and about a year ago he developed schizophrenia & has been tortured by it ever since. We buried him yesterday. Sometimes life really sucks.

i have a question for you, Sir. From what you've said about your life & business, i assume you've had many, many play partners over the years. If so, i'm wondering how you've maintained the passion & compassion that you speak of. For every one of them? That is the gist of what the women at Shadowfind were missing & something i don't want to lose.

i will answer your easier question first. In regard to aftercare, Master Rob always expected me to give him a massage & blow job(s) after a scene. i found that doing this for him was more comforting to me than being comforted by him – if that makes any sense. i am very much a toucher/caresser ... i think you would find that my hands are always moving even when in bondage. By doing this for him, it helped me maintain physical contact while coming back to mental reality at my own pace ... and because i know he liked it so much, i guess it made me feel like i was giving something back ... sort of like a thank you without words. He would become very intense during a scene & i think it also helped him come back down. With other play partners, this kind of "aftercare" never happened, which is likely the reason i never really felt much of a connection with them. Also, i want to mention that while i like to receive it rough, i am very gentle when it comes to giving. Master Rob always wanted me to try the dominant role with others, but it just isn't something i'm capable of doing.

Your more difficult question is regarding where i would go & how i would get there. i assume you're referring to the head-space. i'm laughing because i've tried many times to describe it & always feel inadequate in doing so. First, let me explain that i have a very high-stress career in which i am on-call 24/7 ... and people literally live or die based on the decisions i make. (i am the director of a hospice program.) Under normal circum-stances, it is very difficult for me to shut everything out enough to really enjoy sex. However, in a submissive role i am repeat-edly amazed at how quickly & easily i can make the transition to being fully present in the moment. i think a blindfold is key in that transition ... along with the Dominant persona of my partner. The Dom needs to be experienced, authentic, and also fully present, or it just doesn't seem to work. It also seems like the lower i am made to feel, the higher i can soar. Need i men-tion that flogging is also a requisite? Where do i go? It sounds kind of dumb, but the answer is that sometimes (not always) i fly ... weightless like a butterfly in the clear blue sky. If i am pushed hard enough and long enough, it's like i suddenly disen-gage from my body ... endorphins, i guess ... the body's own heroin. Actually, i was a "stoner" back in the 70s & have some very fond memories of being high, but none compare to this ... and it's not even harmful to one's health! How would you know when i get to that place? i quit moving and become totally re-laxed ... probably with a stupid grin on my face (at least if my mouth isn't otherwise occupied!).

Your other difficult questions are regarding my husband & pre-vious Master. i have been married for 25 years (got married when i was 4!) and my husband doesn't know that i do this – but he is quite pleased with the results. Frequently when i come home after a session, he tells me "I don't know what you're doing, but I hope you keep doing it!" It must be that stupid grin on my face!! However, if he really did know, i am sure that would be the abrupt end of the marriage. He is a good person, but very narrow-minded. When i got started in this, i guess i just felt the need to expand my horizons, and he wasn't interested in going along for the ride ... he quit learning & growing a long time ago. my relationship with Master Rob isn't over. We are still close friends & probably always will be, & he will probably session me again sometime in the future ... but once again, i feel the need to expand my horizons, and our ideas about how that should happen have diverged. He wants me to dominate women, & i am simply not interested in being dominant or being with women. Under his tutelage, i have been with a few women & it just doesn't do anything for me. Thus, i figure – why should i continue down a path that leads to nowhere? Time to switch paths! i think every person has their own certain attributes that we love them for, but no one person can be everything that someone else needs ... or at least if such a person exists, i have yet to meet him!

Okay, enough rambling. i will attach some pictures to give you a general idea of what i look like, but i don't send face pictures over the Internet – can't risk having them get into the wrong hands.

Have a great day!

sharon

November 7, 2003

Steven Toushin wrote:

Hello Sharon,

I am sorry to hear about the young man's death. I have two children of my own, and that kind of tragedy is heart-wrenching. Sorry for his family.

I love the scenes I do. The mental planning and preparation of a scene always excites me. I learn something from every partner that makes me grow. I am also very passionate about my business, which, if we meet, I will tell you a little about. I do not know too many people in the Chicago BDSM community. I have never had to venture out of my world. I am not closeted, but I also do not wear a neon sign advertising my business or lifestyle. I have men and women working for me who in their private personal lives are slaves, submissives, butch fems, straight young women, gay men, etc. I judge people as individuals, not as a group. Most people who work for me want the freedom to be themselves 24 hrs/day.

This Saturday I will be going to the Quad Cities with Jack Rinella. He was asked to speak at a dinner gathering of a local BDSM group that meets monthly and afterwards to have a book signing. He asked if I would accompany him, and I could use the break. A few weeks ago I was at a convention called *Together in Leather*, a regional lifestyle convention. I went to attend classes and to hear a few people speak. The rest of the time I was vending with *kinkybooks.com* (look up that site), which is owned by Jack's slave patrick (who works for me). It was enjoyable; I had a good time. My site, by the way, is *www.bijouworld.com*.

I am not looking for you to switch with me. I do not switch, nor am I looking for you to top or dom with someone else under my guidance. I am one-on-one; that's what I like. When I play, I want to know as much about you as possible. I play with what you like, then expand on that. In a short time I will start new paths to journey on with you. But I need to feel, see, hold you, see you move, how you breathe, your eyes, sounds, etc. All this lets me know where you are going and teaches me how to take you there and beyond. We will talk more on this. A few more questions: how often did you play, what days, and how long?

I very much enjoy humiliation scenes, so I need to know how you have played, and tell you what and how I play, and on what levels I play. Every thing I do, besides the physical, is on mental and emotional levels and intensity, all depending on your experience. Starting out with me will be at an easy pace, very much like Ravel's *Bolero*.

Yes, I do like the lean grace of your body; it is very erotic to me.

Enough for now. Next step will be either talking on the phone, to hear each other's voice (for me, after 9:30pm), or meeting face to face at a Starbucks at North and Wells in Old Town.

Please let me know what is convenient for you. If Starbucks, give me a day and time.

Yours,
Steven

November 7, 2003

sharon smith wrote:

Steven,

i wonder if it's the affinity for "mental planning" that makes the difference between a Dom & sub ... i much prefer to be sponta-neous ... never plan anything ... drives everyone around me crazy.

i looked at the *bijouworld* & *kinkybooks* sites. The Bijou looks like it's only for gay men. True? Or didn't i look far enough?

i'm curious what You mean by humiliation play. That can take many forms. Master Rob wasn't into that as much as i would have liked. i think that's why i was frequently looking for someone else to play with. i've experimented with quite a few fetishes and can't think of anything i didn't like ... some i don't understand, but i love to see people doing things they really en-joy! i've chosen my play partners because of their differ-ences, so i'm pretty much open to anything....like to try new things. i'm not sure if that answers your question or if you wanted to know specific activities? As far as levels of play, that has also varied. The very first time i was sessioned, i had no idea what to expect & not much of a clue what BDSM even was & had only spoken to Master Rob in person for about five minutes. Quite naively, i met him in a hotel room near O'Hare where he pro-ceeded to tie me down & give me over 100 (hard) lashes with a variety of implements ... and i loved it ... but still can't believe he did that! my ass was purple for weeks! Only once have i been able to take that many since then. For a while, there wasn't as much physical intensity & it was more mental control ... lots of assignments & the learning of manners, etc. ... definitely tested my limits. i guess i was a bit of a slacker there ... not sure if i learned something or if he just gave up on trying to straighten me out. A few times i was severely punished for lack of respect (although i think i was innocent in that regard) – think i have that one figured out now (i hope). Any-way, some people have used "whips" that would have to be classified as cute, & others have used quite torturous devices. (That reminds me, one thing i cannot handle is being upside down for more than a couple seconds.) i think i've gotten off the subject here, so will move on to the next question.

In the past, my time was pretty flexible & i could usually be available for anything from a couple hours to a few days at a time. However, i just took a new job & moved to Illinois about three weeks ago so my time is more restricted at present. For the next couple months i can probably only be available on week-ends or early evenings. As far as how often i played, the answer is: never often enough!!! Seriously though, the people i have played with have been either doctors or CEO's & most of them married, so scheduling was always a big issue on their part. i suppose it's been anywhere from 3-4 days in a week to once in a couple months. With all my recent packing, moving, unpack-ing, etc., it's been a couple months now … definitely too long.

i would rather meet you in person than talk on the phone. Actu-ally, tomorrow (Saturday) during the day would be the best time for me, if you have the time to spare. i don't know where the Quad Cities are, but perhaps you will be traveling nearby on your way there? i live in Hinsdale (southwest burbs). Or i could meet you in the city if you prefer. i have the whole day avail-able, so it's up to you what time. i will look forward to hearing from you.

sharon

November 8, 2003

Steven Toushin wrote:

Hello Sharon,

I cannot make it today. I'm leaving at 1pm will get back around midnight-2am. I will be available tomorrow to meet you, so let me know. If we scene, I will learn from you how you have played. We will talk things out. I usually play with what you tell me over in my head to get a feel for you. I will still ask you questions; nothing is written in stone. I improvise based on how you react, your body movements, sounds, your body heat, eyes, response to my voice, etc. I like to put you into a submissive frame of mind up front, usually in puppy play; more on that later when we meet.

I am not big on strict training or Emily Post etiquette or upside down suspension or verbal abuse (I do it when it fits into a scene, your fantasy, or your need). I talk, direct, demand, interrogate, praise, reward, punish. I am also with you at all times, touching you, masturbating you, etc. When I play, it could be a fear scene, utter humiliation, hot wax, knife, breath play, fisting in all positions, and so forth and so on. The first few times we scene will be easy; we will be in the early stages, learning about each other. It is easy to just flog; hopefully, you will be relaxed enough to get into your headspace, for I will be in mine if I connect with you. You don't know me; I'm very flexible and work and play on the positive. If we play together, we will learn more about each other's dark needs, wants, desires, and "must-haves." The level of play will get much deeper and more sophisticated. Also, I play at my home; I have a wonderful open space and a lot of this and that.

By the way where is Hinsdale? How far from Chicago?

Take care.

Steven

November 8, 2003

sharon smith wrote:

Steven,

Without traffic, Hinsdale is about 20 minutes southwest of the city off of I55, near Hinsdale & Burr Ridge, if you are familiar with them.

Tomorrow can probably work. Late morning? Just let me know where and when. I can get directions off of *Mapquest*®, but I have a tendency to get lost in the city, so if you can send a phone number where you can be reached in case I'm late or hopelessly lost, that would help.

Thank you.

sharon

Part III

Getting to Know
Each Other

November 10, 2003

Steven Toushin wrote

Sharon,

It was lovely meeting you. I think you have an inkling about me and where I (we?) will go: the fun, the growth and the heightened levels. Please ask yourself and think about these questions. Do you want to see if we have the chemistry, the respect to go there? Do you want to go there, and go there with me, to scene with me, and later in the future if all the components are there, to serve me? Please answer these questions. If all this is somewhat of what you want, and you want to start this journey with me, let's do a two-month contract (non-binding, not written in stone) If so, let me know when you can get together with me.

Have a good week.

Steven

[Ed. Note: No contract was ever prepared.]

November 10, 2003

sharon smith wrote:

Steven,

It was truly a pleasure to meet you today … and your kiss made it quite difficult to drive away. i have such little willpower … would have followed you back to your apartment if i hadn't started my period yesterday. The feeling i have is that you are just what i've been looking for, and i am excited about the possibilities. To be honest, some of the things you described make me pretty nervous (i.e., knives, hoods) and i'm not real sure how to deal with that. From my perspective, those things (especially knives) would require a great deal of trust, which would take time to develop. i'm not the kind of person who is easily scared, but knives & guns are two things i am very frightened of ... i guess i've seen too many people in the emergency room who were accidentally injured or killed with them. i need to know that you understand where i'm coming from on that, and that you are okay with not introducing them into our play until i am ready (if ever). Strangely, though, the idea that i find most enticing is that you've gone farther to the edge than anyone else i've known. i'm laughing now because i'm always the one who is trying to convince people to go along on some "daring" or "extreme" adventure. It would indeed be a novel experience to be with someone wanting to go farther than i do!

Yes, i do want to go on this journey with you. i don't think i want to do "scening" without also "serving," and i'm not sure what you meant by that ... perhaps some components i am not aware of. i also like the idea of a contract, although i'm not sure what it would involve as i've had no experience in that area. i am scheduled for triage from the 17th to 23rd, so next weekend will work well to get together – Saturday is better than Sunday.

i am looking forward to seeing you again.

sharon

November 10, 2003

sharon smith wrote:

Steven,

i was reading about you on Google this morning ... a very colorful life. We come from such opposite backgrounds, it seems impossible our paths would ever cross. Do you believe in fate?

sharon

November 10, 2003

Steven Toushin wrote:

Hello Sharon,

You are right; I wasn't explicit. I assumed that it is a given with me, serving and play. The serving when we are together and not together is a discussion in itself for later on.

Thank you for your kind words and for being pretty nervous (smile). I am comfortable with anything you request, I feel you will explore your limits at a later time when trust and respect have been established.

The contract is a good idea. I would like to see how we do together first on Saturday, to see how we mesh and if we want to continue. If so, then we will play for 3-4 times and then enter into a contract if all is well. I'm being courteous, and if either of us have any reservations it's best at the very beginning not to continue, like dating (which I know you haven't done in a while). If we should enter into a contract, it will get us to talk more on the dynamics of our relationship and what we want from each other. Your understanding of submissive yourself is what I like about you; you know who you are and what you are searching for. That inner strength is very enticing, alluring to me.

Now you have given me some things to think about.

Yours,
Steven

November 11, 2003

sharon smith wrote:

Dear Steven,

i want to feel you inside of me … your heat … making me melt … breathing your scent... … tasting you … touching you … exploring every inch of your body. Will you let me do this? Do you like to be touched & caressed? i'm trying to imagine what your taste & scent is like … cocksucking is one of my favorite activities … mmmmmmm … never enough. i'm going to have to quit thinking about this, or i'll be melted down to nothing but a puddle by Saturday!

It has occurred to me that i haven't told you my real name. As i'm sure you already know, the last name isn't "Smith" … just a convenient name to use when i don't know the person on the other end of the correspondence. my last name is actually xxxxxxx, just so you know.

Have a wonderful day!

sharon

November 12, 2003

Steven Toushin wrote:

Hello Sharon,

How is your week going? Saturday is coming up, thank god. I'm not religious, but right now it's the right thing to say.

Now I'm going to play a little. I'm day dreaming about how you're going to be, if you will be my loyal, obedient puppy, the sounds of pain and pleasure, how your body moves, the heat of your body, your wetness, to discover how sensitive your nipples are, how far you're going to travel inside yourself.

Saturday will be our first time together, when you will be giving me your submissiveness, which I need, to serve me, which I crave. I am not looking for the moon, but for chemistry and connecting with you.

Steven

November 12, 2003

sharon smith wrote:

Steven,

my week is going very sloooowly, & I'm finding it quite difficult to concentrate at work. Would much rather be serving you
as your loyal, wet & obedient puppy. Only two more days ...
maybe I should practice wagging my "tail" for you ....

Please don't worry; I'm not looking for the moon either. I just
really enjoy serving & what ever happens, I'm okay with it &
will consider it a privilege to have the opportunity to serve you.
However, I must confess that my pussy is throbbing just thinking about you ....

See you soon!

sharon

November 14, 2003

sharon smith wrote:

Steven,

I think I was very near you today – was "lost" in Chicago &
crossed Wells Street several times, but no time to stop & say hi
... would have liked to, though!

I got scratched on the chin by a delirious patient earlier this
week, & it has become a relatively huge wound (for a chin
anyway). God only knows what the guy had under his nails.

Anyway, I'm going to have a doc take a look at it in the morning. It shouldn't be a problem, but in case I'm late that would be why. Hope you don't mind a submissive with a band-aid on her chin. Ought to fit right in with the humiliation aspect of things!

I don't know what to wear tomorrow. Any suggestions?

I'm looking forward to the bizarre & unforeseen ... i think!! Will call when I get close.

See you soon.

Sharon

November 16, 2003

sharon smith wrote:

Steven,

i want to thank you for a wonderful day. Do you have any idea what a special and unique person you are? i wish i would have met you a long time ago. There is a famous painting, and i don't know the name of the artist (Michelangelo?) or the painting, but it portrays two hands touching only at the tip of a finger. That is what it feels like happened today. i feel like there is so much more i want to learn & explore with you. i hope you will be patient with me. It takes a while for me to really speak openly with someone, but it will happen. i guess i've been stung too many times in sharing my thoughts/feelings with people, and so they are not readily available on the tip of my tongue. If you want honest answers, it's better to let me think about things for a while. Actually, i spent a couple hours driving around & thinking after i left you this evening ... kind of an evaluation of where i'm at with everything.

The first thing that came to mind was that i felt really good about myself after spending the day with you ... no guilt, no disappointment, no wishing that things had evolved differently. What i didn't feel was the "loss of self" that i've felt with others in the past. It would take a whole lot to explain that statement adequately, so for now let me just say that it was a different feeling than i've had with anyone either in or out of the bedroom in a long, long time.

The second & third things that came to mind (smile) were that your cock fits perfectly in my pussy (like a lock & key), and that i love the taste & scent of your cock. (Laughing now.) Maybe i really am like one of your dogs ... the crotch sniffer.

Which brings me to the next thing i was thinking about ... your questions regarding humiliation play. i have difficulty with those questions because i don't mentally categorize something as "humiliation" if i enjoy it. So when you ask what i've done in that regard, the answer would depend on how you specifically define humiliation play. Having grown up with & been around dogs all my life, i've often envied their simple & carefree lives & fantasized about being a dog – or any kind of animal for that matter. The fact that you enjoy puppy play simply allows me the freedom to act out that fantasy ... without someone thinking i've totally lost my mind!! It doesn't feel humiliating, but rather it feels validating that someone else would have the same "crazy" idea. Watersports/golden showers is another example of something "unacceptable" that i've fantasized about and, once again, to find someone on the same page is more validating than humiliating.

Chances are that i've fantasized about anything you can think of. Do i have a favorite or fetish or something i've been dying to try? Nothing specifically comes to mind. Some people say they've been disappointed when they've acted out their fantasies. Maybe they don't carry them out to the extent that they should? All i can say is that i really enjoy getting into other people's fantasies because to try all of mine would take three lifetimes, & i wouldn't know where to begin.

One last thing & then i have to go to bed. You asked about specific activities that i like in a scene. i really, really like being fisted. i also like having my hair pulled. And yes, i do like having my ass fucked ... if it's done right. And i appreciate having my face slapped if i get too far out there. (Okay, it was more than one thing ... sorry!)

i'm really looking forward to serving you again & would like to do so on an ongoing basis if that is what you want.

Pleasant dreams ....

sharon

November 16, 2003

sharon smith wrote:

Steven,

Wow! i've been reading the stuff you gave me & am beginning to understand what you mean by levels of submission/serving & connection. Although not explicitly stated, these are things that were implied, things i was looking for in the beginning of my relationship with Master Rob – but they never happened. i have the greatest respect for him & love him dearly, but he was not interested in connecting beyond the physical/mental level. Except for the expression on his face while he was whipping me, i was never really sure whether i was pleasing to him or not. i guess on the continuum between Dominant & asshole, he was more on the asshole side … although i don't like that term because he is truly a good person.

Other play partners were more communicative but were fighting their own inner battles with guilt, fears, identity, acceptance, etc. If i were a very insecure person, it would have been easy to develop a complex because many of them came to the painful conclusion that they needed "time to think" and have withdrawn from BDSM entirely (i.e., the "sex addict"). These, of course, are people who claimed to have 20+ years of experience as a Dom. Others thought they had fallen "in love" & wanted me to seek a divorce, marry them, quit BDSM, and live "happily ever after" in a vanilla relationship. These relationships i ended as quickly as possible.

The reason i'm telling you all this is because i can now see the importance of explicit goals for a relationship from the beginning. i like the contract. It describes the kind of relation-ship i'm looking for. i also like the fact that it's an open-ended commitment, because no one knows what the future will hold … people's goals & needs change over time. However, i think that signing a contract such as this would require more discussion.

First, of course, i would need to know if that is something you actually want or would be willing to do with me. i also need to know how serious you would be about going beyond the physical/mental level. It has become rather easy for me to give myself physically/sexually in almost any way to please a partner, and i enjoy that for what it is; and if that's all it is, that's fine. It is also easy for me to be mentally submissive, obedient, etc., and i enjoy that for what it is. To give myself emotionally is not difficult, but it is beginning to enter a place where many people don't want to go … and i don't want to go there (again) by myself. It is a place that requires trust … a place of vulnerability ... a place where i'm more selective about who i will go there with.

To give myself spiritually is something i haven't done, but if i were to give you my whole life's history, i think you would see that it's something i've always been seeking to do. It is here that i would need to be sure you understand what spirituality means to me ... the depth of the vulnerability & trust.

i told you yesterday that i've worked in the ministry in the past. Part of what i did was to teach classes on things like the difference between spirituality & religion (which have little, if anything, in common), and also classes on defining/identifying the spirit and spiritual needs, and helping people to meet their spiritual needs. Also, in this ministry, i had the rare opportunity to become intimately acquainted with all the world's major religions ... and found that, with the exception of Buddhism, i have less than zero interest in any of them. Buddhism, i feel, has a lot in common with D/s, which i assume you already know according to the quotations you gave me. Although i have no use for religion, i have spent a great deal of time studying & meditating on things of the spirit.

What i feel you need to know up front is that if we were to decide to pursue a relationship on a spiritual level, i think we could end up in a place where neither of us has ever been ... a place of depth & vulnerability, where i've never known anyone who is willing to risk it. For you to know & control me on a spiritual level would be a tremendous responsibility, and i question whether it's a journey you would even want to embark on. i also understand that your definition of a spiritual connec-tion is surely different from mine (different experiences, etc.), and i would need to know up front what your expectations are and how far you would want to go in this area. i guess what i'm trying to say is that i'm willing to travel to spiritual levels of connection/submission if you're interested in or willing to take me there. If not, that's okay too, as long as we both understand from the beginning that it's not a goal. i am very interested to know your thoughts on all of this.

sharon

November 16, 2003

sharon smith wrote:

Steven,

Hmmmm … do you suppose that i have "inner demons" that need to be punished & controlled? Something to think about.

Perhaps D/s is a form of exorcism … from both sides. We are made to feel guilty from the time we're born, & most of us have fashioned our lives around that guilt … should do this, ought to do that … and guilt would naturally lead to anger, which is also unacceptable … leading to more guilt, etc. That is why i said yesterday that you are a rare & unique person … someone who has led an authentic life. i admire that. It requires a lot of courage & strength of character to remain authentic in the face of pressures & accusations. Quite obviously, i have not led a very authentic life, and that is something that has become increasingly apparent to me in the past few years. Maybe that is what i'm looking for … authenticity (smile). And i just thought it was an insatiable sexual appetite! You may be sorry you opened the floodgates!

sharon

November 16, 2003

Steven Toushin wrote:

I did not realize I would be touching and opening the floodgates
of your thoughts so quickly. You have kept them hidden for a
long time.

We talked Saturday (now this is only my opinion) about men
with inner battles, guilt, and repressed anger in the negative.
You brought out their inner demons in a big way. You were the
symbol of woman that they wanted to lash out at. Since you offered yourself to them unconditionally, they could do to you as
they pleased in any way, shape, or form. You accepted all, plus
any punishment they wanted to bestow on your person. The reality of this freedom, plus their imagination and their anger
without any repercussions, was too much for them to bear. As
far as wanting to marry you and lead an acceptable life in society, again guilt reigns. They can take you out of depravity,
become the knight in shining armor, so they can now brutalize
you as their wife or willing woman on the side without ever
thinking about you as a person, your wants, needs, desires. Did
I say I did not have an opinion? Let's play shrink; just My
thoughts.

I asked a question and gave you a few general things to read. I
am delighted that you are thinking about your journey, where
you have gone and where you want to go. I am looking for a
play partner who, if over a period of time, if all things work out,
will be my submissive/slave to serve me, and if I should be so
lucky to find a partner/lover/sub, my sub/slave will serve us
both.

In the early 70s (for 4 years), I had a manservant (Jim K.) who
took care of all the household needs, and at night at dinner

(when we were home) he would play piano pieces from Chopin for my me and my wife.

I have to tell you that I do play with others and will continue. You will not be involved with them; I do not mix and match unless asked. For us to play there will have to be respect and a spiritual bond. All this I will explain. I am and always will be of my own spirit. I like my freedom of thought and solitude. My life has pretty much been as I speak. As I told you, I did not want to make the commitment of caring for another person or persons over the last years. You are married, so that brings a different view to the picture of what you have to offer. If there is anything that I have said that makes you feel uncomfortable or does not agree with what you want and are looking for in a Dom/Master, please feel free to bow out at any time; it's OK.

If you are OK with what I have said and want to continue, then let's do so. Let's talk in person. You let me know when we can meet again. If you do not want to play this time but rather to talk, that's fine.

You're doing good, kid.

Steven

November 29, 2003

sharon smith wrote:

Steven,

Thank you for the surprising evening! It was exactly what i needed, and i hope you were pleased. my pussy & ass were so sensitive all day that i've been having mini-orgasms every time i move. Being the "greedy" little submissive, i'm sitting here wishing i could serve you every night ... would make both my nights & days so much more enjoyable!

i will be in the city tomorrow afternoon ... if you want to make use of any of my holes ....

i've been thinking about the idea of "inner demons," & think i might be an exception ... at least i can't think of anything at the present time. i've had plenty of issues in the past that i've struggled with, but I have a tendency to confront those things directly ... plunging into things that i fear or don't understand, or things that have caused emotional pain, & forcing myself to deal with & do things that i don't want to do. Actually, being married to an alcoholic has been an overall experience of growth because it forced me at a young age to confront bigger issues than many people deal with in a lifetime, & it also forced me to confront my own "less than desirable" traits & either accept or change them. i am a long, long way from perfect, but (at least today) i can't find any trace of anger, guilt, etc. i think BDSM is where i found myself after all the (known) demons were exorcised ... a place of peace. As far as i can tell, my motives are very simple ... i just thoroughly enjoy pleasing & serving ... and cocksucking and fucking ... and pain & pleasure & playing ... and all other hedonistic activities! a.k.a. submissive slut? Then again, maybe i'm feeling this way today because i had the opportunity to serve you last night!!

If you want to reach me tomorrow (Thursday), please leave a message on my cell phone ... my mouth is craving your cock ....

sharon

November 20, 2003

Steven Toushin wrote:

Sharon,

You are so kind. Thank you for your thoughts.

Tomorrow I have meetings all afternoon which all deal with sexuality (it's a rough life) and how to market it on the Internet. I would love for you to serve me and for me to take you as I please. But I can't do it tomorrow.

I am happy you had a good day with those wonderful physical and mental memories of last night.

Let me know when we can get together again. I am enjoying you.

Yours,
Steven

November 20, 2003

sharon smith wrote:

Steven,

Thank you for the phone message. i had inadvertently left the phone in the trunk of my car after the last patient visit & so didn't receive the message until i got home or i would have answered or called you back. Saturday evening should be fine. i just need to figure out how to get from Park Ridge to the city without getting lost!! After seeing patients for the past week, i'm actually learning my way around the south side – but coming from the north will be a whole new challenge!

i want you to know that for the past month & a half, i have been extremely stressed out & testy due to the move, new job, etc. But now, thanks to you, i am feeling really good this week ... high energy, productive ... feel like i've crawled out from under a cloud. Thank you!!!!!!!!!!!!!!!!!!!!!!!! i owe you lots & lots of anything you may desire!!

And yes, every time i think about you my pussy gets all wet & tingly ... and i want to spread my legs & invite you to pleeease come inside ... Sir.

Have a wonderful day!

sharon

November 23, 2003

Steven Toushin wrote:

Hello,

Had a lovely evening with you.

Please tell me about your availability for those 2 Saturday dates. Hope you had some pleasant dreams and a few wet quiet orgasms today.

You need to tell me about how things went last night within you.

Steven

November 23, 2003

sharon smith wrote:

Steven,

Thank you for everything! i really enjoyed serving you last night. For some reason 😊, my ass & leg muscles were really aching this morning – and my husband insisted on dragging me all over creation to shop for a dining room set ... could have used a few jolts of electricity to get me moving! Would have much preferred lying in bed until noon & dreaming about you.

December 20 is my work Christmas party, which will work out well because i'm not enthused about going there anyway, and it will give me an excuse to go out that night (and get dressed up!). As far as i know, December 6 should work, too. Dates for family parties haven't been set yet, but the 6th is a little early for those.

(Smile) You couldn't tell how things went last night? In case you're interested, squirting orgasms are quite rare for me. Never have i had more than one during any one session ... but i seem to be a gushing fountain whenever i'm with you. You seem to have a way of knowing when to keep going & when to stop. You are also very generous in allowing me so much pleasure! i think i have finally met my match (and more) in the area of sexual appetite! So much to look forward to!!!

i liked being your puppy. It does do things to one's mind ... kind of simplifies it, i guess ... makes me feel content ... makes it easy to feel like i am pleasing to you and also easy to know if i'm not (smile). Also, i am now beginning to understand why dogs act the way they do. Being on "all fours" provides a whole different perspective to things ... pretty much makes you defenseless, except for your bite or your growl ... which, in my case, doesn't amount to much!

i will confess that when you were using your knife, thoughts of Jeffrey Dahmer & John Wayne Gacy passed through my mind – and i appreciate the fact that you didn't feel the need to demonstrate how sharp the knife was. It made me nervous/scared, but i was okay with it. Definitely made me aware of the power & control you had over me ... which is the "point" of the whole thing (haha). It is hard to describe the kind of trusting & the desire to please you that were involved in that seemingly simple activity. It was much more a mental (as opposed to a physical) serving.

Electricity ... the jury is still out on that one. i'm sure it is much more fun to watch someone jump than to be the recipient of the jolts ... but anything to please you, Sir.

The singletail whip was a unique sensation. It didn't feel like a whip. It felt like a red-hot pointed object being drawn across my skin with a spark at the end. my ass is still stinging from it ... and need i tell you what that does to me? You have elevated flogging to an art form ... a whole different experience than what i've had in the past.

i had the feeling last night (and also the other times i've been with you) that i was being pushed farther than i could go. That is a good thing, a challenging thing, something i've wanted ... something i suspect you understand. Going beyond supposed limits & at times achieving perfection in other areas of my life has provided me with a deep satisfaction. i am not a competitive person & not even interested in comparing myself to others. However, there is something inside of me that lights up when anyone (including myself) says that something can't be done. i need someone challenging me to go farther to keep me feeling alive. i think you have the strength to do that. D/s has a whole array of challenges (pain, fear, humiliation, serving, etc., etc.)

and levels of each. Exploring ever higher (or in some cases lower) levels is the thing i find so intriguing & exciting. So when you ask/tell me to do something & i say that i can't or won't or don't want to, what i might be saying is that i want to but i just need to be pushed or forced ... and in the end i will thank you for it. Does that make any sense at all? That is why you may get different answers to the same question at different times. It's not that i'm trying to be difficult.

Okay, i am off to dreamland ... to dream about sucking on your tasty cock ....

Hope to see you again soon!

sharon

November 25, 2003

sharon smith wrote:

Steven,

It looks/feels like winter is here! Now i understand why they call Chicago the Windy City. i nearly got blown off my feet while pumping gas today! Are you staying warm?

i will see if i can change my hair appointment to Friday since i'm off anyway ... will be less rushed that way.

my husband told me tonight that he will be starting to work in Indianapolis next week, which will probably mean he'll be spending the night there a few times a week ... which means i will have more free time ... for about the next four months anyway. Hmmmm ... however shall i fill those long evenings? ... i will have a better idea of when i can be available next week by this weekend.

i'm looking forward to seeing you again soon.

sharon

November 26, 2003

sharon smith wrote:

Steven,

my son & his friends arrived here about 2am this morning (such thoughtful guests), and they say they're leaving Saturday night – which means my parents will want to come on Saturday so they can see Don. i'm not sure how all this is going to work out. Is your schedule flexible so that if i end up having everyone here for dinner on Saturday that i could see you on Sunday? With the way these guys operate, i may not know for sure until Saturday morning what is going on.

sharon

November 26, 2003

sharon smith wrote:

Steven,

Perhaps now you will realize how annoying it is to be involved with someone who doesn't know what she's doing from one minute to the next!!! i think my parents are going to come up here on Friday, & then i'll keep my Saturday appointment. Then i could see you around 3:00pm Saturday as originally discussed. Please forgive me. i was born without a planning gene. Trying to think so far ahead is exhausting!

You are always on my mind … and people are wondering what i'm smiling about all the time ….

i hope you have a wonderful Thanksgiving!

sharon

November 28, 2003

Steven Toushin wrote:

Sharon,

Looking forward to filling up your pussy with my fist and then watching you nap on your dog bed, dear puppy sharon.

Your planning involves a lot of people and their schedules at holiday time; big mess.

Have a good Thanksgiving. See you Saturday.

Steven

November 28, 2003

sharon smith wrote:

Steven,

Things have finally quieted down around here. Must have had fifty people in & out of here today. One thing for certain about college kids, they have learned how to consume a lot of beer & food! A nap in my dog bed sounds pretty good right now!

i will see you tomorrow. Will call when i get close.

Your puppy,
sharon

November 30, 2003

sharon smith wrote:

Steven,

Thank You for a wonderful day yesterday, & thank You for allowing me to be Your submissive (and slave-in-training). i will do my best to make You proud, Sir. i want You to know that i meant everything i wrote before about wanting to serve, etc. While i won't deny that i intensely enjoy the "do-me-queen" part, it is the pleasing & serving that i enjoy more. Although, i should probably point out that it is the pleasing & serving that makes my pussy dripping wet. And while i'm on that subject, i will also mention that masturbating for a couple days after i am with You seems to be a necessity because my pussy is so dang sensitive it would drive me crazy if i didn't!

Anyway, i've been thinking about the whole idea of play-ing/submitting/serving & fantasy/reality/ lifestyle & feel like i need to explain something to You. i think the biggest reason i've been looking outside my marriage & exploring D/s is be-cause that is exactly what's missing in my marriage. When i first got married, i expected my husband would be the head of the household, & my job would be to do whatever he wanted & to make him happy. However, i've tried everything possible over the years, and he is not happy with anything i do or have done, and i don't think he even knows what would make him happy. That, of course, does not make him a bad person, but it does nothing to satisfy my innate need to please & serve. Our sex life is at least average compared to most married couples, & sex wasn't what i was specifically looking for when i got started in all this.

What i was looking for was someone who knows what he wants & what will make him happy, someone who is willing to com-municate that to me & who will allow me to do whatever it is that pleases him, & also (very important) someone who will let me know if/when he is pleased. i guess it comes down to the fact that i am happiest when i am doing something that makes someone else happy ... and it doesn't matter to me what that something is. Anyway, it doesn't sound like a very difficult thing to find such a person, but it has been ... which is why i'm so excited about serving You.

If any of this makes sense to You, then i hope You will under-stand that this is why i don't have much to say when You keep asking me what i want or like ... because i want what You want & i am happy if You are pleased. This is soooooooo hard to ex-plain, but it is a very basic thing for me, and i hope You understand what i'm trying to say.

One more thing – in looking at the calendar, i see that my period is due on Wednesday, so i don't know if You will still want me to go with You on Saturday. Please let me know about that.

Have a great day!

sharon

December 1, 2003

Steven Toushin wrote:

Hello Puppy Sharon,

Saturday is on. I am looking forward to it with you. Fix yourself up. Sometime in the following week (you will let me know) we will do the makeup thing.

I am happy that you have thought about what I have asked you. Your answer was well thought out and precise. I think things will work out to both our liking.

Talk to you later. Take care.

Yours,
Sir

December 1, 2003

sharon smith wrote:

Sir,

Fix myself up? Can You please be more specific on that? Is this a formal occasion?

i should know in a couple days what will be happening next week.

Tomorrow is my baby's 20th birthday – and i'm not sure whether to be happy or depressed. As exasperating as they were, i always enjoyed having teenagers in the house … never a dull moment! Of course, in retrospect it's easy to laugh about all the trips to the emergency room, calls from the principal, visits from the police, & all the really stupid stuff he did … could write a book on that!

Thinking about You always.

puppy sharon

Part IV

The Wanting and Needs of Master/Sir

December 4, 2003

sharon smith wrote:

Sir,

i've just discovered colorful email!!! Are You impressed? 😊

i thought maybe it would brighten Your day!

i hope everything is well with You. It's been a busy week around here. i have created a new job for myself ... got weary of sitting in an office, so i'm now going to be a "field supervisor." That way i won't have to deal with all the bullshit and office politics & will have much more flexibility ... now just have to come up with a job description & decide how to spend my time. i'm thinking this could work out very well.

i've also been thinking ... You said something before about explaining the meaning of "Master" and "Sir," and then i think we got sidetracked and forgot about it. Then later You said to use Sir except when we were playing & then to use Master ... What is the difference between the two? i'm also thinking that i am going to need You to tell me exactly what to do on Saturday night because i'm kind of nervous that i'm going to do something wrong & don't want to embarrass You ... i think i told You before that i didn't do very well in the manners course ... and i had a little difficulty concentrating on what You were saying the other night while other parts of my anatomy were being so pleasurably occupied!!!!

i'm looking forward to serving You soon!

puppy sharon

December 4, 2003

Steven Toushin wrote:

Dear Puppy Sharon,

Yes, very colorful indeed, looks fabulous (smiling). As far as Saturday is concerned, you will not embarrass me; you will do well. Using the term "Sir" in public is polite acknowledgment of my position, our relationship. "Master" in private is directly to the very essence of our relationship without imposing it on others. For the time being, this will be the order of things. In time if all goes well with us, I will direct you at times to address me as Master when we are out and about.

I am very glad that you are thinking about what I have said to you, asked of you, and that you are looking into yourself for answers.

Congratulations on your new position at work.

Yours,
Sir

December 5, 2003

Steven Toushin wrote:

My dear puppy,

No, this is not a formal occasion. But I do want to show you off: a little lipstick, eye shadow. You have lovely facial features.

Happy birthday; don't get depressed. It's good that they're getting older. Enjoy tomorrow.

Yours,
Sir

December 5, 2003

sharon smith wrote:

Sir,

Thank You for the kind words! I'll see what I can do with the makeup.

i took Don out for dinner for his birthday tonight, & we were both so full afterwards that we're postponing the cake until tomorrow. Then we'll have cake first and see if we're hungry for dinner after that! He was telling me tonight that he signed up for a yoga class because he figures that will be a good way to meet women in this area. To understand how funny that is, let me tell You that Don is 6'6" tall and weighs 165 lbs. The women are all going to die laughing when he attempts any of the yoga positions ... a knotted-up pretzel comes to mind. I may have to go & take pictures of this!

Your puppy

December 5, 2003

Steven Toushin wrote:

Hello little puppy,

How's your week going?

6'6" and 165lbs: yes, he would look like a pretzel.

Things have been OK. I just don't like gray skies.

Let me know on Saturday about what weeknights work for you.

Take care.

Yours,
Sir

December 5,2003

sharon smith wrote:

Sir,

You must have been writing about gray skies at the same time i was writing about colors to brighten Your day … hmmm … now is that intuition or what!

Did You happen to see the lake this afternoon? i happened to be driving north along Lake Shore Drive this afternoon during the few moments it was sunny, & the lake was awesome, with the water crashing against the shore & the sun shining on the spray – beautiful! i wished i had a camera with me.

i'm wondering what time to meet You tomorrow & where? And should i wear anything special? i have to see a patient in Lansing sometime tomorrow, so it would be helpful to know what time i need to be there. Thank You, Sir.

Hugs & kisses.

puppy sharon

December 6, 2003

sharon smith wrote:

Sir,

Depending on traffic & whether or not the patient dies & when, i should be able to be there by 3pm. i will call You when i get there or if it will be later.

puppy sharon

December 7, 2003

sharon smith wrote:

Sir,

i had a very wonderful time serving You yesterday! i want to tell You that You were looking sooooo sexy when You were talking to the group at that meeting that it was really a struggle to keep my hands off of You! i know every woman there was jealous that i should be so lucky to serve such a perfectly charming & handsome Master!

i also want to tell You that every time i see You, i feel like i'm soaring for days afterwards. The reason i'm telling You this is because i've never felt this way with anyone else before. There was always something indefinable that was missing with other people, and whatever that was, it is there with You. You are the perfect Master for me, and i will do anything to please You. i really wish i could serve You 24/7. The rest of my life suddenly seems unimportant since i met You.

I've also been thinking that if You would ever want to record Your thoughts, i would love to put them in writing – in a book. People have been telling me for years that i should write a book, but i have never felt inspired to do so. i have actually had several professional articles published in the past & have won quite a few awards for writing, so i think i could do it in a way that would meet Your approval. i would truly consider it a privilege to do this for You. You have so many things to say that people want to know and need to hear!

One final thought … i don't know how You manage to leave my ass stinging so much without leaving a mark … maybe that's a secret You could share in Your book!

i can be available Monday through Thursday nights this week to serve You.

Hope to see You soon!

puppy sharon

December 14, 2003

Steven Toushin wrote:

Dear puppy Sharon,

How are you doing? This was a lovely week with you. I do believe that you will learn and serve me well and that you will make me proud. Let me know your schedule next week. I expect to see you Saturday at 2:00pm since I made an appointment for you.

Hope all is well, speak with you soon.

Yours,
Sir

December 14, 2003

sharon smith wrote:

Sir,

I am really missing You & thinking about You all the time. i am sorry i didn't write sooner but just got my Internet connection fixed about 5 minutes ago.

i want to thank You for the wonderful evenings this week. i really enjoyed serving You & hope i will make You proud.

i can be available to serve You this evening after about 4:00pm or 5:00pm, or any evening from now until Thursday, and maybe Friday & Saturday.

Hope to see You soon!

Your puppy

December 15, 2003

sharon smith wrote:

Master,

i had a wonderful time serving You last night. However, my ass is very, very sore & hot this morning, & I'm wishing i had a couple of ice packs to sit on ... and my pussy is so sensitive that i can't keep my hands off of it ... in fact my whole body is so sensitive I don't know how i'm going to manage wearing clothes all day. i'm wishing i could feel Your cock in my pussy this morning ... it is dripping wet for You.

Your puppy

December 15, 2003

sharon smith wrote:

Sir,

i tried the "submissive's secret" this morning & was able to sit down without too much discomfort within a couple hours. i guess those submissives aren't as dumb as they look! i have concluded, however, that a wire brush is quite a wicked instrument. i guess that is one of those things a Sadist enjoys more than a masochist ... but anything to please You, Sir!

Before i forget, i meant to ask You last night about the time & place of Monica's Xmas party. A friend of mine often attends Monica's events but accidentally deleted the invitation to the Xmas party, & when i told her we were going, she asked me to send her the details. i think i told You about Marlene. She was Rob's slave & Mistress to her husband, although she has decided there isn't a submissive cell in her body. Anyway, she & her husband would like to go to the Xmas party, & i would really like You to meet them. They are both very charming, sophisticated, and honest people, & i think You would like them. She is a retired dentist, & he is a pilot for a major airline (i forget which one). They are a lot of fun.

That also reminds me – is this a dressed-up thing, or more casual like the other one we went to?

i've been thinking about Your articles about Dahmer, & the time You spent in prison, & all the other stuff You've been through, & the fact that You've remained such a beautiful free spirit ... without apparent resentment or anger or disenchantment. That is truly a remarkable thing. i've known other people who were free spirits, but life managed to destroy them, & they either died at a young age from things like alcoholism or they became bitter, stifled, angry people. On the other hand, You are not only a survivor, but You continue to flourish & live Your life according to Your ideals. It is an extremely rare person who can say that for himself. You should be very proud of that, and You have my deepest respect for Your integrity & strength of character.

You asked me last week what is different about my feelings for You than anyone else i've been with ... i think the answer has a lot to do with respect. Of course, it might also have a little to do with the fact that You are so charming, creative, sexy, and have the most delightful & delicious cock i've ever encountered!

Your puppy

December 15, 2003

Steven Toushin wrote:

Dear puppy,

You wrote: "I have tried the submissive's secret." What is the submissive's secret?

Sir

December 15, 2003

sharon smith wrote:

Sir,

Regarding the "submissive's secret," it is a "miracle" salve that will heal abrasions, minor burns, bruising, & a variety of skin irritations, usually within 24 hours. There are actually two of them that i know about. One is Rawleigh's Salve, and the other is Petro-Carbo Salve. They are both something that our grandmothers probably used, & most older nurses are familiar with them, which is where I originally heard about them. i later heard about them from several submissives who couldn't go home with marks that would last for days. It seems to be a commonly known remedy among submissives.

Your puppy

December 16, 2003

Sir,

Thank you for the info regarding Monica's party. i forwarded it to Marlene.

I am looking forward to serving You soon.

Puppy sharon

December 17, 2003

Master,

Thank You for allowing me to serve You last night, Sir. However, I have to tell You that You've been hitting my face too hard. One time last week i think i lost consciousness from it, & last night I'm not sure what happened, but i had difficulty driving in a straight line & remembering how to get home. I have a really bad headache yet this morning, and my ears are still ringing.

I have to get ready for work, so will write more later.

Puppy sharon

December 17, 2003

Steven Toushin wrote:

Dear puppy,

Sorry, I will be more careful. I did not read, sense, feel, or think I was hitting you that hard. When I asked you how you were doing, you kept responding that you were doing good, so I took it as everything was OK. I did not see a distressed look in your eyes or face; your breathing and your body were in rhythm. Now that you have told me more, I will modify and change what I do with you in face play (slapping, grabbing, hand pressure in covering of mouth and nose, eyes, etc.).

When I ask you in play how you are doing, if things are not going well within you, you have to let me know. Thanks for letting me know.

Happy you are all right. Again, ooooooooooooooops, sorry.

Sir

December 17, 2003

sharon smith wrote:

Dear Sir,

I'm fine – just missing a few bits of time. i had to chuckle this morning when i thought of the poor guy who mugged You a while back. He must have been in bad shape for quite a long while.

Vibrators … i bought one for myself a few months ago but have never used it. Rob used to use a vibrating egg (in) me, but Marlene is the only one who ever used a vibrator on my clit. She would use it on herself & have this nice mellow orgasm, & the second she would touch me with it i would go through the roof. She found it quite funny that i couldn't hold still & relax … said i was lacking in "self-control" … which is why i bought one for myself, thinking that if i could control it, it would be different. It's one of those maddening things that i want to say, "don't come near me with it," and, at the same time, "don't take it away"! i wonder if any man has any idea how intense the orgasms it causes … And how uncontrollable they are … at least until you can squirm away. Anyway my thought today was that being forced to climax with a simple vibrator has got to be the ultimate loss of control … very different than receiving pain or bondage, etc., where you can retreat into your own little world of pleasure (a.k.a. subspace) and have some sense of controlling your response. So what it comes down to, then, is that if i want to give up control, why can't i just relax & let it happen … then again, perhaps my clit is just more sensitive than others … hmmmmmmmm.

Your puppy

Part V

BDSM and the Realities
of Everyday Life

December 21, 2003

sharon smith wrote:

Master,

i am very sorry, Sir, about not giving myself to You when i first saw You yesterday & not doing what i was supposed to at Monica's. It's not because it was difficult or because i didn't want to. i fully intended to kneel as soon as i walked through the door … but You are always busy doing something else or talking about something else, & i don't want to interrupt You. i don't need You to tell me, but i do need You to pause so i can have the opportunity to tell You why i'm there. If i didn't want to offer myself to You & serve You, i wouldn't be there. At Monica's, i don't know what happened … i just screwed up. i was already feeling bad because i had disappointed You, and the party wasn't anything like what i had imagined it would be, and they didn't really have anything for me to do, & i was trying to make myself useful & feeling like i was in the way & wishing i could just go back & kneel at Your feet. When You walked over by me, i was just so glad to see You, i guess i forgot about everything else. i'm sorry. That was a completely new situation for me, & i was very nervous about doing the right thing(s). i promise i will do better next time.

All of the above is the simple explanation, but there is also something else going on that i think might be affecting things. The last 3-4 times i have served You, i have been fighting the desire to say "i love You." From my perspective, there are multiple problems with those words. First of all, love has not been a factor with anyone else i have played with or served & is an unexpected occurrence now, & i don't know if that's what You want in this relationship. The problem is that i feel overwhelmed with these feelings when You are fucking me … not a reliable time to be judging feelings. However, i feel like the whole rest of my life has become unimportant, & i would walk away from it all in a minute if i could serve You 24/7 ... also something i don't know if You want. i don't want to burden You or scare You away, & so i feel like i need to keep all these feelings in check ... and not go off the deep end. On some level, i think i am hesitant to tell You in person that i want to give You my body, mind, & soul because i'm afraid i won't be able to stop there ... won't be able to control my emotions ... and afraid of being rejected. Loving someone means risking being hurt.

Now, that's about where my thoughts were when i came through the door at home last night (this morning). When i got home, Arthur was drunk & said he was leaving. He had gone through all of my things & cited multiple reasons (all of them wrong) that led him to the conclusion that i was having an affair. He found a phone number among my stuff & called it, & someone named Josh Michaels answered the phone, so he thinks i'm having an affair with this person, and i don't even know who the guy is. The only thing i can think of is that it could be a family member of a previous patient. Anyway, Arthur was extremely hurt & crying & drunk & said he hasn't felt welcome here for the past couple months & that i don't care about him any more, etc., etc. etc. i managed to convince him that he was being ridiculous & not to leave ... but in the middle of it all, i was wishing he would & it would be over. i care about him & truly do not want to hurt him, but there is nothing between us anymore, & i'm not sure if there ever was.

So here i am trying to love someone i don't love, and trying not to love someone i do love ... and screwing everything up ... and i don't know what to do about any of it. i am afraid if i am honest with everyone, i will end up all alone; & i'm afraid if i'm not honest with everyone, i will never be happy.

puppy sharon

December 2, 2003

Steven Toushin wrote:

Dear puppy,

I am sorry for the turmoil in your life and the episode you walked into Sunday morning. Hope today all is as good as can be expected.

I know that your situation is difficult and does take its toll mentally, emotionally and, at times, physically. I know you are not asking me for answers; I do not have any, and I do not meddle in others people's affairs. Not entirely true; we are playing, so I am meddling.

Love is something we have to talk about.

Yours,
Sir

December 23, 2003

sharon smith wrote:

Sir,

First of all, i want to apologize for the message i sent yesterday. It had been about 36 hours since i had slept, & i'm sure it didn't make much sense. i am rather angry with myself today for getting sucked up in all the drunken shit … like taking a step backwards about 15 or 20 years. i didn't think it had the ability to affect me anymore. The real kicker is that he doesn't remember any of it. If i could manage it, i would whip myself for being so stupid.

Second, i don't remember if i thanked You for the makeup. If not, thank You. i've never done anything like that before, and it was fun. i hope You were pleased with the results.

Also, after a getting some sleep, i have realized what a pathetic job i did of serving You at Monica's party, and i am soooo sorry. i was so blown away by the whole atmosphere that i forgot why i was there. i hope You will forgive me and give me another chance. Perhaps Your electric zapper would have brought me back to earth ... or a choke collar & leash – as for those too easily distracted puppy dogs.

i do have to say, though, that i was fascinated in watching the way people interacted at that party. It wasn't anything like i thought it would be. i thought there would be a definite distinction between Dominants & submissives, but there wasn't. Most of the people seemed to be trying very hard at pretending ... kind of like going to a masquerade ball ... or a high school dance. i also thought i would be able to learn a lot by watching other subs/slaves, but as far as i could tell, the only female submissive there was the one we had met before from *scenetalk.net*. She did seem very nice. i'm curious whether the atmosphere there resembled what You see at the Bijou ... and devilishly wondering what would happen if i went with You to the Bijou sometime ... being the only female in a crowd of gay men ... now that would certainly be a humbling & unique experience!

i got some good news today. i spent 3 years working on a project funded by a federal grant & sent in the final paperwork last May. Today i got a letter from them asking me to do a presentation at the National Management & Leadership conference in Washington, D.C. next September ... 2 hours of didactic followed by 20 minutes of Q & A. It's really an excit-ing opportunity. Part of the stipulations in the grant were that i was expected to do a poster presentation at the conference ... never thought i would get an opportunity like this!!! i'm nervous already and it's 9 months away!

One more thing – i got a final request from a patient today – an 84-year-old man with end-stage heart disease. He asked if i would find him a beautiful woman to have sex with him before he died. He said his wife died 10 years ago, & he hasn't had relations with a woman since then. He was very earnest & sincere with this request, & i would love to see him die with a smile of ecstasy on his face. So i'm wondering if You know of any kinky women who might be interested in making an old man very happy? He is African-American if that makes any difference.

Okay i lied – there is one more thing – as things have turned out, i have to work Xmas Day, & the rest of the family is going back to Indiana – so i can be available in the late afternoon & evening to serve You ... a most delightful way to spend the holiday!

i am looking forward to serving You soon ... especially to make up for how poorly i did Saturday. i know i can do better ....

Your puppy

December 23, 2003

Steven Toushin wrote:

Dear puppy,

I hadn't heard from you and was wondering if all was all right. As I started to write e-mail to you, I got your e-mail.

I'm very sorry for what you are going through. It seems never-ending, always with pauses to dissipate the ugliness of the reality. On a bright note, do not let it get you down.

On working on and giving your paper in 9 months, the grant is a fabulous thing; you worked hard for it.

Another good thing: as far as the man is concerned, a woman is available to you for his request.

Tuesday and Friday will be good; let me know.

Take care.

Sir

December 24, 2003

Steven Toushin wrote:

Dear puppy,

Congratulations on your grant! Good going, kid; hard work with heartfelt intentions does pay off. I know your presentation will be wonderful.

Also I found a young woman to fulfill your man's dreams; it is also a fantasy of hers, so we will need to talk on this. She does charge, though: $400 an hour, but we can negotiate.

Congratulations, again.

Yours,
Sir

December 24, 2003

sharon smith wrote:

Sir,

$400 an hour!!! i am definitely in the wrong business!!! It hadn't occurred to me that the woman would charge for it … duh. i would have to meet & talk with her first, & she will need to be very discreet because the man is currently in a nursing home, & they tend to frown on these things. She would also need to understand that there's a significant possibility that the man's heart could quit right in the middle of things. As it is, i estimate his life expectancy to be only 3-4 weeks. We will definitely need to talk more about this.

Regarding the turmoil on the home front, You are right that i am not looking for answers … just letting off steam, i guess. The episode took me very off-guard, & i was just trying to process what happened. i have no intention of dwelling on it. i made a decision many years ago that i would no longer allow myself to be manipulated by his alcoholic bullshit, & it makes me angry that it created any kind of emotional response. i assume from what You said about Your son that You understand where i'm coming from on this.

Regarding love … i think things have become a little blurry for me. i feel like i'm teetering on a fence … or hopping back & forth to both sides. Perhaps that is what You meant by crossing over? Please understand that i have no desire to change who You are. You have been very clear about Your lifestyle, etc., and that is not an issue. What i'm having difficulty with has something to do with knowing how to serve You without knowing what kind of commitment You want from me … meaning that i'm not clear whether You want me to be a play partner, a sub, or a slave. In my mind, love does not exist between play partners or between a Dom & sub, whereas a slave would love her Master. i feel like You are asking me to be Your slave, and that is what i want to do, but before i can make that kind of commitment, i need to know if that is in fact what You want. i know You have explained all this before, but talking about something theoretically & actually experiencing it are two different things and, as i said, things have become a little blurry.

i won't know until late Wednesday afternoon how many patients i'll need to see on Thursday, so at this point i can't even give You an estimate on what time i can be there. i will call & leave a message on Your phone as soon as i know anything. i hope that's okay.

i am looking forward to serving You.

puppy sharon

December 26, 2003

sharon smith wrote:

Master,

Thank You for letting me serve You yesterday. As always, i had a wonderful time. Also thank You for talking to me about the love issue. It helped to clarify things. i am fine with everything You said … just wanted to make sure i wasn't veering off in the wrong direction. Strangely, i've never felt the need to clarify or define a relationship before. Things just sort of happened or didn't happen. But for some reason, i think we will need to revisit this kind of thing again in the future. It is tremendously helpful to me that You know exactly what You want, because i am still trying to figure out what i want as we go along. i know i want to please You in any way i can, but unforeseen mental/emotional stuff is occurring, and i need to know what to do with it. Again, thank You for taking the time to explain.

i have to be at work early tomorrow morning & need to get some sleep. Will write more when i can.

Your puppy

December 27, 2003

Steven Toushin wrote:

Dear puppy,

Happy Holidays. It was a delight seeing and having you serve me on Christmas Day; it was a slice of heaven. As always, I hope the ride home was easy.

I left a voicemail on your phone about your request for a woman. I will put it in writing in this e-mail. Her name is Karen (a.k.a., Femcar). She did get back to me and said yes, she very much wants to do it. It is a fantasy that she has had for the longest time, a last request, having sex with a dying man. I asked if I could give you her cell number so you both can iron out the particulars, and she said of course. Here is her number: xxx-xxx-xxxx. Now you can make all the arrangements directly and quickly. Hope all works out before the man dies.

If it does or doesn't happen, I want you to write me all the details of your conversations with her and the events.

Let me know your schedule. Speak to you soon.

Sir

December 28, 2003

sharon smith wrote:

Master,

Thank You for the messages regarding my patient's last wish. i will be seeing him tomorrow, & hopefully he will be awake enough that i can talk to him about it. i want to talk to him some more about his expectations & the reality of his physical condition & then hopefully call Karen tomorrow afternoon or evening. The fact that he's in a nursing home complicates things & will require some careful planning. Also, i don't want him to be embarrassed or disappointed if he can't do what he thinks he can do.

i hope Your weekend is going well. Things have been rather trying around here. i didn't think i would be able to serve You this week because Arthur is being quite difficult, & i've been trying to keep things under control here, but it's gotten to the point that i don't care any more. i had gotten some cash from my mother a couple months ago for my birthday & had put it in my jewelry box to spend on something special for the new house. When i found a painting today that i wanted to buy, i discovered that the binge he's been on for the past week has been financed with my birthday money. i also discovered on my credit card bill that he spent over $5,000 in bars during the 3 weeks he was in Indianapolis. No wonder he's been acting like a psychotic since he got back. His brain has probably fermented.

So anyway, i can be available Tuesday evening or maybe Friday evening. Also, i have an extra day off work coming since i worked Christmas Day, so i can be available during the day sometime, too. i have to go to a Christmas party on New Year's Day, so I can't celebrate the holiday with You this week ... though i'm sure it would be much more fun!

i am really missing You. It seems like forever since i've served You. i am feeling very out of synch, & a good whipping would help to get me centered ... gets rid of all the bad karma ... sort of like a purification.

Hope to see You soon.

Love,
Your puppy

December 29, 2003

sharon smith wrote:

Master,

i tried calling Karen & got her answering machine so will try again later. my patient was up walking in the hallway today & looking better than last week. i talked to him about the cost of granting his wish. He grinned & said he hadn't thought of that either. Said he will have to think about that. That could be the biggest roadblock, because the nursing home gets his check, & he just gets a small monthly allowance. In a fortunate coincidence, an old friend of mine just started working at the nursing home & has agreed to facilitate the encounter when she is working an afternoon/evening shift. If nothing else happens, at least i left him with a new sparkle in his eyes & a smile on his face, & he'll have something to think about for a while.

i ended up starting my period today, which didn't seem to bother You last time, so if it's okay with You this time, i can be to Your house by about 5pm or so tomorrow as i'll probably be finishing up in Hyde Park around 4-5pm. If You would rather wait, that's fine too. Please let me know.

Your puppy

December 31, 2003

sharon smith wrote:

Master,

i hope You are enjoying the almost New Year. i've had a few glasses of champagne & am feeling rather bubbly! Don had some friends over, & they just left for the city to celebrate ... the girls wearing almost enough to keep themselves from getting arrested. i'm going to have to find out where they go shopping! They have mastered the art of being naked & "dressed" at the same time.

Thank You for letting me serve You last night. It was exactly what i needed, & i'm feeling much better today (even before the champagne!). i am sorry about staining Your quilt. i bleed heavily because i don't use the birth control pill or hormones. i should have warned You.

i have decided i like the singletail whip ... it has long-lasting effects. Every time i move, i think about You. The closet was a good place for me last night, too ... though i wasn't sure where i was at the time ... could tell i was in a small, closed, quiet place. i haven't told You that i normally tend to be claustro-phobic. When i first got involved in BDSM, i was worried i would panic with blindfolds or bondage but, surprisingly, they had the opposite effect. It's like being instantly transported into wide-open spaces ... very peaceful. In fact, the less i can move, the higher i can fly. It probably doesn't do much for pleasing my Master, but it's very relaxing for me, ... which is what i desperately needed this week. Thank You.

The thing i've been thinking about all day is that i really want to be Your property ... Your slave ... to have You use me in any way that pleases You. That looks very simple in writing but it is very heartfelt. i was also thinking about the contract that You talked about in the beginning & wondering if that's something You want to do. i think i would like that.

Wishing i was there serving You now ....

Your puppy

January 1, 2004

Steven Toushin wrote:

Dear puppy,

Please call Karen and let her know the situation with your pa-tient. Also tell her that you had called before but did not leave a message. It is good of her to offer, and I don't want her to think or feel that this is not real or sincere. Lastly, give her your cell number, and let her know what are the times she could call you. I hope this works out; it is a wonderful last request.

Thank you.

Yours,
Sir

January 1, 2004

sharon smith wrote:

Yes, Sir.

i am planning to call Karen in the morning. i am rather difficult for anyone to reach by phone, so i'm hoping i'll get to talk to her in person when i call. Otherwise, i think i'll leave her my pager number, & maybe she can leave a time when it's best to call her.

i am not going to be able to serve You tomorrow night. How about Sunday night?

Your puppy

January 2, 2004

sharon smith wrote:

Master,

i hope Your day is going better than mine. my patient's family revoked hospice yesterday & took him out of the nursing home for unknown reasons, and i am very worried that he may have said something to them about needing money for a sexual encounter. If he did, all they would have to do is make one phone call, & i would lose my license, not to mention my job. He went into a hospital, but i don't know which one, & with all the new privacy laws, i have no way of tracking him down. i am having visions of police officers showing up on my doorstep any minute.

i also found out from my broker today that all the money i've faithfully invested over the past 20 years is gone, due to illegal activities within the firm … will be lucky to get a few cents per dollar when all is said & done.

In addition, my uncle received a diagnosis yesterday of metastatic lung cancer, & the entire extended family has been calling me with a million questions, most of which i can't answer. Of course, they have enough respect for my other uncle, the doctor who delivered the diagnosis, not to call him about it.

Now, my mother-in-law has invited 15+ people to my house for dinner on Sunday, and i have nowhere for anyone to sit because my dining room chairs are still on backorder.

If my life becomes any more stressful, i think my head will surely explode. i am considering locking myself in a closet until next year.

On the brighter side, my son has eliminated 279 viruses from my computer, & it is working much better!!

i have also been offered a clinical vice president position at work, involving a 50% increase in salary … not sure if it's worth it … but nice to have the offer anyway.

And of course, any day in January that is 60 degrees can't be all bad!

i can be available Monday through Thursday nights next week to serve You ... definitely the most pleasurable activity i can think of right now ....

Your puppy

January 3, 2004

Steven Toushin wrote:

Dear puppy,

Based on what has been happening in your life the last weeks and what you have just told me about this past week, anything would be better for you. So then you will serve me, which will please me, which, in turn, will please you and put you in a good frame of mind. Let's add some good punishment, sending you into that other world, and an orgasm. Now wouldn't that be a slice of heaven for you!

Monday and Wednesday will be good; let me know the time.

Sir

January 3, 2004

sharon smith wrote:

Dear Master,

Serving, punishment, orgasm ... always a slice of heaven!!!

i'll be working in the office in Willowbrook on Monday, so it will be around 6:00pm when i can get there.

i am working on realigning my chakras & releasing all the bad karma i have apparently stumbled into. Finally tried out my Jacuzzi® for the first time tonight, with enough aromatherapy that the neighbors should even be relaxed ... and i am now feeling like an open lotus flower. Have also decided to start running again ... seriously considered taking up boxing, but would probably end up hurting myself. After close to a year of inertia though, it will probably be limited to walking to start. Time has a way of moving too quickly.

i hope Your weekend is going well, & i'm looking forward to serving You on Monday.....

Your puppy

What lies behind us and what lies before us are tiny matters compared to what lies within us.

—Ralph Waldo Emerson

January 6, 2004

sharon smith wrote:

Dear Master,

i had a wonderful time serving You last night ... must have realigned my chakras because the multitude of annoyances today are not bothering me in the least ... except for the fact that the family took the doctor's advice instead of mine, & my uncle nearly died as a result – but it looks like he's going to survive the incompetence, so hopefully they'll quit trying to kill him & he'll have some quality time left. Doctors seem to get so caught up in the illusion of power that they forget that both they & their patients are only human. Power without compassion is a dangerous thing.

Anyway, my ass is a rather colorful work of art today, & my pussy is feeling soooooo good … wish i could serve You again tonight! And i do love the taste of Your cock … it would be so nice to taste You every night … and every morning … mmmmm ….

If You still want me to serve You tomorrow, i am working in Willowbrook again, so it will be about the same time when i can get there … i think it was about 6:30pm last night.

Looking forward to seeing You soon.

Your puppy

January 10, 2004

sharon smith wrote:

Dear Master,

i have started writing to You several times & keep getting interrupted.

There has been so much illness among my staff that i've been having to cover on-call myself, & i think someone in Chicago must have left the door open & let all the mental patients out … must be a full moon. i am certainly coming to appreciate a lot more the work my on-call nurses do!! i'm thinking they all deserve a raise.

Also, my uncle with the lung cancer died yesterday, & my uncle who was his doctor went in for emergency heart surgery on Thursday. Needless to say, my phone hasn't stopped ringing since i last saw You.

i am currently about to leave to go in to the office to catch up on some things & just wanted to let You know that i haven't disappeared. Will try to write more tonight.

Hope to see You soon ....

Love,
Your puppy

January 10, 2004

Steven Toushin wrote:

Dear puppy,

Sorry to hear about your uncles.

I do understand a busy work schedule. Like all else, try to get enough sleep so that you do not get sick. Stay warm; it is cold out there.

Sir

January 10, 2004

sharon smith wrote:

Dear Master,

Thank You for the kind thoughts. i thought i was getting sick last night but must have just been over-tired – feeling better today.

The wake is Tuesday night, so that leaves Monday, Wednesday, and/or Thursday nights that i can be available to serve You next week.

i hope You are enjoying the weekend & staying warm & well.

puppy

January 11, 2004

sharon smith wrote:

Dear Master,

my horoscope today says that "Wild ideas will help your love life. Look your best wherever you go – people are watching you, and opportunities are plenty." … Hmmm. Now i'm trying to decide whether You're a Leo or Virgo. Leo is only concerned with financial stuff, so i think You must be a Virgo – which says "A dose of discipline isn't hard to conjure up when you're focused on helping others have fun" … hmmm.

i also found an ad in the paper today for an executive director's job at a south suburban hospice & have decided to apply for it.

i'm used to being in the executive role, & this middle management job i've got now is getting on my nerves. i need something more creative and autonomous & less tedious. So i guess i'll see what happens.

i am looking forward to serving You tomorrow night. It will probably be about 6:30pm when i can get there. i've been thinking it would be nice if You could come to my house sometime, & i could fix You a nice dinner and serve it to You like a good little slave and then ... well, the rest would be up to You.

Love,
Your puppy

January 12, 2004

sharon smith wrote:

Dear Master,

i couldn't sleep last night & was browsing the internet. I came across a site that contained an interesting article; the site was called *www.hypnoland.com*. This is the first time i've seen anything in writing that relates hypnotism to BDSM. It's a topic i've brought up in the past with others & got no response. i'm wondering: would You be interested in talking about it?

Your puppy

January 12, 2004

sharon smith wrote:

Dear Sir,

As much as i hate to do this, i think i better cancel this evening. i think i have succumbed to the cold/flu that everyone has been passing around. i would be happy to give You anything You want, but i don't think You want this. Hopefully, i'll be over it by Wednesday.

Please let me know that You've received this so i know You got the message.

Thank You.

Your puppy

January 13, 2004

sharon smith wrote:

Dear Master,

i have never in my life felt so miserable from a cold. Finally gave up trying to work about 2:00pm this afternoon. That is the first time i've ever taken a sick time when i'm actually sick … much more fun to take sick days to play. i hope You are staying well. The way i'm feeling right now i can't imagine i'll be well by Thursday, & i don't want to take any chance of spreading it to You … probably best to wait.

Take care,

Your puppy

January 13, 2004

Steven Toushin wrote:

Dear puppy,

I am sorry that you are sick. With all the things going on in your life right now, I am surprised you get up in the morning. Sleep and take care of yourself. See you Thursday.

Sir

January 16, 2004

sharon smith wrote:

Dear Master,

i think i am starting to feel better. Made it downstairs this morning for the first time since Tuesday night & planning to go back to work tomorrow. In the midst of my feverish haze the past couple days, i've had an ongoing dream about serving You … in a perfect world where nothing else intruded, and i always knew exactly what You wanted, & You were always very happy. Strangely, Your wife was in the dream too … and it was good … she liked having me there. She had lots of layers of clothing flowing around her & very curly light brown hair down to her shoulders. i got the impression she was a college profes-sor or a Ph.D. of some sort ... sound like anyone You know?

i am really missing You. i expect to be fully recovered by Sunday night & can be available to serve You if You want ....

Hope to see You soon.

Your puppy

January 16, 2004

Steven Toushin wrote:

Dear puppy,

I have been thinking about you and do hope you are well.

As I was writing this, your e-mail came in. Yes, I knew someone just like you described.

Let's get together during the week. Again, let me know when. Rest up and get your strength back.

Sir

January 17, 2004

sharon smith wrote:

Dear Sir,

i hope You are enjoying the weekend. i am feeling much better today! my dining room chairs were fiiiiinally delivered today, so now i have a table AND chairs & am feeling a little more civilized. Also, my son called today. i don't remember if i told You he was accepted into grad school, which is an honor in itself as it was very competitive. Well, he called today to say he won a very prestigious scholarship which means his whole tuition, books, and living expenses for grad school will be covered – which will make the extra two years it will take before entering the work force a whole lot easier on his mind. He is really flying, & i'm really proud of him. This is the kid who perfected the art of a D- in high school. i never thought he would make it through the first semester of college. When i graduated from college with a 4.0 g.p.a. he spent a lot of time & effort harassing me about what a waste that was. Now i get to just sit back & smile as he fully intends to prove he's smarter than his mother.

i discovered the *CastleRealm* website last night. Are You familiar with it? It has some interesting/ enlightening stuff. Other than fiction & stuff on *alt.com* & *adultfriendfinder.com*, i've never had the opportunity to read much about D/s. i guess i entered into the whole thing rather "blindly." It's kind of nice to see that other people have the same thoughts/desires as i do.

Also, i got a thing from our insurance company today that says having sex at least twice a week will improve one's health & can add ten years to your life. Imagine that!!! i knew that serving You was a good thing!! Will have to work extra hard now to make up for missing a week ….

i miss You.

Love,
Your puppy

sharon smith wrote:

Dear Master,

i am going to write a quick note now because i don't know if i'll have access to a computer again before tomorrow night. When i got home from work tonight, i was greeted by a waterfall coming through the garage ceiling. Apparently a water pipe froze & broke & did a lot of damage in the house & garage, & now i have no water. The insurance company & the association are sending people out tonight, & i'll probably end up in a hotel. i am doing an education program all day tomorrow & so won't have Internet access then either. i'm still planning to serve You tomorrow night, but not sure what will be going on around here, so i will call You tomorrow sometime to let You know for sure.

Sheesh! my new year is not starting out too well ... things can only improve as the year goes on!!

Your puppy

January 20, 2004

sharon smith wrote:

Dear Master,

Welllllll, i must say that the emergency troops arrived quickly & were quite efficient. The pipes are fixed, & i have water. The ghostbusters will be hanging around a few days to finish drying the place out, & the garage & half the house will have to be gutted … so things ought to be back to the way they were by about … maybe July.

On the bright side though, the insurance company will have to replace my piano, which i've been wanting to do for years but didn't want to spend the money. i swear there is nothing left to do but just laugh at how ridiculous my life has gotten lately. Last night when i came home, it took me an hour & a half to get through the gate. Yesterday was the first day the gate to the townhomes was functional, & so i was all prepared with my code & procedure. The only problem was that the association neglected to put my code in the computer, & so the gate wouldn't open. i ended up having someone from the fire department come out here at midnight to put in their emergency code so i could get to my own house! i kept looking around thinking i was on Candid Camera or something. Hopefully they've got it straightened out now, or i will have to abide by a 9pm curfew (the time they close the gate), and that would not be a good thing!

So back to the point of this letter – since i will have to take the day off work tomorrow to deal with adjusters, contractors, etc., i should be able to get to Your house earlier than i have been … so i'm wondering how early You would like me to arrive? That is, if i don't get swept away by a tornado … or trampled by a herd of angry elephants … or hit by a meteor!!!

Your wet puppy

Part VI

Puppy's Story

January 22, 2004

Dear Master,

First, i have to tell You my good news. The interview went very well today. The job sounds much more interesting & challenging than what i'm doing now, & they offered me $18K more in salary than what i'm getting now ... and what i'm getting now is $15K more than i was making at my last job 3 months ago. It all sounds too good to be true. i told them i wanted to think about it a couple days, & i've been sitting here trying to think of the negatives that might be involved & can't come up with anything. Of course, i know that everything sounds better in an interview than in real life, but it's very similar to what i was doing in Indiana, about the same size of program, & for an extra $33K i'm pretty sure i can handle whatever they're not telling me ... so i think i'm going to take it. i figure it was meant to be because i wasn't even looking for a job & just happened to see the ad when i was bored & looking at the classifieds one day ... just got lucky to see it. That's the nice thing about luck ... it always changes!

Next i want to tell You that i especially enjoyed serving You last night. i don't think it was anything in particular that we did ... just felt more of a connection to You, i guess ... maybe i'm starting to relax a little more ... didn't think i was uptight before, but maybe so. While i'm writing this i'm thinking about how we all subconsciously bring past experiences into current relationships & expect people to think & respond the way others have before. In my relationship with Master Rob, he quit communicating after the initial "getting to know you" stage, and the rest of the time was spent with me having to write endless letters to other women trying to get them to meet us. With other people, i always told them up front that finding other women wasn't something i wanted to do, & they would always say they had no interest in that either, & the next thing i'd know, they would want the same thing. So i guess even though You said that wasn't something You wanted, i think i've subconsciously been waiting for the "bomb" to fall. For some reason, i feel like last night i/we got past that point & we are moving in a different direction ... kind of a shifting on the inside ... an increased level of trust.

Now, regarding my early sexual experiences, i'm thinking i should tell You about my childhood for You to understand how i ended up being a stoner & sucking a room full of cocks at the age of 14-15 ... but not sure if You're interested in that aspect of things, so will stick to the actual events/activities that i can remember.

Let's see ... the first thing i can remember was my first kiss, & it's kind of funny because i never made this connection before, but it had a flavor of BDSM to it. i was in the sixth grade & had just gotten off the school bus & was walking home when this high school kid (Blake) who lived down the street came & stood in front of me & said he wouldn't let me past unless i let him kiss me. Being a very good little girl, i wasn't about to let that happen. After a lot of resistance on my part, he finally let me go if i agreed to meet him later. i figured i could just avoid him until he forgot about it ... but that wasn't the case. He found me alone later that same day &, when i again resisted, he twisted my arm behind my back & took me out in the woods where i continued to fight it – mostly because i thought it was the proper thing to do. He ended up tying me to a tree with some vines that happened to be there, & then he held my head so i couldn't move & then kissed me very gently ... and then he put his tongue in my ear, & i thought i was going to pass out!! (In retrospect this is all quite funny.) Then he forced my hand in his pants, & he was hard, & it scared me because i naively had no idea what that was all about. Then he became very patient &

big brotherly & explained all about the "birds & bees," & he ended up showing me how to give him a hand job. i ended up being fascinated by the whole thing (an eager student), & we ended up becoming very close friends until i got married & he moved to Florida to become a police officer. He taught me a lot about sex, but we never did have intercourse ... not sure why, now that i think about it.

To be continued ....

puppy sharon

January 24, 2004

Steven Toushin wrote:

Dear puppy,

Congratulations on the new job.

Thank you for telling me about your new level of comfort.

Yes, I do want to hear about your childhood. Describe in detail what you did with Blake (and all other situations), what you went through, and how you felt. I am concerned about your feelings and actions in minute detail.

Sir

January 24, 2004

sharon smith wrote:

Dear Sir,

No one has ever asked me these questions before. i can't even remember anyone else ever asking about my feelings about anything at all i've experienced ... and my own husband has never even asked me anything about my childhood. That sounds pretty pathetic, doesn't it? Now i've got a zillion bits & pieces running through my mind & don't know where to start. i started writing about my childhood, but it sounded too negative so i deleted it, because i actually had quite a happy childhood. It's just that things you would normally think are bad were actually good, & things you would normally think are good were not good. To explain part of it wouldn't make sense, & to explain all of it would take forever. Maybe more specific questions would help.

i can tell You that my relationship with Blake was never a romantic thing. We were never boyfriend/girlfriend ... never went on a date or anything. He was big on philosophizing about life, about people, about destiny ... and he was in love with the color purple. His bedroom was purple, his car was purple, and one afternoon we even tie-dyed all his underwear purple & hung it out on the clothesline to dry – much to the horror of all the neighbors. i got in a lot of trouble for that "obscene" display.

He talked a lot about sex & about what guys wanted & what girls wanted. i believed about half of what he said. Anything we did with each other was a matter of curiosity or just goofing around. One day he demonstrated on my neck what a hickey looked like, & i got in a surprising amount of trouble for that, too ... still don't know why my mother was sooo upset about that. He let me practice giving him hickeys all over for a long time that day. It's a good thing my mother didn't see him! Aside from that first kiss, nothing really dramatic stands out in my mind. We spent a lot of time exploring each other's bodies, touching, asking questions, finding erogenous zones, became very comfortable & relaxed just being together naked. He told me how to give a blow job, but i don't recall ever doing it for him. He liked to pin my hands above my head when he kissed me, but he wasn't into anything kinky. i guess it was an unusual friendship. We would both be dating other people & then get together & talk about it & sometimes experiment on each other before trying something for real with the person we were dating. It sounds weird but it worked well at the time.

i remember when i did have sex for the first time & was bleeding afterwards, it scared me & i went to him & he reassured me (after a complete examination) that everything was normal & okay. It saved me a tremendous amount of anxiety because i thought something had gone terribly wrong. i remember that day, too, that he held me for a long time & told me how happy he was for me. As i said before, i learned a lot from him & also had a lot of playful fun. i never felt threatened or used or taken advantage of. It was more like "Sex Education 101" ... an opportunity that every naive little girl should have. The last time i heard anything about Blake was a few years ago that he had been divorced three times, had been through several professions and at that time he was a nurse of all things!

Love,
Your puppy

January 24, 2004

Steven Toushin wrote:

Dear puppy,

This is a good start. I want more sexual detail on each time you got together with Blake, including how you felt mentally, emotionally, and physically. How would your parents feel if they knew (how they were bringing you up)? Also, what did you and your girlfriends discuss when you two were together during and after the get-togethers with the group of young men? How did it all start (in all detail)? How did the young men feel? What did they say before, during, and after?

I want a detailed description of all this, step by step, in installments to be revised as you go along, of all the activities until you left home. We'll call this a latent diary.

Sir

January 24, 2004

sharon smith wrote:

Dear Sir,

Sex wasn't that big a part of my life when i was a teenager. It was more of a sideshow, with partying being the main attraction … had an extraordinary amount of fun partying … could tell You a lot about that!

i remember when i was in the second grade, i had been coming home from school with slang sex words that the boys at school were using. i would ask my mother what they meant, & she wouldn't know, so she would ask my dad & then come back to me with the answer. i think he would go to work & ask guys at work, because sometimes it would take several days to get an answer. Then she came up with this book she read to me ... i remember it had pictures of female anatomy ... ovaries, fallopian tubes, etc. ... all very technical & meaningless to me ... though i must say that years later when i had my first period, i at least knew what it was – which is more than i can say for most of my friends. Anyway, she read this book to me & then she said that there is only one thing that boys want & that is sex, & that under no circumstances was i to allow any boy to touch me until i got married because no one would ever marry me if i was ruined. (Marriage, of course, was supposed to be the ultimate goal in life.) She made it sound like all boys & men were bad/evil & not to be trusted. This was very confusing to me because i was the only girl among my 40+ cousins, & the only girls i even knew were ones at school. i was constantly being "touched" by boys. If i didn't play with the boys, i wouldn't have anyone to play with ... and how could we play anything if they couldn't touch me? My mother never explained what she meant by "touching," and she certainly never explained what she meant by "sex." However, she made it very clear that this "sex" before marriage was an unforgivable sin. i was left with the impression that the Almighty God would immediately strike me dead if i ever let a boy touch me in any way. She also made it very clear that this was the end of any talk about sex, & the subject was not to be brought up again.

How did all this make me feel? At the time, i was determined to follow her instructions. i guess it kind of made me afraid of boys ... i certainly didn't trust them. It set me up for a lot of senseless guilt & confusion, because obviously i couldn't avoid being touched. Although i soon figured out there were different kinds of touching, i never really knew where the line was to be drawn. Each time i let it go a little farther, i halfway expected to be struck by lightening or something. i guess in a way, i'm still expanding my limits & waiting for the axe to fall … but at least i'm having a lot of fun along the way!

Your puppy

January 25, 2004

sharon smith wrote:

Dear Sir,

i got married when i was 18 … three months out of high school … still had a 10:30pm curfew the night before i got married … had to leave the rehearsal dinner early to get home on time.

i started smoking cigarettes when i was 10. We were visiting some friends of the family who lived out in the country. i was tagging along with my brother & their son John, & we went outside. There were a lot of small buildings on their property. John took us to this one building, & he pulled out … i think it was a calendar, or maybe a magazine … and was showing it to my brother. They were snickering & wouldn't let me see it or tell me what it was. i was being a persistent little pest, & they were having great fun keeping me from seeing it. Finally John said i could see it if i could guess whether it was a nude or a nurse. i figured there would be no reason not to show me a picture of a nurse, so i guessed a nude. Then he made a big deal saying i didn't know what a nude was so i couldn't see it, but the way he was acting i figured out what it was. He then got out some cigarettes & said i had to smoke one before i could see the picture so he could be sure i wouldn't run & tattle on him. So i smoked the cigarette, & i remember getting real dizzy, but i was hooked from then on. my brother left as soon as i took the first puff.

Anyway, John finally showed me the picture and, even though i had never seen anything like that before, being a little brat, i didn't give him the response he wanted. i think i said something like "so what's the big deal?" John was kind of an unusual kid and, thinking he had failed to impress me, he went & got some (probably Playboy) magazines from his dad's collection, & we spent a long time that afternoon looking at pictures of naked women & smoking cigarettes. From then on, whenever we visited with John's family, it was John & i who hung out together, & my brother was left out. We never did anything with each other, but he always had plenty of pictures to show me. It was always fun looking at the pictures with him because he was in such absolute awe of the beauty of the women's bodies.

His family moved to Phoenix about the time i was a freshman, & a few years later he got hold of some bad drugs & ended up developing schizophrenia. He has been catatonic & in a nursing home in Colorado ever since. i went to see him once when i was in my twenties. He didn't recognize or respond to me, & he looked like he was about 80 years old. i never went back.

puppy

January 25, 2004

Steven Toushin wrote:

Dear puppy,

You're doing good.

Now tell me about the partying from 11 years old on up to 18-20, and the different touching the boys would do to you and your friend. Did you object at certain touching? You will get more specific as we go along, and will describe in detail the sexual by-products of the partying. When the sexuality started, did you and the boys look forward to it?

Sir

January 25, 2004

sharon smith wrote:

Dear Sir,

Regarding whether i objected to certain kinds of touching ... by the time i was around 13, i was very self-conscious about the fact that i was totally flat-chested, while all the other girls had breasts. (That was actually a big issue for me up until just a few years ago.) Whenever a guy would reach for my chest, i would be embarrassed & would move his hand down to my pussy, or i would reach for his cock to distract him. Only a couple guys ever saw me without a top on when i was a teenager. i always felt ugly & inferior because i didn't have a set of big boobs. The funny thing is that i've yet to meet a guy who saw that as a problem.

When i was younger, no matter where i went guys would swarm around me & make fools out of themselves trying to get my attention, often in front of their wives or girlfriends ... and i could never understand why. It caused a lot of problems, especially after i had my kids. But i had myself so convinced that i was ugly due to the lack of breasts that i was completely & totally oblivious to the fact that other people were seeing anything else that might be attractive.

i'm not sure where i'm going with all this … i guess the answer to Your question is yes, i did object to certain kinds of touching, but not for reasons one might expect.

puppy

January 25, 2004

Steven Toushin wrote:

Dear puppy,

You write well. What I have in mind (for two reasons) is to get your early years, parental up bringing, attitudes and your sexual awakening in explicit detail.

About being tied to the tree with vines: how did you feel at the time, how did you feel that night and the next day, mentally, emotionally, and sexually?

Tell me about when you first masturbated, and the get-togethers with the boys and your girl friend. Then jump from 18 to how and when you got involved in rough sex, the thought and emotional process into BDSM, then your encounters with all the Dominants in detail.

I am looking for a diary of your sexual and BDSM awakening. If it reads well, I have a wonderful idea for *kinkybooks*.

So, continue writing to me on what I am asking. Do not be shy or I will gladly punish you severely, which is a contradiction, since you will jump at the opportunity to enter subspace, so where's the punishment?

Sir

January 25, 2004

sharon smith wrote:

Dear Master,

Having sexual experiences & having a sexual awakening are two different things & don't necessarily occur simultaneously ....

After being tied to the tree, i remember running home thinking that my mother somehow knew what had happened & fearing that i was going to get in trouble for it. Of course, when i ran in the door, my mother had no idea what had happened & didn't even pay attention to me. i spent the rest of the day in my room worrying that she was going to find out & i would be punished. When i went to bed that night, it finally dawned on me that i was okay ... my body was still the same, i didn't look any different, didn't sound different, didn't move different, didn't disintegrate into a pile of ashes ... no one would be able to tell by looking at me that anything happened ... i was relieved and safe. i don't recall feeling any kind of sexual spark with that experience. In fact, i don't recall ever feeling any sexual spark with Blake, with the exception of one time when i was around 16 & we happened to see each other at a party. i think we would probably have made love that night, but the cops busted the party & put an end to that. In the rapid exodus from the party, i somehow ended up in a car with a half-dozen football players & ended up getting fucked by the star quarterback. i can't even remember his name ... but he was very cute ... tall, dark, & handsome ... the fantasy of every girl in the high school. He was nice but not my type. i don't remember if i ever talked to him after that night.

i don't have any idea how old i was when i started masturbating. i do remember having sexual feelings before the age of five. The reason i remember i was that young is because we moved when i was five. i remember being at a neighbor's house. Their granddaughter was visiting & we were in their pool & then went in their house to change clothes. i remember seeing her naked, & it ignited some powerful, unidentifiable feelings. i asked her to spread her legs, & she let me explore her anatomy. She must have felt something, too, because after that she would always come looking for me whenever she visited her grandmother, & i recall on more than one occasion our play involved that kind of thing. It always made me feel deliciously naughty, and it created a ... hunger? i had those kinds of experiences with multiple girls before i became interested in guys. Come to think of it, the stuff with girls stopped about the time i got involved with Blake. Anyway, i'm getting off track.

i suppose it was somewhere between the second & sixth grade when i started masturbating. i don't remember any details or circumstances, but i do know it happened by accident in the beginning. my clit must have been super-sensitive at the time because a brief touch created intense feelings of pleasure. Once i discovered this source of pleasure, i took advantage of it as often as possible. It seemed as natural as breathing. i had no idea what i was doing, or that it was even a sexual thing. Then i remember one day i was sitting in the living room with my brother & watching TV. I was absentmindedly playing with myself when i noticed my brother looking at me with a look of disgust on his face. It was then that i realized it wasn't something i should be doing in front of people. (Laughing ... i was so dumb.)

After that, my self-pleasuring only took place in bed at night, under the covers, with the lights off … a nightly ritual … and i always slept quite peacefully! The fact that i was doing this was not something i ever talked about to anyone else. i thought i was the only one in the world who ever did it. Eventually, i heard the term "masturbation," but it was always in reference to the idea that it was a bad thing, something to be ashamed of … and that it would cause you to go insane or blind or at the very least, you would never be able to enjoy sex if you had ever done it. i think there was more guilt associated with that than anything else i've ever done. To this day, i've never discussed it with another woman, & it wasn't until i got involved in BDSM that i ever admitted it to a man. my husband still thinks it's a shameful thing, and he has no idea i've ever done it. He sees it as some kind of inadequacy on the part of a person's sexual partner that would lead a person down such a shameful path.

puppy

January 25, 2004

Steven Toushin wrote:

Dear puppy,

You're doing good. Now you need to elaborate on what happened in the car with the football players and the quarterback. What happened in that period of hours and, again, how did you feel during, after and the following days? You are leaving out the sexual details that need to be put in.

Also, you bring up another subject: young girls experimenting; elaborate and detail your feelings. At what age did you start masturbating? Explain to me your difference between sexual awaking and the sexual experience, and what accrued to you mentally, emotionally after your first sexual experiences (seeing a cock, touching a cock, masturbating a cock, etc.) in the different stages of being a teenager. Also, what were your feelings about a dick when you first encountered one, and as time went on? The same about your exploration of your friend's body and pussy.

You're doing good. As you remember things, you will fill in the details. We will then fast-forward to the last 5-7 years.

By the way, is what I am asking of you bothering you in any way? If so, I will stop. If it is not, we will complete this project; this is what I want and desire from you.

Sir

January 25, 2004

sharon smith wrote:

Dear Sir,

No, it isn't bothering me to write about this stuff. It isn't easy trying to remember stuff that happened over 30 years ago, though. i'm remembering things in snapshots, not videos … trying to remember how i felt about them is harder. Had i known i would one day have to explain them, i would have taken notes! 🙂

With the football players … i was pretty stoned and, as i said, already had my juices flowing. When the cops came, everyone started running, & i just jumped in the first car i could find. There were already four guys in the back seat, so i had to sit on … aha – his name was Danny … i sat on Danny's lap, though it wasn't until we were a few blocks away that i even knew it was him. He started running his hands over my legs & ass & saying something about how nice they were. i was about to give him an elbow in the gut but then turned & saw who it was ... he was quite the sexy guy. The other guys started making comments about my ass & legs, & i remember him saying, "no, this one's mine," & the other guys all shut up right away. i relaxed & leaned back so our heads were close together & we talked for a little while. He was very charming. He asked me some questions, like was i going out with anyone, etc. Then we started kissing & making out. At some point, the car must have stopped & the other guys got out, leaving just the two of us & the driver ... i wasn't really paying attention. We spent a long time kissing. He was running his hands up & down my body, not stopping in any particular place ... unusual for a high school guy – they usually got right to the point. He made me feel beautiful & special.

i remember i laid down across the back seat & pulled him on top of me. We were fully dressed but i could feel his hard cock against my pussy. i was wishing he would do something, but he was being very respectful ... maybe inexperienced? possibly shy? So i started rubbing his cock through his jeans & could feel a wet spot almost right away. His kisses became a little more intense, but he still didn't do anything. By this time i was really ready to be fucked, & was about to go for the guy in the front seat if Danny wasn't going to make a move. i remember reaching up & tickling the guy's neck like – this is getting boring back here, want to join us? He ignored me. Danny didn't notice. So i started trying to undo Danny's jeans – not something i've ever been particularly adept at – and hard as i tried, i couldn't get the job done. Fiiiinally, he gave me some assistance, and voila! out popped his erect cock. At that point in time, i had had enough experience to know to be careful or he would cum before i got anything in return. So with my hand, i pressed his cock against his abdomen & just held it there until he relaxed a little. It was funny because he was moaning like a sick dog. i figured there was no way this guy was going to last long enough to fuck me, so i figured i would push him off me & at least try to give him a blow job before he ejaculated all over my clothes.

About the time i was trying to push him away, his buddy in the front seat came to my rescue & made some snide comment. And being the consummate team player with a reputation to up-hold, Danny came to his senses & became more aggressive. In a matter of seconds, he had my pants down around my ankles. He shoved his cock into me & started fucking me like it was his idea in the first place. He didn't last long, but long enough. When he was done, you'd think he just scored a touchdown. He had just fucked a girl, & his buddy was even there to witness it! It was no doubt the talk of the locker room for a while, with lots of backslapping & high fives, i'm sure. How did i feel about it? i got what i wanted, & he was happy, so it was a good day. i honestly don't remember where i went or how i got home after that … probably went back to a party somewhere & got stoned all over again. Never thought much about it after that. Jocks were not the kind of people i was interested in.

Good grief! If it takes me this long to answer one question, You will certainly have a book by the time i answer all of them!

Your puppy

January 25, 2004

sharon smith wrote:

Dear Master,

Young girls experimenting. i guess it was a safe thing for horny little girls to do. As a part of growing up, it was acceptable for girls to see each other naked in the shower, locker room, slumber parties, etc. – the same as it was for boys to see each other. i never really thought about it before, but now i wonder if little boys explore/experiment with each other before venturing on to the opposite sex. With all the openness & acceptance of being gay these days, i wonder how many people just stop there & assume they're gay without looking any farther. When i was that age, i had never heard of such a thing as being a lesbian. Nowadays, kids can tell you what it's all about by the time they start kindergarten. i'm not so sure that's a good thing. Seems like it would prevent some kids from innocently exploring their sexuality in a way that comes naturally & put a label on other kids who do explore. At that age, kids have such a limited ability to think in the abstract or to process their experiences. i think if someone had told me at that age that i was participating in lesbian activities, i would have been really screwed up.

What did we do? i guess we were a little off-center. In the earliest stage, we played a lot of pretend games, like house, school, doctor, etc., except our games were a little different. A favorite game was "mean mother." This always involved pulling the "naughty" child's pants down & whipping her ass ... lots of punishment & torturing of whoever was chosen to be the naughty child on that day ... and all of it involving one's privates. Doctor games always involved a lot of examination, poking & prodding of the pussy ... laughing ... in fact, i don't think anything else was ever examined. The patient always had to be naked for the examination &, no matter what the diagnosis was, it always required a "shot" in the ass & usually "surgery" with toy silverware to correct the problem – and if you were a bad patient & didn't hold still, a jump rope would serve to tie you down for the necessary treatment to take place.

How did i feel about it? i was always an eager participant regardless of my role. We knew it wasn't something our parents would approve of, but we had fun with it. It seemed like a natural thing to do. When we got older, the games changed a little but were still along the same line. We would pretend to be older boys & girls & kiss each other & play with each other's pussies. The "boy" was always bad, & the girl would try to fight him off, but he would pin her down & do what he wanted. (Hmmm … i guess that's why i was never traumatized when i was later tied to a tree.) We played truth or dare, & that always involved sexual stuff. i don't remember anything specific. my feelings about it? i felt very close to a couple of the girls. The rest didn't play the way i liked, some wanting to go too far, and they made me feel uncomfortable. i remember one girl, Susan, who wanted to stick her fingers into my pussy, & i got kind of upset about that & stopped the game. None of our experimenting ever involved any kind of penetration … that would have been crossing the line.

Sexual awakening vs. sexual experiences … i think a sexual awakening has more to do with how you feel about yourself … accepting yourself as a sexual being, liking yourself & your body, liking the way your body feels, understanding what you are feeling. It requires knowledge first, and then acceptance, and results in a freedom to be whoever you are. It's an ongoing thing, perhaps lasting a lifetime, and involves emotions, explorations, growth, and a shaping of your inner self. It may or may not involve another person. A person who chooses celibacy may be as sexually awakened as anyone else. Sexual experiences don't need to have emotions or knowledge or acceptance attached to them any more than does eating or taking a shit or any other body function. Sexual experiences can satisfy (or not satisfy) a physical need in a person who is not sexually awakened. Personally, i had a lot of fun with sex as a teenager, but didn't become sexually awakened until much, much later. There has to be congruence between who you are & what you feel. i don't think that can happen when you're a teenager because you don't know who you are yet. i feel like i'm talking in circles ... time to stop for the night.

To be continued ...

With all of this brainwork going on, i could use a little physical "de-stressing." Have i written enough to allow me the pleasure of serving You this week?

Your puppy

January 25, 2004

Steven Toushin wrote:

Dear puppy,

How old were you (from when to when) when you were experimenting with the other little girls?

Sir

January 25, 2004

sharon smith wrote:

Dear Master,

Experimenting ... probably from around age 5 to about age 12 ... though experimenting for a 5-year-old is quite different than for a 12-year-old.

puppy

January 25, 2004

Steven Toushin wrote:

Dear puppy,

How is your week looking for you to serve me? You must be busy in good thought with the new job offer, your presentation in the fall, and my requests about your young life.

Remember, you will be skipping years. What you do write will have to be very detailed. It will all have truth. We will get into parental upbringing (we will get into that in some detail), feelings, emotions, and very detailed sexual explicitness for erotica, reasoning and purpose.

It will take some time; just answer all my questions. You are doing beautifully.

Sir

January 25, 2004

sharon smith wrote:

Dear Master,

Well, it seems we are thinking about the same thing. i received this e-mail as i sent my last one. i can be available Monday thru Thursday again. Tuesday & Thursday would probably work best ... my period will be light or done by then.

puppy

January 26, 2004

sharon smith wrote:

Dear Master,

Parental upbringing: my mother was always sick & stayed in bed all day for as far back as i can remember. She always kept all the drapes & shades closed – had a phobia about someone looking in the windows. Because she was always sick, i took care of all the housework, laundry, cooking, etc. Again, i remember doing this at the old house, so must have started before the age of 5. my grandmother helped out when she could. It wasn't until about 10 years ago that i learned my mother was stoned on Valium throughout my whole childhood. my father was in the Navy for a while & then worked shift work with a lot of double shifts, so he wasn't around much. He was very distant ... not sure if he even knew i existed most of the time. i was always afraid of my father ... he had a bad temper.

i am mostly Dutch & was raised in the Christian Reformed Church ... a very strict religion. They were very conservative & big on condemning people & had lots of rules, like no dancing or roller-skating or anything that would involve raising your feet off the ground if you were a girl. A very patriarchal religion ... women were second-class citizens & didn't get the right to vote on church business until just a few years ago. We attended church twice every Sunday & also several times during the week.

Twice they tried to excommunicate my "sinful" family ... once because my dad's job required him to work on Sunday, and once because he used "you" & "your" instead of "thee" and "thou" when he prayed. That involved a trial of sorts on a Sunday morning in front of the congregation. We had to stand up front & be condemned by everyone. i remember my mother did a lot of crying. It always upset me a lot to see my mother cry ... scared me.

i remember once when i was in about the 6th or 7th grade, i had this favorite dress that i wore every Sunday to church. i remember it was navy blue with white pinstripes going diagonally across it, & it was a stretchy, satiny fabric that was clingy ... and it was short, but not extremely so ... certainly not any shorter than any of the other girls were wearing. That was when mini-skirts were in style. One of the men in church (i think he was an elder at the time) decided one day that my dress was causing him to "lust in his heart," & so i was marched to the front of the church where he spouted off about what a whore i looked like & how i was causing the men of the church to sin. It was very embarrassing for me. i remember my vision blurring, & i just kind of mentally checked out. my parents never stuck up for me.

In fact, from then until the time i got married, every time i went shopping for a dress, my mother would make a black mark on my leg exactly 2 inches above my knee, & i was not allowed to buy a dress if the black line showed. Fortunately, longer skirts came into style shortly after that incident so it didn't matter.

i was very involved in the church when i was a teenager ... taught Sunday school, bible school, president of youth society, etc., etc., etc. If any job needed to be done, they always came to me. Then when i was going to get married, i went to the consistory to ask to get married in the church ... the church i had spent every Saturday morning cleaning, throughout high school, for godsakes! They refused to let me get married in the church because Arthur was raised Baptist. They said if i married him that it would not be recognized by god or the church. Caused my mother to do a lot of crying again. i believe my words were something like "go fuck yourselves" ... though on the inside i was very hurt.

These are some of the same things that came to mind last week when i started writing about my childhood & i deleted it because i did, in fact, have a very fun childhood ... not sure why these things are coming to mind.

puppy

January 26, 2004

Steven Toushin wrote:

Dear puppy,

I am liking your story. I am looking for a book of sorts. Your story, not mine. This has all popped into my head after your first writings to me. I'll explain when I see you.

Now you said you were experienced enough; explain. Let's go back to my first questions, about you and a cock and the first few times, and the young girl. Answer all the questions and take your time. This is like a first draft, so each episode can be a single piece of e-mail. I want detail and personal feelings. How old were you with the football player? Were there any repercussions at school from the other kids?

You will remember more as we get into it.

Sir

January 26, 2004

sharon smith wrote:

Sir,

i was about 16 when i was with the quarterback. By that time, i wasn't going to school very often, so it didn't matter to me what people there said. i don't recall ever hearing anything about it.

puppy

January 26, 2004

sharon smith wrote:

Dear Sir,

Darcy was my party pal. She moved here from England in the 7th grade. i was a cheerleader at the time, & i remember her coming to the game & sitting in the front row & mimicking all the cheerleaders. The other girls were quite annoyed. i thought she was hilarious ... such a klutz. We became best friends immediately & were together pretty much 24/7 for a few years. She introduced me to my first joint and, depending on the availability of the stuff, we got stoned at least 3-4 times every day. Neither of us ever had a steady boyfriend. We preferred a different guy each night & often shared one between us.

i used to practice with the guys' high school cross country team, & Darcy would sit in the stands & throw water balloons on us or spray us with squirt guns when we went by. We were in the eighth grade, so i must have just turned 14. The guys on the team used to hang out at Tom's house after practice, & Tom had a crush on me, so Darcy & i started going there, too. Tom's parents were always traveling in Europe or somewhere ... i don't recall ever seeing them. He lived in this house that looked like an ancient castle both inside & out ... looked kind of creepy. At any given time, there were at least a half dozen guys there & people coming & going all the time. We would go there & get stoned & listen to music & dance & get stoned some more. Tom was a huge fan of "Kiss," so that was usually playing. That was when the "bump" was popular, too. i would really get into the dancing, especially with Drew, who was Trudy's boyfriend. Trudy was my other good friend, but she lived in the next town & couldn't be there most of the time. Sometimes we would go up to Tom's room to get stoned & just kind of lay around & laugh & enjoy it. There might be anywhere from 4 to 10-12 people sprawled out in that rather small room.

One day we had smoked some good stuff, & i was lying on the bed with my arm hanging over the side, & i felt a hairy head & was laughing about who that might be. The owner of it denied that it was his, so i started smacking him in the head, & he claimed he couldn't feel anything, so someone else started yelling "ouch." That started this whole thing of going around feeling body parts & trying to decide who they belonged to. (It seemed quite funny at the time.) Of course, if you're checking body parts, you definitely want to make sure that every guy has his own cock in his pants & hasn't lost it somewhere. i recall Darcy saying something about hunting for treasure, & we were crawling around amongst all the bodies looking for cocks. We both tended to get a bit hyperactive when we partied. Without too much effort, we managed to uncover them all & were sitting there enjoying the sight & then, being stoned, we were getting hungry … i do believe it was Darcy who brought up the idea of cocksucking … though it might be that we got the same idea at the same time. Anyway, she said she would if i did & vice versa, & so we decided to go for it at the same time … except that i did & she didn't … at least not until i had come up for air. That was my first time tasting a cock … not sure if it was her first time or not. We had a lot of fun going from one to another & comparing flavors & joking around. We used to kid around about that day for a long time after that. There were never any emotional or mental issues involved with it. It was just a good time.

puppy

January 27, 2004

Steven Toushin wrote:

Dear puppy,

Was that your first time sucking cock? Did they cum and where? If in your mouth, how did it taste to you? Did you drink it down? After that day, what were the boys' reaction to all this in the following days? Also, tell me about the first time you saw a cock and the first time you jerked one off. Be truthful; do not make up a story.

Where did you find the time to get stoned, do schoolwork, work in the church, practice with the cross-country team, and be home taking care of your mother? Please explain.

Sir

January 27, 2004

sharon smith wrote:

Dear Sir,

Yes, that was my first time sucking cock. None of them came in my mouth. That would have been gross! After that day, we just continued partying. i already told You about Blake. That was the first time i saw a cock or touched one.

For the rest of it, i was a rather precocious child academically. i was doing chemistry & calculus in the 3rd grade. By the time i got to junior high, i was totally bored with school as there wasn't anything available within the school system for kids like me. i rarely went to high school, just to take tests or to party … certainly never did any schoolwork. The whole object of getting stoned was to kill off brain cells. i was also a pretty hyperactive child … didn't spend much time sitting on my ass. And i wasn't taking care of my mother, just the house.

This is why i don't like talking about myself … too complicated.

puppy

January 27, 2004

Steven Toushin wrote:

Dear puppy,

That was very good.

Again, I want to know about the 1st few times of the various sexual things you did. How did you feel before, while involved and performing, and after? Also, how did it fit into your life with school, church, and parents – this progression of sexual activity?

Were you teased at school by your friends, strangers?

Go over my other e-mails and fill in the blanks. Each thought, again, should be detailed in action, feelings, emotions and circumstances.

Sir

January 27, 2004

sharon smith wrote:

Dear Master,

i was thinking about Tom's house & all the fun we had there, & the house reminded me of my BDSM Session #2. As a bit of background to this story, i had been with Rob one time, which was my initiation into BDSM. i had absolutely no idea what i was getting into when i met him at that hotel room for the first

- 120 -

time. Laughing ... i think that may have been my sexual awakening.

About a week after that first session, he sent me an e-mail telling me to meet him at a certain address in Glen Ellyn. His only instructions were that i was to wear 4-inch heels and be there at 10am. When i questioned him about it, he told me it was a house that belonged to his slave, Marlene. i was really sooooo clueless about BDSM at the time ... not sure if i had even heard the term yet. i assumed i would be meeting him there, & it would just be the two of us for more of what we did the first time. When i got to the house, it looked like a stone castle ... kind of intimidating. my imagination kind of took off trying to picture the kind of people who would live there. i went to the door & knocked.

Marlene opened the door ... surprise #1. Marlene has platinum blond hair, & she had lots of makeup on & was wearing some kind of black lingerie with the nipples cut out. She smiled & said hello. i was ready to turn around & run out the door. Rob then came into the room & put a blindfold on me. He & Marlene then took off my coat, & he led me through the house & up this winding staircase to a bedroom upstairs. He told me to get undressed – everything but my shoes – and then he put a leather collar on my neck. Still blindfolded & dressed only in collar & shoes, i was led back down the stairs, through the house, & told to kneel on the floor with my knees spread wide & my hands resting on my thighs. (The only part of the house i had actually seen at this point was the entryway, so i had no idea where i was. Also, i had not been introduced to Marlene, & i wasn't real sure who she was or if she was still there.)

i was left kneeling on the floor for quite a while & could hear nothing that indicated there was anyone else in the room. Finally, someone else came into the room & was told to kneel along side of me. Our arms were tied tightly together both at the wrist & upper arm, & i could tell by the texture of the arm & thigh that it was a man kneeling next to me. my knees were pushed farther apart & clamps were placed on my nipples & pussy. i was then stroked & teased with large feathers, & my pussy was checked for wetness, with Rob telling Marlene to check also. This unknown man & i were left kneeling there for a while, while i could hear Rob & Marlene kissing & playing with each other. Then i was stood up & was placed face to face with this man. His cock was exactly the right height to fit between my legs & rest snugly against my pussy ... thus, the reason for the 4-inch heels. Rob & Marlene were quite proud of themselves for calculating that so perfectly.

We were then tied together tightly with rope at the ankles, thighs, waists, & chest, & our arms were tied tightly to our sides ... a very frustrating position to be in. To keep us from falling over, we were held up by ropes attached to beams in the ceiling. We were tied so tightly together &, with me wearing high heels, it was quite a challenge to remain upright. Rob & Marlene admired their work for a while & then left the room. At that point, John introduced himself & said he was Marlene's husband. i was pretty tense not knowing where i was or having any idea what was going to happen. John was very kind & pleasant, & he was able to get me to laugh.

Rob then came back & started kissing me & touching me & getting me generally worked up. About the time i was starting to relax & enjoy my predicament, he stepped back & started whipping me with a very heavy flogger ... which had me going back & forth with the force of the blows, much to John's enjoyment. Then John was flogged by Marlene, and our asses were both examined for marks. This went on for a while ... i got 60 lashes i think. i always had to count them & say "thank you, Master Rob" after each one. After about every 5 lashes, my pussy was checked for wetness. It was dripping wet after the first 5. After the lashes were done, Rob pulled the clamps off my nipples, & i thought i was going to die. That was the first time i'd experienced clamps. John gave me a lot of sympathy for that. The clamps had been on for at least a half-hour, if not an hour, & my nipples had gotten so numb i forgot they were there. Rob said he was very proud that i wore them that long. Had my feet/legs not been tied, i would have kicked him. my ass was on fire and, according to the observers, quite heavily marked, so ice was brought out & rubbed all over my body. The warmth of John's body was the only thing that kept me from turning into a popsicle.

Eventually we were untied, & i was laid down on the floor & the blindfold removed. John & i were sitting face to face with our legs out in front of us & our ankles were then tied to a spreader bar. Nothing like seeing someone for the first time in such a position! Rob then sat down behind me & leaned me back in his lap & started playing with my pussy & kissing me. At this point, i wanted him to fuck me so bad i thought i was going to explode ... but that didn't happen. Instead, the spreader bar was removed, & my hands were tied behind my back, & i was directed upstairs, with the others following behind admiring my purple backside.

Upstairs i was led into a bedroom, my shoes were removed, & i was tied spread eagle to a king-sized bed ... didn't know my legs would spread that wide. Then i was blindfolded again. John was then placed on top of me with his ankles tied together & his hands tied behind his back & ordered to fuck me. It didn't work very well & was more frustrating than anything, & he was getting his ass whipped for not performing as ordered. He was then pulled off & ordered to make me cum by licking my pussy. While he was working on that, Rob & Marlene came & sat on each side of me & were leaning over me kissing, which meant that Marlene's quite large breasts were in my face threatening to smother me. i did, however, manage to find a nipple to occupy myself with. It was then decided that i hadn't cum enough, & so

John was sent off to get a (very powerful) vibrator, which he applied, to my clit. It took all three of them to hold me down, & i was still tied to all four corners of the bed.

Then Rob ordered Marlene to don a strap-on, & my blindfold was removed so i could see what was coming. She was told to lie on top of me & fuck me ... very frustrating because she couldn't seem to get her coordination going. Rob was whipping her ass at the same time. Then my ankles were untied from the foot of the bed & re-tied to the top of the bed to give her better access, which worked a little better. During all this, John was tied hand & foot to a chair across the room with his cock standing straight in the air. Marlene was told to kiss me & suck on my nipples. The poor woman was exhausted from trying to use the strap-on. Then Rob & Marlene left the room, & i was left tied with my ass up in the air, & John was still tied to the chair, & we just chatted like we were sitting in a restaurant over a cup of coffee.

Then they came back & untied me & put me in a nice warm bath & washed me thoroughly, dried me off, and dressed me. And we all went downstairs, enjoyed some delicious wine, and were served a very elegant dinner prepared by John & Marlene. i found out during dinner that it had been John's fantasy to be tied to a beautiful woman & whipped & to be ordered to fuck her by his wife. i was very touched to be a part of his fantasy.

i soared for weeks after that day ... so many firsts ... everything was so new & unknown ... but that was the only time we ever did such an elaborate scene.

Your puppy

January 27, 2004

sharon smith wrote:

"And he answered, saying:
Your hearts know in silence the secrets of the days and the
nights.
But your ears thirst for the sound of your heart's knowledge.
You would know in words that which you have always known
in thought.
You would touch with your fingers the naked body of your soul.

"And it is well you should.
The hidden well-spring of your soul must needs rise and run
murmuring to the sea;
And the treasure of your infinite depths would be revealed to
your eyes.
But let there be no scales to weigh your unknown treasure;
And seek not the depths of your knowledge with staff or sound-
ing line.
For self is a sea boundless and measureless.

"Say not, 'I have found the truth,' but rather, 'I have found a
truth.'
Say not, 'I have found the path of the soul.'
Say rather, 'I have met the soul walking upon my path.'
For the soul walks upon all paths.
The soul walks not upon a line, neither does it grow like a reed.
The soul unfolds itself, like a lotus of countless petals."

The Prophet
By Kahlil Gibran

January 27, 2004

Dear Sir,

i am orienting new nurses out in the field today & then have a second interview. i asked to meet some of the board members, so i don't know how long that will take. Hopefully, i'll get there around 3:30-4:00pm & to Your house around 6:00-6:30pm.

puppy

January 28, 2004

sharon smith wrote:

Dear Master,

i woke up to Your scent on my pillow this morning ... thank You. It is a gift.

i don't know what this has to do with anything, but on my way home last night, i was thinking about my childhood & about a time when i was a kid that i almost drowned. i was around 8 or 9, maybe older. i was with my family on vacation at Van Bibber lake. We were on a paddleboat in the middle of the lake, and my father & brother & i were diving off the side of the boat while my mother sat in the driver's seat wearing a life jacket. (She was afraid of the water.) i dove into the water and for some reason, my mother started paddling the boat, and it went on top of me. i kept trying to get out from under the boat, but every direction i went, the boat went the same way. Everything was moving in slow motion. i can still picture it perfectly. The blade

- 126 -

from the boat hit my left shoulder & the side of my head ... and it felt soft ... didn't hurt. Then it was like i was watching myself, & it was very peaceful and warm and soft. i quit moving. i knew i was going to die, and it was okay ... i wasn't afraid. Then the next thing i knew, i was on the deck of the boat and started shaking real bad and crying and i was so cold ... and my mother was crying. She was more upset than i was ... and my dad was yelling at her.

Whenever You put that bag on my head, i think about that day ... not sure why. It wasn't a traumatic experience. It was like going to another world that no one else could see.

Your puppy

January 28, 2004

sharon smith wrote:

Dear Master,

After the scene i told You about at Marlene's house, i remember Rob was worried that the day had been too much for a novice such as me. i remember telling him that when i was tied to the bed, surrounded by the three of them, i felt very, very safe. i felt like an infant in the safety of its mother's womb. That extraordinary sense of safety surprised me at the time, but generally speaking, i always feel that way when playing/serving ... and it isn't anything specific that happens ... just a frame of mind, i guess. It's very similar to that feeling of softness, warmth, and peacefulness that i felt under the water that day.

How strange ....

puppy
January 29, 2004

sharon smith wrote:

Dear Master,

The cocksucking session that i told You about must have been
in the fall of 8th grade, and it must have been the following
summer that i lost my precious virginity ... a couple months
before my 15th birthday. i was staying at Trudy's house because
my mother was in the hospital, and Trudy & i had a job picking
blueberries not far from her house. Her mother was driving us
back & forth to work, and it was too far in the opposite direction for her to come to my house to pick me up. It must have
been July ... blueberry season. Trudy had four brothers. Dave
was a year older than us – tall, fair, blue eyes, reddish blond
hair, and freckles. Teddy was a year younger than us – short,
fair, blue eyes, reddish blond hair, and freckles. (Trudy, by the
way, has dark brown hair and dark skin.) i wasn't at all attracted
to Dave or Teddy. The four of us had a lot of fun together, but
they were like brothers to me.

It was very different at their house. In my family, no one got
undressed or used the bathroom except behind locked doors. my
family was very private ... to the extreme. At their house, there
were no locks on the doors. Her dad & brothers would often just
walk in while i was changing clothes, using the bathroom, or
taking a bath. They would just stand there & talk to me while i
was sitting in the tub! That took some getting used to! It was all
very innocent and natural for them.

Trudy's neighbor, Gary, had a crush on me. He was one of
those tall, dark, handsome, & delicious-looking farm boys. The

problem was that he was so shy he never managed to say more than a couple words to me. i liked him, but he made me nervous. Trudy & her brothers thought we were perfect for each other, & they tried real hard to get us together, but it just wasn't happening. We kind of worshipped each other from afar. It was one of those ridiculous & awful teenage things where they would come & tell me what he said, & then go back & tell him what i said.

So one day, Trudy was busy doing something, and Dave & i decided to try flying this huge kite the boys had gotten. We started walking out to a rye field behind their house and were talking about Gary, with Dave telling me what a great guy he was & how he wanted to ask me on a date, and me telling Dave how awkward i would feel if we were together for a whole evening & Gary never said anything. It was really hot that day, too hot to be out in the sun. We were just walking, talking, and sweating, and then Dave just turned & took hold of my arms & kissed me. i started seeing stars & thought i was going to pass out … probably more from the heat than the kiss. i was so shocked that i didn't say a word. We just turned & kept walking.

By the time we got where we were going, i had come to the realization that Dave was the one i had liked all along. i hadn't acknowledged it because i had thought of him more like a brother, & also, he didn't look like the fantasy guy i was looking for. We spread a blanket on the ground in the middle of the field & managed to get the enormous kite up in the air without any difficulty. It would have caught anyone's attention from a mile away. He staked the kite string to the ground, & we stretched out on the blanket to watch it. We were drinking red Kool-Aid®. He started kissing me again, & my whole body was feeling like it never had before … like electricity from all over my body shooting to my pussy. That's the first time i remember my pussy getting so wet. i was cumming all over the place, &

he had hardly touched me. He was being very cautious & respectful, & i thought i was going to burst. i remember thinking ... "This is Dave ... we shouldn't be doing this ... what would Trudy say?"

By that time, our bodies were pressed close together, & i could feel the hardness of his cock. He was as turned on as i was. We started rubbing each other through our clothes & then stopping & moving away from each other & then coming back together. Both of us were quite conflicted about what we were doing ... but my pussy was creating a flood, & his cock was twitching in his shorts like a puppet on a string. We reached for each other's shorts & managed to get them down to below our knees. He starting fingering my pussy, & i grabbed his cock & that lasted about two seconds, & then he got on top of me, & he asked me if i was okay, & i told him to fuck me. When he managed to shove his cock inside of me, it hurt like hell ... felt like i was being ripped in half. i closed my eyes & just froze ... i was trembling. He didn't move either. It was his first time, too. After a little bit, the pain subsided, & i suppose i loosened my death grip on him. He pumped a few times (i didn't move), and then he pulled out & shot his cum on my stomach.

It was the most horrible & wonderful, incredible thing i had experienced. i wanted him to hold me close, & at the same time i wanted to run away. i wanted to laugh & cry at the same time. It was like a whole new world had opened up. i felt free. i was scared. i wanted more. We both got dressed quickly, pulled in the kite, and walked back to the house not saying a word. When we got inside the house, we went in opposite directions. i was sure everyone could tell from looking at me what had happened. (i found out much later that Teddy had watched the whole thing from an upstairs window.) i went into the bathroom to wash myself off & discovered i was bleeding ... quite a bit. i called my dad to come & get me. Before i left, i found Dave laying on his bed already looking worried, so i didn't tell him about the

bleeding ... just told him everything was okay, & he looked relieved.

We went out a couple times after that, & we fucked a couple
times, but no real relationship developed ... no more sparks. We
went back to the brother/sister type friendship that we had before. It was good that way.

puppy

January 31, 2004

sharon smith wrote:

Dear Master,

i will answer Your questions, but first i want to tell You about
something else.

i saw a patient today ... 33 year old man dying from cirrhosis,
which he developed as a result of Hepatitis C infection. Cirrhosis is really a terrible way to go ... lots of horrible symptoms to
deal with ... very upsetting for families, etc., to watch. And i
always find it most difficult to deal with patients who are my
age or younger, especially with something like this. He didn't
even know until a couple weeks ago that he had the infection, &
he must have had it for 10 or 15 years. Anyway, i'm getting off
track. The point is that this patient reminded me of Trudy's
younger brother, Teddy, who i mentioned pre-viously. As it
turned out, Teddy died of cirrhosis at the age of 33, only his was
due to alcoholism.

During the 2½ hours (!!!!) it took me to drive home from the
city today, i was thinking about Teddy & the stuff we used to
do, & how things had gone so terribly wrong in his life. Teddy

was one of the most kind, loving, wonderful, sensitive, generous, open people i've ever known. He was truly a free spirit ...
but he wasn't a survivor. When life kicked him in the nuts, he
didn't understand it ... he was not able to attribute any kind of
negative characteristic to any other person. He simply did not
understand things like hatred, anger, jealousy, etc, ... and these
are the things that drove him into the ground & ultimately de-
stroyed him. He was defenseless. Teddy & i were very close
throughout high school. We spent a lot of time talking about our
philosophies of life & of people & things like that. He looked
up to me as the "wiser older woman" (haha!). During that time,
nothing beyond an occasional hug ever happened between us.
We did party together sometimes, as he could usually come up
with a bag when no one else had anything. After i got married, i
think he felt kind of neglected.

The first couple years after i got married, Arthur was working
as an over-the-road truck driver, & he would show up at home
maybe once a week for a few hours & then leave again. Our
house became a hangout for quite a few people (i guess they
didn't want me to get lonesome), and we did a whole lot of
partying. Teddy would often show up long after everyone else
went home. i remember one night he parked his bright orange
Volkswagen bug on my front porch & started yelling for me to
come outside. Of course, with the car there i couldn't get the
door open, so i ended up crawling through a window, intending
to shut him up before he woke the neighbors. He was standing
on top of the car, which was at a precarious angle, in danger of
tipping over. We were both stoned. i was laughing at him to the
point of tears, & he was trying to be very serious ... professing
his heartfelt love for me. He then fell off the car & landed flat
on his back in the front yard ... only pretending to be dead. i
managed to stumble over to him to give CPR, and despite my
inability to remember anything beyond slapping him in the face,
he miraculously survived ... and slapped me back ... and then

pushed me onto my back, sitting on top of me and pinning my hands above my head.

i started writing this last night & got interrupted. Now i've got my in-laws coming over for the remainder of the weekend, so don't know when i'll have time to finish it.

Your (upside down) initials are still very clear on my chest ... more about that later, too.

Love,
Your puppy

January 31, 2004

Steven Toushin wrote:

Dear puppy,

You were a delight this week, my puppy. You serve me well; thank you.

Instead of making this project larger than it is and being over-whelming, I am going to ask for 4 letters from you. Some may not warrant much of an answer; give your memory a chance to recollect:

- A. Any arousal from the being tied down and spanked as a young girl when playing with the other girls?
- B. Any bondage of sorts or rough sex of sorts from initially being tied up with your girl friends till early in your marriage?
- C. Did you masturbate Blake, explore his dick, or experiment with Blake? If so, how?

D. What do you mean by fun play?

E. Partying: I need more on this. How often, and what occurred at the parties? When you and your girlfriend sucked off the cross-country track guys, did you continue to practice with the team? Were there any nasty personal remarks from anyone? Did you party with them again, or with just a few of them?

Sir

January 31, 2004

sharon smith wrote:

Dear Sir,

i wish i was there serving You tonight. i must confess that i enjoy serving You so much that i feel rather selfish. You are a wonderful Master ... exactly what i've been looking for. How lucky for me to have found You! It is continuously surprising to me the things that make me feel good. i really liked it when You wrote Your name on my ass & Your initials on my chest. i wouldn't have thought that would mean so much to me, but it did.

i was telling my father-in-law about my new job this afternoon, and his response was, "So you're the top puppy now." i think i may have laughed a little too hard at that insightful comment. Now he's continuing to call me "puppy" every time he talks to me.

i had no idea what was happening when BB [Ed. Note: one of Steven's greyhounds] started licking my pussy the other night. i thought You were using some kind of toy. Your kiss was timed perfectly because it was about a half-second before that when i realized whatever it was, it was wet ... definitely messed with my mind! It's a good thing You didn't ask me about that ahead of time because i probably would have said no. It's something i've thought about before but definitely a big taboo with anyone i've ever known. It was Your kiss that made it okay. And i must say, no human tongue has ever done such a good job. Has BB had a lot of practice?

i'm sorry about wandering off-topic with the last letter. That patient yesterday really got to me.

To answer Your questions, yes, i was aroused by the games i played with the other girls. That's why we continued to play them. As time went on, the games got rougher & more involved ... and more arousing. One girl in particular was as least as aroused as i was. Her name was Holly ... she was (is) Blake's little sister. i haven't heard from her in many years ... wonder what she's doing now. We never hung around together once boys entered the picture. None of the stuff i ever did with a boy ever compared to the roughness of our "little girl" games. The boys all seemed too shy and/or respectful, like they were afraid they were going to hurt or offend me. It was very frustrating. i always get annoyed when i hear women whine that they wish a man would want them more for their mind than their body. Most of the boys i knew were afraid to go past my mind ... had to practically sit on their faces to convince them it was okay to touch me. Even the slightest bit of aggressiveness on their part would have them apologizing & feeling guilty ... and there is nothing like apologies & guilt to take the sizzle out of sex. i had long ago resigned myself to a life of boring sex, never having any idea that anyone else was aroused by the same things as i was. Thank god for the Internet!

Love,
Your puppy

February 1, 2004

sharon smith wrote:

Dear Sir,

i think i kind of answered the second question with the first answer. Other than Blake tying me to the tree, the only guy who showed any promise was Arthur. When we were dating, he expected to fuck me whenever & wherever he pleased, with no argument, or i was history. That required being an exhibitionist of sorts, but never involved any rough play. Once we were married, sex was limited to the bedroom … missionary style. He would never let me suck his cock. i've tried for 25+ years to get him to fuck me in the ass, and that has never happened. When he's feeling especially "kinky," he tells me to get on top, but that's a rare occasion. However, what was lacking in quality he made up for in frequency. Any other married women i've known are lucky to have sex a couple times a month, whereas we were always at least three times a week, usually more, except for when i have my period … he won't come near me then. At this point in time, he's pretty sure something is going on because since i've met You, i've lost interest in sex with him … that has never happened before.

Love,
Your puppy

February 1, 2004

Steven Toushin wrote:

Dear puppy,

How did your day go? That little story about your father-in-law is adorable. I am happy that you were being addressed by your proper name (puppy) today, even if they didn't know the significance of it, while you carried my initials on your chest. I was part of you all day.

Now back to the work: please, in detail, elaborate on the physical and emotional aspects in the girls' play with you, and how you and your friends reacted as "the games got rougher, more involved, more arousing."

Sir

February 1, 2004

sharon smith wrote:

Dear Sir,

There wasn't any emotional aspect to the stuff i did with the girls. i think maybe that's why i don't remember much detail about it. There were probably hundreds of that kind of play sessions, but they had no more significance than anything else we did. i suppose you could say it went from a compulsion to an addiction to an obsession, and i think it stopped because we weren't willing to go any farther with girls & were ready to move on to boys.

i remember the "play sessions" usually happened at Holly's house when i would spend the night. Sometimes we would camp out in a tent in her back yard, & it would go on until the sun came up. If i had to classify it, i would have to say she was the more dominant/aggressive one when it was just the two of us. i don't remember ever spanking her or hitting her with anything. i remember at some point, there was a regular bull whip that she used on me ... don't remember where it came from. There were blindfolds and ace bandages and ropes. She liked to tie me with ropes in such a way that they dug into my pussy. She was big on pussy torture ... used anything that happened to be available ... silverware, jacks, rubber bands, masking tape, rubber darts, to name a few.

i remember one time i was blindfolded & had my hands tied together, & she ordered another girl, Susan, to stick her fingers into my pussy. Susan asked me in a whisper if that was okay, & i told her no, so she just pretended to do it. Holly never knew it didn't really happen. She really got off on being in control & giving orders that night. She had us crawling around on the ground & was hitting our asses with a stick that she had sent someone outside to get from a tree. She also had us french-kissing each other & rubbing our pussies together ... laying in opposite directions with our legs intertwined so there was direct pussy-to-pussy contact. i recall getting turned on by that. She got pretty mean & carried away that night. i think that was the last time we ever played in that fashion. She crossed the line, & we felt threatened ... not so much physically, but more mentally/emotionally. She wanted us to do things we didn't want to do ... things that were reserved for boys only.

puppy

February 1, 2004

Steven Toushin wrote:

Dear puppy,

This was very good; thank you.

I am finished asking questions of your times with the girls, at least for the time being. It does bring up another question. You said you did not play any bondage except for Blake tying you up at the tree.

Did you have any yearnings, wanted to, fantasize about being tied up, spanked, made to crawl, ordered about, etc., with the boys:

    A. Up until you got married?

    B. When married until you had your second child?

And yes BB likes it to, and is good at pleasing, I'm happy you noticed.

You have served me on stolen moments. Serving me over a day or two would require you taking care of my many needs in and out of play. But that is just a fantasy, for the time being.

Sir

February 1, 2004

sharon smith wrote:

Dear Master,

With the new job in the past few months & now again in the coming few months, it would be difficult to take any time off to spend a few days serving You during the week. However, once i actually start the new job, an occasional weekend "conference" wouldn't be hard to arrange … actually easier than trying to explain coming home in the middle of the night. Also, Arthur was telling me yesterday that it looks like his job will permanently require him to be gone during the week … i tried very hard to look disappointed while thinking, "How nice!" So, spending the night during the week isn't a problem, except i'd have to get up at 5am to get ready for work.

Regarding any yearnings/fantasies about BDSM … There was always something missing, but i was never able to identify what it was. i thought the things i did as a child were just that – kid stuff – and never thought any more about it. Had no idea that adult men & women enjoyed that kind of thing. i spent all my time trying to fit into a mold of what i thought was acceptable sexual relations. i guess that goes back to my religious background: i.e., sex is for procreation, not enjoyment … and sexual fantasies are sinful. It was okay to think about pleasing a man, but personal enjoyment was not to be considered. Sex was supposed to be a woman's duty & not a desire or a need.

During the time i was getting stoned, which was up until my second child was a couple years old, i (sinfully) allowed myself to enjoy frequent sex with multiple people, but there were boundaries, both in my own mind & within the people i was with. i simply did not allow myself to think about the things i would really enjoy … things that i didn't think anyone else on earth would find acceptable. i never really explored who i was or who i wanted to be. i just did what i thought i was supposed to do and became more & more empty & drained as time went on.

When i finally did discover BDSM, it was amazing to me how quickly & easily i slipped into the role of a submissive ... it felt like i was finally home ... felt so right ... so free. But, as You have brought up before, i quickly discovered that even within the realm of BDSM, people have lots of boundaries/limits and ideas of what is right or wrong. Again, i think my fantasies were limited to what the people i was with found acceptable.

So i kept searching for someone to expand those boundaries, which brought me to You.

Your puppy

February 1, 2004

sharon smith wrote:

Dear Master,

my relationship with Blake was kind of like a teacher & student. i think he realized how naive i was about boys the day he tied me up; and he took it upon himself to become sort of my sexual mentor. The fact that we were usually naked when together didn't mean anything. We were just comfortable laying next to each other & cuddling while we talked. i masturbated him quite a few times ... as part of my "education." i would practice something on him & then go try it with someone else & come back & tell him about it. i remember one guy had cum the second i touched him, & when i told Blake about it, he had me practice bringing him to the edge & then backing off, over & over again. He would describe to me what he was feeling & told me what to look for, what to listen for, what to feel for and what to do, how to adjust. i got to be pretty good at it with him ... not so successful with others. Although, when i think about it, he must have had a remarkable amount of self-control, so my success was probably more due to him than me.

i remember one time i felt the pulsating at the base of his cock &, in an effort to avoid the inevitable, i clamped my hand over the tip. He laughed pretty hard at that, and i got a lecture about paying attention. When i did well, i got lots of hugs & kisses, & he told me how good i was. When i failed, i got a lecture about patience or paying attention or something like that. He told me that some guys are real sensitive after they cum & don't like to be touched, so i shouldn't feel hurt if they turned away or pushed me away. That turned out to be quite helpful information.

He also told me that different guys like to be stroked in different ways, but the most important thing was to maintain a regular rhythm. That took some practice ... and patience. He would demonstrate on himself, but i couldn't seem to get it quite right when i tried it. i remember he even had me bouncing a basketball trying to develop a rhythm. i also remember he had me look at my pussy in a mirror & describe to him what i saw. That was the first time i had ever seen myself. Then he pointed out my clit & brought me to a climax, & then had me watch while my pussy dripped on the mirror.

It sounds kind of dumb now, but it was quite a learning experience at the time. Everything seemed so natural & normal & open when i was with Blake. It wasn't until later that i got all shy & self-conscious, insecure, inhibited.

During most of the time we were friends, Blake had this very volatile love-hate relationship going on with a girl named

Becky. One day, she smashed eggs all over his precious purple car. He was absolutely furious. i was helping him wash the eggs off the car & noticed his cock was hard, so i offered to ease his distress & he let me. When he came that day, he let out this long, deep moan ... much like You do when You cum. i think Beth's lunacy really turned him on. He eventually married her & then divorced her a couple months later. i heard they got into some real knockdown, drag-out fights before they called it quits ... and he was really such a gentle, patient guy.

Your puppy

February 1, 2004

Steven Toushin wrote:

Dear puppy,

Do you know when you will be starting your new job? Also, how are you for Tuesday and Thursday nights?

You still have a few more questions to answer; you are filling in the pieces beautifully.

Sir

February 1, 2004

sharon smith wrote:

Dear Sir,

Tuesday & Thursday nights are good.

i think i'll just give two weeks notice at work & then am thinking i'll take a week off before starting the new job ... haven't
decided for sure.

puppy

February 1, 2004

sharon smith wrote:

Dear Sir,

Tuesday is not going to work for me. my aunt died yesterday, &
i just got an e-mail from my mom that the wake will be Tuesday
night. We thought it was going to be Monday.

Will Monday work for You?

Your puppy

February 1, 2004

Dear Sir,

i don't remember what i was referring to with "fun play."

Yes, i continued to run with the cross-country team. i really enjoyed distance running, & there was nothing like that available
for girls at the time. It was all business when we were running.
They never gave me a break, & i appreciated that. We continued
to party for a couple years until the guys all gradu-ated. There
was one guy (can't remember his name) who looked down on
me after that day. i guess he thought i was a slut, but he also
didn't like me because i never studied or went to class. i figured
it was his problem, not mine. He never said much to me, just
walked away looking disgusted whenever i was around ... like i
was an annoyance to him. Oh well. Nothing changed with the
other guys. If they talked about it among themselves, i never
heard about it. i tasted most of their cocks again at one time or
another, but never all at the same time. That was a unique experience!

i partied all the time with lots of different people from several
towns ... couldn't begin to remember them all. There was a guy
named Tony that we (Darcy & me) used to buy drugs from. He
usually had some damn good stuff, but it was expensive. We
weren't so good at managing our cash flow, so we would often
come up short for what we wanted to buy. Being such a nice
guy, he would give us a break if we invited him & his friend,
Daryl, to party with us. Half the time i don't even know what
we were smoking, but we went on some pretty wild psychedelic
trips.

i remember one time we were listening to Pink Floyd and when the song "Several species of small furry animals gathered together & groovin' with a pic" came on, i started seeing dancing bears & laughing my ass off. (i had been to Disney World a short time before that & had seen the Country Bear Jamboree ... must have left quite an impression on me, because i saw those goofy bears every time i started hallucinating.) Anyway, i was totally unaware of what was going on around me until the song ended, & i sort of came to my senses. i found myself lying on the floor with my head between two speakers & my pants missing. Tony's head was between my legs, & Darcy was below him sucking on his cock, & Daryl was on her other end doing something ... i couldn't see that far. We were stretched clear across Darcy's living room. They were all as stoned as i was.

It was an incredible experience, because even the lightest touch expanded & blossomed into a life of its own. We switched positions a time or two, but we were all so stoned that we ended up just laying there, half-dressed, and having these vicarious, hallucinogenic sexual experiences. When we finally straight-ened up, even Tony had to admit that was pretty good stuff.

We talked about the experience a lot after that & tried on a few occasions to duplicate it. It was never quite the same.

Your puppy

February 2, 2004

Steven Toushin wrote:

Dear puppy,

I have noticed that you're not ending with "Love, Your puppy."
Any reason why?

I e-mailed you about bondage yearnings. I am going to expand.

   A. When did you start to have BDSM feelings, and did you
      act on them? If you did, how? Or did you suppress them?
      Why?
   B. Were you submissive as a teenager?
   C. Did you allow the boys to be in charge? Did you always
      allow the boys to initiate the sex?
   D. Was Darcy your Dominant in your relationship with her?
      Did she direct how the party and play would go?
   E. Did she direct your sexual activity when together, who
      you were to be with, and what you would do with them?

Sir

February 2, 2004

sharon smith wrote:

Dear Master,

i've been having a bit of a crisis here. my computer completely
died. Not sure what i did to get it started again, just started un-

- 147 -

plugging stuff & plugging it back in, & it turned on. Whew! i thought i had gotten another virus & crashed the whole thing.

No, there is no reason for not ending my letters with "love." i still love You. i am touched that You noticed the omission. It won't happen again.

i am going to answer Your easier questions first. Between the two of us, Darcy was much more outgoing & aggressive sexually. i wouldn't have done anywhere near what i did if she wasn't there. The thing was, though, that for some reason guys seemed to be more attracted to me. So the way it worked out was that guys would start talking to me, & i wouldn't have much to say. So, she would take over & get things started, & i would join in later. When it came to sexual or romantic relationships, i was actually pretty shy & reserved … but plenty willing to go along with anything the others wanted to do. In some other things, i was more of a leader & Darcy the follower … but she had other strengths, too. It all worked out pretty even. So i don't know if you could classify her as Dominant.

There was never any sexual contact between the two of us. If we would share a guy, it was Darcy who would make the first move, & then i would be right behind her … i guess she did tell me what to do in that kind of situation. Hmmm … i never really looked at it that way before. When there was more than one guy, i think she usually gave me first choice. Sometimes she would fix me up with a guy for a date, & then she & someone else would come along. (Laughing) She was always afraid i would get myself in trouble if she wasn't there to look out for me. i think most of the stuff we did was a mutual decision, though now that i'm thinking about it, it's very possible that she was directing my role … hmmm. Well, at least i can say that i was a willing participant.

i need to get to bed now so i'll be all rested up to serve You tomorrow.

See You soon.

Love,
Your puppy

February 2, 2004

sharon smith wrote:

Dear Master,

Now i'm having another crisis. i just found a card on my pillow that Arthur put there before he left this afternoon. It's a good luck card, & it says "congratulations" on my new job. Then it says he is no longer willing to try & figure out what's on my mind, & i can't even read what the rest of it says.

i don't know what the hell this is supposed to mean. i think he's walked out on me.

Love,
Your puppy

February 2, 2004

Steven Toushin wrote:

Dear puppy,

Is your husband able to go on to your computer and read your mail? Might your son have helped him get on your computer?

Just questions, thinking of things he might have discovered that would make him upset, if he has actually left, or maybe it was just a kind note written with a little too much alcohol.

Sir

February 2, 2004

sharon smith wrote:

Dear Master,

He's been acting really strange the past few weeks. i don't know what's going on, but I have decided i'm not going to pursue it this time. i think his mother has been putting ideas in his head again, & i'm tired of fighting it. If he comes back, he does, & if not, i don't care. It's just that the timing really sucks between the house being torn apart & with me in the process of switching jobs & having recently moved & not knowing anyone around here & it being the middle of winter when everything is more difficult to get done anyway. At least i know how to turn the water off now, if something happens with that.

And no, he doesn't know how to use the computer, & he wasn't drinking yesterday, & he hasn't discovered anything except the fiction in his own head. He left the note so i would get worried & upset & go running after him, & i'm not going to do it. i guess it's a stalemate.

i'm sorry to bother You with all this as i know You don't want to get involved in marital issues.

Love,
Your puppy

February 2, 2004

Steven Toushin wrote:

Dear puppy,

Sorry.

Sir

February 2, 2004

sharon smith wrote:

Dear Sir,

i'm confused. You don't have anything to be sorry about. Honestly, if i loved him the way a wife should love her husband in the first place, i would have never met You.

i have to leave for work ... can explain more later.

Love,
Your puppy

February 4, 2004

sharon smith wrote:

Dear Master,

It's after 1am, & i just got home from the wake & subsequent nursing consults.

Too tired to think about writing ... will write more tomorrow.

Love,
Your puppy

February 4, 2004

sharon smith wrote:

Dear Master,

i just want to make sure we're still planning on the same thing. Had switched Tuesday to Monday, but i'm still planning to serve You tomorrow night as You originally said. i need to take care of some stuff at home tonight.

Have a good day!

Love,
Your puppy

February 4, 2004

sharon smith wrote:

Dear Master,

i'm sorry about the short notes earlier. It was a very long day yesterday. Something is wrong with my mother now. i think she's become toxic from all of her medications again. i seriously would like to shoot/strangle/hang all these doctors who prescribe amphetamines, anxiety meds, anti-depressants, sleep-ing pills, etc., etc., etc., to every woman who walks in their office. She was taking 24 different medications, most of them working against each other ... insane!

It was announced at our team meeting today that i'll be leaving, & i was very touched by the response after only being there for 4 months. i had no idea how much it meant to the staff for me to be in the field helping out. After the meeting, my office was full of people for two hours, crying & asking me to hire them at my new place of work ... and these were some tough bitches when i started there ... amazing ... you'd think they'd never been treated like human beings before.

i had a wonderful time serving You the other night ... and You did an excellent job of clearing all the clutter from my mind! i want You to know that i do want to serve You in any way that You desire & not just be a "do-me-queen." i just need You to tell me what You want me to do.

i don't remember where i was on the questions, so will send this now & then go back to the list.

i am looking forward to serving You tomorrow night.

Love,
Your puppy

February 5, 2004

sharon smith wrote:

Dear Master,

Question A is a hard one, because i'm not sure what You mean by BDSM feelings. That can cover a lot of things. i think i've always had a submissive personality ... always wanted to make people happy ... will have to come back to that question.

Yes, i probably was submissive as a teenager. i don't feel like i've changed in the way i feel about things. i'm the same person i always was ... same approach to things, just expanding my experiences. i think i was always submissive, but i never had anyone to be submissive to ... kind of like a seed planted in the ground & never watered. The teenage boys were in charge to the extent that they were willing. i never made the first move ... certainly not the way girls do these days. i never even called a boy on the phone unless he specifically asked me to. i always did whatever the guys wanted ... may have provided a little encouragement if they were unsure of themselves. It's hard to say, because my world as a teenager wasn't defined in terms of domination & submission.

As i said somewhere in a previous letter, i was raised in a culture/religion where the man was supposed to be the boss, the head of the household, the one in charge. As a teenager, i just assumed that all boys were raised to take on that role. As it turns out, very few boys/men are willing to be in charge or to take control of things. i was never attracted to guys that didn't have a dominant personality. i really felt cheated when i got married because Arthur changed the minute the wedding vows were spoken. He went from being a strong, dominant person to being ... a wimp. i really struggled the first few years we were married with thoughts of "this isn't the way it's supposed to be." i neither knew how, nor wanted, to be in charge. i felt very empty.

Now, however, i feel very tired & will have to finish this at a later time when i can think more clearly. i'm off to bed to dream about You!

Love,
Your puppy

February 7, 2004

Steven Toushin wrote:

Dear puppy,

Hope all is well. I haven't received any letters from you.

When you get the time, let's continue; you're doing so well with this.

Sir

February 7, 2004

sharon smith wrote:

Dear Master,

i'm sorry i haven't written. i had a wonderful time serving You on Thursday. i've been so tired the past few days, & now think i'm getting sick again & not happy about it ... feels like the same way it started last time.

Do You have more questions You want me to answer?

Also wondering if You've ever been to Mardi Gras? i'm going to have the last two weeks of February off & am thinking about going. Would You like to go?

Love,
Your puppy

February 8, 2004

Steven Toushin wrote:

Dear puppy,

In your teen years:

A. Did you think, want, fantasize about bondage, being taken roughly?

B. How were You aroused with sex; playing and controlling a cock by masturbating a cock, sucking or fucking?

C. What was Your sexual progression (from the age of 14 to 18) into maturity, and your own enjoyment?

D. Did you get wet, if so only with a guy present, or thinking about a guy?

E. What excited you? Did you fantasize about sexual things when alone?

F.   What was your reputation in school?

Sir

February 8, 2004

sharon smith wrote:

Dear Master,

Someone ought to go into the business of straightening out bills/paperwork when a person moves from one state to another. i would gladly pay someone a large sum of money to straighten out the mess i've got going here!

i slept for 16 hours last night & am not feeling any better today than yesterday ... kind of halfway sick. i'm going to try & see a doctor tomorrow ... must need something to kick my immune system into gear. i seem to be making up for the last 10+ years of not getting sick, all in one year ... enough already! i hope You are staying well.

Question A:

i was awfully busy as a teenager, & i don't recall sitting around thinking or fantasizing very much. i've always liked reading erotic books & remember reading a series of books about slavery in the old south that had me turned on for months. There was a lot of whipping & torture & explicit sex, & i remember fantasizing about being a slave & servicing a master. Darcy got me started on reading that series. i actually read quite a few sexually explicit books as a teenager that involved rough sex, sort of a D/s theme without actually referring to people as Masters/Doms or subs/slaves, etc.

i do remember fantasizing about one guy, Jim B. (not the same Jim i told You about before – Jim H.). i met Jim at a church youth retreat. i must have been about 16. i was one of the organizers of the retreat & was quite busy trying to keep things running smoothly. i had seen Jim & thought he was very attractive, but i didn't have time for socializing.

i was in the middle of trying to direct a bunch of kids to where they were supposed to go when Jim grabbed me by the arm & took me into the woods to this bridge that went over a little creek. It was a private place where kids would go to make out. He sat me down & started interrogating me, asking questions faster than i could answer them. He wanted to know if i smoked, did drugs, had sex, and also about my family, school, social life, etc., etc. He had me so ruffled i could hardly speak. Then he kissed me for a long time, & then he asked me to kneel in front of him & put my head on his lap. He ran his hands through my hair & didn't say anything for a long time. i told him i had to go before someone came looking for me, & he said okay.

For the rest of the retreat, i only saw him from a distance, & we just smiled at each other, never spoke, but i had a huge crush on him. i found out from a friend that he lived about an hour away from me & went to a private school in Illinois. She said he was the most popular guy at the school & had lots of girlfriends, all blondes, and that he treated them all like slaves … made them carry his books, get his lunch, etc., and that he wouldn't go out with anyone unless they "put out."

About a month or so later, we happened to meet again at a church hayride. In the middle of the chaos of the hayride, he grabbed me by the hair & told me to get off the wagon because he wanted to talk to me. (It was funny because i was sure i had been doing a perfect job of pretending that i didn't notice he was there.) So we started walking a short distance behind the wagon, & he said that if i wanted to go out with him, i would have to do whatever he said. i asked him what he meant by that, & he told me to go with him behind this building that was there. He leaned up against the building & told me to kneel in front of him & suck his cock, which i did. While i was doing that, he grabbed my hair & forced my head back & forth on his cock. He said that was only the beginning of what he would ask me to do. About that time, one of the adult counselors showed up looking for him because the group he was with was leaving ... and he just walked away. i spent a lot of time fantasizing about him ... being forced, tied up, rough sex, doing things for him. i would have done anything for him.

i never saw him again. my friend told me about a year later that he had gone to school to become a minister, & a few years later i heard he was minister of a church in Arizona. i continued to fantasize about being his "slave" until well after my kids were born.

Love,
Your puppy

February 8, 2004

sharon smith wrote:

Dear Master,

As is probably normal with any teenager, i was in a constant state of sexual arousal. (Laughing) i would have preferred to omit the niceties of dating & just get down to business. i remember one day i had three guys show up at my door within minutes of each other, and being so skillful at entertaining them, none of them knew the others were there … until one of them gave me a hickey!

One guy was in the back yard (Rick), one in the living room (Mike), and one in the driveway (Tim T.). i was going from one cock to another & recall being incredibly aroused … wishing i could have all three at the same time, & in great fear of what would happen if any of them found out the others were there. There was "long & skinny," "short & thick," & "hard as a rock" (who got caught in his zipper) … a well-balanced diet! Fortunately, i was wearing a bikini, which was easily adjustable in between. i was so wet & ready, but i never managed to get fucked that day. The guy in the driveway (Tim) gave me a hickey, & when i unknowingly went to the living room, Mike saw it. He thought it was something that had been there all along & he hadn't noticed it, but he got the message that he wasn't the "one and only" and left. Then Tim got angry when he saw Mike leave & started yelling at me, which alerted Rick to come & see what was going on. It was quite an afternoon!

In the end, i was left with a very wet & throbbing pussy, & no one to help ease my distress.

i'm not sure if that answers Your question. It's just the first thing that came to mind when You mentioned arousal.

Love,
Your puppy

February 8, 2004

sharon smith wrote:

Dear Master,

These are hard questions ... sexual progression into maturity? What do You mean by sexual maturity?

Yes, i got wet thinking about, looking at pictures of, and being with guys. i never got gushing wet, though, until i got involved in BDSM. i think that's because i never managed to have more than one or two orgasms with anyone prior to that, and the ones i did have weren't nearly as intense.

Love,
Your puppy

February 9, 2004

sharon smith wrote:

Dear Master,

i really miss You over these long weekends ... wish i could serve You more often.

Love,
Your puppy

February 9, 2004

sharon smith wrote:

Master,

my reputation in school ... i suppose it would depend on who you asked. There were 2,500+ kids in my high school. i knew all of them in my class & most in the three classes ahead of me. i got along with everyone, & never hung out in any particular group ... was never concerned with my reputation. We bought our house from a guy who graduated with me, & he remembered me as being the smart one. It didn't seem to matter how much i partied or had sex. People still thought of me as the smart kid & the good girl. There certainly were girls whose reputations were ruined when they ventured into the sexual realm ... but they were pretty much bimbos to start with. If anything, people respected me too much.

People want to categorize you by one characteristic & expect you to fit into their conception of what you should be. i would rather have been the slut than the smart/good kid. (Laughing) i was one of those people who were often chosen to represent the school. i remember going on a delegation to the state capitol with a handful of honor students. i was so stoned i could hardly walk when we were introduced to the governor & our state representative. Everyone had to know i was stoned, but no one said anything.

Growing up in the seventies was an unusual time. Our teachers were the liberals, protesters & stoners of the sixties. It wasn't unusual to have a teacher escorted out of school for flipping out on drugs. i remember an art teacher on LSD who thought he was a black spider & was trying to climb the wall ... quite entertaining. We were allowed to smoke inside the school, & there was no limit to the number of days you could miss, no dress code, no locker searches. We could come & go as we pleased throughout the day. We all had a good time. Things really tightened up a couple years after i graduated. Kids nowadays aren't allowed to have any fun.

i've been thinking that my life isn't all that interesting for a book. It would be more interesting to add a parallel diary from Your perspective & have the two separate paths come together at the end ... or intersperse what we're doing now (from Your perspective) with stories from the past.

i miss You.

Love,
Your puppy

February 9, 2004

sharon smith wrote:

Dear Master,

i hope all is well with You. i haven't heard from You in a while & am starting to worry. i hope You haven't gotten sick. i went to see a doctor today even though i was feeling fine by the time i got there. He thinks i never got completely over the respiratory infection i had back in October & that's why it gets better & then keeps coming back. So he gave me an antibiotic, & that should be the end of it ... thank god!

i miss You & am worried that something happened to You. If everything is okay, i can be available to serve You Tuesday, Wednesday, and/or Thursday this week.

Hope to see You soon.

Love,
Your puppy

February 10, 2004

Steven Toushin wrote:

Hello, dear puppy,

I have not been feeling well and have also been very tired. I hope to feel better in the next few days. Let's look for Thursday.

Your letters have been good, and that makes me smile; thank you. But we need to continue. So here are more questions:

A. Any other girls involved with you and Darcy, or was it just you two?

B. The parties: at what age? Were they once a month, every 2 months, etc.? Who was there? What happened?

C. How did you feel physically, mentally, emotionally the first few times you masturbated a cock, sucked a cock, and fucked (during and after)? What sexual things did you enjoy or excited you the most?

D. Tell me about the first time you saw a cock cum, felt, touched cum, tasted cum.

E. How did you react to your BDSM submissive feelings? When did you start acting on them?

Sir

February 10, 2004

Dear Master,

i am soooo sorry, Sir. i must have given You my germs, & i'm feeling really bad about that. i hope You will see a doctor right away, because that seems to be the only way people are getting over it. What can i do to help You? You shouldn't be outside walking the dogs if You're sick.

i hope You don't end up as bad as i was a few weeks ago. Please get well soon.

Love,
Your puppy

February 10, 2004

sharon smith wrote:

Dear Master,

Darcy & Trudy were my closest friends from junior high onward. i also became good friends with Bess by the time i was 15-16. Trudy had a good friend named Carrie who hung out with us, but she had a psycho mother & was a little too neurotic for my taste. Darcy also had a good friend named Kathy who was a lot of fun. She lived in a mansion on a large horse farm, & her parents traveled a lot, so we partied there pretty frequently.

Darcy had horses she kept at a stable, & i used to go to the stable & horse shows with her to help with the grooming & be her #1 cheerleader. Darcy rode English & Kathy rode Western, but we often went to the same shows ... camping out & lots of late night partying. Horse people are a unique breed ... lots of alcohol & rowdiness. There were plenty of other girls that came & went at various times, but these were my most enduring friends.

As far as any sexual exploits go, Darcy & Carrie were the only ones who got involved in that. i went on a few double-dates with Trudy, but she had horrible taste in guys & was a bit of a prude. She was a bona fide virgin on her wedding night (laughing), then it took her over 10 years to figure out how to get pregnant ... oh, to have such problems!

Kathy was a late bloomer when it came to guys ... kind of quiet & shy & neglectful in her appearance. She ended up being a very beautiful, elegant woman & a doctor. i still see her once in a while when she comes back to the midwest to visit her family. The parties at Kathy's house were usually pretty big as she had a brother who was a year older & sister who was a year younger. Plenty of sex & lots of fun going on in that house most any time of the day or night.

Love,
Your puppy

February 10, 2004

sharon smith wrote:

Dear Master,

i read the Bijou Chronicles on *scenetalk.net*. You left us all hanging! There needs to be a Part 7. What happened at the end of Your probation in 1996 that You had to go back to prison? Was that during your divorce when your ex-wife turned you in?

It seems so strange that while You were going through all those trials/difficulties/battles, i was oblivious to it all, just living a relatively peaceful, small-town life with no idea that such a thing as BDSM or "rough sex" even existed, much less that battles were being fought for my sexual freedom. It's hard to fathom that anyone would have the strength & dedication to go through what You did. People like to claim their right to free speech, but when the going gets rough, it is a very rare person who will risk everything to defend that right. i'm quite certain i couldn't do it. If i were You, i would be very angry at the injustice of it all … but there doesn't seem to be a trace of anger or self-pity in You. What is Your secret? i keep thinking that i wish i was there to somehow make things easier for You. Also thinking i would like to see some of those controversial movies some time … and would like to have seen the look on the prosecutor's face when she was showing them in court. i bet she loved every minute of them. Why else would she be so dedicated in prosecuting the case?

i still think You should write a book about Your life … it has been much more fascinating and exciting than mine. People may not be able to relate Your life to anything in their own lives, but You've done so much that i'm sure many, many people have fantasized about that i'm sure they would want to read it for the vicarious experience. i'm thinking it could really be a best seller!

Love,
Your puppy

sharon smith wrote:

Dear Master,

i hope You are feeling better today & taking good care of Your-self. Please let me know if there's anything i can do to help.

There were so many parties i don't know where to begin. i was only allowed to go out socially three nights a week (until i got married) ... though i always managed to make it to a party on church nights, too (Monday-Wednesday-Sunday). There were also parties somewhere daily after school & usually during school. Darcy & i got stoned daily before school, which means we/i often didn't make it all the way to school.

i remember one day we took off in my car (a yellow & black Maverick that looked much like a bumblebee – a.k.a. the "buzzmobile"). We were pretty stoned, & i was driving down a country highway when Darcy decided to climb out the passen-ger's window ... and onto the windshield. She was making faces at me through the windshield, pretending to be a squashed bug, & i was trying to see past her, never thinking to slow the car down to a reasonable speed ... or to stop & remove this im-pediment to my vision. She then decided to stand up & be a giant hood ornament ... with her legs spread apart & arms up in the air. i was trying to yell at her through the driver's window to move out of the way because i couldn't see when i lost control of the car, & it spun out & ended up in the middle of a field. It's a total miracle that she wasn't killed. At first i thought she had simply vanished, but then i found her lying on the ground a short distance from the car ... and laughing her ass off. All she said was "What a rush!"

i still can't believe she survived ... i had to have been going 50 m.p.h. We had just bought a whole bag of "columbian gold" & spent most of that day having our own little party in the middle of that field. We laughed a lot about that day afterwards ... definitely some good stuff.

We were actually on our way to "party bridge" and "gypsy's graveyard" that day ... two sites of typically good parties ... many fun memories. i remember being at the graveyard one night & being extremely stoned, & apparently everyone else was in the same condition. i was with a guy named Kelly (the only male Kelly i've ever known – but definitely all male!). We were passing around a joint when someone dropped it – a major tragedy!!! There must have been twenty people there crawling around on the ground looking for the dumb thing. People started out picking up tiny sticks claiming they had found it, & as the search progressed people were coming up with large rocks & tree branches & all sorts of outlandish things, claiming to have found the joint. There was much discussion about the shape of the joint we were looking for & that it was decidedly big like a cigar, which of course led to the idea that some guy had stuffed it into the front of his pants, which naturally led to a pants-check, which meant that any objects found in one's pants that resembled the shape of a joint must be tested to verify that it was indeed the missing joint. Thus (and i have no idea how many of us were testers), we attempted to toke from any long, cylindrical objects we found hidden inside of one's pants. We were on a mission! Since none of us could stand very well, i recall we all ended up in a rather large pile of bodies ... resulting in a lot of shared sexuality, so to speak ... and a lot of laughing while discovering random body parts ... lots of fun.

i also remember going to a number of parties at Crazy Clyde's house. He was in his twenties & lived in a nearby town that was at one time a resort town with hundreds of small cabins built nearly on top of each other. It had become a place of permanent residence for many of the financially less fortunate, as well as a first home for young people starting out on their own. The homes were maybe 500 sq.ft. at most & usually had only two rooms. Clyde's house was divided into two rooms by those long fringes like people used to hang in doorways. One room was filled by his bed, & the other had a small couch, sink, & refrigerator. The house was always lit by candlelight only; and there was always incense burning. Clyde was about 6'8" & had very long, kinky, black hair & black eyes ... quite intimidating in appearance ... and he rode a Harley. i was halfway scared of him, but he was a gentle, easy-going guy.

Most of the people at these parties were quite a bit older than me, but i had started going there with a friend, Jane, who was dating Clyde at the time, & he always invited me back, so it became a place to go when nothing else was happening. He often had prostitutes and biker-girls at the house ... way out of my league at the time (and still is!), so i usually just sat quietly & got stoned & observed what was happening around me. It was a very sensual place ... naked women wandering through the house ... Clyde would often have 4-5 of them in bed with him while other people just casually chatted & partied a few feet away. It was kind of surreal. i never felt very comfortable there, but as i said, it was a place to go when nothing else was happening.

i met Clyde again when my younger son was on the same little league team as his son ... in a very conservative, religious town. At first, i didn't even recognize him with short hair & a clean-cut appearance ... but he was still huge & still rode a Harley. He turned out to be a wonderful father, little league coach, and pillar of the community.

i could tell You about a lot more parties, but i think/hope You get the general picture. We definitely had a lot of fun regardless of whether or not sex was involved.

Love,
Your puppy

February 11, 2004

sharon smith wrote:

Dear Master,

i was always fascinated with cocks from the first time i touched one. i remember it felt spongy (half-way erect), & in half a second it grew & became hard right before my eyes! It was like magic ... and all i had to do was touch it! And so many sizes & shapes ... just like opening a present, you never knew what you'd end up with once it started to grow. Those were the days when everyone wore skin-tight jeans, & i always felt i was doing a great service by releasing those poor constricted cocks so they could breathe.

Masturbating & sucking cocks ... i always thought it was fun ... though wished i could play with them longer. Things would go too quickly, & then that was the end of my fun. Actually, as a teenager i didn't give a lot of thought to the guy's pleasure. It was mostly for my own enjoyment that i liked to play with them. i often thought how fortunate guys are to have such an entertaining appendage.

After the first time i was fucked, i was scared, & i also felt like i had just been transported to another planet where no human had ever gone before (to borrow from Star Trek). It was kind of like everything else in the world suddenly disappeared, & i was floating in outer space. i felt the same way the first time i was whipped ... like i was in a dream. i never had any regrets in either of those cases ... and in both cases, i instantly knew i wanted more. Physically, in both cases, i was hurting ... but it was a pleasurable & exciting kind of pain ... the kind that keeps you warm.

Now that i think about it, i also bled after my first fuck, as well as after my first BDSM session. Sex was initially painful for me for quite a while ... not sure if that was due to lack of experience on the guys' part, or if i just didn't get as wet back then. Once things got going, however, it felt soooo good. i will never get tired of that feeling. i don't remember having any remarkable orgasms in the beginning ... but the whole inside of my body would feel all tingly & floating. Have You ever had a dream that You were falling & then suddenly wake up? That's what it felt like ... or a fast moving elevator, or a roller coaster. It was like every drop of blood in my body would rush to my pussy, & it was completely out of my control ... and my pussy was so delightfully stretched & filled & alive. Cocks were entertaining & fun to play with, but having one inside of me excited me a lot more ... and still does. i've often thought how nice it would be to have one inside of me 24/7 ... and i don't mean a dildo ... it's just not the same.

Thinking about all this has created a desperate need within my pussy right now....and Your cock fits so perfectly ... perhaps some fucking would make You feel better, too?

i hope to serve You very soon!

Love,
Your puppy

sharon smith wrote:

Dear Master,

i am worried that You are seriously ill and in need of a nurse to come & take care of You ... and i just happen to know of one who is available ... one who will do anything to help You feel better ....

i started reading a book tonight called *"The Story of M."* It's a true story (memoir) of a woman's entrance into the world of D/s. She does a much better job of describing her mental/emotional experience than i have done in the letters i've been writing to You. (Of course, she only describes her recent experience & isn't trying to remember stuff from 30 years ago!) i've only read the first few chapters, but there is something hauntingly familiar about it. At one point she described how she used to have this recurring dream that she lived in a house where she kept discovering new doorways leading to unexplored rooms, & how exciting it was to go into those rooms & discover things that she didn't know were there. i had that same recurring dream for many years. i even remember having that dream as a teenager & waking up afraid from it. As the years passed, i became more comfortable going into those rooms & also found them very exciting ... wanting to prolong the experience rather than wake myself up. The strange thing about it is that her dreams stopped when she met her Master ... and i have just realized that i haven't had that dream in quite a while, either.

i have tried to explain that vivid & persistent dream to various people over the years, but no one could seem to relate to it ... yet she describes it so perfectly ... like she was actually there in my dream. She also writes that her Master always insists that she tell him what she is thinking & feeling and, despite how difficult it was for her, this communication helped her to "resolve any inner conflicts and move to a much higher level of awareness and profound relaxation." The reason that struck me is because with all this thinking back on my life, i've been wondering what in the world was wrong with me going from one guy to another & all the partying, etc. It has just occurred to me that all of the things i did prevented me (purposely?) from having a deep emotional attachment to anyone. On some level (though i would never admit it at the time) i was aware when i got married that that particular relationship would never require a deep emotional attachment, & so it was a safe thing to do. i don't mean to delve into psychoanalysis here, but the way this woman writes about it is very familiar, and i am wondering if what leads a person to become submissive is the fact that maybe they have difficulty honestly expressing their emotions … or forming an emotional attachment … perhaps out of a fear of rejection … and perhaps it's all more of an emotional/spiritual need (unexplored rooms) than a sexual one ….

Love,
Your puppy

February 13, 2004

sharon smith wrote:

Dear Master,

i love You.

Your puppy

February 13, 2004

sharon smith wrote:

Dear Master,

i am now officially unemployed for the next two weeks! They had a going-away party for me today & sent me home with 4 bottles of wine & lots of cards & gifts. People were crying & giving me hugs like i'd been there forever instead of only 4½ months ... sheesh! Many of them want me to hire them at my new job. It was a valuable learning experience, but i don't think i'll miss the place ... mass herding of patients is not my style ... i prefer a more personal touch, even if it means less profit. The people (patients) in the Chicagoland area don't even know what quality care is ... far too much greed & far too little compassion in these large health care organizations ... very sad. So on to better things!!

i thoroughly enjoyed serving You last night, & i hope You were pleased. my tender nipples & ass have kept You in the forefront of my thoughts all day! For some reason, Your initials turned out to look a little like hieroglyphics, but i still like them **:)**

Since i dumped on You before about my marital issues, i want to apologize for not answering Your questions better last night. My husband showed up here late last Friday night & started bitching about trivial domestic stuff, so i just went to bed, & he slept in the spare bedroom. i was gone all day Saturday, & when i got home he was drunk, so nothing else was discussed, & he again slept in the spare bedroom. Sunday i wasn't feeling well & slept a lot, & he just pretended like nothing ever happened, & i kept myself busy ignoring him. i fixed dinner before he left, & he bitched about that & then gathered his stuff & left without saying goodbye. i haven't spoken to him since. We are living in two separate worlds & have been for a long time. Basically we've stayed together for the past 20 years for the kids' sake & for the financial benefit of the two incomes. He realizes that the salary at my new job could make me financially independent, & the kids are old enough to be on their own, so there's nothing to keep us together anymore. He wants me to get angry & fight with him, but i just don't care enough to do that. As far as i'm concerned, he can do whatever he wants, & it's not going to affect me.

i was looking back at the list of questions & think i have answered them all. Have been thinking, though, that if the letters are going to be published, people's names will need to be changed. [Ed. Note: the names to which she refers were changed] Although it's highly doubtful that any of them would ever read it, it's a small world ... and i don't want anyone to recognize themselves & get upset.

i think about You all the time & hope to serve You again soon.

Love,
Your puppy

February 14, 2004

sharon smith wrote:

Dear Master,

i am thinking about You & would rather be there to help You celebrate Valentine's Day than anywhere else. i miss You.

Love,
Your puppy

February 15, 2004

sharon smith wrote:

Dear Master,

Is something wrong?

Love,
Your puppy

February 15, 2004

Steven Toushin wrote:

Dear puppy,

Everything is good; thank you for asking.

I have been at *Vicious Valentine 7* this weekend. I've been leaving early, coming back late, and have not looked at my e-mail. *VV7* has had a profound (positive) effect on me, because of a man named Guy Baldwin. I am going back now for the rest of the day, and I will explain when we see each other again.

Back to the questions:

    A. Why did you have senseless guilt and confusion about being touched?

    B. How long we're you involved in the church, and at what ages? What did you do, how much of your time did it take per week, and for how long?

C. Tell me about when you were a cheerleader, your friendship with the girls, and your relationships with boys.

D. How did your parents feel about the parties, missing school and the boys? Any punishments?

Sir

February 15, 2004

sharon smith wrote:

Dear Master,

Vicious Valentine? i am disappointed ... You said one time that You wanted me to go with You to that, & i was looking forward to it ... but didn't know when it was ... and have been languishing in boredom all weekend ....

Love,
Your puppy

February 15, 2004

Steven Toushin wrote:

Dear puppy,

It was an OK event.

For me, though, it was extraordinary. I have to keep rethinking it over and over. I will tell you about it when we meet.

Sir

February 15, 2004

sharon smith wrote:

Dear Master,

What in the world could have been so profound and extraordinary??

i don't know when You want to meet ... my period started today.

Love,
Your puppy

February 15, 2004

sharon smith wrote:

Dear Master,

my parents didn't know about most of it. i wasn't allowed to date until i was 15, & i had a 10:30pm curfew until the day i got married. i was only allowed to go out 3 times a week until i got married. i always worked, though, and between that & church events & babysitting & spending the night at friends' houses, i managed to stay out late any time i wanted. i got in big trouble for coming home with a hickey on my neck one time.

One time when i was 15 & my parents were gone, i took my dad's truck and went & got Darcy, and i remember coming home very stoned, & my parents were really angry & yelling. i was sitting in this chair in the living room, & there was a light shining right in my eyes, & it took all my concentration just to sit still & not laugh or zone out from the light. i couldn't even begin to speak clearly or answer their questions about where i'd been … just sat there staring at the light. Prior to going home, we had all been laughing at each other, because we were so messed up it looked like we had all been crying. Anyway, my parents were furious about taking the truck, but they had no idea that i was stoned, & they must have thought i was crying in remorse. i remember it was a strange feeling to have all this going on inside of me right in front of my parents, & they were so wrapped up in themselves that they couldn't even see the obvious. i wanted to scream at them to shut up and just look at me and quit being so stupid.

For the most part though, i was invisible to my parents. my mother was wrapped up in her own health issues, & my dad worked shift work, so i rarely saw him. my grandmother would sometimes stay with us when my mother was in the hospital. She & i got along very well, & i would curtail the partying for the most part when she was there because i felt guilty about lying to her or leaving her there by herself, & i didn't want to disappoint her. She was a hard-working & tough woman, but not strict. She trusted & respected me & set high standards, but she didn't have a lot of ridiculous rules. i was closer to my grandmother than any other adult when i was growing up. She died shortly after my first son was born, & i still miss her … a lot.

The most memorable trouble i got into was when i was 17 & my mother discovered a large bag of pot in my purse. It was the night of mid-year graduation, and Darcy & i were planning to do some heavy-duty partying. i was fixing dinner for the family & feeling really good about our plans for the evening when my mother walked in carrying the bag. i don't remember what all was said but i wasn't allowed to go to the graduation, & people kept coming to the door looking for me. i was trying to covertly explain to them that i was in serious trouble, and they were all worried & scared for me.

The big thing that happened from that was that the next day, my mother called Darcy's mother & told her all about it, & Darcy's mother forbid her to talk to me any more because i was such a bad influence on her … and that was pretty much the end of our friendship. i had been closer to Darcy's mom than my own, and i was really hurt that she would do that, & also that Darcy would do what her mother said.

Anyway, that happened to be the time when my future husband entered the picture, & i started routinely partying with him instead. He had a whole different group of friends who were into drinking instead of drugs. They were also into racecars, which was kind of exciting at the time, and he had the fastest car around. i remember several occasions being in his car & outrunning the cops … amazing we ever survived. For some reason, my parents liked him, & they would let me go out with him even when i was grounded … which is how i got started seeing him. It's kind of funny, because i used to have to get the newspaper before my parents looked at it so i could remove the page with the police blotter, so they wouldn't see his name there on a weekly basis. That eventually proved to be a valuable lesson for me in raising my own kids … never try to pick your kids' friends for them! (laughing)

Another favorite of my mother's was a very handsome & charming guy who happened to be the biggest drug dealer in NW Indiana. She would see him around town, & he always struck up a friendly conversation with her ... she didn't even care that he wore an earring! He was always welcome in our house, & i would just sit there & grin while the two of them chatted away. She still asks about him occasionally.

i didn't attend school the whole second semester of my junior year, & in May, a couple weeks before the end of the year, the school called my mother wondering where i was. i didn't get in any trouble for that ... just had to take all the tests & stuff in a span of a couple weeks. Nothing more was ever said. i didn't really understand the lack of interest with that, except the goal my parents had set for me was to become a secretary until i got married and had kids, & then i was to be a stay-at-home mom, so i guess education wasn't a priority.

i also neglected to go to catechism for a couple years, & my parents were called to appear before the church council on that one ... definitely got in a lot of trouble over that! i had to spend every waking minute for weeks making up all the missed work, & then had to be cross-examined by the church elders. In that church, kids were expected to go through 8 years of rigorous catechism in order to become members, but no one ever did the whole thing, & they were still allowed to join the church. It was upsetting to me that i was the only one who was held to the 8-year requirement. The same elder who claimed my dress caused him to lust in his heart was the one who wouldn't lay off on the catechism requirement. He seemed to think it was his god-given duty to make my life miserable. The funny thing about that is that he ended up having five children of his own, & all five of them turned out to be a total waste of human flesh ... lots of babies born out of wedlock, disabling drug/alcohol problems, & none of them can even hold down a job & all are living off of welfare. He isn't quite so outspoken these days about what a bad job other people are doing in raising their kids.

It reminds me of when You were talking about different kinds of revenge ... how sweet it is!

Love,
Your puppy

February 15, 2004

Steven Toushin wrote:

Dear puppy,

You remembered, puppy, my golden rules:

1. I do not have time to waste with people who are users and abusers; people whose lives are negative; people who are self-destructive and hateful; people who judge and condemn others based on their narrow moral and mis-informed beliefs of right and wrong; and people whose agenda only benefits the greed of a few.

2. Overall, most people are fine, and they do wish you well, but you should never do better than them.

3. As for revenge: The best form of revenge is living well, with a good heart, with happiness and a smile.

Sir

February 16, 2004

sharon smith wrote:

Dear Master,

i was captain of the cheerleaders in the 6th, 7th, & 8th grades ... captain because i got the most votes during tryouts because i was the only one who could do runs of back-flips, etc., across the gym floor. i had no interest in basketball or football or cheering, but i did enjoy the gymnastics & athleticism of it all. i wasn't close with the other girls on the squad & kind of did my own thing. They were all kind of bimbo-ish & spent all their time fixing their hair & make-up & giggling about boys. They were only there as a status symbol ... totally uncoordinated & un-athletic. i went to a few of their slumber parties but never got into their silly games. i got weary of it all by the 8th grade & didn't try out after that. Jocks & cheerleaders were not my cup of tea.

Love,
Your puppy

February 16, 2004

sharon smith wrote:

Dear Master,

i was very involved in the church up until they refused to marry me. i taught Sunday school, Vacation Bible School, was an award-winning Calvinette (kind of like girl scouts), four-year president of the youth group, served as regional delegate for both Calvinettes & youth group, put together the Christmas program for a couple years, organized bible studies & social events, served on various committees, and was the designated person to welcome new kids into the church & show them around. i spent every Saturday morning helping to clean the church & prepare it for Sunday services. i prepared the sacraments & baptismal fount.

Everything i did was very heartfelt & sincere, despite the routine criticism from various people. i managed to separate my sincere belief in god from the hypocrisy of church people. my focus was on pleasing god. i had developed my own sense of god from what i had read in the bible … a kind, loving, benevolent, forgiving god … as opposed to the angry, condemning, judgmental, fire & brimstone god the church preached about. The god i believed in loved everyone the same, regardless of who they were or what sins they had committed, & it broke my heart when i would bring people into the church & they were later kicked out due to stupid man-made rules that were impossible to follow. i left the church when i got engaged & didn't return until after my kids were born, but during those years away from the church i still continued to believe in god. What happened after i went back to the church is another whole episode.

Reading over this, You are probably thinking i was a hypocrite for partying, etc., while professing to believe in god, but my over-riding belief was in the commandment to "love god with all your heart, & love your neighbor as yourself," and as long as i was doing that, i didn't see it as a conflict of interest … though, in reality, it probably was. In fact, i had many more honest & deep spiritual conversations with my partying friends than with anyone in the church, which was none that i can remember.

Love,
Your puppy

February 16, 2004

Steven Toushin wrote:

Dear puppy,

Stop teasing me as you write!

I have more questions:

A. What kind of church was it that your family and you went to when you were growing up?

B. What was the culture and denomination?

C. When did you go back to church after you were married?

D. Why did you go back to your church after they treated you so meanly?

E. Before you got married, did your husband attend church?

F. When did he start going to church after you got married?

G. Did he attend your church?

H. Did you attend church together?

I. Is he still attending church and how often?

J. Is the drinking a sin in his eyes? Was it ever a sin in his eyes?

K. Did you ever try to get him to see the drinking problem?

L. Did he ever accept the fact that he has a drinking problem? Did he ever get any help?

Sir

February 16, 2004

sharon smith wrote:

Dear Master,

Wow, those are some loaded questions!

The church i went to while growing up was the Christian Reformed Church. It is almost entirely Dutch people ... who actually believed the mantra, "If you're not Dutch, you're not much" ... which is why my marriage was so disapproved of. My husband is not only Hungarian (Roma), but also was raised Baptist, which is nearly the same as being heathen in their eyes ... even though both are Protestant religions. (Interestingly, i am only half-Dutch. my father is what he calls "Heinz-57" & was raised as a Methodist.) However, i was raised in a culture in which the only truth in this world was what the Christian Reformed Church professed, & everyone else was dead wrong & would definitely burn in hell. Even the thought of questioning the church or exploring other religions was enough to get you disciplined by the elders.

i went back to the church because i wanted to have my children baptized. It was about the same time i gave up the sex & drugs ... i think my oldest son was about 4-5, & the younger one was 2-3. It's hard to explain, but even when i rejected the practices & beliefs of the people in the church, i still believed in the god who was behind it all. That was definitely what could be called "compartmentalizing." i went to church every Sunday to worship a god, but i couldn't stand any of "his people." In fact, i always dreaded the thought of someday getting to heaven only to find myself eternally surrounded by such hateful bigots ... professing to love their neighbor as themselves while at the same time doing everything they can to destroy anyone who is slightly different. i've never understood that thought process ...

how anyone could think that because their ancestors were born in a certain place that would make them better than anyone else … especially since they all claim to be descendents of Adam & Eve. How ridiculous!

i said that Arthur was raised Baptist, but his mother didn't discover religion until he was close to junior-high age. His father has never stepped foot in a church in his life. My husband did the church stuff as a kid but was never fully indoctrinated as i was. He never had anything he strongly believed in. His mother has a unique kind of a "magic" belief system in that she prays for things & expects them to just magically happen, without any effort on her own part, and when they don't happen, she just pretends that they do. i think it has a lot to do with the fact that her parents were gypsies, & her father an alcoholic. She has always believed that the "evil spell" that was placed on her father was passed on to her children. Two of the five are alcoholics. i think her belief that it would happen had a lot to do with it. My husband is the one in that family who is most concerned about pleasing his mother, & he thinks she has some kind of special knowledge about a lot of things, regardless of how illogical they might be. i guess it's a sense of powerless-ness & belief in fate, along with not taking responsibility for one's own life. Anyway, drinking is not something that causes Arthur to be rejected by his family. It's more like it's evidence that his mother knows what she's talking about.

When we were engaged, Arthur was plenty willing to go through the motions of attending church with me. Even though he didn't have any specific beliefs of his own, he considered it the right thing to do. When they refused to marry us, we ended up getting married in his mother's church, but we only went to services there a couple times. When i went back to the Christian Reformed Church, he refused to go with me. That was at a time when his drinking was at its worst. However, he did manage to sober up the day the kids were baptized & stood at the front of the church with me for the ritual. He was always angry with me for going back there. It wasn't until we moved to another town that he started attending church. It was such a socially expected thing to do in that town, & he realized that if he wanted to work anywhere, he would have to show up at church. We attended the American Reformed Church there, which is also Dutch, though slightly less strict than the Christian Reformed. He enjoyed the socializing & eventually became a Deacon.

It was while he was a Deacon that he suddenly decided we had to follow all the silly rules put forth by the church (i.e., no shopping or traveling on Sunday, no dancing or roller-skating, etc., & i was supposed to dress like i was 95 years old!). He developed a belief system with a lot of senseless rules, but he never saw alcohol as a problem at that time.

Once, shortly after i first went back to the church, there was an incident in which he picked up the kids when he was extremely drunk & drove them home (about 25 miles). It really upset me (to say the least) that he would endanger the kids' lives like that, & so i threw him out. After about a week of living out of his car, he admitted that he was an alcoholic & went to a mental health center for help. i think he went twice, & then i let him come back home, & he never went back. The problem continued for about another 5 years, with me fighting it & getting angry/upset with him, before i finally decided to let it go. i think i explained the rest before. He currently doesn't think alcohol is a problem, & i am getting increasingly upset with him because he has started getting Don to drink with him. He's been leaving a case of beer here for Don every week when he leaves for Indianapolis. Now that he's going to be here all the time again, i can see there will be a problem, & i'm going to have to do something about it before it gets out of hand. It really pisses me off because Don flourishes when his father isn't around to harass him.

i think that answers most of the questions. i'll work on Don's story later.

Love,
Your puppy

sharon smith wrote:

Dear Master,

Senseless guilt & confusion about being touched ... is there a female alive in this country who hasn't felt that way? From my perspective now, i don't see what the big deal is ... yet there isn't a day that goes by when i don't hear from a real person, or something in the media, regarding anxiety or anger or fear over a woman's body & where, why, when, how it should be touched or who can touch it. Our society has a body phobia ... as if we don't all have the same parts or something ... don't see that in primitive societies. Guilt, secrecy, & shame about our bodies are forced upon us from the time we're born. It's an amazing testament to the natural, inherent need that, despite all the mental garbage, we even manage to procreate. How can it be anything else but confusing to a young girl to be told that something so intrinsically enjoyable & natural is bad & must be avoided? It's an artificial imposement & obviously not a universal awareness, & it has a profound impact on how every woman views herself & her own integrity. Girls/women are supposed to pretend to be chaste virgins appalled by any form or mention of sexuality, when in fact none of them are ... and yet the charade continues ... leading to guilt & shame per-petually transmitted from one generation to the next. At the same time, girls &

women are expected to look sexy & attrac-tive ... just don't touch the merchandise.

Love,
Your puppy

February 16, 2004

sharon smith wrote:

Dear Master,

i need to continue my outrage.

Have You ever noticed how when little girls are growing up in this country that we acculturate them to believe that there is only one body type/one look that men find attractive, & every-thing else is inferior to that ideal? ... How 99.9% of women in this country are unhappy with at least one, if not many, aspects of their physical appearance? i was reading a thread on *bond-age.com* yesterday that started out with a woman wondering if there was anyone out there who wasn't turned off by a woman wearing glasses. All these men started writing in saying that a woman wearing glasses was their biggest turn-on, especially if she was also wearing a business suit ... which all the women found to be unbelievable/incredible. Then the topic drifted to what people (both men & women) found attractive & unattrac-tive in the opposite sex. It was quite interesting & surprising.

It seems there is a complete lack of communication/ understand-ing between men & women on what is attractive ... and so many people have undergone surgery to create their own ideal look when, in fact, there are many people of the opposite sex who preferred their original appearance. It just seems like such a tragedy that so many people, especially girls, are so ingrained with an unachievable fallacy that they spend their whole lives agonizing over what is wrong with them & are blinded to the fact that they are fine just the way they are. It is a pet peeve of mine that any time i am around women, they are constantly talking about what is wrong not only with themselves, but also with other women ... which often becomes vicious & cruel ... kind of a pecking order of inferiority complexes. If it wasn't for the nature of the website, i would make copies of the discussion & hand them out every time the topic comes up.

Okay, that's my "ranting" for today. i'm sure nothing in general is going to change, but at least people are starting to talk to each other about it.

i miss You. Had a long & unusual dream about You last night ....

i can be available to *serve* You any night this week.

Love,
Your puppy

February 16, 2004

sharon smith wrote:

Dear Master,

Welllll ... i will be happy to serve You tomorrow, but i feel it necessary to inform You of my limitations:

1. It will be messy;

2. My asshole is still very sore from last week & requires a hiatus; and

3. i have to go for a physical for the new job on Wednesday morning, & i'm not sure how much of my body will need to be exposed. So it's up to You. i will certainly understand if You'd rather wait.

Love,
Your puppy

February 16, 2004

Steven Toushin wrote:

Dear puppy,

Thursday is fine; it gives me a chance to get some writing in. I will be sending more questions later on.

Sir

February 16, 2004

sharon smith wrote:

Dear Master,

Thursday sounds like a long time to wait, but it's probably a good idea considering about all we could do tomorrow is play cards ... although a four-hour cocksucking session while You write could be a definite possibility ....

i got an e-mail advertising a web site called *love4animalsex.com* & checked it out, & now it has me wondering exactly what Your intentions are between me & Your dogs ... and also thinking that the story You told me about the woman & the horse may have been true. Obviously, my pussy wasn't the first one BB tasted, & now i'm wondering what other "experience" he's had. i will admit that in the past i had thought about having a dog lick my pussy but had never given it any serious consideration & definitely never thought it would really happen. The rest of the stuff on that web site would never have occurred to me in the farthest reaches of my imagination. So if You have something else in mind, i would very much appreciate knowing about it ahead of time because it's going to require a whole lot of mental processing. Actually, if You could address this before i see You on Thursday it would be really helpful as my brain has kicked into overdrive, & i'm not sure whether or not i should start panicking.

Thank You.

Love,
Your puppy

February 17, 2004

sharon smith wrote:

Dear Master,

i think You are avoiding my question ... and it's not putting my mind at ease.

Specifically, what kind of experience do BB, Desperado, and Pirate [Ed. Note: Steven's greyhounds] have? my mind is on overload because i've just seen pictures/videos of women actually being fucked by dogs, horses, and a variety of other animals, not to mention sucking their cocks and/or jerking them off ... the aforementioned of which i would have assumed to be physically impossible! Good grief! my family has always bred dogs, & i saw plenty of them screwing but had no idea a dog's cock got so large or why they were so helplessly stuck together afterwards (or "knotted" as my new education has revealed).

Are You familiar with that website? It has a format just like *scenetalk.net*, which leads me to believe that the stuff on it is real, & these people are talking like it's a common & ordinary occurrence to be fucking all kinds of animals. i am rambling here because the thought that this might be what You have in mind has me feeling a little overwhelmed at the moment. However, i am dealing with it ....

You should have heard me panic when Master Rob first brought up the idea of me being with another woman ... and i managed to survive that, as well as a lot of other "firsts" since then. This was just never a conceived-of option on any list of things to try. 😊

Love,
Your puppy

February 17, 2004

Steven Toushin wrote:

Dear puppy,

You're going into overdrive at the moment; is that because you have a week or 2 of free time?

The woman and the horse story was true. All stories I might tell you of other women, experiences, and scenes will be true. I have no reason for them not to be.

Yes, BB and Desperado do have experience, as do BB and Pirate in other areas. Ask me about that.

As far as future scenes, let your imagination take flight then tell me, or better yet write me, since you are more expressive in e-mails than face to face, about what your imagination conjured up. And, of course, you will tell me how you feel about that.

More questions:

A. With your friend Darcy, what did you mean by a different guy every night? Shared? What did you and Darcy do, and why?

B. Tell me about your first few times seeing a cock cum, the first few times you tasted, and/or swallowed cum.

C. At the party with the team, what were the boys saying to you? What were they saying to each other when you were pulling out each one's cock and sucking on it? How did the party end? Did you jerk them all off? If so, how did you feel about each exploding dick?

Sucking on me for hours sounds delicious.

Sir

February 17, 2004

Steven Toushin wrote:

Dear puppy,

You have me softly laughing. I do not know the site you're talking about.

Yes, I have been in involved in all things with dogs. At this time, I really have no thoughts about anything further with my boys. Their experience has been being played with and being sucked. They are fixed.

Where is your imagination going? Maybe I should tie you up and have everyone have their way with you.

I can't leave any marks, your pussy is full of blood, and your ass is recuperating; that just leaves 1 hole.

Sir

February 17, 2004

sharon smith wrote:

Dear Master,

Well, i'm happy You are amused!

And relieved You "have no thoughts about anything further," so we can put an end to my over-active imagination. i must have too much free time on my hands!

Love,
Your puppy

February 18, 2004

sharon smith wrote:

Dear Master,

Will there ever be an end to all the questions about my childhood? i feel like i'm answering the same ones over & over & over, & i don't think there could possibly be anything more to say. i could think of a lot more interesting things to write about. Not that i'm complaining or anything, but this is getting rather tedious. After this set of questions, can we please skip to something else for a while?

During the time i was friends with Darcy, neither of us ever had a steady boyfriend or went out with the same guy more than once or twice. We were with different guys all the time, whether it was partying, making out, or just goofing around. Sometimes we were with one guy, or two, or half a dozen.

Have i told You about the salesman she picked up? She was babysitting somewhere in town when this guy came to the door selling encyclopedias or something. He was a very poor college student with shabby clothes & holes in his shoes. He was living in a run-down hotel in town for the summer & drove this rusted out junk car. He looked like he hadn't eaten much for a while – pretty pathetic-looking in my opinion. Anyway, she felt sorry for him & decided he must be lonely, so she offered to buy him dinner & show him around town in exchange for him going in to the liquor store to purchase some beer (with her money). After she made this "date," she decided she didn't know whether she could trust him, so she called me & insisted i go along on this excursion of goodwill. Since i had never seen him, she convinced me to go by telling me what a fun & cute college student he was ... ha!! One look told me otherwise. He looked like a homeless person living in the street, & he had the personality of a park bench.

We had dinner at her father's country club, & the guy barely said a word or even looked up the whole time. After dinner, we got back in his car and Darcy pulled out a joint to get things going, & the guy freaked out. He had never been around anyone smoking pot before & acted like he was scared to death of the stuff. Of course, this put the light of the devil in Darcy's eyes, & she decided we were going to have fun with him. i just wanted to go home & put an end to the monotonous evening, but Darcy & i proceeded to smoke a couple joints while this extremely nervous guy was driving. She then started teasing him & asking about his sex life & if he had a girlfriend, etc., which made him even more nervous. When she found out he was a virgin in every way, i knew i was doomed. Darcy was sitting in the middle of the back seat & i was in the passenger's seat in the front, & we were going around the courthouse square in the middle of town when she reached up & grabbed his crotch. i thought he was going to cry & pee his pants at the same time. She told him to pull over in front of the liquor store & go in to buy the beer. The poor guy was scared to death of her, & i was afraid he was going to go in there & call the cops.

A few choice words were exchanged between the two of us while he was gone. However, he did come back with a six-pack of Miller beer, & when Darcy told him to, he opened one & drank it right down. We headed out of town with her making sure he rapidly drank one beer right after another until they were all gone & he was pretty sloshed. At some point, i had become the designated driver when he couldn't stay on the road. i think that must have been his first time drinking beer, because i've never seen anyone get so drunk on a six-pack. We ended up at a county park, way out in the country, with him so drunk he could barely hold his head up. Then Darcy decided we would teach him a thing or two about sex, so we undressed him, & she started kissing him while i played with his cock. We were both pretty stoned, so we were laughing the whole time, & he was moaning like a sick cow. When she suggested trading places, i refused as i had no intention of kissing him & taking the chance of having him throw up on me, so i became the designated cocksucker. He had this tiny little, skinny cock that went a long way in explaining why he was still a virgin. Darcy decided he would never have the courage to fuck anyone unless we helped him out & saved him from a life totally void of sex. i have to say that i was not a willing participant in any of this, but we both ended up fucking him before the night was over.

By the time we got back in the car, he seemed to be feeling pretty good & was laughing & joking with us, & i figured everything would be okay. We drove him back to his hotel & then walked to Darcy's house. She went back to the hotel a couple days later to see how he was doing & found out he had quit his job & moved out. We never saw him again. The poor guy is probably still having nightmares.

Love,
Your puppy

February 18, 2004

sharon smith wrote:

Dear Master,

Do You know that if i didn't have a job i had to go to every day, i would spend all my days thinking about You & would never accomplish anything?

i miss You.

Love,
Your puppy

February 18, 2004

sharon smith wrote:

Dear Master,

i don't remember swallowing any cum when i was a teenager. Guys were kind of funny about that. They never wanted to cum in my mouth, & i never pushed for it because ... i don't know ... i guess i didn't think it was a sanitary thing to do. (Laughing) It seems i have come a long way since then!

i liked the pre-cum ... no real taste to that & no need to swallow. It kind of let me know the guy was interested and/or i was making progress ... even though, from what i can remember, the guy was always hard before i started sucking him. Unless the guy was drunk, it normally didn't take but a few moments, & he would pull out of my mouth or push me away & either finish himself off or fuck me. If he didn't fuck me, it was always the same ... there seemed to be a point where guys figured they could do it better themselves. Maybe that's because i had no "rhythm."

i kind of approached cocksucking like one would lick an ice cream cone ... more for my own enjoyment than the guy's. The first time i saw a cock cum, the biggest surprise was how quickly it got soft afterwards ... which followed my surprise at how quickly it had gotten hard in the first place. Such a fun toy! From what i had heard about it, i expected to see this thick, creamy, white stuff & so wasn't real sure what i was seeing. From the way he reacted though, i figured things must have gone the way they were supposed to. i really didn't know what had happened ... so young. It didn't take long to figure out that the whole goal of any contact with a cock was for the guy to cum, & i always felt very pleased with myself when it happened.

Aside from Blake, i don't remember any guy ever even acknowledging the fact that a girl had the capacity to cum. In fact, i'm not sure i was aware that a girl could cum from being fucked. Condoms were rarely used, so it was necessary for the guy to pull out before cumming, & i guess it never progressed to the point where i had a full-blown orgasm by being fucked. It's significant how things have changed since then. Pregnancy was, of course, a concern, but the idea of possibly getting an STD never even entered my mind.

i'm not sure if all this answers Your question. However, i am sure that if it hasn't, You will ask again!

Love,
Your puppy

February 18, 2004

Steven Toushin wrote:

Dear puppy,

Too much idle time? Then think about ways to serve, to make my life easier. That is your duty, puppy.

I am almost finished with the questions on your early years.

A. How long were you seeing your husband before you got married?

B. What kind of exhibitionist sex were you doing?

C. Were you having sex with other boys while you were going with your future husband?

D. Were you having sex with other men after you were married? What were the situations? Why, how often, what kind of sex, and with whom?

E. You mentioned that men swarmed around you after you had your children; what did you do about that?

Sir

February 18, 2004

sharon smith wrote:

Dear Master,

How to make Your life easier … will definitely think about that. Any suggestions?

Question A: i met my future husband on July 4, 1976 (bicentennial celebration), and we were married September 2, 1978. So i knew him for a little over 2 years, but we didn't start "dating" until January of 1977. So, technically, we had dated for ... 1 year, 8 months. He surprised me with an engagement ring on Christmas, 1977. i had become pregnant in late summer of that year & had a miscarriage after only a couple months. When i was pregnant, we thought we were going to have to get married, but the subject was never brought up again after that until he gave me the ring. So i became engaged during my senior year of high school & was married 3 months after graduation ... 2 months before i turned 19.

Question B: i'm not sure what You mean by exhibitionist sex.

Question C: We didn't see each other exclusively until we got engaged. i remember having sex with one other guy during the time we were engaged. That was kind of by accident when i went to a party with some friends ... didn't intend for it to happen. Neither of us really took the relationship too seriously, though, until after i got pregnant with our first child. If it weren't for my mother, we probably would have been engaged for a while & then broke up. i never asked him, but i think he must have bought the ring when i was pregnant & then decided to give it to me since he already had it. We had actually split up a couple weeks before that when i decided he had a drinking problem. He never actually asked me to marry him ... just gave me the ring & i put in on. When my mother saw it, she went into full-speed-wedding-planning mode. She planned the entire thing right down to what dress i would wear & what date the wedding would take place. i had no vote on anything. It wasn't until they started having bridal showers for me that it actually dawned on me that i was getting married, like it or not. Our friends were all making bets at the wedding reception that it wouldn't last a year, & neither of us thought it would either. Now, 25 years later ....

Question D: Unbeknownst to me, my future husband had quit his job the day before we were married. Then he spent the next few months on a constant drinking binge, so our sex life was non-existent, including the honeymoon. i spent a lot of time alone & confused. When he made it home, it was because one of his friends drove him there & carried him to bed. i became very close with some of his friends & occasionally had sex with them while he was passed out in the other room. After a few months, i got rather pissed off & insisted he get a job, so he started driving a truck over-the-road & showed up at home un-announced about once a week for about a day at a time. During the truck-driving years, i always had a lot of people showing up at my house to party at all hours. People would just walk in af-ter i'd gone to bed, & the next thing i'd know they would all be in bed with me ... or there would be people camped out in other rooms having sex ... or we'd all be in the living room/kitchen getting stoned out of our minds. There was generally a lot of flirting & playing around. i occasionally had sex with someone; nothing serious, just for fun.

i'm going to have to finish this tomorrow. Have to get to bed now or i'll be late for my appointment in the morning.

Love,
Your puppy

February 18, 2004

sharon smith wrote:

Dear Master,

Question D: The thing is that i never even had the slightest idea that i might be seen as attractive. i couldn't figure out why i couldn't even walk through the damn grocery store without being bothered. Going to social events like weddings or going to bars usually left me upset because guys would make idiots out of themselves right in front of their wives, & the women would think i was doing something to ask for it. They would be angry with me & get in big fights with their husbands, & i would feel very hurt by the whole thing.

It kind of came to a peak one night when i had gone to a bar with Trudy & her husband, Ricky. A couple guys that i didn't even know got into a fistfight over who should be able to talk to me. It was a bad scene, & i just headed for the door to get out of there as fast as i could.

i was outside crying & upset when Ricky came looking for me. The two of us went for a long walk with me blubbering about all my frustration and anger, & he just listened. We were walking down the middle of a railroad track (and i can still see this perfectly) when he stopped & took me by both arms & turned me to face him. i don't remember his exact words because he talked for quite a while, but the gist of it was that he told me none of it was my fault, that i wasn't doing anything to ask for it, & that it was the guys' problem. Then he told me how beautiful i was, & what guys were seeing in me. It was like being hit by a ton of bricks … i had to sit down. We talked for a long time, & he never once tried flirting or making a pass. Then when we decided to go back inside, he gave me a big hug and, of course, that was when Trudy had decided to come looking for us. All she saw was the hug, & she was furious.

Anyway, as a result of that talk, i made a few changes. i switched from contacts to glasses & started wearing baggy clothes, no make-up, & a different hairstyle … and it worked! i think the glasses were the big thing. i also avoided looking at anyone or talking to anyone when i went anywhere, & i quit going to bars. i had a few problems after that when i would get dressed up to go to a wedding or Christmas party or something, but it wasn't a daily ordeal. i was blissfully frumpy!

Love,
Your puppy

February 20, 2004

sharon smith wrote:

Dear Master,

Have i told You lately that i love You?

i guess i've become suspicious of people over the years, especially people involved in BDSM, and so i'm continually surprised/pleased/delighted by Your honesty and openness ... no hidden agenda. You are a very special and unique person, and i feel honored to have the opportunity to serve You.

On the way home last night, i was thinking about Your experience with Guy Baldwin (and wishing i could have been there to witness & share in Your moment of honor). Again, i was thinking that Your life would make a much more interesting book than mine. The things i have read that You have written have recorded events that occurred. However, the question that people (myself included) would be fascinated in understanding is "Why?" How did You get to a point where You were willing to sacrifice everything for the sake of ... sexual freedom? integrity? freedom of speech? The process of the thoughts/emotions of someone who is willing to stand in the face of persecution, and the strength of beliefs/ideals of someone who is willing to continue to fight for them, are what people want to read. It's the stuff that makes for heroes. It would also, i suspect, be quite a controversial book and have a flavor of eroticism. And if done right, these are all components of a best seller. Furthermore, a book like this would create a legacy so both You and everyone else would remember and know that Your efforts were not in vain. It would also be a catharsis for both You and Your children, since they also lived through much of what took place.

Now, having said all this, i want to add that i don't think this is the kind of book that a person can write about himself. Which brings me to my idea … i would like to conduct & record a series of interviews with You, and also with people from Your past/present (for credibility) and put together a book that would be part biography, part philosophy, part history and, hopefully, challenging, inspiring, and thought-provoking. What do You think?

Love,
Your puppy

February 20, 2004

Steven Toushin wrote:

Dear puppy,

You have time on your hands and are over-thinking.

Thank you for the offer, but I would have to think about that. Right now your story is THE STORY.

Enjoy your day.

Sir

February 21, 2004

sharon smith wrote:

Dear Master,

Maybe i was just inspired! 😊

Then again, maybe i do need something to occupy myself ....
😊

Love,
Your puppy

February 22, 2004

sharon smith wrote:

Dear Master,

i hope Your weekend is going well.

i've started a project that will keep me busy for a long, looong time ... cleaning out files/file cabinets. i can't believe i still have all my notes, etc., from nursing school. They are crumbling to dust when i touch them. This is perhaps a project that has been put off for too long!

my parents were here today, too, & we had a nice visit (unusual). my dad was talking about his mother & grandmother (her mother), which is a side of the family i knew very little about. He said his grandmother used to own a building somewhere on North Wells Street back in the 1910-1930s that was a restaurant/tavern on the first floor, with 3-4 apartments upstairs. Her husband was an engineer on a merchant marine ship on the Great Lakes & in the Caribbean, & he died at sea when he was quite young, so she raised her three children over this bar on Wells Street. my dad couldn't remember exactly where it was or what it was called, but isn't that a coincidence? my grandmother could have been raised very near to where You are living.

Hope to see You soon.

Love,
Your puppy

February 23, 2004

Steven Toushin wrote:

Dear puppy,

Have you finished all the questions? If so, here are some more. We're moving up in time now.

    A. Did you go back to your church, or any church, after you were married, or when you had your children?

    B. When you were having sex with other men after you were married, was it once a month or at what frequency until you had your 2nd child?

    C. Did you embrace any BDSM activity during that time?

    D. When did your sexual desires come alive again within you to make you go out searching?

E. Did you know at that time you were looking for a Dominant/submissive relationship?

Sir

February 23, 2004

sharon smith wrote:

Dear Master,

After approximately 14 hrs today, my office-cleaning project is completed, & i can actually see the floor & desk!!! Found all sorts of things i thought i'd lost forever. i'm pretty impressed with myself.

i think i answered all the previous questions, so will start on these.

A. i went back to the church when my second son was about 6 months old because i wanted to have the kids baptized. i had to appear before the council & go through a couple hours of cross-examination, but then they welcomed me with open arms. It was a few months before that when Arthur & i were separated & went through counseling. It was after that when i decided i wanted to do this for the kids' sake regardless of whether or not he approved. my involvement with the church was a big problem/issue for him for quite a few years.

B. i really have no idea of the frequency i had sex with other men. i suppose at times it was maybe once a week & other times it was maybe a couple/few times a year. It was when my older son was around 4 years old that he saw me kissing Lenny (Arthur's best friend), & i decided it was time to clean up my act & be a more responsible mother.

C. No, the idea of BDSM-type activities never even entered my mind. i think i was having sex with other men because i was lonely. It was usually with close friends & would start with deep conversation & emotional connection & just kind of naturally progress to sex ... frequently with Arthur passed out in the next room. It was usually a tender & romantic kind of thing.

D & E. There were a whole lot of things that happened between the time i decided to be a responsible mother & when i first put the ad on the Internet. Basically, all of my ideals & things i believed in proved to be false, & i felt like i had wasted my life away trying to be what i thought i was supposed to be, & i was just tired of it all. i'm not sure what possessed me to put the ad on the Internet ... curiosity, i guess. It seemed to be anonymous & risk-free, & i really didn't think it would come to anything. In fact, the idea of actually meeting a stranger from the Internet didn't enter my mind. It was just a way to entertain myself. However, as it turned out, the ad was more honest than i ever knew at the time. To paraphrase, it said that i wanted someone to tie me up, spank me, and fuck me as often as possible. i got hundreds of replies from (mostly illiterate) men describing in endless detail their enormous cocks & what they were going to do with them. It got to be quite boring, & i was deleting them after reading the first line. After about a week i had lost interest in the whole thing.

Then i received a letter from Rob. In that letter he said he was a doctor & had over 30 years of experience as a master of domination and submission. He said he liked my profile & asked if i would be interested in training as his submissive. Nothing about his cock or body fluids or my tits or pussy, etc. He seemed very mysterious, as well as intelligent. i had never heard of anyone referring to themselves as a master & had never heard of domination & submission, but something about the authority in that letter made me very hot & wet ... and he never even mentioned sex. That was the only letter i responded to. i don't remember what all was said, but we corresponded for a couple weeks, & i was very eager to meet him. When we finally met, i wasn't at all attracted to him physically, but the way he talked to me made me melt in my seat. i still had very little idea of what BDSM was all about, but he had some kind of power over me that i had never experienced before & couldn't explain.

i know it sounds ridiculous & dumb, but i was hooked. When i (naively) met him at a hotel a couple weeks later, the experience was like ... an awakening. It was like i had found what i had been looking for all my life, only i hadn't known what it was i was looking for. It was like i was finally home. And i do have to say that it wasn't the "rough sex," because he never (ever) fucked me. It was the submission & being controlled that created an indescribable peace like i had never felt before. There was absolutely no question in my mind that this is what i wanted. What happened during that session is another whole story.

i can be available to serve You anytime between now & Friday evening.

Love,
Your puppy

February 23, 2004

sharon smith wrote:

Dear Master,

i have managed to break four nails since yesterday, & my poor little fingers are in pain to type with. Other than that, i am having a very good (productive) day. How about You? i thought i answered these questions in the last round, but i assume You want more detail?

A. my older son had bought me a computer for Christmas & set it up when he was home on Thanksgiving break. i had taken a week of vacation the first week in December to go Xmas shopping & so had some time to explore the Internet in private. Prior to that, i had only used it for research/professional stuff. As a bit of background, this was when my older son was a freshman at college, so he had been away for only a few months. Also, it was about a month after we had to send our younger son to live with relatives in Tennessee because his life was being threatened by people who had close political ties to the county prosecutor, & so he was being prosecuted (framed) for stealing a car & attempted murder. He was 17 at the time, but they wanted to try him as an adult. We had to move him out in the middle of the night.

Anyway, for the first time since the kids were born, the house was very quiet. Our house had been a gathering place for teenagers for quite a few years & so it was ... empty. Starting a couple years before that, i had really started putting some effort into spicing up our sex life. Arthur was ... amused by that. He had become very involved in the church (religious fanatic) a short time after i had become disenchanted with it all and, as a result, had developed some highly conservative (extremely boring) ideas about sex. However, he was plenty willing to have sex as often as i wanted it, so our sex life was actually better than it had been in many years because his new-found religion required him to come home at night. Nonetheless, there was no connection between us once the kids were gone.

i'm kind of getting off track here, but the point is that i was bored, disillusioned, and felt like i was living someone else's life instead of my own. (Laughing) Might that be called the "bored housewife syndrome"? Anyway, that's where i was when i discovered the web site & impulsively placed the ad. i guess the basic feeling was that i had done everything a good wife & mother was supposed to do, & everything was fucked up, & it was time to change course … although it was a lot more complicated than that. i discovered the web site by accident when i clicked on the wrong place on a pop-up & just perused some of the ads out of curiosity. The site was *adultfriend finder.com*. The ads sounded enticing … people were having fun with sex … stepping outside the boundaries imposed by society & religion … and there were so many of them. It was like there was a whole world that existed out there, & i knew nothing about it. i felt quite deprived that all the while i was trying to be this chaste, virginal, "Mrs. Cleaver" supermom, all these other people were doing what they really wanted.

It must have been a rare moment of insight when i said i wanted someone to tie me up & spank me, because i don't recall ever thinking about that before writing the ad, and i don't recall seeing that kind of thing in any of the other ads. Where the idea came from might be something that psychoanalysis might reveal … perhaps subconscious desires/fantasies that i had never acknowledged? … maybe felt too guilty about it to ever speak of to anyone in person, but i could do so with the anonymity of the Internet?

In any case, placing that ad was the best decision i've ever made.

Love,
Your puppy

February 23, 2004

Steven Toushin wrote:

Dear puppy,

You stated that you sent your son out of state because he might be killed. What were the circumstances? Where did you send him? With whom did he live, and for how long?

Sir

February 23, 2004

sharon smith wrote:

Dear Master,

i've started to write this story several times now, but it's such a complicated story it would be a book in itself.

Don ending up in Memphis was the culmination of many, many things that occurred over several years. Some were his own fault, & some were the fault of others. He had created a bad reputation for himself, & there were people who would take advantage of that. The events immediately preceding his exodus from Indiana started on the day the World Trade Center was bombed. A "friend" of Don's reported his car stolen that night & accused Don of stealing it. It was found the next day floating in the Kankakee River with the CD player missing. This same kid had stolen a CD player & speakers from Don's car a couple months earlier. Don had confronted him about it & told him he wouldn't turn him in to the police if he gave the stuff back. The kid, of course, denied it, but he later told one of Don's other friends where to find it ... which, quite coincidentally, was in the woods behind the first kid's house. So Don & his friends went & got the stuff, but it was ruined from setting out in the rain. Don never turned the kid in, but kept telling him he wanted to be paid for the stuff. (i'm having a real mental block here because i can't remember the kid's name ... never thought i'd be able to forget it ... last name was Will).

Anyway, Will kept saying he was going to pay Don, but he never did ... Don wanted $100. Then Will had a birthday for which he received a brand new, expensive red sports car from his father. This was about 2-3 weeks before 9/11, which, if i remember correctly, was on a Tuesday. On that Sunday (9/9), Don had enough of being put off regarding the cash, & so he confronted Will & said he was going to the police. Two days later, Don was accused of stealing the car. Now, when we heard the accusations, i wasn't so sure that Don didn't do it. He had been arrested about 6 months earlier for stealing the wheels/tires off of a car. The reason he got caught with that is because he stole them from a neighbor & then was dumb enough to put them on his own car & drive it around, not to mention getting arrested for doing burnouts/donuts while he had them. Those charges were made out to be much worse than the actual crime, & he was facing quite a bit of jail time for that. We had been working real hard with him trying to convince him he wasn't cut out for a life of crime. For the first time in several years he had a steady girlfriend (Maranda) & seemed to be making an effort to straighten up. So i was pretty upset when the police came to arrest him for stealing the car.

He was still a minor at the time, so they had to release him to us. The Sunday after 9/11 was Maranda's birthday, & the two of them went out & were planning to come back to our house for birthday cake. We heard them pull in the driveway. Several car doors slammed, & we heard voices ... didn't think much about it. A few minutes later, i got a phone call from the neighbor across the street saying we better get outside right away because there were some kids trying to kill Don. We got outside in time to see Don & another kid hit the ground, with Don (luckily) landing on top. (Don was 6'6" and about 160 lbs.; the other kid – a football player – was a little taller & about 100 lbs. heavier). We both started running as Don pulled back & hit the other kid in the face. Arthur grabbed Don as he was hitting the kid for the second time, & Don walked away. The other kid came at me, then turned and swung at Arthur. i ran in the house to call the police. There were about 20 kids who had come to watch the fight, & it was pretty chaotic.

When i got back outside, Arthur was trying to restrain that kid, and there standing against one of the cars was Will with a big grin on his face. We later discovered Will & this other kid had come, armed with golf clubs, to kill Don … only Will had chickened out because so many other people had showed up. Anyway, we all ended up at the police station. Don's hand was shattered, quite deformed, and swollen. The other kid was in the back room when his parents came in to the station. After his mother saw him, she came back out in front by us & started screaming at Don & threatening him. She said a lot of nasty things & started pushing Don, claiming Don had followed her son & tried to kill him. She ended up having to be restrained by the police. They took her son to the hospital … we later found out his jaw was shattered, & he spent about a month in the ICU with severe head injuries.

The police interviewed all of the kids who were there, & they all had the exact same story … this kid had followed Don home & tried to start a fight, & Don kept walking away until the kid grabbed his shirt & tried to throw him on the ground. Don landed on top & hit him twice … defending himself in his own front yard.

Don was arrested & charged with battery with the intent to kill. It so happened that the kid with the broken jaw … his parents were major contributors to the county prosecutor's campaign fund. And the kid himself was a star football player & had never been in trouble with the law. The facts of the case didn't matter. The prosecutor wanted to try Don as an adult for the stolen wheels, stolen car, & attempted murder, all at the same time, & send him to jail for 20+ years. i was hugely upset, to say the least, because i knew Don was not a fighter & would never hit anyone unless he had to, & there were so many witnesses to corroborate his story. So we got a lawyer & planned to defend him.

In the meantime, the kid's mother was going around town telling everyone Don had attacked her son & tried to kill him, & she was going to take revenge. We started getting threatening phone calls, rocks were thrown through our windows, and our mailbox was blown up. After about a week, Don was released by the doctor to go back to school. The other kid's brother was a teacher at the school. The first day Don went back, the brother cornered Don (who had his arm in a cast) & tried to start a fight with him. Don wasn't about to fight with anyone as he was still in a lot of pain, so he tried to walk away (as i had always foolishly taught my kids to do). The brother took a swing at him just as an administrator came down the hall & then claimed Don had swung first … so more charges were brought against Don, & he was suspended from school.

The threats & vandalism kept getting more bold & severe, and each time we called the police, & they didn't do anything about it. i even had some of the threatening phone calls recorded on my answering machine, where the kid's cousin & brother had identified themselves. It had gotten to the point where we were all afraid to be living there, & we were afraid to go anywhere else because someone from that family followed us everywhere we went … even the grandmother got in on it.

Then, after about a month & a half of being harassed, Don finally had a bit of luck. Maranda was home from college & was talking to an old friend who happened to be dating a friend of Will's. This girl told Maranda that her boyfriend, two other guys, and Will himself had staged the car theft for the purpose of blaming it on Don ... because Will was afraid of losing his baseball scholarship if Don turned him in for stealing the stereo equipment. Don had suspected this all along, but we had no proof. So we took Don & Maranda up to the county sheriff & had them tell the story. They went to the girl's house, & she & her mother verified the story, & then the boyfriend confessed.

So, now Will was really in trouble. We had gone home & the police called us & said to lock the doors & stay away from the windows, because, when they had gone to arrest Will, his father had thrown a punch at them & had gotten away & was coming after Don. It was several hours before they called back & said they had arrested Will but still hadn't found his father. As it turned out, it was Will's father who had ordered him to kill Don in the first place because Will had told him Don stole the car. (In case You can't tell, we were dealing with true Kentucky hillbillies ... Will, his father, & the friends of the prosecutor.) The deputy was pretty shook up himself the second time he called, & Arthur told him he wanted to get me & Don & Maranda out of there, but Don wasn't allowed to go anywhere because of all the charges against him. The deputy called the prosecutor & got her okay, & Don, Maranda, & i got in to the car & drove to my brother-in-law's in Tennessee. Will's father was arrested a couple days later.

Don spent about 7-8 months in Tennessee & then came back home & still had to face all the charges. We went through two lawyers & many thousands of dollars. He didn't get any jail time, but still got a lot more punishment than he deserved, considering that, by that time, everyone knew he was innocent of three out of the four charges. The other kids were never charged with anything & are all in college. Will wasn't kicked off the baseball team & is currently playing baseball for IU where my other son also goes to college. Because Don's senior year was so screwed up, his grades fell, & he wasn't able to take the college exams & wasn't able to go to college like he always planned.

And that was the short version of the story!

Love,
Your puppy

February 23, 2004

Steven Toushin wrote:

Dear puppy,

I asked for a story and got a story; that was some story.

Tuesday and Thursday are good.

OK; let's start on the current times:

    A. What caused your decision to place and ad on the Internet?

    B. What sites did you look into, and on how many sites did you place an ad?

    C. When you first placed your ad, what kind of responses did you get, and which ones attracted your attention?

Sir

February 23, 2004

sharon smith wrote:

Dear Master,

One more thought regarding that last question: i had taken the exam for certification in pain management the week before placing the ad. Perhaps it was all experimental research?

Make that two thoughts. i think i spent my whole life feeling guilty about everything under the sun until i got involved in BDSM. Since then ... no guilty feelings about anything. Go figure!

One more thing. i am going to have lunch with my soon-to-be medical director tomorrow, & i am wondering if it would be okay if i get to Your house early, like around 4-5pm? That way i won't have to come all the way home & turn around & go back.

Do You think Your employees would mind if i suck on Your cock while You finish working?

Love,
Your puppy

Part VII

Discovering BDSM
or Falling into BDSM

February 23, 2004

sharon smith wrote:

Dear Master,

Shall i assume it will be okay to arrive early then?

Question B: In the beginning, *adultfriendfinder.com* was the only site i put an ad on. Rob told me about *alt.com* at our first meeting, & i put an ad on there a few months later. It was through alt.*com* that i met everyone else. However, for some reason Rob preferred *adultfriendfinder.com*, & it was there that he told me to put the ad as a couple looking for a woman. That was less than two months after he first sessioned me. i had a free ad on (i think it was) *matchmaker.com* for a couple weeks until it expired, but that site didn't look too interesting at the time. i did the same thing on a couple other sites ... can't remember the names.

Question C: Up until i heard from Rob, the only replies i got from that first ad were from guys who found it necessary to describe their cocks in explicit detail, & also tell me in explicit detail what it would feel like to have their "enormous" cocks in my pussy and their "gallons" of cum all over my body. i do remember one guy saying how he was going to take a cigarette & make burn marks all over my body while i was tied to a chair & gagged for something like 24 hours. Also, there was a guy who sent a picture of some woman who had "slut," "whore," etc., written all over her body in something red. i got the impresssion that all the guys who responded were just getting off on writing the letters ... couldn't imagine that they actually thought i would want to meet them after reading stuff like that. They all sounded like lunatics.

Shortly after i met Rob, i got a very nice letter from a guy also claiming to have 30 years experience in D/s. He told me a lot about himself, & his approach to the whole thing. i wrote back to him a couple times & learned a lot about BDSM ... he was much more communicative than Rob ever was. He also seemed to be quite concerned about my safety. If i weren't already involved with Rob, i probably would have met him.

After that, the replies slowed down a little and went in another direction ... guys looking for love and marriage. None of them looked interesting enough to respond to. For the most part, my impression of *adultfriendfinder.com* is that most of the people are on there to get their kicks out of writing letters & looking at pictures, and they will never meet anyone in real life. *Alt.com* was a little better in that respect, but there were a lot of people on *alt.com* who seemed to be just sending a form letter to every ad that was posted. In fact, i would often receive the same exact letter from the same person on multiple occasions.

i am looking forward to serving You soon.

Love,
Your puppy

February 24, 2004

sharon smith wrote:

Dear Master,

i'm ready to leave & still don't have a cell phone, so i will stop by around 4-5pm. If You're busy, i'll just go shopping or something.

See You soon.

Love,
Your puppy

February 23, 2004

Steven Toushin wrote:

Come to the office; my employees will not pay us any mind.

Sir

February 25, 2004

sharon smith wrote:

Hello Dear Master!

i hope Your day is going well! You wore me out so much last night that You inspired me to finally get off my lazy ass & start running today. Only went a mile & thought i was going to die, but at least it's a start. i've concluded that a person over 40 gets out of shape very quickly. (Of course, i'm in total denial that smoking has anything to do with it ☺.)

On the way home last night i was feeling sad about Pirate. Making the decision to have my dog Buster put to sleep, & then actually being there when it happened, was one of the hardest things i've ever done, so i know what You're going through. It's been almost 4 years since Buster has been gone, & i still don't have the heart to get another dog. Pirate is such a sweetheart; it just doesn't seem fair. Anyway, i was thinking about how, in a way, it's easier with people because we can talk to them, & they can understand what's happening to them. They can communicate what will make their final days most meaningful. One of the things that our hospice patients often find most pleasurable/meaningful is being given permission to eat anything they want … no restrictions. So i was thinking that what Pirate needs is a big juicy steak all to himself. Of course, You would know what he likes better than i would, but i'll bet he would thoroughly enjoy a steak. And yes, i know i've got too much time on my hands to be thinking about such things!

Also (with my currently excessive time for thinking), i am wondering what You are thinking about all the stuff i've been writing about my past. Because i'm only identifying specific types of "events," i feel like You are getting a skewed idea of who i am. Sex was actually a very small part of my life until i got involved in BDSM, and even then it was not a big part of my life because the people i played with were either married (with highly restricted schedules) or lived halfway across the country. i felt lucky if i got the chance to play with someone (anyone) once a month.

The reason i was thinking about this is because of some of the things You said last night. Being rather thickheaded, i am slowly starting to grasp the extent of Your experience … outside of the Bijou & making movies (which i have never seen). It just seems important that You know that my experience has been very limited, very isolated, and very vanilla. Even the Doms i've played with have had very narrow views about what is & is not acceptable. So, You are a whole new experience for me. i'm not sure where i'm going with this, except to say that (lucky for me) we seem to have come together from two totally different planets … and i am light-years behind You in knowing what it's all about … and i just want to make sure You understand that. i may even need some remedial education! 😊

Love,
Your puppy

February 23, 2004

sharon smith wrote:

Dear Master,

i woke up this morning thinking about You & wishing i were lying next to You so i could offer You my pussy … and anything else You might want.

It's so nice to have the luxury of staying in bed until the sun shines through the skylights. i felt like i was being bathed in the warmth of Your scent … just stayed there for a couple hours thinking about You & wishing You were here.

i have this extremely thick & fluffy down comforter on my bed (it's like sleeping in the clouds), and when you press on it, it releases a big puff of warm air. This morning when i pressed on it, it filled the air with Your scent … made my pussy all warm & throbbing & wet. It kind of annoyed me that my son still lives here or i could invite You into my fluffy cloud.

i still haven't showered or gotten dressed … am sitting here naked as i write this. So much to do today, & i can't seem to get started on anything ….

Love,
Your puppy

February 28, 2004

sharon smith wrote:

Dear Master,

What a beautiful day! my cat even decided it was nice enough to sunbathe on the deck. i hope You were able to get out & enjoy the nice weather. i did eventually take a shower and get dressed, & then spent most of the day shopping. Didn't accomplish what i needed to, but it was too nice to stay home. We're having some friends up for the weekend. They've been having trouble with ghosts in their house, which is built on an old Indian burial site, and they want to go to this witchcraft place in LaGrange to see about getting rid of them. Ought to be interesting!

You said to start writing about the present, & i don't remember where i left off, so will start with the 1st session with Rob. Now that i'm thinking about it, i don't know what possessed me to get involved with him in the first place. He said he had 30+ years of experience, & i always just took him for his word. He seemed to know what he was doing, but from what You've said, i'm guessing now that he was lying about that. He lied about a lot of things. In the beginning, he told me he was a doctor, but he wouldn't tell me what kind of doctor or where he practiced. Eventually, many months later, i found out (but not from him) that he is a child psychologist, not a doctor. It also took several months to find out his last name. i actually think he is very dominated by his wife, as he seems to be quite afraid of her. To say he is discreet doesn't describe it ... paranoid is more appropriate. No matter where we went, he was always looking over his shoulder like someone was going to see him. i would always have to make the reservation & put the hotel room on my credit card, because he couldn't use his. Sometimes he would give me cash for the room before he left. We could never be seen entering or leaving the hotel together. He also had me pay for the ads on *adultfriendfinder.com* & *alt.com* for the same reason, which became the "straw that broke the camel's back." They were ads looking for a woman to join us so i could explore my "bisexual nature," something i never wanted to do in the first place. It was costing me over $100 a month &, after writing about 20 letters a day over two years during which he found only a couple women who would meet his qualifications, i finally told him i wasn't writing any more letters or paying for any more ads. It took a couple e-mails to convince him i was serious, & i haven't heard from him since. Perhaps i should have had "doormat" tattooed on my forehead. Oh well, live and learn.

Anyway, back to the first session. He called me at work a couple days before we were to meet & told me exactly what to wear: black dress, 4-inch heels, gold choker, gold dangling earrings, red lipstick, black satin & lace bra & thong. i had to go shopping for a couple items. We were to meet at a hotel near O'Hare, & that was the one & only time he made the reservation. It was one of those "nice" hotels where all the customers only stay for four hours. i was to be there at 9:30am. When i arrived (late), he was already in the room & had his toys all laid out & covered with towels. i went in & hung up my coat, & he sat down on the bed & told me to kneel in front of him. He asked me if i was nervous, & i said i was very nervous. He asked if anyone knew where i was, & i said no. He asked if i wanted to call someone, & i had to laugh because i couldn't imagine telling anyone i knew that i was meeting a stranger in a hotel room.

Then he just leaned back & stared at me for a while. i couldn't look him in the eye … never could. He has intimidating eyes. Finally, he told me to go stand in the corner with my legs spread & hands behind my head. He left me standing there for a while which is probably the best thing he could have done, because it gave me a chance to calm my nerves a little. Then he started gently running his hands over my body & up under my dress … kept telling me to stand up straighter. Then he grabbed my hair

& took me to the middle of the room where i was again told to stand with my legs apart, hands behind my head, eyes closed ... and (for some reason) my mouth open. He walked in circles around me a few times & just lightly touched me a couple times ... told me to spread my legs wider, move my hands to the lower part of my back. Then he took me by the arm & took me over to where he had his toys laid out. When he uncovered them & pointed out a couple things, he had what can only be described as a gleam in his eyes, & he asked me what i thought of them. At the time, i had no idea what i was looking at, so i just smiled & said they were nice.

He told me to lie down in the middle of the bed with my legs spread wide, & he was pacing back & forth at the foot of the bed. He told me to raise my ass off the bed & do a couple things, & then turn over & get on my hands & knees with my face on the bed. When i put my head down, my eyes started burning badly, & i lifted my head up again. That made him angry & he yelled at me ... don't remember what he said. Then he told me to pull the covers back on the bed & lay face down in the middle. He blindfolded me & tied my hands & feet to the four corners of the bed & put a couple pillows under my belly so my ass was sticking up in the air. He said that each time he hit me with the whip, i was to say, "thank you, Master Rob" and then the number. He then whaled on me full force with what seemed like every piece of equipment he had, & he had some pretty heavy-duty stuff. With that being the first time i was whipped since i was a child, i think it took a while for my nerve endings to wake up, because the first 20 or so hurt but i was able to lie perfectly still. Actually, i was afraid to move because i really had no idea what was going to happen. my later hypothesis was that the pillows underneath me cushioned the blows. After about every 5-10 lashes, he would play with my pussy, & by the time i had gotten around 20 or so, my pussy was gushing wet. By the time it had reached about 40, my mind was gone somewhere else. If i remember correctly, he gave me around 80-100 lashes that day, & there came a point where i was floating & in a very peaceful place. my ass was black/ purple for weeks.

Then he told me to turn over, & he again tied me to the four corners of the bed, got on top of me, & started to kiss me. When i started to kiss him back, he bit my lip hard enough that it started to bleed & swell up immediately. i had lifted my head to kiss him, & he grabbed my hair & yanked my head back while he had his arm behind my back so my back was arched way up & my mouth was bleeding & what did i do? If i remember correctly, i started begging him to fuck me. Instead of doing that he put one of those vibrating eggs in my pussy, which drove me crazy. i had never felt anything like that before.

The next thing i knew, he was fisting me (also a first), & i was having one orgasm after another & going wild. He had his arm in me up to his elbow, & i could feel him pounding on my cervix. It hurt like hell, & i didn't even care. Then i started bleeding very badly, & he immediately stopped. i was begging him to keep going, but he got real upset. He would always panic at the sight of blood. i think he was real scared of getting HIV or something (and bringing it home to his wife). He always used a glove to fist me. Anyway, he immediately stopped & untied me & told me to go into the bathroom & clean myself up.

When i came back, he was on his back on the bed & had undressed. He told me to suck his cock & then to give him a massage. i spent a couple hours alternating between the two … and that was about it. When we were done, we got dressed, & he kissed me & sent me on my way. That day & the day we were at Marlene's are both very memorable to me, because everything that happened was brand new to me.

Love,
Your puppy

February 29, 2004

Steven Toushin wrote:

Dear puppy,

Thank you. This was very helpful and definitely insightful, but now I need to ask you some more questions. Questions, questions, questions, questions; when will he ever stop asking me questions? Answer: until the 12th of never.

A. In what sequence were the e-mails you forwarded to me sent to you?

B. What is the timeline?

C. What did you apologize for?

D. I know that you discussed this before, but it seems that he was very concerned in picking up other women.

E. Were the words and acts of punishment and discipline your fantasy or his? Did it ever deviate?

F. Again, I am repeating a question that you have already answered, but how often did you see MR [Ed. Note: "Master Rob"] in the beginning of your relationship, the middle and the end of your relationship?

G. How often did you correspond, and what was the focus of your correspondence?

H. Was the relationship sexual, and what was performed by each of you?

Sir

February 29, 2004

sharon smith wrote:

Dear Master,

That's a long time! my poor little fingers will be worn down to nubs! What does it cost to print a 1,000-page book?

In answer to Your questions, i sent you the e-mails from Rob in the order they were written. The first one was shortly after i met him, & the last one i sent was from about a year ago. There are plenty more if You want them ... that's why i had to clean out the inbox: it was full. Marlene had called to say her e-mails were bouncing. i thought the dates would come through when i forwarded the e-mails or i would have added them.

What did i apologize for? i'm not sure which time You are referring to ... he would get angry with me & not tell me why, & i would apologize for everything under the sun until i hap-pened to hit on the right thing.

There was a very small range of things i could talk about without getting in trouble. It took me a while to catch on to that. It pretty much stifled the communication, which is why it deteriorated into him telling me to write letters, & me telling him i had done what he said.

He started telling me to write the letters to women probably about three months after i met him. He was obsessed with finding other women, but they usually came with husbands or male partners, which he didn't usually approve of. He always said he wanted me to explore my "bi-curious nature" (which didn't exist), but on the rare occasions that we actually met anyone new to play, it was about 2% bi, & 98% him & her.

The words & acts of punishment ... i think he felt it was his duty as a Master. i could never figure out why he was so hard on me & not on any of his other subs. He always said i needed to be controlled ... that i craved it. The others could laugh & talk & move around, etc., & i was always expected to be silent & sit/kneel in a certain way & most often was blindfolded ... though i must say that i was usually the center of attention when it came time to play! i always wished he would be more affectionate to me, though, like he was with the others.

One thing i do know is that i could never get him to budge on anything. i was halfway scared of him ... kind of a love-hate relationship. His discipline & punishments were quite severe, so i definitely tried to never make the same mistake twice.

In the beginning of the relationship, i saw him about once a month. There were only a couple times i saw him more often than that. He always had time to meet other people for coffee, but no time to play. The fact of the matter is that unless i could provide other people for him, he didn't have the time for me. And the frustrating thing about that was there were plenty of people who wanted to play with me, but they had no interest in him and/or he had no interest in them. It was all quite a futile exercise. He would talk like he really wanted to meet someone, & then he would sabotage the whole thing ... and then i would have to write hundreds more letters.

Anyway, back to the frequency of our actual time alone together. i think there were only 3-4 times in the last year i was with him. Still don't know why i kept going back & asking for more. We corresponded at least daily. Sometimes he would send 10-15 messages in one day with lists of names to write to. i wish i had saved some of the messages i sent to him. In the beginning i had gotten quite descriptively eloquent about the experience. i asked him a couple times if he had saved any of those letters as they would have made quite a good book, but he never responded to that. By the time i had known him about 6-8 months, about the only thing i felt safe in writing was either benign stuff about the kids, work, etc., or else in direct response to what he asked me. By about halfway through the relation-ship, it was almost like we had become partners in the search for other people, & talking about them was the majority of our communication. i could never make him understand that wasn't what i wanted. i kept hoping he would give up on the idea, but instead he kept getting more & more obsessed with it.

Was the relationship sexual? i guess that depends on how You define sexual. He only tried to fuck me one time, & that didn't work out too well. He would play with me when we were together … vibrators, fisting, clamps … and i would suck his cock. Mostly it was bondage, whips, discipline, rituals for me … and a long massage for him.

Love,
Your puppy

Part VIII

Master Rob

Steven Toushin's Comment:

At my request, puppy sent me these e-mails between her and her former master, and between her and Marlene.

My opinion of her former master is "Charlatan Master" or, as another friend says, "Insta-Dom: just add computer." I expressed to puppy my opinions on part-time manipulative fantasy people who read a little and then pass themselves off as knowledgeable, caring, and nurturing teachers of BDSM and who call themselves "Dom" or "Master." This also includes the female Dommes, of which there is also an abundance. I feel that this group makes up about 70% of the people who play, be it cyber, stolen moments, secret lives away from their spouses, lovers, and friends.

There is nothing wrong with these BDSM feelings and yearnings – but be truthful about your lack of experience; be honest about it. You are already coming out, or are out in your fantasy life; to the people you are playing with, be truthful about what you do, have done, and who you are.

I felt a varied sampling of Rob's ("MR") e-mail was in order to explain and show puppy's journey through the fringes of the BDSM world, a world that a serious submissive/slave has to venture into. It is the same for Tops/Dominants/Masters, wandering through the maze of fringe fantasy bottoms/ submissives/slaves.

Something else: in the BDSM subculture, the abusers and cheaters have found a place to hide. They give themselves a scene name, read a bit, talk in chat rooms, and post on websites, and they throw around phrases and words as they search for prey. Be careful.

Steven Toushin wrote:

Dear puppy,

I forgot to ask, you said that it seems that you only saved the good mail from MR. What was the gist of the bad mail? Did you save any of your e-mail to him?

Sir

sharon smith wrote:

Dear Master,

The good mail was when he actually talked "to" me. The bad mail was when he talked "at" me. The thing that struck me when i was going through that stuff last night was how the letters he wrote to other people (& then sent copies to me) were nothing but lies. Of course, his early letters to me were also lies, so i shouldn't be surprised. i was fairly new to e-mail when i met him & didn't even know i could save the letters i sent until several months had gone by. Then i purposely had the "sent" option turned off for a while, because my kids were home & my computer was in the kitchen ... not much privacy. i just looked at the "sent" folder for that account now, & the earliest thing in there was from last summer, when i was talking about selling the house & getting the new job, etc. ... nothing too interesting.

You asked how many people i contacted that we actually met or played with during the three years. i wrote thousands of letters for Rob. Out of every thousand letters, we were lucky to meet one person/couple ... maybe 5-6 meetings in all. Of the people we actually met, the only couple we actually played with was Susan & Raj. The others were either not acceptable to him, or they did not want to play with him ... just wanted to play with me by myself.

Right from the beginning, Rob wanted me to dominate another woman. He wasn't at all interested in us meeting with a dominant woman, but only a submissive one. Obviously, the reason for that wasn't so much that he wanted me to dominate her, but rather that he wanted to dominate her himself. It wouldn't have been any fun for him if the other woman was dominant, & he couldn't control her. i told him from the start that I couldn't do it, but he kept insisting. i tried it with Susan, & it was a fiasco. She just lay there like a dead fish, & i had no idea what to do with her. Fortunately, it only went on for about a minute before Rob & Raj stepped in … Rob, of course, pairing up with Susan.

Both Tammy & *NaughtyNurse* were only interested in a bisexual experience. Neither of them wanted anything to do with him. His insistence on me being dominant with both of them was … i don't know what. i guess he thought that when we got together with them, he would be directing the show, & getting involved in the action, too. He liked the idea of him being dominant to someone who was being dominant to someone else. He kept dictating to me what to write to them, & they both became offended & cut off communication. They weren't at all interested in BDSM. They just wanted to try the bisexual thing. He couldn't seem to grasp that fact. i think both of them were left feeling very hurt by the correspondence.

That's the thing that bothered me most about the letter writing … all the lies & false pretenses. What's wrong with just being honest? He always had me tell people he was 6'1" when he was actually about 5'8" … like no one would notice?

Anyway, back to the idea of me being dominant … Whenever we met anyone under that pretense, they could tell right away that it wasn't true, & he would get angry with me for not playing the part the way he wanted. That's what was behind the remark about me not being worthy.

We had met with Tammy & her husband, and Rob was upset because he said i wasn't aggressive enough in "seducing" her ... like i would have a clue as to how to seduce a woman. i mean, if there was ever an instance where i was sexually attracted to a woman, i might have some idea of what a woman is looking for in another woman & could try to do whatever that is ... sheesh!

Of course, Tammy actually wanted to get together with me until he had me sending her letters telling her how i was going to tie her up & whip her ... scared the shit out of her. Then, when she said she was no longer interested, he kept telling me to write more stuff. i think she felt like she was being stalked ... poor thing. She will probably never have the courage to explore anything again.

Love,
Your puppy

s*haron smith wrote:*

Dear Master,

i removed Rob's e-mail address, but am otherwise not editing these. [Ed. Note: they were subsequently edited for spelling, punctuation, etc.] Discretion & privacy are of extreme importance to him, so please edit out any references to his family, etc. Thank You.

This was the earliest letter i still have. It was written shortly after we first met.

Love,
Your puppy

Rob wrote:

sub sharon,

I am both impressed and intrigued with the nature and depth of your introspective nature, in general, and your insights into the etiology and core features of your BDSM yearnings. I am also pleased that you followed up and did the assignment that I gave you, and it also spoke volumes about why you're in this experience.

Suffice it to say, you have tremendous potential as a submissive. First, you answered the one key question, which I posed to you as you sat across from me: namely, what is your main role? You wrote that you would try to please me. That, in and of itself, is the central component of being a submissive. Your needs are served by and through serving the needs of your Master, period. I will dominate and control you as never before and, in that relationship in which you become the (an) object, you will have no choices. Thereby, you will arrive at the "freedom" you have been seeking all these years.

On another level, you have had many seemingly diametrically opposed strong drives and forces at work within your soul. I will dominate you and give you the control, discipline, pain and, hence, security which you crave. The result will be the integration and enhancement of your being.

You have apparently had these intensive feelings in the core of your being for years and years. I want you to continue to pen your thoughts and send them to me.

I will contact you regarding an initial training session as soon as I firm up my schedule.

Master Rob

sharon's Comment:

This was written shortly after the first time we were at Marlene's (the second time i was with him). i think i described that scene in response to one of Your questions.

Rob wrote:

sub sharon,

I am pleased that you trust me as you do and feel safe with me. That has been, and always will be, my intent.

I am also happy that you are being open as to your feelings about your BDSM sessions and experiences. They help me to better understand where you're at with it, and to be sure it's all on course. It also helps you to get to know yourself better. As far as "weird," not at all. The feeling of being totally secure and safe, like in the womb, while being tied up, is just where I want you to be. The truth is that you arrived at "sub space" and that special place of feeling secure very early on in the process – like immediately. It is where a submissive goes when she completely gives up control and "power" to her Dom and Master. It usually takes a while. I think it is the result of our good chemistry and your being as ready as you were, and my expertise in recognizing it.

Now is a good time to tell you this: you are a "true" submissive. I have met a few throughout my thirty odd years of doing this, but not many. You have the potential to go very, very far with this. I was and am extremely delighted with how you obeyed me and submitted to Me and respected my commands. I thank you for striving to please me and for succeeding as well as you did. I was there for you and will continue to carefully and lovingly guide you, if that is what you still desire.

Master Rob

sharon's Comment:

Rob wrote a poem for me shortly after the scene at Marlene's, & after i had a fit about writing the letters to all the women.

Rob wrote:

for sub sharon

> you relented and detailed your method to masturbate
> in attempting your horny home abstinence to satiate.
>
> Your lack of sex gives you a fit,
> so I'll need to titillate and arouse first your clit.
>
> And soon your undulations will be felt
> after I whip your ass with my thick belt.
>
> I know you feel safe as my sexual slave
> and more pain and use do you crave.
>
> Though not sessioned now for some time,
> I sense your wantonness doth pine.
>
> You've pleased Me and know how to obey
> lest you know Master will make you pay.
>
> You will be red, hot, bruised on your seat,
> then aroused your Master's cum you will eat
>
> and massage and caress me head to toe,
> naked, my sub's servitude to show.
>
> In short measure you've had new explorations,
> strangers, multiples and female sensations.
>
> All meant for your growth and erotic gain,
> but all directed by Me to show you such pain.

you are my property and in my control
and you'll fully pleasure Me with your body and soul.

Of Me you've asked for a fuck
if pussy I require you to suck.

Well, my submissive in waiting
I hope your dreams are not abating.

For, if from your Master you want a good fuck,
you must first perform well as my slut.

you obey and behave as my tramp,
then I'll attach to your erect tits taut my clamp.

There's one thing I've left unsaid
that throughout you'll be tied hard to the bed.

And while orgasmic below your wet mouth I'll be kissing,
now, my sub, you know what you've been missing.

And if the truth be further told,
your eyes also covered with my special blindfold.

MR

Rob wrote:

ss,

I guess that you are just a very willing subject. After all, isn't
giving someone else total control over you what you need?
Such a choice speaks to the ease with which you are hypnotized, be it for ninety minutes by a stranger or a briefer period
by your Master. I am pleased that the "phenomenon" of sub

space and the experience lingers. The best part of it all is that you are completely at my mercy as to what "direction" it will all take. Somehow, at a deep, intrinsic level, you truly crave such a power exchange. I am actually happy that you give this all such introspection and attention. Your desirability, for me, as a submissive is not only your desire to totally please and obey me, but also that you understand that D/s and BDSM is, at the core, a mental process.

It will be unlikely that I could spend much time in the city with you that weekend, but I'll give it some thought.

Have a good day.

MR

Rob wrote:

sub sharon,

I am happy that you also felt so relaxed, centered and "out there." You truly entered "subspace" and more. You have arrived at a very special place in your development as a submissive. Yes, more frequent sessions would get you there more frequently. Also, the atmosphere makes a difference. Hence, a home setting with proper hooks and wall mounts works even better.

Your description of your experience was flowing, cogent and rather eloquent. Hold down the fort well today and next week.

MR

Rob wrote:

ss,

Set it up for tomorrow at 1:00pm in your name. I'll demonstrate flogging and whipping sue to Raj, and then you and sue will play together. Let sue know that I do not have the strap-on as it's at Marlene's. Reassure her that we are healthy, and mention that you hope that they are as well. Tell them that we use precautions, and that Marlene even used a condom on her strap-on. Tell them we're looking forward to being together. Page me if there are any problems. Try to get a first floor end room on the north side by U.S. 30, as there is a private entrance right there.

MR

Rob wrote:

ss,

You are a bright and sensitive soul, quiet, but very observant.

I felt very badly about sue, mainly because I had no idea that she felt anything other than pleasure. I asked her over and over how she was, and she kept saying, "relaxed," "great." I also felt that it was Raj's responsibility to look over her as he knew what he and she wanted. I stopped whenever she said to stop. Raj, as I knew, only wants sex and you alone. He is much less caring about sue's welfare than his own. That is why I would not permit you to do what he wanted, along with health concerns. It is also not very respectful of Me for Raj to be writing to you directly. You will not reply to him but will continue to forward all e-mails to me.

I have tons of consults to do today and tomorrow, reports, etc., and Yom Kippur this Sunday evening and Monday. It is the holiest day in our year. We will go to Chicago for dinner with our three daughters; they are making dinner.

I'll get back to you when I can and talk more about yesterday. If I get time, I'll call you. I don't like to see anyone upset.

MR

Rob wrote:

ss,

Get an e-mail address for writing sue directly. Also, forward all of her letters to Me.

It is not appropriate for Raj to be writing you, or for you to be replying. In the future you will not write to anyone without My permission. Your replies, though, seem honest and reflective of my sentiments as well.

MR

Rob wrote:

sub sharon,

Your correspondence to susan was fine, as it reflected your sincere and honest feelings. I realize, too, that you wrote to also protect Me and my interests, etc.

you will also write *couple2pleaseF* and *verysexycouple3*, *adult friendfinder.com.*

MR

Rob wrote:

ss,

I understand you better than you know. You are bright, extremely caring, obedient, attentive, curious, and brave. You are, however, rather naive and overly trusting. I've known that for a long time and have been focusing on it in my own way. You were fortunate to have trusted me as you did, as I'd never do anything purposely to harm you. I've walked away from scenes when I knew that a woman was too sick or scared. I don't need to harm or use people. The pleasure for me is to see them grow in their submission and as people.

I really knew that Raj could not be trusted. He was too anxious from the get go, too quiet, and he wanted me to loan you out and to give him a sub to perform with a dog or animal. I would never do those things. I guess that I'm trying to tell you that I know that you get real hard on yourself when you think that you've made a "stupid" mistake. As your Master, I'm telling you that you no longer have the right to beat up on yourself. That privilege is mine and mine alone! I do not fault you for being naive and getting duped. I want you to grow from it and become a better person as a result and to continue to not be afraid. We can walk the narrow bridge of life in fear if we choose. I elect to not be afraid, but to proceed full speed, with my eyes and ears open.

I have lots more to tell you about you, but it'll have to wait. I have dozens of cases to dictate and am nowhere near having my manuscript ready.

I'm sitting here writing to you via the Internet with my window open and cool breezes coming through my study. I'm thinking how strange it is to be able to correspond with anyone in the whole world right from where I sit.

My goal for you, sharon, is for you to feel very good about yourself and to explore your self and your submission as a means of gaining a sense of balance and peace. Think of it as "special" karma. Besides, you found Sue; I think she will be a real asset.

Send Me your available days for next week.

MR

Rob wrote:

sub sharon,

I am acutely aware of most of what was occurring. Like you, I know and feel more than I sometimes wish to say. I know that you felt caught in the middle, and I know that your intention was to protect me from feeling rejected by susan. I have broad shoulders, and any feelings or comments that susan may have towards me will not damage my psyche. I do, though, appreciate that you were "looking out" for your Master.

I had two primary concerns. The first was that I have been attempting to train you to be totally respectful and obedient. The essence of BDSM and serving, and being a "true" submissive and then a "slave," is dependent on the submissive's ability to "please" her Master. The cosmic glue of it all is the "mental servitude," based on trust and proving that you will spare nothing to satisfy your Master's desires. In the context of such a bond, the other stuff that happened would have been miniscule. When I felt your disrespect and disobedience, the rest fell apart.

The second concern, and regarding the crisis, was that I wanted to give you some space to deal with the tragic deaths in your family. That was, and is, a lot for anyone to bear.

In the scheme of things, this is merely adult play or diversion, or whatever and however you wish to label it. Family is family. Life is life. Loss is loss. Related to that, I wanted to also give you time and space to work this out in your head and to come to your own conclusions. You did do that.

For the record, you needn't be too jealous of susan. I see you as far brighter and much more caring, sensitive, sexual and sensual than she is, and you certainly give a much better massage. I get bored easily in relationships and will bring "new blood" in at times, but only to enhance what is already there with the other relationship. I had not sessioned anyone but you since May, when I last saw Marlene. And, for the record, susan is very conflicted as to the role of a submissive. The only purpose for which a "true" submissive exists is to serve her Master. Her satisfaction is secondary or inconsequential, and she is only gratified when and if her Master so chooses. In the Eastern style of serving, i.e., Geishas, it is even a higher, refined art. In the Western mode, a sub awaits her Master's command, whereas in the East, the submissive strives at all times to "anticipate" her Master's needs, to know him so well that he will be "taken care of" before he even asks.

Enough. Tell me how you are healing from your losses and about the weekend of family visiting and mourning. Life is truly short. Since you are so much younger than me, I must be selective and picky and focused in what I do, as I do not have the same time to work with as you do.

I may let you serve me this Monday, but I have to see what I can get done in the next few days.

Master Rob

sharon's Comment:

Hmmm … i'm surprised i saved this one. This was when he was very angry with me because i didn't want to be the go-between for him & Susan.

Rob wrote:

sub sharon,

I will grant your request to assist you and "tell you what to do." Please note well that I am doing this after careful deliberation and for a few important reasons. First, you are coming "back to your senses," somewhat. Second, it is my responsibility to exert maximum control over you. Third, you essentially made the decision, yourself, that "you want only to serve Me."

You will write susan and tell her "that you only want to serve Master Rob," and that you do not have your Master's permission to do otherwise, nor do you wish to request it. You will send me a copy of this and all future correspondence to susan or from susan and/or anyone else.

I am more pleased that your "tone" is more respectful, obedient and reverent than it has been of late. I will not tolerate your rudeness and lack of respect, and I was totally displeased and disappointed in you for such insolence. You know better and, if you don't, you will.

Do you grasp the essence of this message?

Master Rob

Rob wrote:

sub sharon,

I am pleased that you received such quick and excellent job prospects.

Yes, you never know what or who you'll end up finding on the Internet these days.

Also, I was very pleased with the letter you wrote to susan. I am also happy that you wrote it immediately. Your attitude and level of servitude have improved. I would like to do a three-some with the primary focus of my watching you and susan play together.

Futttrader? Give them a quick note to say that we both need to set up our work and play schedule this week and want to know if they're still interested and want to meet for lunch Thursday. If they write back in the affirmative, tell them we'll give them a location in the Westmont area for 12:45pm lunch.

Beverly is about 95th Street or 111th, just north of Oak Lawn, I think.

Gee, a new job and your own apartment? How soon can it happen?

MR

Rob wrote:

ss,

Quiet is good as long as it's not the "calm before the storm."

You will be deluged with job offers.

No reply from *futttrader*?

I want you to reconnect with susan. I would like to see the two of you again involved with each other in play, and I have some other ideas as well. Carbon me in.

MR

Rob wrote:

ss,

you may also tell susan that this Friday would not work for Master Rob.

MR

Rob wrote:

sub sharon,

Thanks for keeping me "abreast" of the communications be-tween you and Sue. you will continue to cc me in on all e-mails.

I had wonderful holidays with my family and feel extremely at peace.

you may keep your own *adultfriendfinder.com* ad, but I will keep your password and login name and check it daily. you will not open any messages until I have seen them first.

I'll have to see what tomorrow looks like, but as of now I don't think it will work. I have just gotten online and must go straight to my writing. I am submitting a professional manuscript and have an editor's deadline.

I plan on writing sue and will send you a carbon and let her know that I'm doing that and that everything, between you and me, is aboveboard.

Send Me your available days for the next two weeks.

MR

Rob wrote:

ss,

It is almost 7:00am, and I need to be on the road and get tons done as I am off tomorrow to meet with my urologist in the city.

Don't even reply back to susan. I sense that she is being devious.

Stay in touch.

MR

Hmmm … it seems i only saved the nice ones!

Rob wrote:

sub sharon,

I am pleased that you followed through on your assignment so graciously. I appreciate the effort and the "improved" attitude. Now, was that all so difficult? I'll just have to whip you more and make you my "little pain slut."

Just write *couriouzcpl* on your own and see what you get back. As for *annettecl*, write her and tell her you're intrigued and interested, and you want to meet them and bring your partner, who is very experienced in the lifestyle. Note to her that discretion is most required as we're in the area professionally, etc. If she "bites" (pun intended), we'll figure out a place, probably the Star Plaza, mid afternoon.

Happy you're sounding much better. Keep the good karma coming and stay "in balance."

MR

Rob wrote:

sub sharon,

I was pleased with you and how well you are serving Me.

Don't bother to write anyone for now. I may have some new profiles for you to contact soon.

I'm fine but very busy.

Take care and be sure to get some exercise. It improves cardio functioning, especially while engaged in smoking cessation, and also increases one's ability to serve her Master.

MR

Rob wrote:

ss,

I am most pleased that you strive to serve and obey me in such a sincere and unconditional fashion. There will be ample opportunities for you to continue to prove your worth, and for Me to expand your limits and test your will.

MR

Rob wrote:

ss,

Hope you're doing well.

Can you schedule some time this Thursday, mid-morning, to possibly meet Nick and Nora and *ChgoCpl* in Chicago? If so, write to *ChgoCpl7928@yahoo.com* today and see if they can meet for coffee or an early lunch.

I have to be at Northwestern Hospital early this Thursday.

MR

Rob wrote:

ss,

I don't want you bored while I am away. You will write to every new ad on *adultfriendfinder.com*, beginning today. There are many good ones, including:

> *newbutsexy*
> *couple 4792*
> *cnr*
> *wiopencouple*
> *Funcouple*
> *honeybrippr*

and more, including some in Hammond and Valpo.

Stay with it or you'll be punished.

MR

Rob wrote:

sub sharon,

Happy that you got away a bit and had a good time in Mishawaka.

I don't know the name of the newer resort or operator at French Lick. By now, you're probably right to assume that you not need to speak French. Doesn't "French Lick" have a nice ring to it?

I accept your apology for being yingy and yangy. I expect you to smooth out your moods so that I can whip your ass and body into multiple shades of blue, purple and bright pink.

Write to *wnerinbi* and elicit further interest and see if we can meet her to give her what she seeks. I was going to punish you for opening that e-mail, but I will let it go this time.

Be well and stay in touch daily.

MR

Rob wrote:

sub sharon,

I worked all day on Saturday and Sunday, and went to a black tie wedding in Chicago. The son of very close friends was married. It was a beautiful wedding, but we didn't get home until 2:30am, and I am not a night person.

Write to all of those ads, including *pmba* on the Gallery. Tell them our roles and experience levels, that I don't switch, and that we are patient, loving and respectful. For those who are interested more in exploring partners and not necessarily BDSM, write something more vanilla. In all cases, suggest that we'd be willing to meet to discuss compatibilities and options.

Take care.

MR

Rob wrote:

ss,

You will get to claim your spanking (whipping) soon, and you will "Sir" Me in my presence. you are showing Me respect.

I know that your time has been and will still be limited. However, I will now expect you to check the new Gallery listings on a regular basis and reply.

Whatever happened to *DOMSWB*! Check the mailbox and reply; they have a different ad. If you still have their number, call.

Tentatively, I am trying to schedule dinner this Thursday around 5:30pm with a new couple near Hinsdale and I294.

Yes, it was hard to not go full throttle yesterday. It will happen soon.

Hope that your mother is well and that you had a good visit.

I'm not sure that I want to go forward with that couple. They wrote and said that they want to play with us. More on that later.

MR

Rob wrote:

sub sharon,

Yes, I felt quite good, almost too relaxed to function. I was very pleased.

You can have Bobbi contact me on or after January 6. Also, write to *luvs2teaze2001*, in Chesterton, on *adultfriendfinder.com*. Tell her how much you want to again be with a woman, and that I'll be there to join in the fun.

It is not unusual to feel the pain of the whip more now than in the beginning. It is a strange, but not too uncommon, phenomenon. Marlene experienced it as well. Then, just as the pain increases, you will begin to take more and to ask for and need more pain.

I understand your memories regarding family traditions. I guess that they vary for all of us. A sense of belonging and identity is central for all of us.

Stay in touch.

MR

Rob wrote:

sub sharon,

I wrote earlier from a public computer and wasn't sure if it went through.

I just wanted to tell you that you've sounded quite good of late, rather energized. Could it be that you're more centered since I last saw you? Maybe you really enjoy being whipped?

MR

Rob wrote:

sub sharon,

Call *redtop*, as she gave you her number, and check availability for next week. You will also write back to the reply we got, the one I opened, who lives in Chicago, who is bi and wants a couple. Send me a carbon.

MR

Rob wrote:

sub sharon,

Just got our computer back up.

Send me *redhead*'s phone number. Send her an e-mail and tell her I'll be calling her to make plans.

Talk to you soon.

MR

Rob wrote:

sub sharon,

Write *abad1* on *adultfriendfinder.com* today. Emphasize your slim, smooth body, firm nipples, and warm, multi-orgasmic body that loves men and women. Emphasize, too, that I come with you as your Master and participate.

MR

Rob wrote:

ss,

Also write *NaughtyNurse* (check the messages). Don't tell her that you are submissive, as I indicated that we were both dominant. This will be a training exercise for you. Also, she plays with or without her husband. Let her know we'd like to meet her for coffee or lunch, and somehow indicate that we want to do fetish play and domination with her. Don't suggest that he be involved.

MR

Rob wrote:

sub sharon,

Thanks for your good wishes; I'm finally feeling semi-healthy. I at least slept for eight hours. and my cough has subsided.

I checked the sent messages and am pleased that you have followed through with all of the assignments. You are doing well, becoming quite the woman of "arts and letters."

I'll contact *ftttrader* and *patandmike*. A note of caution regarding *PlayToyWife*: I'm unsure whether or not he plans to bring his wife to meet us. Also, if, in fact, he really did bring four men to a motel room to do his wife, then that raises issues about STDs. Few of the recent ads with whom we're corres-ponding stress health and safe sex.

Give me your available days next week at this point when you can massage my aching muscles.

MR

Rob wrote:

ss,

You are to write letters to all of the following no later than this Sunday evening at 10:00pm. All are *adultfriendfinder.com* profiles:

> *ssls62032*
> *weshareyou111*
> *makemetremble*
> *qcouple (*see Gallery*)*
> *jewels1126*
> *screeneme*
> *pinkprl*
> *Hellokitty_32*
> *Goldeyes_35*
> *1fajita*
> *justakiss2*
> *sexymaria32*
> *xjustbetween2or3*
> *yourlittleslut2*
> *N2fw*
> *kelly4usexy*

MR

Rob wrote:

sub sharon,

Thanks for your warm, sincere birthday wishes. I really like the card! It gives me ideas as to how you can serve Me. I have a feeling that you wouldn't mind being bound and gagged with hot candle wax dripping on your breasts as long as you could also feel the pleasurable pain of my whip across your wanton ass and entire body. You do love the whip, don't you?

Yes, I don't think Kathy will work out for exactly the same reasons you suggest – she is too needy. Stay in touch with her, though.

MR

Rob wrote:

sub sharon,

I wrote to *luckeus* and *Roc Lexi*.

I want you to write, now, to *kristine73*. She looked at our profile and is interested.

Here are the others you are to write from the Gallery:

> *smartsexyjoe1*
> *Kat_Tom_sxycpl*
> *MarkandLindsey*
> *fukmygf*
> *raycey*
> *daytimers*
> *ShyButWilling*
> *Naughtypair2*
> *illinoiscple819*
> *spiceycouple31*

I spoke with the couple whose number you gave me. They are very interested in meeting us. What is their handle? Please send me your tentative availability next week and the week after, for coffee or whatever.

Take care.

MR

Rob wrote:

ss,

Write to these ads on *adultfriendfinder.com:*

> *ChgoCpl5532*
> *22zwing*
> *Illinoiscpl2*
> *Orgrinder*
> *teewinontone*
> *HwknTitan1*

MR

Rob wrote:

ss,

Your recent lapses in respect and obedience are part of your development as a submissive. You will be appropriately disciplined for such behaviors.

I read each of the letters that you wrote and liked them a lot. It shows a better effort and attitude on your part. You will write two other nice letters to *sweetjane60614* and *bacdraft*; they are in the new photos in the Gallery.

I am most angry (perhaps very concerned is a better word) at your smoking relapse. I realize that it is highly addictive. I will not allow you to self-destruct. You will renew your efforts, and I will help you. I do not stay angry at my submissives very long, just long enough to discipline you and teach you not to be so forgetful the next time(s).

Stay in touch as instructed. I'll see what next week looks like. Send me your available days.

MR

[Ed. Note: In response to Steven Toushin's question to puppy asking about the lapse of obedience above, puppy replied:

i'm not sure what the particular lapse in obedience was. It usually had to do with the idea that i wasn't showing the proper respect. There was an incident early last summer in which Marlene had arranged a play party at her house in Rob's honor. Kate had flown in from Ohio to be there, & it was supposed to be for the whole weekend: Friday morning to Sunday night (Rob's wife had gone to Arizona for the weekend). Anyway, the five of us were there, & Marlene had this whole elaborate weekend planned, with gourmet meals, fine wine, et al. Then Rob decided after dinner on Friday that he had to go home. Marlene was upset because she had gone through a lot of work, & she felt it was very rude for him to leave, especially since Kate had come this far just to see him. Personally, i was used to that kind of thing from him & didn't think anything of it. However, i did tell him that he had hurt Marlene & Kate's feelings, & they were very disappointed that he didn't stay. He was furious with me for saying anything, i got several vicious e-mails about it … as did Marlene. i held my ground for a while, but eventually i caved in & apologized for being so disre-spectful. I know, I know … that probably wasn't the right thing to do. There just wasn't any arguing with him. It was either apologize, or it was over. i guess he hadn't pushed me far enough yet.]

Rob wrote:

sub sharon,

I am happy that you are blessed with such good feelings and feel so thankful. I was pleased with the excellent letter that you wrote, and you even remembered to send me a copy. You are making progress. You will continue to write to all the new pro-files on the Gallery while I am gone.

Thanks for your good wishes for the trip. I need to run some errands and then pack. We leave late morning tomorrow and return late evening this Monday. Have a wonderful Thanks-giving!

MR

Rob wrote:

sub sharon,

I can't say that I got much sleep last night either, but I am at least somewhat more oriented. We did get to see some sights in NY, including Ellis Island, Statue of Liberty, Ground Zero, a few museums, Times Square, SoHo and two musicals, "Mama

Mia" and "The Lion King." We were somewhat "locked in" to times because our friends had several pre-nuptial events, dinners, etc. It was our first time in NY, and we really liked it. Our daughters love NY and are exploring moving there. Barbara was offered one job by a family member at the wedding. It is in Jersey, but she could certainly live in NY. She can also get a lateral transfer to her company's office right on Times Square as they are looking for CPAs to fill their new headquarters, which we visited.

Here is what you will do with the various and many potential play partners, many of whom you have so well cultivated. You will tentatively set up Pat and Mike for this Thursday somewhere not farther than the O'Hare area. you will make phone contact with Pat and have her tell you on the phone, again, their interests and expectations. Do they want to just watch? One of their replies stated that they just want "oral" the first meeting. Is he bisexual?

I wrote to *Partycpl9524*. You are to write to *PlayToyWife* and show interest in us meeting. Wait a while to write back to *seeksmore2002* as he took a long time to get back to you.

Call *babette* at the number they left and see if they'd travel out here. You will write, today, to *GraphicCpl* and offer to patiently and lovingly teach them. I like their ad. You will also write to "*Just_Rock1*," a new Gallery ad. Tell them that we have a few select, fit, attractive professional couples as well but wish to be with them first. You will then write to *venus2112*, *lucky couplewi*, *ChiRosie*, and Tim and Jean.

Keep up the good work.

MR

Rob wrote:

sub sharon,

It was a wonderful trip. I am exhausted due to getting in late and now have to tend to the backlog and head into the office.

You've done a nice job with the correspondence. I'll look it over again when I can and decide if you continue to write to them or if I take over.

Hope to whip you long and hard real soon.

MR

Rob wrote:

ss,

I had this great fantasy. You get this neat apartment. Since you are not inclined to top and be a Mistress, I make you "The Madame." These couples reply, and you schedule them. I arrive for our morning meeting, and you tell me who is scheduled. I then tell you to "prep" *roc lexi* for a double dildo session at 9:00am and then to schedule todd and laurie for 2:00pm, but to be sure to leave a break in between for us. What do you think, Madame?

There are three more for you to write: *maybe2871, lennanddave*, and *Gfunk6869* – they are all new on the Gallery.

I will count on you to keep up all of the replies while I am gone.

Talk to you later.

MR

[Ed. Note: Steven Toushin asked puppy:

Did Rob think that you were getting an apartment on your own outside of husband and children? Where did he get this thought of you being a Madame and that you would provide a play nest for him? Was he going to pay for this?

puppy responded:

The idea (fantasy) of getting an apartment & me being a "Madame" came about when i took the job in Illinois, & the house in Indiana wasn't sold yet, & we didn't have any place to live yet in Illinois. i was going to get an apartment over here while my husband stayed there until the house sold & until i found a house here. i thought it would be more convenient for Rob & me to get together, rather than having to go to a hotel. He had other ideas ... which i was disappointed with, since i had absolutely no desire to prepare other women for him to play with. The only time he showed interest in anything was when the possibility of other women was involved.

As it turned out, I ended up living in a hotel for a couple months, & he could never find the time to stop in to see me ... but he was upset because i didn't have computer access while living in the hotel & so i couldn't write any letters.

No, he would never pay for anything like that (laughing). We met a couple for dinner at a restaurant in Chicago one time, & the bill came to about $100. i thought he was going to have a panic attack. i ended up paying for most of it. He couldn't use a credit card because his wife would have found out, & i don't think his cash allowance was much more than that for a whole week.]

Rob wrote:

ss,

You have developed into an obedient and loyal submissive. You just need to be whipped and used on a more regular basis and serve Me more regularly. You also need more diversified BDSM experiences to take you farther.

Gurnee is about 30 minutes or more north of O'Hare, where Great America is, and Northbrook is about 10 minutes north of O'Hare off of I294. The Westmont area is much closer for them than us; just tell them we're coming in from Indiana.

If someone is not interested in BDSM, just reply to their interests. My sense is that they do have some curiosity about BDSM play since they know our profile. You might want to say that we'd be happy at anytime to introduce them to it, but it's not a requirement for our playing.

We're going into the city this afternoon. Zoie wants to see the Freida Kalo exhibit at the Mexican Fine Arts museum, and we'll meet our daughters for dinner somewhere.

MR

Rob wrote:

ss,

I am actually pleased with your renewed positive manners, respect and favorable attitude towards your Master. Your manners are actually improving. It is the subtle "refinements" which distinguish a good sub from an outstanding one. You're learning. I have much to teach you still.

I'll be in further contact with you. In the interim, you must continue to inform me each morning of your cigarette count. Did you do so this morning? I have a plan for you to stop smoking that will involve something other than non-stop, 24/7 whippings and plugging all cavities or burning your nipples with your cigarettes.

MR

Rob wrote:

sub sharon,

I appreciate your clear and honest words and am pleased that you wish to obey and serve this Master. I am also happy that you now understand, and even value, the distinction between sex versus developing your self through control, discipline, pain, and submission. There really is a major difference. You are developing very well. I would not waste my time with you if I were displeased.

Be well and keep that good karma and balance.

MR

Rob wrote:

sub sharon,

I can't meet you tomorrow as I am very, very behind on my work and must meet this deadline for my manuscript. We'll try for next week. I will definitely control you and whip you and keep you quiet, aroused and contented as you please Me as I desire.

MR

sharon's Comment:

This was after Rob had ignored me for quite a while (as punishment). i had complained that he was always too busy to see me.

Rob wrote:

ss,

Yes, I accept your apology.

However, you can expect to be properly punished for your now twice delinquent non-reporting of daily cigarette count and, especially, for your disrespect shown to your Master by your "sassy and bitchy and rude attitude." I will not tolerate either disobedience or especially any lack of respect by my submissive.

You will look at *autumntide*'s reply in our mailbox and carefully compose a reply to attract her. Send me a copy.

I know that you have your hands full with work and were also disappointed that we could not meet lately. Trust that I, too, am over-loaded on my end. Years and years of my tireless efforts to put together my own health clinic and dream are now at a critical point and require my total attention.

I am not "blowing you off."

Master Rob

Rob wrote:

ss,

We're on the same page with Kathy and Dianne. Don't spend too much time writing Kathy, but continue the dialogue. She seems unrealistic in what she wants and what we want. I think that Dianne is struggling with whether or not she would do this with us alone should her "nervous" husband not want to do it with her. I think that she wants to respect her spouse's needs and balance them against her own desires. We will meet with him and give him a chance to talk and to feel comfortable and see what he wants and reassure him about limits.

Thanks for wanting to serve me. I need this week to catch up. My daughters are either coming here tomorrow for dinner or we will leave early for the city and have dinner there.

I would like for you to serve me next week. Send me your available dates the next few weeks.

I will write Dianne and arrange lunch this Saturday at noon.

MR

Rob wrote:

sub sharon confused,

No hidden agenda. I do not wish to communicate with nurse Kathy but want you to do so. I will try to clear up time during the day on a weekend to meet with Todd and Laurie and the Deerfield woman, but I can't commit yet. Cannot do evenings for now.

There is only the one woman to whose profile and interest you called my attention on that *alt.matchmaker* account. No interest on any other *adultfriendfinder.com* or *alt.com* account.

We will meet D and J tomorrow for lunch. Call that resort in Chesterton and see if their restaurant is still under construction or is now open for lunch. Leave me a voicemail with the answer and your number where I can reach you.

MR

Rob wrote:

ss,

I will meet you tomorrow at 2:45pm in the back area near the restaurant at the Radisson. Come through that back or side area door. I don't have a name, yet, of the woman we will be meeting, but she is very eager and anxious to meet us (especially you). In fact, her hubby can't get off of work, and she asked if we'd still meet with just her. She wants to be with you, but also in a threesome or foursome.

MR

These are e-mails between Rob and Dianne.

Dave Smith wrote: [Ed. Note: another pseudonym Rob used]

Hi,

Yes, we would both be happy to meet with you alone and are sorry that your husband can't get off of work. Sharon and I will meet you at 2:30pm tomorrow afternoon at the Radisson Star Plaza. Just meet us by the main, front lobby door; there are some couches. We'll find you and then get coffee or a drink. We are kind, pleasant and easy-going. We look forward to seeing you and talking about mutual fantasies and interests. Please confirm that you will be there.

Take care.

Rob and Sharon

J and D wrote:

Rob and Sharon – Thanks for meeting with me yesterday. I spoke to Jerry about another meeting, and he is agreeable. I want to be up front and tell you that I sense he is still somewhat nervous. He says he can't imagine watching someone "hurt" me. In the end, I can't predict if he will be willing to go forward.

We generally work days, but could possibly take a day of vacation if you want to meet during a weekday. We do have a toddler so, for an evening or weekend meeting, we would have to plan ahead to arrange a sitter.

Dianne

Dave Smith wrote:

Dianne and Jerry,

Sharon and I were happy to meet you.

We understand Jerry's concerns and initial anxieties. Rest assured, as we emphasized, nothing will occur that you do not wish to happen, and all limits will be respected. Sane and consensual apply at all times. You will not get "hurt" for the sake of being hurt, but only if you so choose to experience erotic pain leading to arousal.

We would be happy to meet you both for lunch this Saturday at noon to talk.

Rob and Sharon

Dave Smith wrote:

Subject: Re: Assignments

Dianne and Jerry,

These are your initial assignments to begin to prepare both of you, though at this point more so Dianne, for your role and training as a submissive under My tutelage. For these assignments, Dianne, I want you to show Jerry your writing before "submitting" it to Me. It will also serve as a basis of discussion between you and Jerry. I want Jerry to know, at all times, where you are at with your submissive desires.

1. Go to the website *sexuality.org*. Go to keyword "partner checklist." Complete the checklist in detail and send it to Me as a straight e-mail, not attachment.

2. Describe, in as much detail as possible, your three salient fantasies.

3. Give Me your reactions to whatever readings you've completed regarding *The Story of O* and the *Beauty* series.

Please feel free, both of you, to ask questions at any time.

Sharon and I look forward to a safe, sane, consensual, sensual, erotic, growthful and fun experience.

Master Rob

Dave Smith wrote:

Subject: Re: Mentoring

Dianne,

No, I am not Gorean. I'm not that "far out." Gor is fictionalized and follows the many novels of John Norman. It is ritualistic and bizarre.

Be assured that cleanliness/safe sex/safety are primary for us as well.

We will talk more about your concern, at this point, of being completely tied up and helpless in your first session. I will certainly not force it upon you; but, on the other hand, I do not want you to categorically begin to rule things out which you may well enjoy and get "turned on" by.

I am pleased that you are both interested in being mentored and in exploring your erotic sides and in learning to be a submissive.

There seems to be a lot going on at work, and I hope that your positions are both secure.

Let me know as soon as you know about meeting dates.

Regarding your serving me as a full-time sub, I will explain the etiquette and role that you will play in more detail when we talk and meet.

MR

Rob wrote:

ss,

I was thinking about Jerry and Dianne. I want you to write to Dianne, femme-a-femme. You have her e-mail address. Don't use the one I forwarded. Compose a new one with your own address. Tell her that you hope that things are settling down with their jobs, that all is well, and that you've been thinking about her. Say something as to how much you were looking forward to being with her and slowly exploring her body, and vice versa. I want to see if she is still interested. Feel free to add more erotic stuff as well.

MR

Rob wrote:

ss,

You wrote an outstanding letter to Diane! Her response leaves me thinking that she backed out of wanting to do this, especially now that she has nothing but time on her hands.

I will have to see when I can meet with Lisa and Mike next week.

Not sure about tomorrow's availability, as I might need to cover for someone. I'll let you know.

MR

Rob wrote:

ss,

Looks like I have no indication of prostate cancer, but the prostate continues to enlarge, which is why the Flomax® stopped working. I will be on Proscar® for six months to shrink the prostate and will, hopefully, avoid surgery.

A few quick things before I go to the office. First, I did write Tammy a quick note last week and thought I sent you a cc. In any case, she did reply and said that they were interested, would be in touch, and did not want BDSM. Tammy said she'd like for "sharon to be aggressive with her." Write to Tammy and tell her that you'd be happy to do that for her, and that we'd both like to make her feel good. Ask her to let us know a bit more about what else she might enjoy. I don't want to be pushy but want to continue the contact.

Second, regarding susan, if you feel you'd like to reply. you may. If you do, be your honest self and tell her what else is going on in your life, that we're active with other couples and individuals, and that we're planning for a sub and slave party in our dungeon at Mistress Marlene's. You may want to suggest to susan that she contact Master Rob for permission to use one of his other lithe, sensual subs to service her Master.

MR

Rob wrote:

ss,

Not a problem. We will probably have to wait until I get back the week after this.

I know what your sexual and personality proclivities are. I am pushing you to see if you would be willing to try to be aggressive with Tammy. If it is not possible, then you are not worthy of serving Me. Page Me with you phone number when you get this. I may have time to call you to talk about all of this.

You have an assignment that must be completed by noon tomorrow. You are to go to the Gallery on *adultfriendfinder. com*, to the page with Nick and Nora. Don't write to them, as I already have; they will call us when they will be coming back to the area.

I want you to write to EVERYONE on the rest of those pages and all of the following pages. The woman with her eyes covered wants mentors, so be sure to add that we will be mentors.

There is a Dom/slave couple. Indicate what our roles are and that we perhaps we can get together, two Doms and two subs.

MR

sharon's Comment:

This is a copy of a letter he sent to Tammy. She had gotten angry because i was sending him cc's of my correspondence with her – as i had been ordered. This is his effort to fix things – all bullshit & lies.

Dave Smith wrote:

Dear Tammy and Bob,

I just want to clarify what I hope is just a misunderstanding. First, and again, Sharon and I truly enjoyed meeting you. It took some effort on all of our parts to travel so far on short notice, but I take that to mean that we were all serious about seeing one another in person. We were not disappointed. In fact, ever since then, we have been discussing how much we will both enjoy making Tammy feel very, very special – aroused, tingly, wanton and wanted. In fact, having learned over lunch that this would be Tammy's first bi experience, Sharon went shopping for a new strap-on. Sharon has a most unusual, sensual, loving touch. I have been massaged by dozens and dozens of women, and Sharon is by far the best. It is because she is a kind, caring and patient person. It's not unusual that she became a nurse.

We have many couples and individual women with whom we are meeting, and we do not lack for sincere, sensual people to be with. Our intention is to make your fantasies come true for you both. Therefore, Sharon has posed questions to you, Tammy, to learn more about what you seek so that she and I can take only the best of care of you. Likewise, we are not pushy and do not want to proceed if you think that this is not what you want. Since Sharon and I, together, will be with you, Tammy, she wanted me to know what was going on so that we could fine-tune our "encounter" with you. Because of our and my being known, professionally, we sometimes go "undercover" with these handles. Suffice it to say, we want this to be fun for everyone.

Hope that this finds you both well.

Sincerely,
Rob

Rob wrote:

ss,

You'll have many job offers and will struggle with which one to actually accept. you won't even have to come close to selling your body. If you did, though, I would be your manager, as it would be a most lucrative venture.

I do want you to get a better handle on the replies and organize them somehow. Keep up with the "hot" prospects, and don't let them slide.

I can probably free up time on Wednesday but have a business meeting in Merrillville from 7:30-9:00am, so it would have to be around 10:00am. I do want to start to meet people, so think about setting up coffee, lunch, coffee, etc. Set up some time the following week as well. We'll find time for you to serve me "*tête-à-tête*" as well.

Write Veronica of *alt.matchmaker* as she seems nice.

I leave at 1:00pm tomorrow, so I'll write again tomorrow.

MR

Rob wrote:

ss,

This great weather is an omen of good things to come for us all.

I am pleased with your correspondence to Veronica. They appear to be a couple I'd like us to be with. I'll let you reply forthwith in your own sincere and direct manner. Keep just a few things in mind to be sure to get in. First, emphasize our own concern to maintain total discretion and to keep this private as we are known in the medical/professional field, etc. That will be a lead-in as to why we do not send pictures. Then, relative to all of that, stress how it is our preference and best experience to merely meet for coffee or lunch to assess compatibilities and talk *tête-à-tête*. We do not have the time or interest to cyber *ad nauseum*. Focus, as well, on your desire and that of your Master to more intimately and intensively explore your bi-curious nature within threesomes and foursomes. Find out a bit more about her level and types of submissive/BDSM experiences and stress that I have a vast amount of experience in BDSM.

I am also pleased that J&D wish to meet. I'll write them and send you a copy. I do not yet know when I can meet, but it would be Thursday, most likely, as that is also when you're free.

Keep Thursday free. I'll let you know about Friday, as I've not heard back from *luckeeus* or *Inigma* regarding lunch on Thursday.

MR

Rob wrote:

ss,

I think you might need a sabbatical or leave of absence if these couples pan out. For sure, you will need an apartment.

I'm about to head to the health club as a work break.

A few things: One, what's up with the other Sharon in Deer-field? We will want to meet her.

Two, Todd and Laurie, aka *luckeeus*, seem open. Read the e-mails when you get home. Todd suggested that you write Laurie, and I think it's a good idea. I think his intention is to get you two connected and help bridge her anxiety. I suggest that you get her regular e-mail address, and then send a cc to you, and then forward me a copy of your cc to her. Also, forward me copies of all of her replies to you.

Three, anything doing with that other ad you placed?

MR

Rob wrote:

sub sharon,

Tentatively, you will massage me this Friday, and we will then go to lunch to meet Marcia, per *adultfriendfinder.com* "hot lunch" posting and reply. She will be the next woman in your life. I will e-mail her to confirm and then let you know.

MR

Rob wrote:

ss,

The reply from *foreveryoung55* looks interesting. They are new and want to take it slow. Their names are Kelly and Joe, and their e-mail address is *jkstonfa@xxx.com*. I gave them our first names. I want you to write them and keep in touch with them.

MR

Rob wrote:

ss,

I just got home and am exhausted as I've been up since 2:00am. Zoie is at school late for conferences. I'm going to have dinner, watch the news hour at 6:00pm, and either go to sleep or watch the NCAA games.

We have two good replies. Check *adultfriendfinder.com* and write to Suzanne and the one below, the younger couple. I can free up Thursday per usual, and also Monday, just for meetings. Those two couples I referred to on *adultfriendfinder.com* want to meet as well. See what you can do to arrange meetings, even just coffee back-to-back a few hours apart. Maybe we could do two coffees and one lunch on Monday and get it knocked out.

MR

Rob wrote:

ss,

What other day(s) next week might you be available to meet another couple for coffee or lunch?

MR

Rob wrote:

ss,

Hope that Don had a successful day with jobs and school.

Let me know your schedule and availability for this week. As it turns out, the couple is very interested in meeting in the Woodfield area but wants to do it the following week, not this one, on Monday or Wednesday. Let me know about those days as well.

My father-in-law left and now I'm trying to catch up with my own work.

Don't check any e-mail replies on our account until I've done so first or I'll whip each cheek 100 times for a total of 200 and then start all over again.

MR

Rob wrote:

ss,

I want you to follow up with all of the *adultfriendfinder.com* replies. Don't send more pics to that couple that wants to see more. Offer to meet for coffee.

There is another couple; the man wants you and his lady to speak first, and you can offer to do that. We will not meet them in Woodfield but closer to Hinsdale; tell them I come from Indiana.

MR

Rob wrote:

ss,

No, I didn't do anything with the profile. This is what you must do. First, change the password on the account and page me with it. Next, or first, call *adultfriendfinder.com* at 888.575.8383 or 650.847.3151 and tell them that our profile has somehow been deleted, that you are a Gold member in good standing, and that you want it to be immediately reinstated.

I may not have time to write again today. The weather in Phoenix is not great. We are essentially going to visit my father-in-law who is eighty-eight and look at assisted living facilities for him. We will stay with him in his apartment. He lives in a retirement complex.

Call *adultfriendfinder.com* ASAP. My pager works nationally.

Be well.

MR

Rob wrote:

ss,

I got your message and am heading out to pick up Zoie and then to Midway.

Tell *adultfriendfinder.com* that you did not alter the profile and do not want to lose time awaiting approval as a "new" profile. Be sure to stress to them that you are a GOLD member; they advertise that GOLD members get priority technical assistance status, etc. Be sure to leave me a voicemail as soon as you get home to do so.

Thanks for the good wishes. Be well (and horny) for your Master.

MR

sharon's Comment:

This was the day of my 25th wedding anniversary, & i was homeless, living out of a suitcase. We had sold the house & hadn't found anything else yet. The quiz Rob refers to was a list of 4-5 questions that he sent me. They consisted of things like "Are you homeless?" "Are you stressed out?" i don't remember what else. Simple questions about what was going on in my life at the time.

Rob wrote:

ss,

Thanks for the update and swift completion of your quiz. You passed with flying colors, but not nearly as colorful as your pale white wanton flesh will be when I finally catch you with my whips.

Happy 25th!! It is a milestone, and you should make a point to celebrate – after you get settled. As you well know, it is an accomplishment to both live so long and to be with the same partner for so many years.

If that couple is available Friday, daytime, I'll book something, maybe lunch, but you cannot come into the restaurant with your suitcase – promise?

You have quiet strength and determination. You'll end up with a home and great new job; I'm certain of it.

I'll take care of *adultfriendfinder.com.*

MR

This was Rob's last e-mail to me; i did not e-mail back.

Rob wrote:

ss,

Your *adultfriendfinder.com* account remains inoperable.

You must call and speak with a supervisor and get it straightened out.

You will be whipped long and hard.

MR

[Ed. Note: This is an e-mail to Steven Toushin.]

sharon smith wrote:

Dear Master,

The following e-mails are between me and Marlene, mostly about Rob.

As an interesting tidbit, Kate was a Marine when Rob first met her, & she re-enlisted after the fiasco last summer & shipped out to the Middle East just before Christmas. i haven't heard any more about her since then, so i hope she's okay. She has a pre-teen daughter at home.

i should have read these before i sent them to You, because Marlene specifically said she wanted to keep the stuff about Rob being manic-depressive confidential. i don't like the idea of breaking a trust. i really do not want to hurt any of the people that i've mentioned in the letters. i honestly didn't think anyone would find any of this interesting enough to publish it, or i would have paid closer attention to what i was saying. i do want to read all of it before You send it to a publisher.

This series of letters started when Marlene returned from a month-long trip to Singapore, and she had started by telling me all about the trip. They do have a lot of fun when they travel. She had asked if i had seen or heard from Rob lately. i don't remember if i told You that she had gone with me to Shadow-find in August. Kate was supposed to go too, but she had backed out in the end. The idea of going to Shadowfind was something the three of us came up with the weekend that Rob abandoned us. Rob was furious that we wanted to go. i was the stupid one who told him about it, never thinking he would be upset by it. He blamed Marlene for the idea, & they had some very heated exchanges over it. i put a huge amount of effort in trying to mend things between the two of them.

Marlene is very big on discussing things, expressing thoughts & feelings, etc., whereas i just wanted everyone to get along. The two of us had spent a lot of time talking about Rob as well as Kate while we were in Michigan. Anyway, when she got back from her trip, around the middle or end of September, she was still simmering about the stuff that had taken place over the summer. That was at a time when i was still living in the cheap hotel & rarely had access to a computer, so the e-mails got stretched out over the next couple months. i mostly told her about my new job, house-hunting, kids, family, etc., etc. i told her about how stressed out i was & how Rob had become in-creasingly obsessed with the letter-writing, & that the only time he was interested in seeing me was if it involved meeting an-other couple for coffee Then after i would go to extreme lengths to accommodate his schedule, he would find something wrong with everyone, & then become even more obsessed with the letters.

Basically i told Marlene that i had had enough & that i was getting nothing out of the relationship except stress and frustration … which i definitely didn't need at the time. i don't know if You understand what a difficult conclusion that was for me to come to. If it weren't for Marlene's support & You coming to my rescue, i probably would have eventually gone crawling back to him with my tail between my legs. i still don't understand how i managed to get myself lost in such a dysfunc-tional relationship. Then again, when i think about it, throughout most of the relationship the only information i had about BDSM was either from Rob or from fictional books. The rest of the Doms i played with were just playing … nothing serious.

It wasn't until last summer that i got the chance to talk to anyone at length about the lifestyle. i guess i just jumped into things too quickly and too naively, but that's the only way i know how to do things … all or nothing. So i will just have to record it as a valuable lesson learned. i was pretty much in a mental/emotional black hole just prior to meeting You. i don't think i ever told You that the reason i originally sent You the "wink" was because of the picture on Your profile (i didn't have access to the profile itself). In Your picture You were smiling, & You looked like You knew how to have fun, and fun was what i needed. i think it must have been fate, since You are the best thing that's ever happened to me, & i don't think i would have understood that, except for everything that had gone on before i met You.

Love,
Your slave puppy

[Ed. Note: The following e-mails are between Marlene and Sharon.]

Marlene wrote:

Sharon,

You wrote: "I feel like there is no D/s relationship at all, but rather Rob is just using me to feed his addiction for looking at nude pictures on the Internet. It may sound selfish, but I think I can find something better ... someone who can meet my needs & have a relationship beyond just giving me orders to write letters to strangers. I just feel like the whole relationship is going nowhere, & it's time to move on."

Sorry, in retrospect I realize I didn't begin to answer your concern – just told you what was happening (or not) with me. It seems like you need either to meet MR in a neutral, public place to tell him how you feel or, better yet, write him similar to what you wrote above. If he wants to change/negotiate, and you want to give the relationship another chance, then you can meet in a neutral place to set new limits. You don't ever have to apologize for how you feel. And, of course, you never want to be in a compromising position unless and until this whole thing is settled to both of your satisfactions.

You are attractive, intelligent, and caring – and deserve to be treated as such. It's a Master's duty to nurture the submissive, and I believe the basis of everything is a healthy respect for each other's needs. Exploitation is not the basis for serving.

That said, I share my layman's observation of MR, which John concurs with and which I ask you to consider and trust you to keep confidential. I've felt for a long time that MR exhibits symptoms of manic-depression. Most times, he has too many things on his plate (multiple projects that never come to fruition, running in six directions giving consults, having you write people with little likelihood of success, waking early to undirected bursts of creative activity, and I'm sure there are more). Then typically, like after our last day here, he seems to just crash, impolitely leaving us all here the next day, as if dealing with taking Kate to the airport or having lunch with us was too much. Am I thinking correctly? Please tell me if I seem off target.

I'm not saying MR isn't kind, or devoted to his family and profession, or insightful, or fun – just excessive, and lacking direction and follow-through.

Unfortunately, I've seen (in the San Francisco scene, our Kate, the Michigan weekend at Shadowfind, etc.) that dysfunction runs rampant in the BDSM community. You are a breath of fresh air, with high self-esteem and the strength to tell MR (of course, in a respectful way!) how you want to be treated, and to move on if he can't meet your needs.

Thanks for sharing your feelings with me

Marlene

sharon smith wrote:

Marlene,

That's okay, I didn't expect you to solve the problem … I was just venting. I've spent a tremendous amount of time & effort trying to figure MR out, but it's obvious he doesn't want to be known. Communication has been completely one-sided, with me telling him everything there is to know about me, & him telling me nothing about himself. Even then, when I tell him about some big issue going on in my life, the most I get is a cursory one-line response, followed by orders to write more letters. I was feeling completely overwhelmed last week when I told him I couldn't write any letters for a while, & the only response I got was an order to write more of them.

I guess it was a wake-up call … and what it did was cause me to lose respect for him. Maybe it's just my state of mind right now. I just feel like I need some kind of reciprocal emotional connection & empathy, or my "submissive well" is going to dry up. I want to find someone who is more interested in helping me grow as a submissive, rather than using me to make notches on his bedpost. There are, no doubt, a lot of dysfunctional people involved in BDSM, as in anything else, but I also think there are people, such as You & John, who are caring, open, honest, and capable of a D/s relationship that goes beyond wielding a whip.

I sent MR a message last Friday that simply said "You are not listening to me" followed by a lot of exclamation points. I haven't heard from him since then. It was probably disrespectful, but I do not feel like saying anything else to him at the present time, nor do I feel like meeting him in person to discuss it. I have written to him almost every day for three years & have said everything there is to say. It's time to move on.

I'm sorry to unburden on You. Venting is quite therapeutic. You are very kind & caring to "listen."

Sharon

Marlene wrote

Sharon,

Wow, that's some mental abuse you've been getting. Congratulations on seeing the light and moving on.

As I was alluding to before, one of the things I believe is that you teach people how to treat you. How interesting that, after months of little or no contact with MR, the same Friday you put an end to the shit you were getting was the day I got the call from him. Then when I was less than eager to see him myself (and perhaps when we next meet it will only be for some kind of closure), I can imagine what fuel I added to your fire. No apologies here – you get what you give, and respect is a two-way street.

Anyway, I did write back with possible dates I could meet him, and that it could be wherever he decided, either for coffee somewhere or here at my house, but it would be strictly to take stock of where we were and either renegotiate the parameters (like what has he been doing the last six months, and with whom, as I'm highly concerned about safety issues), or move in different directions. It wouldn't be for any kind of scene. I haven't heard back from him, and have in the meantime filled in some of the dates that I was formerly available – but I'm teaching him how to treat me.

Your insight is invaluable ... if only he'd known what a Pandora's box he opened when he didn't return that Saturday morning when we were getting to know each other better!

Marlene

Part IX

Puppy's Travels through Dominant Cyberland

February 29, 2004

Steven Toushin wrote:

Dear puppy,

Questions:

A. At what point did MR tell you to undress?
B. How often did you meet with MR?
C. Was it always at the same motel?
D. About the different types of play: can you recall 5 or 6 different play dates and what happened in each one?

Sir

February 29, 2004

sharon smith wrote:

Dear Master,

i hope Your weekend is going well & You got a chance to enjoy the beautiful weather! i'm kind of worried that i'll oversleep tomorrow & be late on my first day ... I'm getting too used to this not working thing.

Regarding that first session, Rob undressed me when he took me back to the center of the room right after i was standing in the corner.

There was anywhere from a week to three months between sessions ... usually at least a month. His wife is a schoolteacher, so summer months were out of the question, as i eventually figured out.

There were two motels we went to, the one near O'Hare (Galaxy Inn) and the other (a Best Western) in Westmont. One time we went to a Best Western in Merrillville, but he was so paranoid the whole time that we never went back. That one was actually a whole lot more convenient for me because it was only a half-hour from my house, as opposed to 2½ hours away.

The second time i saw Rob was at Marlene's house, which i already told You about. That was about a month after the first session. About a week or two after that, i met him again at the Galaxy Inn. i don't remember much about that time, except he went over a lot of protocol/manners, etc. He also put a collar on me & led me back & forth on a leash. Probably about a month after that, i met him at the Best Western in Westmont. When i got there, he told me that another couple would be joining us. It turned out to be a young couple that he had met via the Internet & had played with one other time. They were married & looked like they were in their mid to late twenties. The girl was quite pretty, & the guy looked like a nerd … and had a personality to match. i got the impression that he had spent his whole life jacking off in the bathroom with *Playboy* magazines & never came in contact with a real-life female until he somehow very miraculously got hooked up with his wife.

Anyway, before they arrived, Rob had me clean all his toys & lay them out on the counter in the bathroom. When they arrived, we exchanged short introductions & then sat on the bed … Rob sitting between the girl (can't remember her name) and me. The guy had to stand. Rob asked her about her limits, & she said no animals or children. He also asked them who was the Dom & who was the sub. She said she was submissive, but it was quite obvious she was the dominant one of the couple. i don't remember what else was said, but we talked for a while.

Then Rob took her over to a corner & had her stand facing the wall, & he told the guy to take me over to the opposite corner. He told the guy to undress me but he couldn't manage it, so i did it myself. At the same time, Rob was undressing her over in the other corner. Then he took her to the bed & tied her face down. He then brought me to the bed & did the same thing. He gave her, i think, two lashes & she was crying & very upset & angry. So he came around to my side of the bed & gave me about 20-30. i was blindfolded, so i don't know how they reacted to that. Then he started playing with her with the vibrating egg (his favorite toy), & i don't know what else.

Rob told the guy to take care of me. The guy just started endlessly shoving his finger in & out of my pussy like a robot or something, & i quickly figured out why this girl wanted to meet someone who could teach him a thing or two. Due to the logistics of tying two people to the same bed, i ended up having the freedom to move around quite a bit & so, after a short time, i was able to get the blindfold off & turned towards Rob & the girl to try to communicate to him that i needed to be rescued from the moron. Rob told me to kiss her, which i did, and she responded quite nicely. Then he told me to suck on her tit. When i did that, she let out this scream like she was in pain. Then he told me to finger her pussy &, again, the response was a scream of pain. At that point her husband started shoving his finger in & out of my pussy again as if to distract me from causing this terrible pain to his wife. Sheesh, i barely touched her ... way too nervous & jumpy for me. Rob tried doing something to her. She screamed again, & he got mad & gagged her, & bound her arms tightly to her sides so she couldn't move. i could tell that she was really angry about that.

During all this, the guy just continued to robotically finger-fuck me & watch what was going on between Rob & her. i remember Rob eventually removed the gag & straddled her face & had her suck him, which she seemed to enjoy. In the meantime, i took

- 302 -

matters into my own hands & told the guy to fuck me. He went through several condoms before he could get one on without ruining it, but he did fuck me ... in that same robotic manner, while he watched his wife the whole time. She got upset about something (and i don't think it was because he was fucking me), and she decided the play session was over. Then the two of them used the hot tub for a little bit, while Rob stretched out on the bed & i gave him a massage. Then they left.

After they left, Rob started talking about how well he thought the session had gone. i couldn't believe my ears! i didn't want to say anything negative & make him angry, so i just left. After stewing over it a couple days, i finally explained to him via e-mail that i didn't want to meet them again & why. He never really understood why, but said if i didn't want to, we wouldn't play with them again. i don't know if he ever met them again by himself or not.

It was right after that when he told me to put an ad on *adult-friendfinder.com* as a couple looking for a woman. i protested about that quite a bit, but eventually did as he asked. i figured it might take a month to find such a woman, & we could play once, & that would be the end of it. How wrong i was! He had me writing at least 20 letters a day, & i had to save copies of all of them so he could make sure i did it right. He always picked out the profiles i was to write to. It seemed like he was picking ones that had nothing in common with us & wouldn't be interested in anything in our profile. The whole thing was extremely frustrating to me, & i hated every minute of it, but he wouldn't respond to anything i wrote to him unless the day's letters were written. So i kept writing them. After about 2-3 months of this, i was beyond bored. It was apparent that i wouldn't be seeing him again unless i successfully found another woman to join us, & that wasn't going to happen because no one who replied was good enough for him.

At that point, i put an individual ad on *alt.com* & got quite a few interesting replies. i started corresponding with a guy who said his name was Donald Lester. He came across pretty strong via e-mail ... more rude & crude than i preferred, but i just wanted to find someone who was different from Rob. i had to go to my cousin's wedding in Schaumburg, & so we agreed to meet there in the afternoon about an hour before the wedding. From the sound of his e-mails, i wasn't too sure i could trust him & figured that way he would know people were expecting me somewhere at a certain time. He pulled up next to me in the parking lot of a restaurant & motioned for me to get in his car, which i did. i barely had the car door closed, & he reached down the front of my dress to grab my breast. He said he was checking for implants & was glad i didn't have them. (Laughing ... like if i had implants, i would choose such a small size!) Then he reached up the bottom of my dress & acted a little put off that i was wearing underwear. He put the car in gear & started driving, & i just sat there a little shocked by what had happened so far. He started chatting & seemed really nice, though, so i figured it would be okay. In the two minutes he was driving, he told me far more about himself than Rob had in 6 months. We went to another restaurant & he parked the car, & we got out & started walking. While we were walking, he was feeling my ass & determined that i was wearing a thong, so things weren't as bad as he thought. He was really quite funny.

We went into the (very elegant) restaurant & sat at the bar. He ordered us some wine & appetizers, & we started talking. He was very straightforward & definitely not shy. After a couple glasses of wine, i was pretty outgoing myself, & we were having a good time. Then he told me to go into the ladies room & take off my panties. When i came back, he asked to see them. It was funny because we were the only ones sitting at the bar, & the bartender was standing right in front of us throughout this whole thing. He told me to turn & face him & spread my legs. i had on a short snug dress, so when i did this it went up pretty high & he had to adjust it to keep my ass from showing. While adjusting it, he managed to start fingering my pussy. i'm not sure if it was him, or the wine, or the fact that we were in a public place with people walking around right next to us … but, in any case, i was really turned on by the whole thing & found it impossible to sit still. He kept playing with me & damn near had his whole fist in me right there on the bar stool, with the bartender nonchalantly standing in front of us washing glasses. i was ready to climb up on the bar & spread my legs & beg him to fuck me. Instead i kept leaning forward & biting his neck & telling him we had to get out of there before we were arrested.

During all this time, he had me rubbing his cock, & it was pretty obvious that he was turned on too. We exited the place in a bit of a hurry. When we got back to his car (in the middle of a very busy parking lot) he told me to pull up my dress & turn over so he could see my ass. Then he started spanking me & then opened his pants, took out his cock & told me to suck him. While i was on my hands & knees doing that, he was spanking my pussy & i was having a very powerful orgasm & then he came in my mouth. We then put ourselves back together, & i was already late for the wedding so he took me back to my car, & i left. i was the happiest guest at the wedding … except my pussy was tingling the whole time, & i don't remember anything at all about the wedding itself!

Love,
Your puppy

February 29, 2004

sharon smith wrote:

Dear Master,

Donald Lester is married, still has a teenage son at home, and owns his own computer business. i saw him several times that summer. He was mostly into a sort of exhibitionism ... had his hand in my pussy no matter where we went, & he had me sucking his cock on sidewalks & in parking lots & hallways every chance he got. i kept telling him i was holding him totally responsible if we got arrested. He was really very charming, polite, and a lot of fun. He called himself a master, but was really just more into playing. He would stop & buy miscellaneous stuff from a hardware store or someplace on his way to meet me. i never had any idea what he would bring next.

i remember one time he stuffed my pussy with four golf balls while we were in the car & then had me walk into the restaurant threatening to whip me if i lost any of them. One of them fell out as soon as i stood up, & he bent me over the car, pulled up my dress, & spanked me right in the parking lot. When we got inside, we sat at the bar, which was quite crowded. We drank some wine, & he fed me calamari ... laughing the whole time because i didn't know what i was eating. Then he started fishing the golf balls out of my pussy one at a time & had me lick them clean before sticking them in his pocket. The bartenders in this place were much younger & not nearly as discreet, & they were enjoying the whole thing immensely, though no one else seemed to notice what was going on. The golf balls became a routine thing after that. A couple times he fucked me with the golf balls in place, which i found to be quite stimulating ... had some gushing orgasms with that. He dripped wax all over me once. It wasn't hot wax like You used though. Sometimes, he tied me with plain white rope he had gotten from the hardware store. He had a couple small, cute floggers that he used a few times … they tickled more than anything. He also had what he called a cane, but it was actually a very thin, flexible dowel rod. He liked to use that, & it definitely stung. He used regular wood clothespins on my breasts once. He had me shave my pussy for his viewing pleasure once. Once he had me bend over a chair & tied my hands to the front at the bottom & tied my ankles to the legs in back, & then he just walked out of the hotel room & left me there for about an hour. He was really into water sports & what he had done was go downstairs to drink several cans of iced tea so he would have plenty of piss to bathe me in.

For the "water sports," he would have me kneel in the bathtub, & he would cover me in piss from head to toe. He would pee in my mouth, but i never swallowed it. Once, after he had done this & then told me to take a shower, i came out & he handed me a cigarette (he hated smoke) and told me to smoke it, & then he handed me a glass of pee & told me to drink it. i managed about two sips & that was all i could do, but he was pleased with that.

Donald is the one who decided he was a "sex addict," which kind of annoyed me because he said he had 20 years of experience as a master, & he picked that particular time to decide he was a "sex addict." One of his friends talked him into the diagnosis, & the two of them went through a twelve-step program similar to Alcoholics Anonymous. He was intensely serious about it. He was a very loving & compassionate man & very devoted to his family. Once he started with the twelve-step program, i saw him two more times & tried to convince him that it was okay to be "addicted" to sex because every healthy adult should be. His wife had refused to have sex with him for something like 15 years, & he felt guilty for looking for it someplace else. He thought if he was a good husband and father, he should be able to do without. Incredible!! He had gone from a charming, charismatic, fun-loving person to a depressed, hollow, guilt-ridden shell. Twice after he started the program, he "gave in" to his impulses, & we played & had a lot of fun. The last time, as we were leaving, he kissed me & gave me a hug & had tears in his eyes. i never saw or heard from him again. Someone really screwed with his head.

Love,
Your puppy

February 29, 2004

sharon smith wrote:

Dear Master,

Before i get started on another episode … i can be available to serve You Monday thru Thursday this week ….

Back to Rob … During the summer that i was being entertained by Donald, i continued to write the daily letters for Rob. Every week he would ask me what days i could be available to serve him, & i would tell him, but he always claimed it wouldn't work out in his schedule.

i think it was late July when i got a reply to my individual ad on *alt.com* from a couple. i thought i was corresponding with the woman who said she was a Domme & her partner a submissive. We corresponded for a couple weeks, & then they wanted to meet me … which was unusual because every other woman wanted to correspond forever but was never willing to meet. So i thought, aha! this may be the one who will satisfy Rob's requirement that i explore my "bisexual nature." i wrote her & told her about Rob, & told Rob about them, & within a few days, the four of us were able to meet for coffee. When we met,

Susan seemed very shy & submissive. Rob asked her a lot of questions about her experience, & she seemed to be quite experienced & know what she was talking about. i could tell that Rob really liked her immediately. Her partner, Raj, was less talkative & seemed to be very inexperienced ... and hard to figure out.

Anyway, we decided to meet the following week to play. Rob & i got to the motel room first. He was always very strict about being on time, & they were late. He kept looking out the window & pacing back & forth, & about a half-hour after they were supposed to be there he saw her pull in, & she just sat in her car, which made him angry. He had me call Raj on his cell phone, & he was stuck in traffic & ended up being about an hour late. Rob was pretty upset about all this & took his anger out by whipping me while we waited for them.

When they finally came in together, he told her to sit on the bed & Raj to sit across the room on a chair, & i was told to kneel in front of him. He talked to them a while about limits, etc., & then he blindfolded Susan & had her stand in the middle of the room. (This was after she told him that blindfolds were a hard limit for her.) Then he told me to undress her ... which i did with much difficulty because she had on some kind of complicated bra/corset thing that was impossible to undo. By the time i was done, we were both laughing pretty hard. Then i was told to sit in the chair, & Rob proceeded to do some stuff with her ... don't remember just what. Then he put a collar & leash on her & led her back & forth – all the while with the blindfold still in place. It was pretty obvious she was upset about the blindfold, but she didn't say anything because Raj was supposed to be her Master, & he never said anything.

Then Rob tied her face down on the bed & gave her a few lashes. She had told him she couldn't go home (to her husband) with any marks, & he seemed to be careful about that. He then had her turn on her back & retied her. He told me to get undressed & get on top of her. This kind of freaked me out because the whole scenario was supposed to be that she was going to top me, & she supposedly had all this experience topping women. i knelt on the bed between her legs & desperately looked at Rob to tell me what to do next. He told me to kiss her, which i did & got absolutely no response. Then he told me to suck her nipples ... again, no response. All this time i was still on my hands & knees above her, & Rob was apparently not happy with that because he took his heaviest flogger & started whipping my ass, causing me to fall down flat on top of her. Once i was lying flat, he continued to whip me, & Susan got upset because she thought he was hurting me. i was actually enjoying it & appreciating the diversion. By the time he was done, i had my face buried in her neck & was breathing heavily.

He told Raj to get undressed except for his underwear, & he did the same. Rob was kind of homophobic & would never be completely naked in the same room with another man. He directed Raj to pull me to one side of the bed, & he moved Susan to the other side. Raj was very ... sexual and ... passionate, and he was kissing me & masturbating me & had me gushing wet. Although this wasn't what i had expected (it was supposed to be Susan & i together, & she had said there would be absolutely no swapping of partners), i was enjoying myself & just going with the flow. Raj told me to ask Rob if i could suck his cock & when i did, Rob said no.

So we continued on with a lot of motion on our side of the bed. On the other side of the bed, Susan was laying perfectly still without a sound. Rob was kissing her & touching her & fisting her, and she was lying there like she was dead ... just like she had done with me. (She had also said that fisting was a hard limit with her.) With the way Rob was acting so passionately with her, i was starting to get a little jealous. i was only going along with Raj because i thought that's what Rob wanted me to do. i turned toward Susan & Rob ... i guess to kind of remind them i was still there ... and Raj pulled me back. It was kind of hard to ignore him because he definitely knew how to push my buttons. He was all excited about my squirting orgasm as he had never seen that happen before & thought it was just a fairy tale.

At some point, Susan reached across me to Raj & actually laid on top of me to get to him. When she did that, Rob picked up the heavy flogger & hit her ass. She then clung hard to Raj, & then Rob hit her again. She then said it was time to go, & she got up & started to get dressed. Rob gave her a hug & a kiss, & i did the same to Raj. Then i decided to take a shower, & when i came out they were gone.

Rob was very worried that Susan was angry with him. i told him that whatever it was, she would get over it. It was really quite obvious that something was wrong. That night, i got an e-mail from Raj saying that Susan was really upset because Rob whipped her & that she was refusing to talk to him (Raj) as well as us. He made it sound like it was all Rob's fault, & it kind of upset me that she was being so unfair. i asked Raj for her e-mail address, & he refused to give it to me. A couple days later i got an e-mail from Susan via my *alt.com* account. She said that it was never her that i was originally corresponding with, that Raj had lied about everything, & that Raj was a dangerous man. The message was quite cryptic, & it scared me. i was worried that she was in danger. i wrote her back, & over the course of the day got her phone number, & we spoke on the phone. She was upset with Raj & not with us. She felt that he knew her limits & should have stopped things (protected her) when those limits were crossed. He had lied to her about everything & had imper-sonated her throughout all the correspondence. It was a big ordeal, but we ended up talking for a long time & became friends.

i passed the info about what happened along to Rob as he was feeling really bad that he had done something wrong. Then he started corresponding with Susan himself. Susan had zero interest in Rob, but he talked her into meeting us for a threesome. That seemed to go okay as Rob was very careful not to do anything that would go beyond her many limits, & it was mostly her & me together for him to watch. Rob became rather obsessed with Susan, & she kept telling him she had no interest in him, but only in me. He talked her into meeting us one more time, & he tried to make it more about him & her, & she got quite moody. Then he tried talking her into meeting him by himself, & she forwarded me the e-mail he had sent her along with a note that she was very upset by his message. i was at work when i got the message & didn't have time to deal with it, so i forwarded it back to both her & Rob along with a note that i didn't care what went on between the two of them but to just leave me out of the middle of it. He had been continuously asking me what Susan was saying about him (which wasn't anything nice), & she was continuously asking me what he was saying about her. i'd had enough of the juvenile games & honestly didn't care what happened between the two of them.

Well, my little note infuriated Rob, & i got a nasty note back from him demanding an apology. It was a whole big ordeal, & i was angry about being put in the middle of it. He didn't speak/write to me for a long time. This took place over two years ago, & Rob has been obsessed with her ever since.

Coincidentally, i got a note from Susan last Friday that he has started writing to her again & wants to meet her. She has always been very blunt & straightforward, telling him she is not interested, & he just doesn't get it … and it's not my problem anymore!!!!!!!!!!!!!!!!!!!!!!!!!!!!

Love,
Your puppy

March 1, 2004

sharon smith wrote:

Dear Master,

What has happened that You've quit writing to me? Is it something i've said/done?

Love,
Your puppy

March 1, 2004

Steven Toushin wrote:

Dear puppy,

Good luck on your new job; hope it is more enjoyable than the last.

No, I haven't quit writing; in fact, that is all I did this weekend (the next columns of the Bijou Chronicles). I got so involved in completing writing projects that I lost all track of time.

I read all your e-mails this morning. You're doing great. I would like some more information on play dates with these two men. Also, how has BDSM has filled a void (if I can say that) in your life and your well-being (your fulfilled feeling and the growth inside of you)?

Tuesday and Thursday are good.

Sir

March 1, 2004

Dear Master,

Okay ... just checking! Whenever Rob was angry with me, he would just quit writing. i would be in the dark as to what i did wrong & would just have to start apologizing for everything i could come up with until i would happen to hit on the right thing. i know You've got a lot of stuff going on right now & hope You've been able to get some projects completed.

i think my new job is going to be better ... feels like a better fit. It's more like the job i had in Indiana ... more administrative & less clinical. i don't do well in middle management ... prefer to be the top dog ... or the bottom puppy!! 🐻

i'm going to step backwards a bit on the story line ... Anyone i played with other than Rob was for the purpose of fulfilling some particular fantasy that i had at the time, something that Rob found unacceptable. With Donald, the goal was to have my ass fucked & to see what the "water sports" was all about. Never got around to getting my ass fucked by him. That was something i wanted to try for the past 20+ years & had a heck of a time trying to find someone to do it! Several people said they wanted to but never did. Donald did have me lick his ass (a first), but that's as far as the ass play actually went.

With Rob, the play sessions after that were all about the same ... kneeling, blindfolds, bondage, being flogged, cocksucking, and massage. When i told him i liked the fisting & the collar/leash, he never did those things again. In fact, i learned rather quickly that anything i told him i liked never happened again ... best to keep those things to myself. i'm not sure why i continued to serve him for almost three years because he drove me absolutely crazy. He was the only one that ever sent me into "subspace" though ... just something about him. i asked him once if he was hypnotizing me ... he just smiled.

Early in the relationship, i remember trying to explain to him how i felt this incredible peace & freedom when i was with him ... like the whole rest of the world just stopped & i felt totally present in the moment. my job at the time was very intense, 24/7, & it was like taking a mini-vacation whenever i served him. It was an escape from having to be the one in charge of everything & having to make all the decisions & have all the answers & all the responsibility. (Laughing ... and now i've gotten myself into the same kind of job!). All i had to do or think about was obeying him ... and that gave me the freedom to relax enough ... to forget about everything else for a few hours ... to be totally focused ... i guess it allowed me to get in touch with myself enough to experience intense pleasure. i guess it took all of the things he did to get my attention enough that it was impossible to think about anything else.

When i had sex with my husband, my mind was always somewhere else (and still is). It's hard to feel sexual pleasure when you're thinking about work, family, etc. It got to where all i had to do was kneel at Rob's feet, & i was ready for anything he wanted ... and the lower he made me feel, the more peace & freedom i felt, and the more i wanted to please him. It's hard to explain because it all sounds so contradictory. The more he took away & the more i gave, the more i received ... like becoming empty & being filled at the same time.

Rob always had me reading books like *The Story of O* (his favorite) and the *Sleeping Beauty* trilogy & the *Marketplace* series. i used to fantasize about being kidnapped & forced into a life of total slavery like in the books ... never have to worry about anything again ... no decisions ... just do what you're told ... and, of course, lots of sex!

Another (and maybe the biggest) thing was just being able to make someone happy. i think i spent my whole life trying to do that & never felt successful. my husband is never happy with anything &, even when i do what he says he wants, he then decides he's not happy with that either … and believe me, i've tried everything under the sun! The same with my parents, patients, and staff, and at the time i got involved in this, my kids were teenagers & naturally impossible to please. It just gave me a lot of satisfaction to be able to please SOMEONE … make SOMEONE happy if even for a short time.

How has all this helped me to grow? i've always believed that all people are the same, no matter who they are or what they've done with their lives … everyone has value/worth and needs to be understood & loved. The only ones i would condemn are those who condemn others (i.e., pious church people) and even then, i feel sorry for them for their ignorance. my "adventures" in BDSM have brought me into intimate contact with people i would have never otherwise met, people who others would condemn, and i feel very privileged to have had the opportunity to meet & connect with them … especially people like You who share my views about people. Somehow, knowing that there are other people who think like me helps me to be more patient with small-minded people who can find nothing better to do than criticize & condemn everyone else … gives me a different perspective...keeps me from getting angry with them … if that makes any sense.

Also, anytime i do (or survive!) something i didn't think i could do, i feel like i'm growing … expanding my horizons. Although i did a whole lot of protesting about being with a woman, it ended up being a growing experience. It's not something i'm interested in & would have never tried if i hadn't been forced into it, but it was a growing experience … actually, i think being with a woman somehow helped me to be more accepting (less critical) of myself, if that makes sense … that's kind of strange ... will have to give that some more thought. i guess overall though, the whole thing has made me more accepting & less critical of myself ... perhaps the reason for the feelings of peace & freedom.

Okay, i've got to get to bed because ... i have to go to work tomorrow. Dang! i was really getting used to that life of leisure!

Looking forward to serving You soon!

Love,
Your puppy

March 3, 2004

sharon smith wrote:

Dear Master,

Good morning, Sir!

Just want to tell You that i was really stressed out by the time i got to Your house last night (almost turned around & went home before i got there), but i was feeling exceptionally good/relaxed on the way home. Thank You!

You are quite the artist with the whips. Somehow You manage to leave my ass more tender the next day without leaving a mark than Rob ever did, & he always left my entire ass purple.

i will be thinking about You every time i move today!

Have a wonderful day!

Love,
Your puppy

March 3, 2004

sharon smith wrote:

Dear Master,

Guess who i heard from today ... Rob. Just one line: "Do you miss me?" How funny, after we were just talking about him last night! i think i will wait about 6 months & then say "no" ... just to be ornery.

To continue with my adventures in BDSM, the same summer i met Donald, which was the same summer i met Susan & Raj, i also met a guy from South Bend whose name i can't remember. He was also on *alt.com* claiming to have many years (maybe 10?) experience as a Master. i guess intelligence & experience were what i was always looking for, and he seemed intelligent, so i figured what the hell ... and drove the 2½ hours to South Bend on a Saturday to meet him ... at a T.G.I.Friday's. i remember he gave me horrible directions & i got lost, but i still got there before he did.

When he got there, he walked over & stood in front of my car, & i had to make quite an effort to keep from laughing. He had on these plaid shorts down to his knees with socks up to his knees & a striped shirt & a baseball cap ... not to mention being quite overweight & bald. i thought it had to be a set-up. No one would look so ridiculous on purpose. But i figured i had driven that far & had the whole day, so i went into the restaurant with him, & we sat at the bar. i figured a couple glasses of wine would make the meeting a little easier to digest.

He was one of those guys who likes to show off. He made a big deal of putting his arm around me when we walked in & talking loudly to everyone in the place ... rather obnoxiously. He spent a long time telling me about all his toys & things he was planning to build, and how everyone in the bar knew him because he went there every night, and about all the women he had played with ... on and on. It was pretty obvious he was just making things up as he went. Now i'm laughing because You won't believe what i did. i drank 4-5 glasses of wine, & then he asked if i wanted to go to his apartment ... and i did! He had told me about this prestigious, high-paying job he had as a computer programming consultant, and he lived in this tiny apartment that looked like it had been (sparsely) furnished by K-Mart ... and it was a total mess.

When we got there, he ran around gathering all his toys to show me, and he brought out this yellow bra & panties that he wanted me to put on. So i put them on & they were about 20 sizes too big ... looked like something my grandmother would wear. Then he proceeded to try out every toy he had. (By the way, this was also supposed to be someone who wanted to fuck my ass ... but, again, that never happened.) He had these suction cup things that he was pretty proud of, & he used them on my clit & nipples ... and was all excited because my nipples started leaking when he used them. i don't remember what else he had ... some rope, blindfold, & lots of junk stuff ... quantity being more important than quality. He kept talking about this one woman he was with & how he had started out as a sub but she told him he should be a dom.

i don't remember much about what happened but by the time the wine wore off, i was ready to go. i ended up getting a flat tire on my way home that day. With it being really hot that day, i wasn't wearing much. It was so funny, because i pulled off the side of the road & sat in the car for a while hoping someone would stop & help me. Finally, i decided i better see if i could find the spare tire. i opened the trunk & was bent way over trying to get to the tire under the floor, & by the time i stood up, about 6 cars had stopped to help. All these guys were arguing about who was going to change the tire & how it should be done ... and i was standing there all embarrassed because, as i said, i wasn't wearing much. It was just a day when i should have stayed home! But ... it gets worse.

The guy started e-mailing me, telling me how he was building this whipping bench & suspension thing & how he was spending so much money on it & how he needed my height & the size of my wrists & ankles so he could make it just right. i tried to politely tell him i wasn't interested, & he kept writing about all this stuff he had ordered for me. He also sent me a list of activities that he wanted me to rate my interest/experience in. Anyway, i was feeling guilty about all the trouble he was going through ... so i agreed to meet him again. When i got there, his whole apartment was full of stuff he built ... and again he tried out everything he had. Both times i felt like i was being run through an obstacle course.

Then he decided he was going to make dinner for me, but he had nothing in the house. So we got dressed & went to the grocery store, & he did what appeared to be a month's worth of grocery shopping, often running back a few aisles to get something he forgot & leaving me standing there for long periods of time thinking i must be insane. Anyway, he finally made dinner & then started telling me that i was the most beautiful woman he had ever been with (no big surprise there!), and how he wanted me to get divorced & marry him so i wouldn't have to be doing things like this, & how he was going to take care of me & make an honest woman out of me, etc. i got out of there as quickly as i could & ended up having to be quite rude to get the point across that i wasn't interested.

The really funny (or maybe unfunny) thing though was that Susan told me a few months later that she met this guy who said he knew me and referred to me by my full name. It was the same guy! He told her what a slut i was & how he broke up with me because i was so in love with him & wanted to marry him. It made her quite angry that, after she told him she was a friend of mine, he went into great detail exaggerating to her about everything we did, just like he had told me every endless detail of what he had done with that other woman. The guy was just a real creep. Needless to say, Susan didn't accept his offer to take her back to his apartment. She was quite upset about it. i thought it was quite funny ... although i did send him a threatening e-mail about what i would do if he ever referred to me by name to anyone else. i will just chalk the whole thing up to very poor judgment on my part.

Oh, well, i guess there has to be some humor in one's life.

Love,
Your puppy

March 6, 2004

sharon smith wrote:

Dear Master,

Thank You for the lovely evening.

Sometime it would be nice if i could spend the night, so i don't have to get dressed, etc., & drive home ... though it would probably disrupt Your sleep if i got up at 5:30am.

Sorry i didn't write yesterday. Have been getting into this new job so much that i'm working on stuff at home & losing track of time.

Going shopping now, so will write more later.

Love,
Your puppy

March 7, 2004

Dear Master,

i hope Your weekend is going as well as mine. Very successful shopping today! 9 dresses, 6 tops, & 2 pair of earrings ... and all on sale! But everything is for summer, & i still don't have a thing to wear for spring.

Also, while i'm thinking about it, i can't serve You on Thursday or Friday next week. Monday, Tuesday, or Wednesday are good, though.

You asked about my definition of "Master," and i told You it is evolving. Actually i never really thought about a "definition" until i met You. i remember Rob telling me that the difference between a sub and a slave is that a sub has the option of saying "no," while a slave cannot say "no." i asked to be his slave, but he always referred to me as his submissive. That seems kind of funny now because in the three years i knew him i only said "no" one time, & that was when he cut off communication with me. No one ever defined "Master" to me ... at least no one ever said what i could expect from him as a Master or defined what made him a Master. The closest they came was to tell me i was to obey & respect them and call them Sir or Master.

i suppose in the beginning my idea of "Master" revolved around the books (fiction) that i was reading ... mostly a romanticized version. i wanted someone who was stronger ... more stubborn? ... than me, someone who would stand up to me & not let me have my own way. That doesn't really sound right, though, because i wasn't at all looking for a fight or anything. It's just that most men (including those who called themselves Master) always backed down the minute i voiced an opinion about something. Then (and my husband is the perfect example) after they go along with whatever stupid idea i had at the time that turns out to be wrong, i hear about it forever. i guess i just wanted someone who would stand up for what he wants and/or believes in ... and i thought a "Master" would do that.

i fantasized about someone who would take charge of everything ... tell me what & when to eat, wear, do, say, etc. The problem was always that i wanted to give (serve) much more than any of them wanted to receive. i wanted it to be my whole life, & they just wanted to play when it was convenient for them. Let me refine that statement a little ... the ones i wanted to serve just wanted to play at their convenience ... and the ones that wanted it to be more than that ... i guess i didn't feel they happened to be "worthy" of being served. Anyway, i played with enough people to know that none of them wanted to be totally in control ... it was all just a game (role-playing) to them ... not something they were serious about ... not something that was an innate thing ... who they are.

i think in the beginning, my idea of a Master was someone who was like a god ... powerful, commanding, just, knowledgeable, dependable, faithful, loving ... someone to worship and serve ... someone perfect (as i said – a romanticized idea). As time went on, i realized (especially with Rob) that the men who called themselves "Master" were only "strong" during a scene and were weak & submissive in the rest of their lives. Furthermore, they were only strong during a scene because i so freely gave myself to them. They didn't just take what they wanted. i guess, in a way, it's just the opposite with me. i control & get/take what i want in the rest of my life and only give up control when i am with someone to whom i want to give up control ... if that makes sense. That has become quite apparent to me in that i was not happy in a job where i had to answer to someone else ... was not in charge.

i think that's why i am so fascinated with You. To live a life that is congruent inside & out … i've never met anyone like that before. i wouldn't even know how to do that … although, i guess with the kind of work that i do, it is the needs of the patients that are the primary concern … so the "serving" just isn't in the direction of the lines of corporate authority.

Anyway, back to the topic at hand … to me, i think the meaning of the word "Master" became less over time … probably more realistic, less romanticized. i became less concerned with my ideal & more open to whatever came along … meaning that i was okay with whatever commitment (or lack thereof) and whatever intensity of relationship or play that a person who called himself "Master" wanted. i always enjoyed whatever it was & never felt hurt or anything when it was over.

So, i guess my definition of "Master" is whatever my Master says it is and whatever he demonstrates himself to be. Of course, i still harbor the fantasy of being owned & being a full-time slave to a full-time Master … and fantasies have a way of becoming reality sooner or later.

Love,
Your puppy

March 8, 2004

Steven Toushin wrote:

Dear puppy,

Lost Internet access this weekend, so I did not get your e-mail or send out e-mail.

I read your e-mails; thanks for answering that question. You communicate very well in writing.

Now, more questions:

A. Who were the next men you were with?
B. What was the communication like with these men? Be specific with each one.
C. How did you connect up?
D. What did they have to offer you that you decided to be with them?
E. How long were you with each one, and what were the scenes like?
F. What did they call themselves?

Thursday is good.

Sir

March 9, 2004

sharon smith wrote:

Dear Master,

What are You so busy doing? Did You get switched over to the new server? How's Pirate doing?

i got a bill today from the court in Memphis for when i had to sign over custody of my son, Don (talk about a slow court system!). It got me thinking about all that stuff again. i think that was the hardest thing i've ever done ... cried for the entire 12 hours it took to drive home. All the hopes & dreams i had for him went up in smoke, along with everything else i believed in & stood for. For the first time in my life, i didn't feel safe ... emotionally i guess ... or spiritually. All the things i thought were there to protect & defend turned out to be mirages. Up until then, i had done a good job of denying all the institutional (church, school, government, legal, judicial, etc.) corruption, & i guess it kind of hit me all at once. That was about a month before i started the journey into BDSM.

The reason i'm telling You all this is mostly because i don't remember what i've already told You ... so please forgive me if i'm repeating myself ...

i think at the time i started corresponding with Rob, i was trying to deal with more emotional/spiritual pain than i could handle ... and i think it was originally a desperate attempt to escape ... maybe an attempt to punish myself ... maybe because i was helpless to protect my son ... from the things i had taught him to respect & honor. Although i didn't know much about what i was getting into, it turned out to be quite effective at numbing the spiritual/emotional pain ... the physical pain & bondage took over, all-consuming ... and, for the span of a few precious hours, i felt light & free ... and there was no emotional risk involved because, at the time, Rob was virtually a stranger to me. In fact, i think it was his lack of emotional attachment that kept me going back.

On the other hand, i threw every ounce of my emotions into serving him.... ... i think it was when my feelings got too strong that i had to start looking for other people to play with. Rob was (is) probably the most stubborn & detached person i've ever met ... but he was exactly what i needed at the time i got involved with him. However, life goes on & things change. What i wanted from him (as a Master) was to make me feel numb & to clear out the cobwebs, so to speak. In return i was quite happy to do anything to please him. i told myself it was all about him, but in reality i now think it was all about me.

So, anyway, when i got the court bill today, all that stuff came flooding back to me, & i realized it no longer has the power to cause so much pain. Thus, it is no longer an escape i am looking for in being submissive. So when You asked about the other people i've played with over the past three years, it occurs to me that all of them, including Rob, were negative experiences … running away from something instead of moving towards something. Being with You is the first positive experience i've had … a new direction.

All this goes back to what i was saying the other night about an evolving definition of "Master." A short time before i met You, my concept of "Master" was wiped clean … or rather, what i was looking for in a Master changed … and i think i realized i was in this as much for myself as the person i serve … meaning, i guess, that i wanted to feel good about myself as well as making the other person (You) feel good. (That's quite an admission to make for someone who's always played the martyr!)

Actually, i think i was still coming to that realization after i met You … and maybe even because of You.

Even within my marriage, it was never about me being happy or feeling good about myself … like it was some terrible & selfish thing to feel good. The ironic thing, however, is that the better i feel about myself, the more i can release the (emotional) stranglehold & simply enjoy You for who You are … and "allow" You to define what You want a Master to be … which i am (slowly) grasping as time goes on … had to start with the remedial education class!

Okay, it's 1am, & i have to get to bed, so i will quit rambling.

i miss You.

Have a wonderful day!

Love,
Your puppy

March 9, 2004

sharon smith wrote:

Dear Master,

i hope Your day is going well. i'm pretty proud of myself today
(especially considering i only got a couple hours of sleep last
night). Managed to get us a contract with a pharmacy that will
save at least $300K directly per year, not to mention many,
many hours of labor & overtime … now if i could just get some
kind of commission on that, it would be a really great day!!

Sorry about the middle-of-the-night rambling last night. Whatever it was that i said made perfect sense at the time, but today
i'm not sure what i was talking about. You can probably delete
that from any copies You're making of this stuff.

Now to answer Your questions, the next man i was with was
also someone i met on *alt.com* … can't remember his name. He
said he was an anthropologist currently working as an editor (of
what i don't remember) and lived in "Printer's Row" (i don't
know exactly where that is). He said he was married, but his
wife lived in NYC, & they had an agreement that they could see
other people. Said he was living with his sister & nephew. i met
him at that big mall in Schaumburg … at the Cheesecake Fac-
tory. i had this adult/child role-playing fantasy that i wanted to
try out, & there aren't too many on *alt.com* who were interested
in that. We had lunch & talked for quite a while … he did most

of the talking as You might expect :) He was an odd man ... kind of hard to describe ... almost like he had two personalities. He wore an expensive suit, but looked all disheveled ... like a little boy who wears a suit once a year. He was very intelligent, but he had this strange breathless way of talking ... like someone might interrupt him before he said what he wanted. At the time, i just figured he was a bit eccentric due to being an anthropologist. He was actually kind of dis-appointing to meet in person, & i ended up making up an excuse to leave. There was no sexual attraction whatsoever. He walked me to the middle of the mall, & it was kind of weird because he held my hand & started swinging it back & forth like he was having a wonderful time, & then he suddenly let go & kind of withdrew into himself ... like he was afraid to touch me. Anyway, i said a quick goodbye, & we went in opposite direc-tions with me planning to never see him again.

i don't remember just how it came about, but i did end up seeing him again. i was at a conference in Indianapolis for a few days & had agreed to meet him in Kankakee & spend the night with him before going home. It was a long, slow drive. i had been up since about 4am & didn't get there until around 8-9pm. He had gotten a hotel room & told me to call him when i got there, & he would come down to get me. When i got to the parking lot, i was dialing the phone, & he came out of nowhere & knocked on the window. Scared the shit out of me! i just had a vague feeling there was something not right about him. We went up to the room, which was very elegant. The bed was on a raised platform at an angle in the corner, & there were plants all around it ... very pretty for a hotel room. i was exhausted & hadn't eaten all day, so i suggested that i could change clothes & maybe we could go out for dinner. Instead, he said he would go get some fast food & bring it back to the room, which was also fine with me. He then left in a big bustle & hurry.

i started looking around the room. He had left a briefcase open on the dresser, so i looked inside of it. It was full of knives & those pinwheel things (Wartenberg wheels?). The fantasy, as i said, was supposed to be role-playing ... adult man & little girl. Although i had told him about my BDSM experiences, there had been no discussion of that kind of thing taking place between us ... certainly no discussion of knives. The thing was, though, that it seemed he left the briefcase open just so i would see the stuff ... so i rationalized that it would be okay ... probably because i was too tired to panic. i ended up falling asleep & woke up when he got back – about three hours later! And all he had brought back was a milkshake! i think he must have told me to get undressed before he left because i remember being very cold, and a milkshake was the last thing i wanted. i remember he started kissing me. He was fully dressed, & all i had on was thigh-highs, & he was fascinated with how they felt. Then he had me kneel in front of him & suck his cock ... which was the tiniest thing i had ever seen. It didn't take very long for him to cum, & when he did, he started yelling "fuck, fuck, fuck" really loud, like he was very angry ... which was very uncharacteristic for him because he normally spoke very quietly.

Then he blindfolded me & tied me to the bed, & i remember he used the pinwheels on me, & i was worried he would do something with the knives, but he didn't. i also remember he fisted me & licked my pussy ... don't remember much else. i think we both fell asleep in the middle of things. Never did do anything with the role-playing.

The next morning i got up & took a shower & expected to spend the day with him, but he said he had to be somewhere. Again, i figured that was the last time i would see him. Again, i was wrong. He started writing to me about stuff he was fantasizing about, & it sounded kind of fun. i figured maybe he was nervous before & was loosening up a bit, so i agreed to meet him again in the city this time. He was very specific about wanting me to dress very gaudy like a whore ... 5-inch heels, fishnets, a very short tight skirt that almost covered my ass, leopard print blouse with no bra, & lots of gaudy jewelry. i met him at a parking lot ... i think it was on State Street. It was pouring down rain & very windy & cold. i got in his car & he drove quite a distance & went to this fetish toy store. We went in & were looking at stuff, & he bought a butt plug. Then we went back to his car, & he drove almost back to where we started from (i think), & we went to a theater. He bought tickets to a movie (matinee) that he figured no one else would be watching. Then, between the ticket counter & the actual theater, he stopped about 3-4 times for various reasons. It was beginning to get annoying because i had been with him for several hours, & all he did was drive around & mess around ... like he had planned every second & it had to be exactly as he planned or it wouldn't work ... but he couldn't just enjoy himself because he was too busy with this agenda in his head.

Anyway, we finally got to the theater, & there was only one other person in there. We sat in the very back row. i remember he finally started playing with my pussy, & i was pretty sprawled out with one foot on the chair in front of me. He fisted me ... i remember he had very small hands. Then he put in the butt plug, and then it was like he was just playing the whole thing out in his head ... like he was getting annoyed that things weren't exactly as he envisioned them. He told me to pull out his cock, & then he kind of just lost it ... like it wasn't just right so there was no point in continuing. We left in the middle of the movie.

He had made reservations at this Chinese restaurant that had private booths for couples ... i would recognize the name if i heard it but can't think of it right now. i think it used to be a theater ... just a block or two west of State Street. Anyway, he had my juices flowing from the little thing at the theater, so i figured i would play with him on the way to the restaurant ...

not part of the plan! He was obsessed with taking this round-about way through the city & didn't want to be distracted by me.

When we finally got to the restaurant, he had to drive back & forth in front of it & then pull up in a certain place for the valet parking. Then he messed around doing something while i was standing there in the rain, & then he told me to go inside & wait for him. It was a good 10-15 minutes before he finally came inside. We were ushered to one of the private booths & had to sit exactly right. He had me put the butt plug back in, & his plan was that i was to get under the table & suck his cock. However, the booths weren't as private as they were advertised to be, the restaurant was quite crowded, the waitress overly attentive, & he was getting annoyed that we couldn't do what he had in mind. We had dinner, & i played with his cock a little, but it was just obvious that things weren't going as he planned, & so i was rather relieved when he decided the evening was over.

A few days later, he wrote & told me he had to think about some things & didn't know how long that would take so i shouldn't wait for him. i wrote back & wished him well and that was the end of that.

Love,
Your puppy

March 10, 2004

sharon smith wrote:

Dear Master,

After the last guy i wrote about, i was a good girl for a long time. Rob had been angry with me, & i had finally figured out what it was about & decided i better mind my p's & q's for a while & concentrate on being his perfect little subbie. Even managed to make it through the dry spell in the summer without running off to find someone to play with ... such an angel!

The following winter, Rob couldn't seem to find time to see me, & i was getting bored & frustrated and ended up reviving that adult-child role-playing fantasy that never got played out. At about that time, this guy from *alt.com* wrote to me saying he wanted to be my daddy & went into this whole scenario about what he wanted to do. i even remember his name ... Rich. He was a cop/paramedic, single, and lived in Cleveland. Interestingly, he was in his early thirties. Everyone else i played with was older than me ... most in their late fifties. He wanted me to call him "Daddy Rich," and he called me "baby sharon" ... which should have been an omen of what was to come. i agreed to meet him in Michigan City for a weekend. He got a room in a cheap hotel & met me in the parking lot. He looked & acted like a typical cop (ex-football player) ... big ego, throwing his weight around, making sure everyone knew he was a cop. Normally, i don't care to be around that kind of person, but he seemed kind of nice anyway. He carried my bag up to the room, & i barely got through the door when he told me to strip. Then he pulled out this giant-sized plastic pants & a diaper, & i thought "uh-oh – this is more than i bargained for." He put them on me & then decided we were going out for dinner, only my jeans wouldn't fit over the thing so he had me put on a pair of his sweat pants. i felt totally ridiculous, & so was plenty happy to oblige when he insisted that i drink several beers. (i can be really stupid sometimes!) Of course, after drinking a few beers i had to pee … and of course, he wasn't about to let me go to the ladies' room. He really got into the mean daddy/naughty baby thing, & i will have to say that by that time, i was finding the whole thing pretty amusing myself. Since my bladder was about to burst, i ended up flooding the diaper while sitting in the middle of the restaurant. (i can't believe i'm telling You this!) So i wanted to get out of there ASAP, & he made a big deal about checking the diaper & announcing that i would have to be punished.

We went back to the hotel & he told me to strip & then he (painfully) handcuffed me to a chair. Then he brought out this big wooden cutting board & started beating my ass with it. It hurt like hell, & i thought he was going to break a bone or something … definitely not a safe thing to be hitting someone with, especially when the one wielding it is built like a linebacker. After that, if i didn't move fast enough to do what he said, he threatened me with that "paddle," & i moved a whole lot faster … though he kept making things impossible & would use it anyway. He had me doing all kinds of things & would stand there watching me & working his cock until he got himself so sore he could hardly stand to be touched.

He was into water sports & shit play, lots of cocksucking, vibrators, humiliation play, anal plugs, slapping, and i don't remember what else. Not that first weekend but a few months later, he was the first one to finally fuck my ass. He was also into a lot of mindfuck. He was really very cruel & brutal when we were playing, but very thoughtful & sweet outside of that. We would go for walks on the beach & feed the seagulls & watch the boats, etc.

Because he had to drive so far to see me, we would always meet for a weekend … i probably saw him 4 times over the course of about 6 months. i was his first experience with BDSM. He said he was always into diapers & often wore one himself when home alone, & it meant a lot to him that i would let him put one on me. He shared a lot about himself & his secret desires/fantasies/needs. There were times when i felt very close to him. He was very outgoing, social & aggressive in his everyday life ... not someone you would ever expect to have a secret diaper fetish. The problem was that he kept calling my cell phone at the most inopportune times, & he was one of those guys who fell in "love" & wanted me to marry him ... said he wanted to keep me in diapers 24/7. i didn't mind the play because it meant so much to him, but it was not something i could do all the time.

However, he was very open-minded & willing to try anything the mind could conceive of. (Laughing) He always wanted me to connect him with someone who could mentor him to become a skillful BDSM Master ... might You be interested? i'm sure he would be happy to come to Chicago for lessons.

Love,
Your puppy

March 11, 2004

sharon smith wrote:

Dear Master,

When i saw Rich, it was for 2-3 days at a time, and 90% of the waking hours were spent playing, so describing a full scene would be rather difficult ... hard to remember. He was very big on verbal humiliation. i remember he took me to a store & bought several pairs of satiny full-coverage panties ... and very ugly ones at that. He had me wear them for a few hours, & then he put them on my face & had an unusual amount of fun calling me "panty-face" & kept telling me to say how much i loved wearing my panties on my face & sniffing them. Of all the things i've ever done, i really hated that … mostly because i don't like anything covering my nose & mouth … a mental thing i guess … thinking i can't breathe. Besides that, it just wasn't something that even remotely turned me on. There was no arguing with him, though, because i definitely didn't like that damn wooden cutting board he would threaten me with. He really got off on sniffing & licking my panties. He would take them home with him & write for weeks about how he would sleep with them on his face & could still smell my pussy. He must have either had an extraordinary sense of smell or a very vivid imagination!

Rich would talk pretty much non-stop when we were playing. He got very descriptive with name-calling, though i can't remember now what he said other than calling me a slut, whore, et al. He liked to have me stand with my nose in a corner & my pants around my ankles & would order me to play with my pussy while he watched & wanked himself. He was constantly wanking himself & would always complain about how sore he was. He also kept apologizing about the size of his cock & the fact that he couldn't cum every 10 minutes for three days in a row. (i think he may have believed a few too many locker room stories!) The first time i was with him, he had spent several days beforehand jacking off in anticipation & wasn't able to cum at all when he finally got there … a huge disappointment for him.

Another thing that really turned him on was to have both of us wear these giant plastic pants, & he would push them aside & fuck me while we were wearing them. He also liked fucking my ass because i let him do that without a condom. As far as water sports, that was mostly with the diaper thing. One time he had me lie on the bed & pissed all over me, without considering the fact that he was soaking the bed at the same time, & we had to sleep in it for the next two nights … a lesson learned. He never did that again!

As for shit play, he would take a dump in his hand & then use it to finger paint (smear) all over me. He especially liked drawing a moustache. Again, he would be yanking on his cock the whole time he did it. This all sounds kind of dumb in writing, but when i was with him, i was just fascinated by how intensely he got turned on by it all.

He considered me to be very experienced & wanted me to teach him how to do BDSM & how to be a Master or else hook him up with someone who would teach him. i was his first experience outside the world of vanilla sex. It was like he had 30 years of fantasies built up & was trying to fulfill as many as possible when we were together. It was fun just to watch & see what he was going to do next. He was also kind of refreshing because he was very honest about his lack of experience & very open about all the things he had fantasized about. He repeatedly talked about how it was "so cool" that i would go along with everything. But alas, it ended up that he wanted me to marry him so he could make an honest woman out of me. He also kept calling my cell phone several times daily while i was working, which got to be a real problem. He was an interesting experience, but definitely not someone i wanted to spend time with on a regular or long-term basis.

Love,
Your puppy

March 12, 2004

Steven Toushin wrote:

Dear puppy,

In the golden shower and scat scenes:

    A. Did you find enjoyment, fulfillment, a void being filled, and/or a need for humiliation that was invigorating?

    B. Was there any sexual thrill in this type of humiliation?

    C. If you didn't like it, was he the wrong person to be doing these scenes with?

    D. Would you have liked it with another Dom?

    E. How many times did you repeat these scenes, and were they different each time? Meaning, how did you inwardly feel about each time?

Sir

March 12, 2004

sharon smith wrote:

Dear Master,

Once i got past the obvious aversion to the scat, i did enjoy it. (i had gotten used to the golden showers with Donald.) In the beginning, i think the thrill was in the fact that these things were so taboo. i don't know what kind of void these things would have filled. i think it was the humiliation that turned me on. There's something about both scat & golden showers, though … it's kind of like a gift … an extreme form of intimacy … like it's an honor to receive it. It depends on how much the other person enjoys giving it.

i think it's like that with anything, though. The thing that turns me on the most is when the other person is really into something, really turned on by it. However, i must confess i do enjoy any kind of "messy" sex. There was limited enjoyment with Rich because it seemed like he was playing out fantasies in his head ... like he was going down a checklist of things to try ... not fully present in the scene. He also seemed to be struggling with ... the power? ... of being given permission to do anything he wanted. Actually, it was more like he was struggling with the freedom of being given permission to do what he wanted ... a mental thing – like once he could, was it really okay?

Anyway, i have enjoyed golden showers & drinking You more than anyone else because it just seems so natural ... more intimate ... more of a gift that i feel honored to receive. It's that way regarding anything with You, though, because You are actually present & don't seem to be playing some fantasy in Your head ... not in a big hurry to try everything listed in the "BDSM handbook" ... more of a connection.

Regarding the last question, i was only with Rich maybe 3 times. He got braver each time with how far he would go. As far as how i felt inwardly each time, it got to be too much, not so much with the scat/golden showers, but with the whole thing. He got to be too brutal, like he was the macho cop arresting & brutalizing some street scum. After about a day & a half, i would feel emotionally bereft, & he wouldn't let up. It was just too much for too long. He was a nice guy, but he didn't know what he was doing.

See You soon!

Love,
Your slave puppy

March 13, 2004

sharon smith wrote:

Dear Master,

i'm trying to remember how this writing project got started. Seems like i must have written hundreds of pages by now.

Michael is the last person i was with before i met You. i met him via *alt.com* about the same time i started corresponding with Rich. Must have been about a year ago. Michael is one of those guys who searches *alt.com* every day & writes to every new profile that appears. i think his handle is *MasterMotts* ... or maybe *luckymotts*. i don't have access to the profiles, but i'm sure he would still be on there. He is married with, i think, 6 adult children (very family oriented), owns his own very successful business, & is worth many millions. His wife has been sick for a long time, so no sex on the home front. i don't remember the early correspondence & don't even remember who contacted who first. i do remember him telling me before we met in person that his one leg was amputated when he was a teenager. He later told me how it had happened: as a result of a botched knee surgery. Because of that, he had lost a basketball scholarship to one of the big 10 schools ... don't remember which one. His wife (who was his girlfriend at the time) stayed with him through the ordeal & was his source of strength & later success. He adores her.

Anyway, i met him one afternoon at a Chinese restaurant in Westmont. He is a large man, both height & weight, in his late forties, "white" hair which i would call gray but he claimed it's blond, very self-confident, charming, polite, sophisticated, deep baritone voice, lives in Naperville. He said he had lots of experience as a Master ... i think it was about 10 years or so. We had lunch, & he told me a lot about himself & why he was involved in D/s & about his business. i remember we were sitting in the middle of the restaurant. i was wearing a suit (skirt & jacket) and didn't have a blouse on under the jacket and, after politely asking, he unbuttoned & reached inside the jacket to "fondle" my breast, all the while carrying on a conversation like nothing was going on. Fortunately, i had my back to the rest of the customers so i don't know if anyone was paying attention. If so, he didn't seem to care.

He was very different from anyone else i had been with ... just seemed to be very at ease & natural about everything. We decided to meet again about a week or two later & ended up back in Westmont at a Best Western. He met me in the parking lot, & we walked in together, which was very different than Rob who would never dare be seen entering or leaving a hotel with me. When we got to the room, he sat on the bed & had me stand in front of him, & he undressed me down to the black lace garter belt, thong, & black nylons he had instructed me to wear. Then he just kind of ran his hands over my body, exploring every inch. He used a vibrator, whips, & leather cuffs, & he fisted me. He took off his artificial leg to play, which made me feel kind of uncomfortable. He had to fuck me a certain way ... with me lying on the edge of the bed & him standing next to it ... i guess for leverage.

He was into ass-fucking & said he was going to train my ass so he could do it without hurting me ... which i appreciated because he had quite a large cock, & my ass was still virgin territory at the time. He sent me home that day with various sizes of butt plugs that i was to wear three days a week. Again, being rather stupid, i remember i wore the first one three days in a row & ended up with a very sore ass. He got quite a laugh about that ... he had intended that i should wear it every other day.

When i saw him a couple weeks later, he was pleased with the results ... spent a lot of time "opening" me up but said i wasn't ready to be fucked. He was quite patient, & the ass-training went on for a couple months before Rich beat him to the target. Rich's cock was quite a bit smaller, & it was still a while after that before i could handle Michael. He did eventually fuck my ass a few times, but never without being quite painful ... though i think he permanently stretched it out ... which, when i told him that, he thought was quite amusing.

He also used to do this intricate thing with ropes over a door in which i would be suspended with ropes everywhere, & then he would whip me, & i would spin around like a puppet on a string ... hoping to have my back to him when the next lash hit, but that wasn't usually the case. He laughed about that, too....said he was going to tie bowling balls to my feet to hold me still.

The last time i saw him was in August, about the time my house sold & also the day before i went to that Shadowfind weekend. Michael traveled a lot, & he left right after that to spend a couple months in Europe. Since then, he's left a few messages on my cell phone, but i haven't returned any of his calls. He was nice, but there was just never a real spark there, i guess ... just not something i wanted to continue. His big focus in life was money & what he would buy with it, & i'm just not that impressed with the things money can buy. The last time i saw him, he made me guess how much his watch cost ($30K) ... that just turned me off. Seems like there would be something better to do with that kind of money than spend it on a watch.

So that's the end of my story. i was pretty much celibate for a couple months before i met You ... and since then, i have had no desire to look anywhere else because You are so perfect in every way!

i miss You.

Love,
Your puppy

PS: i did just think of something else ... Marlene had a party for Rob at her house last May. That was kind of interesting ... so maybe one more episode in the sub saga!

March 14, 2003

Steven Toushin wrote:

Dear puppy,

How is your week? How is the new job going?

I have to start going through all your e-mails and organize them; that should take me a while.

Please finish the last request, and I think that is it for a while. If there are things you want to add that you feel were left out, that you feel that would fill in and be important, please do so.

See you this coming week.

Sir

March 14, 2004

sharon smith wrote:

Dear Master,

i miss You. It's been a long week. i hope all is well with You & You have all Your computer stuff straightened out. We lost our entire database at work on Thursday, which put a lot of I.S. people into a panic. As of Friday afternoon, they could see it but couldn't get to it … i'm not sure what that means, but it doesn't seem to be a good thing. i had a house full of Mexicans here all day yesterday fixing the drywall from the flood. None of them spoke English … just smiled a lot. Looks like they did a good job, though. Now we just have to paint & re-stretch the carpet, & things will be back to normal.

my role and place with You as my Master … i'm not sure how to answer that. It is whatever You want it to be. i am Your puppy, submissive … According to the definitions i've heard, i'm not Your slave. i suppose in all reality i am an occasional diversion in Your otherwise busy life. i'd like to say i'm making Your life easier, but that doesn't seem to be the case. The thing that is different about You is that i'm very much sexually attracted to You, & that wasn't an issue with anyone else … kind of clouds things up. You are not as strict as the others, yet right from the start You've managed to get me to do things i have (or would have) refused in the past. Also, i admire/respect You as a person, not because You demand it, but because i honestly do … which also wasn't the case with anyone else. Respect was demanded without reason except by virtue of the role of "Master" … or the size of the whip. Also, when i am with You, i am only thinking about You, which is why i'm speechless (surprised?) when You ask me something about myself. i think that's a very subtle thing that You do, & i'm not sure You even realize You're doing it … although i do know that You (deviously) take me right to the edge & then keep me from going over into my own little world. (Laughing) i guess that means my role & place is that of a toy to entertain You.

Serving You is more real & less fantasy. With anyone else, i spent a lot of time fantasizing about what i wanted them to be & do. Hence, the handle "*subrosafantasia*" (sub-rosa = secret, fantasia = fantasy). i don't fantasize that You are someone else. You are what You are … and Your imagination/experience is beyond anything i could come up with. i do fantasize about being Your full-time slave, but i understand Your situation & that's not what You want and my own situation also being an impediment at the present time. i feel like i'm rambling & not sure if i'm answering Your question. my role & place is that i want to please You in any way that i can … whenever and however You want … because it makes me feel good about myself when You are pleased/happy … also makes my pussy very wet!

i can be available any day this week.

Love,
Your puppy

March 17, 2004

Steven Toushin wrote:

Dear puppy,

I am going over and listing all of your e-mails. I have not re-read them yet to put them in any order.

I think I have a few more questions.

A. Your encounters with those masters: how did they leave you in terms of fulfillment?

B. Did you have a craving and a wanting to explore in more detail?

C. If so, when did you know the search would continue?

D. Did you know what to expect, what a Dominant would bring out in you?

E. When did you realize that this was your path?

F. Where do you want this journey of yours to end up?

Sir

March 17, 2004

sharon smith wrote:

Dear Master,

There was always something missing ... something different with each one of them. Rob & Donald were the only ones i called Master. If the two of them could be combined into one person, it would be good. Rob was not able to fuck me and, as You astutely noted, that's kind of important to me. Donald was more into exhibitionism & just playing & not so much into D/s ... very enthusiastic, though. Rob was very reserved, & Donald seemingly carefree. As far as feeling fulfilled, sometimes after seeing Rob i would feel really good. Just as often, however, i would cry on the way home ... not sure why ... i don't think it had anything to do with him or anything that happened ... though i never did that with anyone else. They all had their own little thing that they were into, and i guess i was more interested in trying it all. i remember the first time i met Rob, he asked what my limits were, & i told him i didn't know because there were so many things i hadn't tried. How was i supposed to know whether i liked something if i never tried it? He thought that was a dumb answer, but it was the truth. Fulfillment ... not really ... but i did always have fun & never regretted anything.

Cravings ... i would have to say that my appetite for BDSM (and all things sexual) far surpassed that of anyone else i was with. The encounters never happened often enough & never went far enough. i think most people find more pleasure in fantasizing about something rather than actually doing it, whereas i prefer the doing much more than the fantasizing. i could never figure out how a person could be so intense during a scene, & then just live off that encounter for a month or even several months. It's kind of like people who spend months planning for a vacation & enjoy fantasizing about it more than the vacation itself, & then they spend months afterwards showing the pictures to everyone they see. Personally, i don't think i've ever planned a vacation until the day i left, & most often never knew where i was going until i got there ... and probably had more fun ... and if i remembered to take a camera, i would usually forget to take any pictures 😊! (laughing) i guess that's why i need someone to take charge of things ... bad memory.

By the way, i do want You to know that i purchased some golf balls this evening ... now just have to remember to bring them with me tomorrow night! There must have been 50 different kinds of golf balls in the store ... long, short, hard, soft, fast, slow, etc., etc. ... people must have thought i was a bit odd laughing about which kind of balls to choose ... finally decided to go with cheap since they will probably be lost rather quickly.

Now that i've gotten way off the subject, the next question was when i knew that the search would continue. It was always a spur-of-the-moment thing. Rob would frustrate the hell out of me. Every week he would ask me what days i could be available, & i would tell him at least 3 or 4 days, but he could never manage to find time except on days when he knew i had something else scheduled. It was pretty obvious that he didn't want to find the time ... just sadistically testing my patience. He actually thought i would sit around forever waiting for him. So, i figured, why should i make myself miserable & frustrated? If he didn't want to see me, i would find someone else to satisfy my "cravings" ... after all, anything is better than nothing.

i would turn my *alt.com* profile on &, within a few hours, there would be dozens of replies, & within a few days i was no longer miserable & frustrated. Then i could wait patiently for however long it took him to find time in his schedule. i seriously think he would have killed me if he knew what i was doing. He honestly thought he was successfully teaching me to be patient. He spent all his time telling me to do things he knew i didn't like & didn't want, & if i did everything he said, my "reward" was that i got to see him once every 2-3 months. If i weren't entertaining myself with other people, i probably would have given up on him within the first 3 months i knew him. i still don't know what possessed me to keep going back to him for so long. It had ceased to be enjoyable long before it was over. He just had this grip on my mind that i couldn't seem to shake loose ... definitely know i don't ever want to get involved with another psychologist!

Did i know what to expect about what a Dominant would bring out in me? Not in the beginning. i was quite surprised at my reaction the first time. If i thought i was going to react like that, i probably would have been too embarrassed to show up. After the first couple times & the first couple people ... it must have been conditioning, like with Pavlov's dogs ... all it took was a certain touch or word or ritual, & i knew i would become hopelessly ... wanton? (for lack of a better word). And the more people i played with, the more "triggers" seemed to develop. The humiliation thing surprised me, too. In everyday life, i tend to get embarrassed easily. Would have never expected to enjoy something like that. And pain ... normally a minor scratch causes undue distress ... but from the hands of a Master/Dom, a totally different reaction. i have to say that i still find it pretty amazing how it all works. It's like my brain becomes completely rewired the minute i see You, & i react/respond/feel things differently than any other time.

The rest of the questions are going to have to wait because i can't stay awake any longer ... think i will go to bed & dream about sucking Your cock ....

Love,
Your puppy

March 19, 2004

sharon smith wrote:

Dear Master,

i hope You're continuing to have a good week! i am spending too much time working & trying to fix too many things at once ... can't even think anymore. Finally got a new printer at home so can at least get some stuff accomplished at night without a dozen people waiting in line to tell me their issues. i have to admit this job is a little more challenging than i thought it would be. It's hard to fathom how the program could be in operation for 15 years & be such a mess. my life seems to have been reduced to two things ... on the way to work in the morning, i'm preoccupied thinking about You, & on the way home (or to see You), i'm preoccupied thinking about work ... feel like i'm on a time delay & need to switch that around ... might improve the concentration. It's pretty bad when i have to stop to think about what my own son's name is!

i believe i still need to answer the last two questions about when i realized this was my path, & where i want this journey to end up. The first time that i served Rob it felt so right, so congruent ... like i was doing what i needed to do ... like i was finally home. i knew right away that this was something i wanted to continue to explore. i really don't know where this journey will end up. i tend to be a perfectionist, so i expect the journey will continue until i become a perfect slave, & since that's probably not possible, i expect the journey will take me to increasingly deeper levels of submission. i'm finding it more & more difficult to lead a double life. Feel like i'm hanging on to something that has lost all meaning & importance, but i can't seem to cross the line. How do i walk away from everything i've spent the majority of my life working for? And how can i not? i wish i had discovered all this before i got married & had a family. Yet, i don't think i would have had the maturity and ... self-confidence? ... to appreciate it back then. That seems so contradictory ... i haven't thought of it like that before ... to have enough self-confidence to be submissive. Anyway, the destination of my journey will depend mostly on my traveling companion and where he wants to take me. Perhaps a forthcoming sequel to "the puppy papers"?

i wish i was there serving You tonight ....

Love,
Your puppy

March 21, 2004

sharon smith wrote:

Dear Master,

i miss You. Have You gone on vacation? i woke up this morning so horny that even Your dogs would have sounded good.

i've been thinking about some things ... first, i am seriously considering getting hypnotized to quit smoking. i was talking to one of the paramedics the other day, & she said both she & her husband had smoked 2 packs/day for 20 years. They were both hypnotized last fall, & neither has wanted a cigarette since then. In the past i've tried everything from quitting cold turkey to patches, pills, gum, etc. The only thing i haven't tried is hypnosis. i think i haven't tried that because i'm afraid it won't work, & that would be my last hope. Whenever i've talked to people who have done this, they always say there has to be something either that you strongly don't like (like a particular food) that can be associated with smoking, or something that you strongly want that can be associated with quitting. The problem is that i can't think of anything i don't like enough to make any difference, and, while i very well know the benefits of quitting, that isn't enough to make a difference, either. So, anyway, i'm trying to get myself motivated to do this, & i'm wondering if i make an appointment if You would be willing to go with me. The best motivation i can come up with is if i could convince myself that it is something You absolutely insisted on.

The second thing i've been thinking about is that it really bothers me that i can't seem to implement Your most simple request. i know i've talked about this before & can't believe i'm still stuck in the same place. i think i must be misinterpreting Your body language, because i am very happy to do anything at all to help/please You, but then when i see You, i always feel like You would rather do stuff Yourself, & i don't want to mess with stuff that You don't want me to … which actually means i am being polite. i would be much happier if You were sitting down relaxing while i took care of everything else for You. So i've decided i need to become more aggressively submissive (how's that for an oxymoron!) and just do what i want to do (serve You), regardless of what i perceive at the time … if that makes any sense. i will personally feel much better when this little piece gets fixed.

Love,
Your puppy

March 21, 2004

Steven Toushin wrote:

Dear puppy,

Yes, I will go with you to a hypnotist, and, yes, stop being passive and serve.

Tuesday and Thursday of this week are good. I moved the meetings over to Monday and Wednesday.

Is there anything left on the writing agenda?

Sir

March 21, 2004

Dear Master,

Thank You, Sir. There is a hypnotist near where I work in Har-vey. i can try to make an appointment there for next Saturday, or maybe an evening if they're open later – unless You know of someone closer to You. Please let me know what would work best for You.

i hadn't really thought of it as being passive, but i think You're exactly right. Seems i've gotten passive & submissive mixed up. So much easier to see that in someone else than in myself. Thank You.

Tuesday is good. i have a late afternoon meeting on Thursday, but should be able to leave by 6-6:30pm, so would just be a lit-tle later getting to Your house, if that's okay.

Still missing You ....

Love,
Your puppy

March 21, 2004

Dear Master,

i think i've answered all the questions that You sent. i thought of something else to add the other day, but now i can't remember what it was. Will have to let You know if/when it comes back to me.

Love,
Your puppy

                              March 24, 2004

sharon smith wrote:

Dear Master,

Thank You for being so patient with me.

Love,
Your puppy

Part X

A Slave's Heart

March 25, 2004

sharon smith wrote:

Dear Master,

i was talking to my mother tonight, & she was telling me about a kid that lived next door to us when i was growing up. He was one of those kids that everyone picked on mercilessly. Even his parents harassed him all the time. Due to all that, he became a fighter & generally got in a lot of trouble … kid stuff. He was actually a nice kid but never stood a chance … mostly just because he had buckteeth. As he got older, he got arrested for things like shoplifting, public intoxication … little stuff like that. Then about 15-20 years ago he broke into a store & just vandalized the place & ended up getting sentenced to life in prison for being a habitual criminal. Then a couple months ago, he was released from prison, & the first thing he did was buy a lotto ticket … and won $10 million!!!! i think that is so cool. This is definitely a guy who deserved a break. It's kind of like a payback for all the abuse he's endured all his life. i hope he spends every penny of it on himself & says "screw you" to everyone who goes knocking on his door asking for money.

Also, i looked up that *bondage.com* website You talked about. The forums there look a lot more interesting/insightful than *scenetalk.net*. i think i had a very narrow view about D/s before i met You … probably because i only had contact with narrow-minded people … probably more along the lines of Tops and not Doms or Masters. Now i'm curious why You ever gave me a second thought. i am no different than the woman You said went into it blindly & was injured, & You thought she was a fool. There couldn't possibly be anyone who got involved in BDSM more naively than i did. i had never even heard of it, much less read anything about it. In fact, everything i participated in up until i met You was done in isolation without any awareness that there is a whole community of people involved in this as an everyday lifestyle. Well, i did meet those few women at Shadowfind, but they seemed to be societal outcasts who had formed their own little "club." It's hard to explain, but i feel like there is … an awareness … that is slowly sinking in.

Just when i think i'm starting to understand everything, i realize i've barely touched the surface, & there's a whole world of potential left to explore. i hope You will understand if i occasionally pause in fascination at the dynamics of it all. You said something last night about my *alt.com* profile saying that i wanted to be a slave. That is what i want … to be Your slave … but i don't think i truly understand what it means, and i don't think it's something that i can just read about or decide to do & then do it. It's more like You said in Your last set of questions … a journey … or a process … or maybe an evolution of sorts … not something that can be turned on & off. Actually, it's a lot like becoming a nurse … you study and practice and work at it for years, and then one day you suddenly realize – that's who i am, not because i have a degree or a label or a particular job or because i do certain things, it's just who i am. i feel like a child who is just learning to ride a bike! This probably all sounds ridiculous to You. Very uncharacteristically, i suddenly feel like i want to take this "journey" very slowly … to savor every step … and to have You point out the signposts along the way.

One more thing … what You said last night about serving isn't something i've ever considered as an option, because i've never known anyone who would allow that kind of (presumptuous) service. Once again, a whole plethora of possibilities and something that will involve a gradual understanding of what will please You. Hmmmm … perhaps with time, i will be able to anticipate Your every thought … though i can't imagine You ever being that predictable ….

Love,
Your puppy

March 27, 2004

Steven Toushin wrote:

What about your appointment with the hypnotist? Let's figure out a time.

Sir

March 27, 2004

sharon smith wrote:

Dear Master,

i've lost track of my calculations, but i think next Saturday i will be PMS-ing … not a good time to attempt to quit smoking – been there, done that, & feel fortunate to have not killed anyone! How about the following Saturday?

Love,
Your puppy

March 26, 2004

sharon smith wrote:

Dear Master,

When i first got involved in BDSM, when i first met Rob, the thing i wanted was for someone to "take" control. i didn't want to "give" it, & i didn't want it to be a power "exchange." i wanted it to be taken, & i wanted to find someone who enjoyed, got excited about, got off on, derived a great deal of pleasure from, the "taking" of control. i always got more excited with the "taking" of control than any actual activities that took place.

One of the topics that i was reading about on the *bondage.com* website the other night was started by a woman who said that she found it quite easy to be "submissive" to her Master, but she was unable to "yield" to him, which is what he wanted. She defined being submissive as doing the cooking, cleaning, running errands, laying out his clothes, keeping his juice glass filled, running his bath, etc., and being generally attentive, but she found it impossible to "yield" to his desires, sexually or otherwise. my thought when i was reading that was that i am just the opposite of her. To my way of thinking, this woman was in complete control … the typical "vanilla" housewife, simply doing what needs to be done, when & how she wanted, and the more "attentive" she was and the more she did for him, the more control she had. It had nothing whatsoever to do with him except to make him helpless because she decided what he was going to eat, drink, wear, etc. It happens every day, everywhere. i fail to see how that is being submissive. All women have done those things throughout history. Am i wrong on this?

Personally, i spent a great deal of time for many years trying to take care of my husband & do what i thought he wanted. Consequently, i was left in charge (in control) of everything, & no matter what i did to try to make him happy, he was never happy. For example, he wanted dinner on the table when he got home from work, so i would rush home from work & make a nice dinner every night, but he would never show up, & then he would get angry when the food had to be thrown away. He wanted me to pay the bills, but he didn't like the way i did it, so i would do it his way, and he didn't like that either. I would decorate the house the way he said he wanted it, & then he would tell everyone what bad taste i had. He wanted me to work, so i worked, & he complained that i wasn't home. He wanted me to stay home & take care of the kids, so i did that, & he complained that i wasn't working. He wanted me to get an education & work at a high-paying job, so i went to school, which he was very unhappy about, & then went back to work, which again he was not happy with. So i worked part-time, & he complained i wasn't working enough. He hated shopping, so i would buy his clothes for him, & he never liked a single thing. i would even bring home 20+ shirts for him to pick one, & he wouldn't like any of them. He didn't want me talking on the phone or going out for lunch with friends. At one time, he even got rid of all the phones. He alienated all my friends, & then harassed me because i didn't have any. i took care of everything with the house, the yard, the kids, the pets, the vehicles, and anything else that needed to be done. Then i would sit & worry to the point of becoming physically ill because he wouldn't show up for days at a time, & i was so afraid he was lying dead along the road somewhere, & i would be expecting a police officer to show up on my doorstep any second.

Anyway, the point of all this babbling (besides that i apparently have more baggage than i thought) is that i spent about 20 years trying to make his life as easy & stress-free as possible. In return, i was routinely yelled at & told i was stupid, fat, ugly, useless, lazy, pond-scum, etc., etc., etc. ... usually while i was cleaning his whiskey vomit off the carpet or the broken dishes off the floor, etc. Throughout all of that, i was totally devoted to being "submissive" to him in a similar manner to what the woman on the website described. Then i finally came to my senses & decided i had to let it go. i quit doing anything for him. i did whatever i wanted, whenever i wanted to, & he was left to fend for himself, & if he killed himself or someone else while driving drunk, it was his problem not mine ... a complete emotional disconnection. It was an approach i had to take to keep my sanity, not to mention my health … and it has actually worked quite well.

On the way home last night, i was thinking about what You said, & i started crying because i felt like i was disappointing You & not able to please You & if You had any sense, You would toss me aside & move on. And i was trying to figure out how i could go to see You, wanting more than anything to serve You in any way You want, & then when i get there, i become speechless … frozen in place. i asked myself if, like You said, maybe i wanted to be punished or forced or make it part of an agreed-upon scene. i don't play games … i don't do or not do something because i want to be punished or because i want to manipulate You into doing something. i appreciate being punished if i mess up, but that isn't the reason i mess up. Being "forced" makes things easier for me, but You are not forcing me to do anything, & pretending that You are is avoiding the issue, & it would all become just a pretend game that we would both quickly lose interest in. That much i have figured out from my experiences in the past. If it were part of a scene it would be the same thing. When i am with You i don't divide it into scene & not scene. i don't pull a "submissive hat" out of my bag & pretend for a few hours, & then put it away & go back to my regular life. It goes with me & is a part of my everyday life. i don't wear a sign announcing it, but it's there.

i think about You all the time, & Your presence is always with me. When i'm with You, it's because i want to be, & anything i do is because i want to, not because it's part of a scene. Does that make sense? It's not like this is a scene, & it starts at point A and ends at point B, & anything between those two points is different than anything outside of those two points. When i offer You my body, mind, and soul, that is very sincere and, as far as i'm concerned, it is open-ended and includes anything at all that You want, whenever You want it.

So, back to the original question of what is keeping me from doing what i most want to do. By the time i got home last night, i had concluded that i am afraid of something, but i don't know what it is that i'm afraid of. So i tossed & turned & didn't get much sleep last night trying to figure it out (which is why i was writing so early this morning & unable to operate a computer correctly!). As of this morning i hadn't figured it out, which is why i was writing random thoughts that came to mind. As of this afternoon, i think i'm beginning to figure it out. It makes absolutely no sense, but somehow that one simple phrase represents crossing a line to a deeper level of commitment … and i am afraid of being hurt. So the question then becomes, why am i afraid of being hurt? Ironically, i think it has something to do with one of the reasons i was attracted to You in the first place … Your experience. You have had many submissives/bottoms/slaves/play partners, or whatever You want to call them, who have come & gone, and i am always expecting that the same could happen to me at any time. It's a pretty shaky limb to step out on.

Hmm … that sounds like a trust thing, doesn't it? i think what i need is to know that if i cross the line, that You will be there. Please don't get me wrong … i am not looking for some long-term or monogamous commitment. i just need something concrete to let me know that You are not going to just disappear without notice & leave me lost in space. That is all i know, & my brain is weary of thinking.

Love,
Your puppy

March 27, 2004

Steven Toushin wrote:

Dear puppy,

Yes, every thing you've said made sense. I need to bring things up for discussion and to know your inner thoughts. What you think and how you feel are important. Your inner thoughts make up an important part of you and who you are. You know I do not analyze (I am not a junior shrink) or judge (I do have my inner opinions and I do rant on about things, especially politics), for I am in no position to judge, since my shortcomings are many.

You are right about the fact that I could be gone tomorrow. I have never hidden that fact. But so could you. I do not live in fear of being hurt. I welcome the warm, endearing thoughts I have of you. And if, for any reason, we do not see each other again, I know that I knew you and that you gave to me your love, warmth, and a smile that will last forever.

Sir

March 27, 2004

sharon smith wrote:

Dear Master,

Yes, You have always been very open & honest, & that is a very big reason why i was attracted to You in the first place – and still am. There is nothing about You that i would want to change. (smile) i sometimes have a hard time following Your train of thought, but that's okay because people often have a blank look on their face when i'm going off in a dozen different directions at the same time, & i'm glad to know i'm not the only one who does that😊 .

Aside from the misleading fact that i've gone through quite a few Doms in the past couple years, i am the kind of person who makes a commitment & then sticks with it long after it should be over ... perhaps a defect in my wiring. Except for Rob, i never made a commitment to any of them. With Rob, it was a one-sided thing, & i knew he was lying to me the whole time ... no real heartbreak when it was over. On the other hand, i feel like You are the One i've always been looking for, & i think i would be heartbroken if You suddenly disappeared. i am willing to risk that, but there needs to be a sort of inner shifting (re-alignment) that takes a bit of time ... kind of a self-protective measure. i think there are things that could be done to speed up the process, yet i think that would skip over some pieces. Maybe that's what i was talking about the other day when i said something about going slow (because i sure didn't know what i was talking about after i sent that message ... i hate slow!!). Dang! i don't normally make things so fucking complicated ... feel like i'm talking in circles & not zeroing in on what i'm try-ing to say ... whatever that might be, i don't know. Maybe the thing to do is if You would send me far out into subspace (over the edge?), & then leave me there for a while to clear out the cobwebs, cleanse the mind ....

Love,
Your puppy

March 29, 2004

Steven Toushin wrote:

Dear puppy,

Monday and Wednesday you will be coming over. Crossing over that line: for me or for you? The commitment will have to be something that you want for yourself, something that fills your need and gives you pleasure. It is a selfless act. I will be the Master of that commitment of your very being, for I am a selfish Master and will take it gladly when offered, only if it is sincere. Only then will you begin to learn to serve me in the ways I want to be served. In turn, I will hold your commitment, you, in the highest regard to take care of, respect and protect.

Sir

March 29, 2004

sharon smith wrote:

Dear Master,

There isn't anything i do that is not sincere. It gives me much pleasure when You are pleased. If i think You are less than pleased, i feel lousy ... worthless. So, yes, i need to please You to feel good about myself. Is that selfish or selfless? i would have to say both. It's kind of odd, i guess, because to be successful, influential, beautiful, rich, famous, powerful, etc., is all meaningless to me. What is meaningful to me is to make someone else's day brighter, to put a smile on their face, to ease their suffering, to give them hope, a boost up ... things like that make me feel good. Is that any less selfish than the person who derives pleasure from being successful, influential, etc.? i don't think so. Anyway, it's a very small step from those things to a D/s relationship.

Like i said before, it is Your pleasure that gives me pleasure. The thing that is exciting/satisfying to me is that You continually expect more ... and the more i can give to You the happier i am ... despite the fact that i may hesitate at some things. It is when You continue to ask for or push for things or simply take them that i can get past my own hang-ups, and it is then that i feel like i am really doing something to please You. Does that make sense? What's important to me is that You want and find pleasure in the things You ask of me ... the more selfish You are, the happier i will be. Sheesh! It seems like the more i write, the more is left unsaid ... much easier to just do it & not think about it!

Love,
Your puppy

March 31, 2004

sharon smith wrote:

Dear Master,

i hope all is well with You & You are enjoying the beautiful spring weather. i spent most of the day yesterday working on the dreaded taxes & got everything off to the accountant (my brother-in-law) this morning. Seems i get more disorganized with each passing year ... have about deteriorated into one of those people who brings in grocery bags of receipts to dump on his desk.

i went to a Cancer Support Center fundraiser at the Olympia Fields Country Club Friday night with 3 of my staff. It was one of those "have-to-make-an-appearance" things that none of us were enthused about. It was funny because we went out for dinner & drinks beforehand, & then were late getting there, only to find there were a couple thousand people there, & no one would ever know whether we showed up or not. So we walked through the door & within about two minutes, a photographer came up to me & asked if he could take my picture, so three of us got in the picture (proof that we were there!!), and then left right afterwards. It turned out to be quite a fun evening, despite the short foray to the fundraiser.

My husband is done working in Indianapolis now, so he will be home most of the time, & he's already getting on my nerves with the constant bitching, complaining, & general negative attitude. The marriage works much better when i don't see or hear from him for 5 days out of the week! So anyway, now that he'll be here every night, it won't make any difference if i see You on a weeknight or weekend.

Which reminds me ... You have mentioned several times about doing a "fisting demonstration" ... i'm wondering when/where that is going to be because if it involves traveling somewhere, i will need to know ahead of time.

i was cleaning out the inbox of another e-mail account last night & came across some early letters from Rob and am wondering (if i can figure out how to delete any identifying info) if You would want to include a couple of them in the book? They kind of explain his perspective of D/s and, thus, my experience with it, too ... although i think most of the more descriptive ones had previously been deleted.

i miss You. i have been having long dreams about You every night ... perhaps that internal shifting i was talking about before ....

Love & kisses,
Your slave puppy

April 1, 2004

sharon smith wrote:

Dear Master,

Thank You for the lovely evening! i hope You are coping with the loss of Pirate. He will be missed.

When i got to work this morning, the clinical supervisor brought an envelope to me & set it on my desk without saying a word. When i finally got around to opening it a couple hours later, it was her letter of resignation, effective tomorrow. i about had a heart attack because she is the only other one there who knows what she's doing. i would be in deep shit without her! After a few minutes of panic, i confronted her with it, & it was an April Fool's joke! i don't think i've ever been duped so successfully! Or been so relieved it was a joke! It took the rest of the morning to recover.

Love & Kisses,
Your slave puppy

April 7, 2004

sharon smith wrote:

Dear Master,

Thank You for a wonderful evening! i was feeling like #$%&*@ on the way to Your house last night & feeling soooooo much better on the way home! i hope You were pleased.

i'm thinking You may have hit on something last night ... perhaps i am lazy ... well, at night anyway ... hmmm? i'm actually quite productive until around noon ... though have been rather hyper tonight ... must have gotten my battery recharged.

Thinking about something else You said ... we had our team meeting this morning, & i couldn't keep from laughing at my "drama queen" (lesbian) social worker ... never thought about it before, but so true, so true!

Also thinking about what You said about branding ... sounds extreeeemely painful. Were You serious about that? i do want to be Your slave.

See You soon!

Love,
Your puppy

April 9, 2004

sharon smith wrote:

Dear Master,

Yes, i had a wonderful time last night. On the way home a song came on the radio with the line "I'm on top of the world ... looking down on creation ... and the only explanation I can find ... is the love that I've found ever since You've been around" ... a perfect song for how i was feeling.

i didn't get home from the association meeting until after 10pm tonight. What a nightmare! It sounds like they're going to sue the developer, but that will take 4 years &, in the meantime, the property is worthless for resale. i was hoping to sell in the fall of this year.

If You don't mind😊, i want to answer Your previous question first since i've been thinking about it all day. Had started writing several times in the past few days but was making it more complicated than it needed to be (imagine that!). Loving You feels different, but i couldn't figure out exactly how. "Wider" is a good word ... more expansive ... and deeper, too. On the way home last night, it dawned on me (or maybe "mooned" on me) that it's different because it doesn't make me miserable ... it makes me happy. It doesn't drain me ... it fills me. Before that, i had concluded that what is different about it is You. You don't seem to be afraid of it for one thing. Your openness & honesty cause me to trust you more, & i feel safer with You than anyone else. i don't feel like i have to hang on to You to keep You from self-destructing ... don't have to fix You or hold You together. You are a whole person, & so i can love You because i want to, not because i have to. i guess it's a purer kind of love. Do i love You "enough" to be Your slave? Yes, more than enough. When did i figure that out? No certain time ... gradually over the last few weeks and months ... maybe i'm still figuring it out. i guess You will just have to trust me that it is "enough."

Also, i have to tell You i had quite a laugh this morning. One of the hospital VPs has been working on a project in the office next to mine all week. This morning he came in my office & said he had been watching me all week & if i was a model, i would make $2,500 per day because i have such "perfect posture" and move with such "grace." A picture of me sprawled over Your chaise having my ass fucked and crawling around on Your floor with the dogs flashed in my mind ... i think i may have laughed a little too hard. "Graceful" isn't quite the word i would use to describe it!

i love You.

Your slave puppy

April 10, 2004

sharon smith wrote:

Dear Master,

Let me see ... i remember You said to write an essay on what it means to be a slave ... and i know You said something else, but i don't remember what it was ... think i may have been a little distracted ....

> *slave* (n) 1. a person that is held in servitude as the chattel of another; 2. one that is completely subservient to a dominating influence; 3. a device (as the typewriter unit of a computer) that is directly responsive to another.

—Webster's Ninth New Collegiate Dictionary

Being Your slave would mean that You own me. i would be Your possession/property to do with as You please. There would be no limitation as to how, when, or where You might choose to exercise Your ownership. Ideally, it would mean that my only purpose in life is to serve You. i'm not sure how that would work out, given the fact that i also have other responsibilities. It would be up to You to define what You want. For me ... having never been a slave, i don't have an agenda. i don't know what it would mean in everyday life. i don't need to know. i don't normally think about things beforehand ... just do something & figure it out as i go along ... enjoy one day at a time & not worry about what's next.

To me, being a slave is more a matter of degree ... a deeper level of trust, of giving up control, of devotion, of serving, of flexibility or moldability (if there is such a word – and i don't mean the green, furry stuff). It seems to me that it would be a very peaceful place ... and, ironically, a place of freedom, where i would also be safe and protected. Most of the time, i seem to get in my own way when it comes to connecting with other people ... and other people do the same thing. i suppose it's a self-protective instinct.

To me, being a slave would mean making a connection in which nothing is reserved, nothing hidden ... and my "self" doesn't get in the way ... a kind of fusion ... removing of boundaries ... being totally open to anything at all. As i said a while back, i don't think it's something that happens overnight ... like one day you're a submissive and "poof!" the next day you're a slave. It's more of a gradual process, of pushing limits, and i will count on You to let me know when/if i get there.

i would consider it an honor to be Your slave.

> Being your slave, what should I do but tend
> Upon the hours and times of your desire?
> I have no precious time at all to spend,
> Nor services to do, till you require.
> Nor dare I chide the world-without-end hour
> Whilst I, my sovereign, watch the clock for you,
> Nor think the hollow of your absence sour
> When you have bid your servant once adieu;
> Nor dare I question with my humble thought
> Where you may be, or your affairs suppose,
> But like a loyal slave, stay and think of nought
> Save, where you are how happy you make those.
> So true a fool is love that in your will,
> Though you do any thing at all, she thinks no ill.
>
> —William Shakespeare

i love You.

Your slave puppy

Appendices

to

The
Puppy Papers

Appendix 1

Puppy's *alt.com* Profile

I am a gentle, loving  & obedient submissive who thrives on pain and humiliation. Looking for a strict but sane Master to please. I am slender, attractive, and intelligent. I am a very horny little slut who needs firm control, discipline, & guidance – & lots of attention for my very wet pussy.

Looking for: Men, Couples (man and woman) or Groups for performing only (little/no contact) or active participation.

Ideal Person: A man or couple who is experienced, clean, and sane. Someone who enjoys being served by a humble and loving slave. Appearance doesn't matter, as long as you are clean and not obese.

Gender: Woman

Birthdate: March 24, 1960 (44 years old)

Lives in: Chicago suburb, Illinois, United States

Activities Enjoyed: Age Play; Arse (Ass) Play; Blindfolds; Bondage; Breast/Nipple Torture; Clamps, etc.; Candle Wax; Chastity Devices; Chains; Collar and Lead/Leash; Depilation/Shaving; Infantilism/Diapers; Discipline; Dildos (Handheld & Strap-ons); Exhibitionism/Sex in Public; Fisting; Gangbangs; Handcuffs/Shackles; Hair Pulling; Masochism; Nippples; Doctor/Nurse Fetish; Oral Fixation; Spanking/Paddling; Pain; Power Exchange; Role Playing; Master/Slave; Toys; Vibrators; Whips.

Height: 5 ft 8 in

Body Type: Average

Drinking: I'm a light/social drinker

Education: BA/BS (4 years college)

Race: Caucasian

Appendix 2

Steven Toushin's *alt.com* Profile

 I have a lot of history, and this is just a little of it. I have chosen to travel a different path in life from day one; it is for me as natural as breathing. My life is not one of definitions. I'm a happy dreamer who at times gets lost in my own mind. I am a pleasant man with an easy-going temperament and disposition, who is quietly strong in character. I'm pretty direct in my approach to relationships and life. Good sense of humor (Python, Richard Pryor, Alan King, Marx Brothers, George Carlin, absurd), good listener. Attractive, with gray in my hair, lines on my face, physically fit (work out regularly). My business of 34+ years (The Bijou Theater in Chicago) is very much off center, very unconventional, adult sexual alternative extreme lifestyles; The Bijou is the oldest gay adult theater and sex club in the U.S. (I am not gay or bi.) I made adult and s&M films (slave & Master video) from the 1970s through 1999. My films have been shown at the Kinkfilm Fest and Cinekink Fest in New York. Adult entertainment on the Internet: *bijouworld.com* and *kinky books.com* (since 1994). Gay, fetish, kinky, s&M video mail order company (since 1978). Attend and vend at lifestyle events like *Black Rose, Beat Me in St. Louis, Vicious Valentine, Together in Leather*, etc. Have had many legal trials for being in my chosen profession.

I do not fantasize about being a Dom: I am not a cyber dom; I'm not a weekend or a pretend Dom. I've been a Dominant/Master/Top, playing and creating scenes for 40+

years. Back then, this was just rough sex, or S&M. My experience comes from living my life, playing, loving my personal lifestyle. Again, I've been doing all aspects of rough sex a long time. I am not a 24/7 lifestyler, *per se*. I like sexuality and humor in time spent together. I like sex in my scenes; I'm a light player; I'm a heavy player.

Here are a few essential foundation qualities that I have as a Master/Sir/Dominant/Top: passion for this lifestyle and scening; as well as compassion for the woman slave/sub/bottom I am with, beginning, during, and after play and time spent together. My need is to be compassionate and understanding of her needs, wants, and desires as a human being and as a woman. I must have and feel a connection with you, or else the play or relationship will not work for me or you, whether it be for the evening or forever. These qualities are not in conflict with sadistic, cruel, punishing, mentally and emotionally imaginative play. They enhance the experience and push you to greater heights. Control is a given; out of control is unacceptable.

A safeword (red) is an absolute. A Master/Sir/Dominant/Top or slave/sub/bottom who plays without it is a fool looking for trouble. A safeword expands conversation and play; don't leave home without it. I am compassionate in all forms of power exchange. The power I have is the power you give me. I am attuned to your body movements, heat, eyes, and your sounds; my dear, this is our dance; we are creating our own ballet. This control and power I will use to bring you the pleasure, the pain, the wants and desires that you need and crave, which brings me tremendous excitement. The circle is complete; the energy travels back and forth; it gets intense; mentally, emotionally, physically escalating to subspace and release.

I do not need or use my play partners, subs, and slaves to entice, solicit, and procure for me other play partners, subs, and slaves. If I have to use others, than I am not worth being with. My personality, character, integrity, experience, compassion and passion are what I have to offer. You make the decision to be with me, or not to be with me.

I have a unique private play space: a dungeon loft that is open and airy. Known in my community, I'm good to excellent at my craft, depending on my partner knowing, exploring herself, and letting me in, communicating.

Married twice, plus relationships (I do date). I live with four greyhounds and several large parrots in downtown Chicago. Enjoy walking by the lake; enjoy Chicago's ambience. Enjoy going out. Enjoy being home, theater, movies, dining out. Enjoy most music (Dinah Washington, Nina Simone, Marianne Faithful, *Cirque Du Soliel*, jazz, blues, rock, folk, etc.), comedy clubs, s&M clubs, etc. My lifestyle is very offbeat, entertaining, creative, and fulfilling. I write a bi-monthly column, The Bijou Chron-icles. If you're interested and you want to know a little more about my history in BDSM and my adult sexual businesses, go to *bijouworld.com* and read The Bijou Chronicles. It will give you an idea on how I view the world, my opinions, sex, BDSM, etc. I need to create and accomplish. I associate with people in many different life-styles and of all ages. Life has a way of humbling a person. The world is not perfect, and neither am I (except in discipline play; smile). I live with a margin of error.

I am an attractive man who wants an attractive (slim/ athletic, average) intelligent female submissive who is independent in character and thought. Feels good, understands, accepts her submissiveness, finds strength and knowledge in her submissive journey. A woman whose private motivation and natural inclination are towards

BDSM. Has masochistic, hedonistic tendencies. Who is sensual, seductive, and sexual. Who enjoys kissing, spankings, floggings, singletails, bondage, chains, rope, mind games and mindfuck in play, role play, humiliation scenes, discipline play, electric and wand play, hot wax, suspension, knife play, hoods, gags, puppy play, fisting, pussy play, pain, pleasure, love-making, etc. A woman who needs and gets tremendous satisfaction in pleasing and serving her man, her Master. I am looking for a warm friendship, a companion, a lover, a play partner – or just a play partner. Almost all the profiles say nothing. When responding, please take the time and write some things about yourself. Must include photo, and must live in Chicago.

Looking for: A woman for active participation.

Ideal Person: An attractive, intelligent woman who is independent in character and thought, who does not make choices and decisions based on how the world would judge her. Feels good about herself. Has character and integrity. Listens to others. A woman who is passionate about life, and this lifestyle, who wants passion in her life. Takes care of her body (must be slim/athletic, average) and mind, has a creative imagination. Who is easy-going, fun loving, has a sense of humor, can laugh at herself, and has a warm, happy, positive disposition. Appreciates a compliment. Will respect other people's lifestyles and opinions, as she would want others to respect hers. Reads, keeps up on current events, enjoys her own company. Will volunteer her time for a good cause. I enjoy the company of many types of women. Professional women who are in high-powered, stressful positions, who are always in control and who crave a release only in the bedroom (so as to get her batteries recharged). Women who have the need to give up control in the bedroom and in time spent together. Women who want a 24/7 with a man, or women who want a part-time Dom/Master, or play.

A woman whose private motivation and natural inclination are towards BDSM, has masochistic, hedonistic tendencies. Sensual, seductive and sexually submissive, who enjoys kissing, spankings, floggings, singletails, bondage, chains, rope, mind games, mindfuck, role play, humiliation scenes, discipline play, electricity and wands, hot wax, suspension, hoods, gags, knife play, puppy play, fisting, pussy play, pain, pleasure, love-making, etc. Who has a need to please and serve her Master, her man, and gets tremendous satisfaction from doing so: this woman will be well appreciated. A submissive woman who feels the warmth of a smile, a caressing touch, an admiring glance. A woman who likes, wants, a man strong in character. There are a lot of pretend, fantasy bottom/sub/slave profiles, those who are "me, myself, and I" people, who play the fantasy in their heads; to those of you: please do not bother to respond. For those of you who are genuinely beautiful submissive women, I would love to hear from you. Thank you.

Appendix 3

Rob and Sharon's Profile

My Master, age 57, is very handsome, athletic, fit, dominant, patient, and kind. He is a very experienced Master and wants to help me explore my bisexual nature in a threesome with another woman. I am 41, submissive and attractive, but not very experienced. We are both professionals and, due to the nature of our work, we must be discreet and cannot send pictures over the Internet. If you are interested in trying new things & exploring your sexuality, we would love to hear from you.

Appendix 4

Puppy's Timeline

April 10, 2004

Steven Toushin wrote:

Dear puppy,

Your story is finishing up beautifully. There is information needed to clarify and clean up your history, and that is a time line.

- A. What is the year of your birth?
- B. What years did you go to high school and, about how many kids went to your school?
- C. What state or states do you live in, and during what years. Where in each state: southern, northern, or middle?
- D. What was the year that you stopped having sex outside of your marriage? You said that was when your 2nd child was how old?
- E. What years did you give birth to your children?
- F. What year did you place your first Internet ad?
- G. What was the time frame with each of the men until you met me?

Sir

1959 – i was born

1966 – started first grade

1971-72 – 6th grade (Blake)

1975 – got my driver's license! – sophomore

1976 – Bicentennial; met my future husband, Arthur, on the 4th of July

1978 – graduated from high school (June) & got married (September) (age 18)

1981 – birth of my 1st son Dale (age 22)

1983 – birth of my 2nd son Don (age 20)

1987 – went back to school

1991 – graduated from college (age 31)

2000 – older son graduated from high school (May), sent younger son to Tennessee (November), placed ad on *adult-friendfinder.com* (November), met Master Rob (December)

2001 – met Marlene & John (February), met Donald (June), met Susan & Raj (August), met the guy from South Bend (July or August)

2002 – met the anthropologist (winter)

2003 – met Michael & Rich (spring), went to Shadowfind (August), moved to Illinois (October), met You (November)

i think that covers everything!

So i went to high school from 1974 to 1978. i'm guessing there were about 2,500 kids in the high school, since there were about 650 in my class. i lived in northern Indiana all my life until moving to Illinois last fall. The town i lived in during the school years was much larger than any town i lived in before or after. The others were small farming communities with a total population of 1,000-2,000. The town i lived in for the past 15 years was the same one i lived in until the age of 5. i am related to almost everyone else who lives there. It is a very closed & very religious community … outsiders are not welcomed. Their claim to fame is that they are in the world record book as the town having the most churches per capita. That is where i was living when i got started in BDSM.

Love,
Your puppy

Appendix 5

Steven Toushin's Greyhounds

"He was a friend of mine; he never had no money; I paid for his bones; he was a friend of mine."

—From the song "He was a Friend of Mine"
Sung by Dave Van Ronk

Big Pirate (Hawkhill Pirate) 1995-2004

Best friend to GoldDust Pearl (Goldie), Desperado, and BB Gun, as well as sweetheart of Ms. Charlie (a big solid Rot), Pirate was the loving friend of the Bijou office and of anyone who knew this big, beautiful, dumb guy. He was a slim 85 lbs., and he never raced. Pirate was too scared; he had no heart for racing.

He was scared of cats and would hide behind someone and cry, always looking for a place to hide if the cat got too close. Noises and small dogs scared him, too. My job was to protect him from Lions, Tigers and Bears. Pirate was just a big, lovable, dumb guy.

Pirate will be missed by his sweetheart, Ms. Charlie, who sexually harassed him on a daily basis; he couldn't get away from her! She would chase him around the office and pin him against the wall with her solid body, then she would stand on her tiptoes and kiss him, not letting him get away. When he was lying down, she would lie next to  him, put her nose touching his, and kiss him. If he moved his head, she would hit him with her paw ("When I'm kissing you, you do not move away from me!"). Pirate was the only one who could take anything away from Ms. Charlie; if anyone else tried, she would growl and snap. But when Pirate would do this, she would go to him and stand over him, trying to steal it back. They always made us smile and laugh.

Going out and walking with Pirate was an elegant experience. He majestically pranced, with his head high by my side, and he would never stray or pull. In the office, he stayed near patrick, and he would whine when he wanted something. In response, patrick would ask "What's the problem now, Pirate?" patrick looked after the big boy, always taking care of the problem, and spoiling him rotten.

I could not protect Pirate from cancer. He stopped eating and could not get up or go to the bathroom. His last night, his last meal was a rib dinner. All the dogs and I stayed at the office that night, and I slept on the floor next to him. I knew that the next day I would be putting Pirate to sleep.

In the morning, everyone in the office wanted to spend time saying goodbye. When it came time to go, BB Gun came over and laid down in front of Pirate, would not move, and would not let me get to Pirate. Ms. Charlie, who was tied to a filing cabinet, started to drag the cabinet to get over to Pirate. Let me tell you it was tough.

BB Gun

I picked Pirate up and carried him down the stairs to a waiting van that brought us the few blocks to the vet's office. My daughter, Sydney (who designs the Bijou website) and Claudia went with me. Pirate trusted me to take care of him; he was scared, I held his head in my right hand in my lap, and I placed my left hand on his heart so I could feel his last breath when I told him I loved him.

I am so very thankful to have had Pirate in my life, to have been able to give him a home, to love him, and to be loved by him. He was a best friend of mine.

—Steven Toushin

To find out about adopting a retired greyhound racer, go to _www.greyhoundsonly.com_.

Back: GoldDust Pearl (Goldie); Left: BB Gun; Right: Desperado; Front: Pirate

Appendix 6

More About Steven Toushin

This picture was taken during my first obscenity arrest in 1969 for the film "Flaming Creatures," by Jack Smith, which is considered an underground classic.

I do not have a clue what to say about my life, and me since it is not over yet. But this is a little about me, a little of my ego.

The Puppy Papers is one of many things I am doing in my world of sexuality. My businesses have included: theaters; sex clubs in Chicago (still going), San Francisco, and Indianapolis; gay bathhouses; massage parlors (prostitution); and adult bookstores. I made films: straight, gay, and S&M (Slave and Master videos in the early to middle 80s.). The Bijou Video Catalog is the bible of gay video. On the Internet, my site is *www.bijouworld.com*; I'm a partner in *www.kinkybooks.com* with Jack Rinella's slave, patrick; and I write a column for *Cruisin* magazine on my life, politics, BDSM, and bullshit.

Throughout the years, my businesses have had over 200 busts, and I have been arrested 48 times. I've been through 12 jury trials (4 of them federal trials) and numerous bench trials. For being in my chosen profession, I've been to prison (federal) twice, and I have been in the legal system as a defendant every day from 1970 to date (2004).

I have had the good fortune of playing roughly with a lot of wonderful women during the past 40 years, and I do not see any signs that it will let up. I am not a public player; public to me is foreplay. I like roughness, intensity, and sex.

I'm not crazy about people who have names that start with Master/Mistress (just had to stick that in).

There are many more things I have done and have been through. What I am doing today and will be doing tomorrow, though, is more exciting and interesting to me than what happened yesterday.

Thank you for reading this book. I do hope you enjoy puppy's story.

—Steven Toushin

Shameless Plugs & Advertisements

BIJOU VIDEO • The Gay Film Experts Since 1969 •
www.bijouvideo.com

Bijou Video started selling gay video in 1979. In 1987 the Bijou Video Catalog was born and soon became the bible on gay video until 1995 when it was moved to the internet and where it became a free resource for everyone. It's still the best information resource for gay porn that you'll find any-where.

We specialize in gay adult film from the 70's, 80's and early 90's. Of course we also carry all current and new releases in all formats. Hands down, we are the best site on gay video and kink/fetish film in the world.

While you're visiting www.bijouvideo.com be sure to read the Bijou Chronicles, articles written by Steven Toushin that have been published in several gay magazines in Chicago.

www.KinkyBooks.com
Celebrating Healthy Sexuality

KinkyBooks.com was created in October 2000 as a way of bringing attention to the large variety of books available to the BDSM community. There have been are far more books available on kinky subjects than you'd imagine and many of them have gone out of print from lack of exposure.

By searching out the various publishers and bringing books together in one place KinkyBooks hopes to make them available to many more people than would otherwise be the case. You can find more than nearly 400 alternative lifestyle books, reviews by TammyJo Eckhart, and advice from Jack Rinella and Mistress Constance at our web site www.KinkyBooks.com. Or find us in the vending area at many BDSM events across the country. KinkyBooks.com supports our community in celebrating healthy sexuality.

Other books you might find interesting:

Erotic Surrender: The Sensual Joys Of Female Submission by Claudia Varrin, Citadal Press, 2003 $15.95 Non-fiction
Sexually submissive women often feel misunderstood or ignored. Erotic surrender shatters the myths about S&M relationships and emphasizes the emotional and physical benefits that can be derived from sensual submission, and guides you toward a newfound sexual enrichment that can heighten intimacy and trust inside and outside the bedroom.

Erotic Fairy Tales: A Romp Through the Classics by Mitzi Szereto Cleis Press 2001 $14.95 Fiction
Fairy tales historically boasted licentious themes before being cleaned up for the consumption of children in modern times. Seasoned erotica author Mitzi Szereto restores the explicit sex in these 15 tales — and adds some provocative surprises of her own.
Each tale is prefaced by a brief introduction telling its history and the sexual culture in which the work was originally composed.

The New Bottoming Book by Dossie Easton and Janet Hardy Greenery Press 2001 $14.95 Non-Fiction
Almost a decade ago, the first `Bottoming Book` taught tens of thousands of people that bottoming - being a submissive, masochist, slave, `boy` or `girl,` or other BDSM recipient - is as much an art as topping. Now, the completely updated revised `New Bottoming Book` gives even more insights and ideas about how to be a successful, popular bottom!

Rhapsody: To Touch the Face of The Goddess by Mistress Steele Unbound Books 1998 $11.95 Fiction
Published in late 1998, Rhapsody has become a solid favorite. This is a Fem/fem S/m erotica book which takes a searing look into the mind and soul of a young woman discovering her sexual, sensual and erotic nature. This is the kind of book you want to share and share until the pages fall out!

The Ethical Slut by Dossie Easton and Catherine A. Liszt Greenery Press, 1998 $16.95 Non-Fiction
Guide to exploring non-traditional relationships. Details about meeting needs, managing jealousy, making agreements that work for all concerned & build a life full of all the sex & love you want. an easy, straight-forward, non-graphic discussion of non-monogamous relationships.

Haughty Spirit by Sharon Green Greenery Press, 1999 $11.95 Fiction
This story is about Meriath, an arrogant goddess who angers a god stronger than her and is "put in her place" by him. There are three "mini-stories" in the book where she becomes mortal and is cursed to "serve" the first man she sees at all times. She at times is treated cruelly by the men around her, but in the end the men who deserve it get their "just desserts."

Exhibitionism For The Shy: Show Off, Dress Up and Talk Hot by Carol Queen Down There Press, 1995 $14.50 Non-Fiction
Carol Queen is now a famous sex educator who describes herself as a recovering shy person. In 13 chapters and 3 appendices she helps understand what holds us back from exploring and fully enjoy-ing our sexuality and offers exercises we can use to move into a more fulfilling passionate life with ourselves and with others.

Shameless: Women's Intimate Erotica: Woman's Intimate Erotica by Hanne Blank Seal Press, 2002 $14.95 Fiction
There's something for everyone in this collection of 18 fictional first-person pieces. S&M, pregnancy and physical disabilities, a panoply of sexual orien-tations and configurations, power dynamics between genders. Settings range from Port-au-Prince to the Midwest.

The Survivors Guide to Sex: How to Have an Empowered Sex Life After Child Sexual Abuse by Staci Haines Cleis Press, 1999 $24.95 Non-Fiction
Sex-positive and daring, Haines ably discusses common negative reactions among survivors, such as withdrawal and dissociation, and suggests ways to move on. Her chapters on "Sexual Response and Anatomy" and "Masturbation and Self-Healing" may come as a revelation to women who have repressed their sexual feelings.

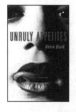

Unruly Appetites: Erotic Stories by Hanne Blank
Seal Press, 2003 $14.95 Fiction
Marked by Blank's fantastic imagination, each deftly written story flaunts a bold, sensual lyricism and dy-namic characters that titillate and inspire. No shrinking violets here, this book features intelligent women who know what they want and how they want it, and in the process deconstructs quaint and antiquated notions about women's sexual lives.

Tricks...To Please a Man by Jay Weisman
Greenery Press, 2004 $13.95 Non-Fiction
*The latest of Jay Wiseman's "Tricks" books,
it gives some basic tips as well as some
creative ideas to make him moan and beg*
you for more. *For those who haven't had much experience, or worry that he might be a little bored with the
same-old-same-old (and don't know how to change that),
this book is a treasure chest of ideas and information If
you don't find at least several ideas to spice up your sex
then you need to hang out your prude shingle!.*

Taboo: Forbidden Fantasies for Couples by Violet
Blue Cleis Press, 2004 $14.95 Fiction
*What is your deepest, darkest, sweetest, most
stunningly wicked fantasy? Taboo will feed you erotic
stories of forbidden desire like fingerfuls of warm
chocolate dripping onto your tongue. Here are
twenty-two superbly written erotic stories featuring*
couples who want it so bad they can taste it—and they do, making
their most taboo erotic fantasies come true.

**Big Big Love: A Sourcebook on Sex for People of
Size and Those Who Love Them** by Hanne Blank
Greenery Press, 2000 $15.95 Non-Fiction
*Realistic and entertaining info on sex, love and
romance for everybody from the chubby to the
supersized. How to improve your self-image, find
partners, have great sex in spite of physical*
limitations, Big, Big Love spells out how to overcome those "problems" in plain English. It's about time!

Screw the Roses, Send Me the Thorns! By Phillip
Miller and Molly Devon Mystic Rose Books, 1995
$24.95 Non-Fiction
*Fun, approachable, chatty, and insightful. There's
clear explanations and detailed tutorials for begin-
ners, solid advice, safety measures, steamy
suggestions, plenty of black-and-white photographs,*
useful and humorous drawings. The chapter on finding partners
and sharing your fantasies with existing partners is be invaluable.